The Ballad of Stitch and Doe

The Ballad of Stitch and Doe

Daniel Rose

The Ballad of Stitch and Doe

It is the mark of an educated mind to be able to entertain a thought without accepting it.   Aristotle

When they come to take you down
When they bring that wagon round
When they come to call on you
And drag your poor body down
Just one thing I ask of you
There's one thing for me
Please forget you knew my name
My Darling Sugaree
Shake it up now Sugaree
I'll meet you at the Jubilee
And if that Jubilee don't come
Baby, I'll meet you on the run

I get to where I'm going by walking away from where I've been.

Pooh. A.H. Milne

Prologue

"Funny, it doesn't look at all like you."

I was examining the flyer in my hand and comparing it to the face which stood in front of me. It was a long stretch, but there was a vague resemblance, despite the fact that the person in question had pulled her baseball cap low and adjusted the myopic lenses which perched upon her nose. It was a uni-lens, although such detail could only be observed when up close. Not that this mattered much, the bulk of the problem laying more in time than in space.

"It's my senior picture from High School," she commented, as if reading my mind. "God knows she wouldn't have bothered to pull anything more recent, because the bottom line is that she really doesn't want to find me. You see, it's not really about finding me; it's all about making the effort. And all she has to do is make that effort for the next two years, and then she can cash in on the big old life insurance policy she took out on me when I was a kid."

It sounded like a plan. A nefarious plan, but a plan nonetheless. I looked at my traveling companion and looked at the Missing Person's flyer again. Had she really looked like this a mere twenty-five years ago? I mean, we all go through changes in our appearance, but Jeezus…

The girl in the picture was so clean cut, with a tidy no nonsense hairdo and a pristine neck which was not defiled by a rope-like tattoo. Plus she had a little meat on her bones; something my traveling companion was a bit lean on (to make a bad joke). Who knows, maybe she ate better back then. Our present diet of half-eaten Burgers scrounged from dumpsters and questionable bottles of wine stolen from passed out bums was not what you'd call the cream of the crop. Still talk about meth-head skinny!

I checked my own reflection in the glass doors of the building we'd wandered into, praying that I wasn't following in her footsteps. I was met with an image which stood out in stark contrast to the institutional green walls of the building in which we were located. I was pleased to see that I still maintained a bit of my former bulk, although I had shaved off a few pounds since my quarter pounder days. However, the rest of the reflection did not bode well if you were someone who didn't want to be noticed. Great God, was that really me? With my African top-not and muscular frame, I looked like a Maori tribesman. All I needed was a bone between my nose and I'd be good to go.

"Let's get out of here," I whispered, fearing that if I raised my voice too high, someone would call the cops. Hell, it had happened before.

She looked at me with intensity, or at least as much as one can muster when one lens is missing from your glasses.

"Not until I get what I came for," she insisted as she sidled over to a row of Post Office boxes. She singled out a key from the ones she kept strung about her neck. It was a mystery how she managed to select the right one since she had close to a half dozen of the frigging things, all which bore the same number. Seventy-seven. How she'd managed that one was beyond me, but she had her ways.

I waited with my heart in my throat. No make that my stomach in knots. That's a much better way to put it since any chance of that part of my anatomy finding some degree of relief hung on the success of her mission.

It was long moment. They always are. Hunger will do that to a guy, especially when they'd been used to three square meals a day for most of their life. I waited while she inserted the key and pulled out the contents. Most went in a wastebasket, being the crap all Post Offices so graciously supply for their patrons. But one letter remained in her hand. Slowly, she slipped a ragged fingernail beneath its seal and then, the sun came up on her face.

I could tell even from a distance what lay inside. A royalty check? I couldn't believe my eyes. She'd actually sold enough books for a royalty check? And what was the amount she was waving in my face? Oh my God! A whole seventy-five bucks. Oh well, Thank you, Lord, anyway. At least we would eat that night. And then? Well, we'll see.

Chapter 1
Noone
AKA Doe
1985-2008

It all began with the TDA accounts. No, scrap that. Since it probably began years, even decades, before that. I was marked from birth or so it seemed. Or at least from the day my mom decided to name me after her favorite rock star: Peter Noone of the Herman's Hermits.

The Herman's Hermits? Why on earth couldn't she have picked a cooler group? Lord Knows there were enough of them in her day. Led Zeppelin, Pink Floyd, Jefferson Airplane, Cream, the Jimi Hendrix Experience. Yeah, the list goes on and on. It was the Golden Age of Rock, and the music that came out of it was so good that future generations continued to listen to it.

Oh, we millenials had our own shit, mind you. Old standbys like The Beatles and Queen, rappers like Eminem, sweethearts like Taylor Swift and Beyonce, and even some hand-me-downs from the Generation X like Nirvana and Pearl Jam. I, myself, tended to favor the latter since they epitomized both my angst and slacker attitude. In fact, the first one of those bands rocked so close to the bone that at one time I almost changed my name to Kurt after one of their major players.

But then I sat down until the mood passed because by that time it was no easy deal to change your name. Not like in my mom's era when

3

all you had to do was write the social security office and tell them you'd been married, divorced, murdered, or born again. Whatever....

So Noone it was, and Noone it remains, and no wonder I feel so much like a fish out of water. In fact, I probably relate better to fish than I do to most of the people I know.

Not that I wasn't curious about the humble origins of my name. Yes, even as a young whippersnapper, I was the kid with a thousand questions.

"Where did it come from? Why Noone? What was so special about Herman's Hermits?" I asked one day.

From my perspective they'd been sort of second rate compared to the other bands that were out there at the time. And their songs, especially the one about Henry the 8th? Jeezus. A ten year old could come up with better lyrics than that. So there had to be some deeper forces at work.

Besides, at the time I'd been hanging with a kid at the beach by the name of Sun, a contemporary who, like me, came from the Era of Far-out Names. I'd figured him to be named after a celestial body, kind of like Moon, one of Frank Zappa's daughters. But noooo... He was quick to inform me that it was much more complex than that, his mom being a very very complex person.

"Ok, then," I'd persisted. "Come off with it. What's the big secret?"

At which point he'd smiled and told me some crazy tale about how his mom was convinced she'd been impregnated by some pond spirit and that his name was actually taken from an I-Ching hexagram and meant *lake at the foot of the mountain*, the place where said spirit resided.

Well, that sounded great, and gave me hope that maybe; just maybe, my name had some kind of spiritual significance as well. Which was why I'd decided to ask.

However, the answer I got was far from the one I'd sought since my good old mom—who was always renowned for her extreme candor—simply told me that she named me thus because it was at a Herman's Hermit concert where she lost her virginity, an event that didn't even lead to my conception because the math was all wrong.

Boy, it must have been some earth-shaking event if it was able to top all the rest of the stuff that happened at that very same concert. Stuff like chicks getting their arms broken as they struggled to worm their way into first row seats. Reminds me of those lines by AC/DC.

> Better lock up your daughter
> Lock up your wife
> Lock up your back door

4

And run for your life
The man is back in town

Yeah, this is when it all started. With the British invasion, and many felt it signified the beginning of the end as far as American family values went. Because it quickly went downhill from there as those Fabulous Fifties degenerated into the Sensational Sixties. Yeah, lock up your daughters, indeed. And my mom was one of them, the kind of lost soul who ran away from home at the ripe old age of sixteen to join the Merry Pranksters.

And as for me. I just got stuck with the name of Noone, which if you haven't figured out by now loosely translates as No one. And the only silver lining is that my namesake was one of the few rockers to live to a ripe old age and actually prosper. Yeah, even though he was a card carrying member of AA at the tender age of nineteen, he managed to come through it all relatively unscathed. Word has it that he's been married to the same woman for forty-six years and at sixty-four still looks great. He's in possession of a full head of hair and a Twitter account and is even touring again. Boy, it can't get any better than that, considering most of these guys are burned out or dead before they hit thirty. Yeah, if I could only be so lucky, but luck is not exactly my forte. As the TDA accounts were so kind as to demonstrate. Regrettably, I have a sneaky feeling that fate has other plans for me.

That's right. Fate and her fickle fingers, and I was one hundred percent sure of the gender. It had to be a woman, all flighty and faithless, a real fair weather friend (or fuck buddy if you chose).

Now I'd like to say I don't believe in fate, that I don't like the idea of being victimized by the capricious little bitch. I'd like to say we make our own way in this world and are not subject to the slings and arrows of outrageous fortune. However, I am a bit on the walking wounded side as I speak. So it's a little hard to mouth the positive platitudes. So I'll skip the shit about *change the way you look at things and the things you'll look at will change* and that bit about *being captain of your own soul.* Because it's all a bit too raw right now, too close for comfort.

Oh, I know it's just a temporary state. I was always an easy going kind of bloke. A bit like my namesake. And I was always fairly good at bouncing back from all the crap that was dealt to me. Lord knows, I've had a lot of practice. My life has never been easy. To say *I ain't no senator's son* is putting it mildly. No, I'm the poor slob hat gets shipped off to war and shipped back in a box. The cannon fodder if you're the aggressor; the collateral damage if you're simply caught in the line of fire.

Whatever the case, it's all synonymous with lower class loser and my story could very well be a guidebook for any who seek public assistance.

It begins with my mom. Where else? Since without her, I would have only been a gleam in my father's eye. Ok, so what about dad, you say. Well, let's just say he was a contributing factor to a miserable ten years during which I rarely slept under the same roof for more than a year. To say we moved around a lot would be putting it mildly. By my eighth birthday I was in and out of more schools than most kids see in their entire career, and every single move was motivated by an inability to cough up that month's rent. That's because we were a single parent household and way below poverty level.

So there you have it. There was no dad in the picture. In fact, his mere name was a mystery to me as well as any other details concerning his life. Why, mom didn't even know what state he currently lived in! So scratch any possibility of any child support.

Therefore, we struggled since my mom belonged to that class of laborers which is considered unskilled and therefore unworthy of a working wage. Not that she didn't try. Poor girl, she'd do just about anything to make a buck. Oh, she drew the line at hooking, but sometimes I wondered why since most of her jobs fit the description of legal prostitution. McDonalds, Walmart, phone solicitation, restaurant work, toilet scrubbing. All were the sort of jobs that don't pay enough to get by which is why she needed to work them in tandem.

Then, by the time I was eleven, she'd finally landed a pretty good one in a child care center down on Flagler Avenue. It was semi-permanent with a contract that went year round, so for the first time in all my years, we finally stayed put in one apartment complex. But it still didn't pay enough to cover the bills. So she was forced to supplement her income by working nights at a nearby pizza parlor. Sometimes she'd come right back from her day job and, after slopping me a few Tacos and parking me in front of the TV, she go right back out to deliver pizzas until one o'clock in the morning. It was a brutal life for her and a lot of times she'd be sick for weeks on end. But she kept it up, never missing a beat. It was a lucky thing we lived in Florida, or I swear she would have dropped dead from pneumonia. As it was she probably had a walking version of the disease.

When I got older, I would help out, or at least perform my own version of helping. Hell, I had to if I ever wanted a soda or a candy bar! At first, it was small shit like picking up golf balls that had been lobbed off into the woods and then selling them back to the country clubbers. It wasn't much but it paid for those few small essentials that every kid must have. Later though I was able to get a job stocking the shelves at a local grocery store. I was only thirteen at the time, but the guy I worked for was able to get around the labor laws somehow. It was a job that, at two dollars an hour, had me rolling in dough. I thought I'd hit the jackpot and was even able to save up enough of my profits to buy my first surf board. Boy, did I ever think I was king of the Curl. For two years I did nothing but surf and party. I was heading for a career as a beach bum and proud of it.

And that's when the shit hit the fan for the first time. I was the one who saw the letter first. It was lying in a pile with a bunch of shiny catalogs and ads from Bi-Lo and Piggly-Wiggley. Since we didn't get much in the way of personal mail, I was curious. So curious, in fact, that I was just about ready to rip into it when mom burst through the doorway. She was wearing the red and white checked cap the pizza delivery company demanded. I hated that hat, but had I known it would be the last time I'd ever see her in it, I would have ripped it right off her head and placed it behind glass. Because it was to signify the end of an era, and it was an era that, for me, had just begun.

Not for her though.

"Gimme that!" she screamed and, not used to such outbursts from my normally docile mother, I surrendered the letter, dropping it at her feet. Now this was not meant as disrespect but mostly done because she scared me. But what she did next really put the fear of the Lord into me.

First she thumped me on the head in an act that went completely against her nature. (I can count on one hand the number of times my mom had ever used any physical force against me.) Then, after ripping open the letter and scanning it, she immediately began to jump up and down. Well, I have heard the term *jump for joy*, but this bordered more on the ecstasy one experiences when one has seen God. OK, so maybe she had seen God because her God always did have a greenback.

"We're rich! We're rich!" she exclaimed with such vigor I swear it shook the roof beams off the cheap apartment building we called home. And then, she performed one more act which was totally out of character. She ran to where I was still holding my aching head and swept me up into her arms. (Did I mention her lack of physical contact swung both ways, embracing both the good and bad sides of the force?) I was dumbstruck and stood there like a limp rag doll. What else could I do? She surely wasn't communicating in her usual way which was either to snarl some instructions at me or inform me that she was too tired to talk.

I waited, knowing the truth would come out and when it did, it came in a way that rocked my young world for good. Gone would be the dawn patrols to catch the early morning smokers. (That's what you call a wave that is blowing foam sideways on account of a north wind). Yeah, gone with the rest of the lingo. Making the drop, hitting the lip, jacking, point breaks, pearling, peeling, ricos… Gone too, was making fun of shubbies and paddlepusses and worrying about the men in grey suits (sharks). Yeah, I'd even miss that!

Gone. Gone. Gone.

Because we were moving to Ohio. That's right. A state so boring you can't even find a good joke about how boring it is. Ohio, inspiration for stupid kid games like the one about the hunter who was chasing a rabbit through the woods when it went into a hollow log. So the hunter cut the log in half, and then in half again and… Oh my God, somehow you end up with the name of this deplorable state. Yeah, Ohio. What's round at both ends and high in the middle? ☺HI☺

Except I wasn't smiling and high was something I was never going to associate with Ohio.

But not so for mom. It was a real turning point for her and a *Godsend* as she continued to state over and over again.

A *Godsend* the way her own mom, a grandmother whom I had never met, had undergone an epiphany while on her death bed, one which had led her to track down her one and only daughter. A *Godsend* the way Grandma Mysterious had changed her will and instead of leaving it all to her nine cats, had penciled in a new recipient, her long lost daughter, who twenty-some years ago had run off with this weird band of robbers by the name of The Merry Pranksters.

I didn't know it at the time, but apparently I had clinched the deal. There's nothing like the existence of a grandchild to soften an old fart's heart. Think of all those scam calls that begin with *your grandson in jail and needs ten grand for bail* and you get the picture. Maybe it has something to do with senility or maybe it's just the way we get at the end, all sentimental and forgiving, but once Grandma Mysterious had caught wind of her daughter's progeny, this was all it took. The lawyers had been called Johnny on the spot and a real will drawn up. And as for the cats, well they were there to greet us when we unpacked the U-Haul which held all our earthly possessions.

I remember them quite well since I am a self-professed cat person, albeit one who has been deprived of the company of such furry felines by the sheer fact of living places which enforced a strict No Pets policy. There was a big black and white Kat Kong named Precious who ran the harem. A spayed male, he was the only Tom amongst them. The rest were females and some were daughters and granddaughters of the original, and they all looked about the same to me. However to the old lady's eye they had always possessed some sort of distinguishing mark or characteristic. Maybe that's why she named them after the seven dwarves. Sleepy, Sneezy, Doc, Dopey (the catnip junky), Grumpy (who loved to piss in my shoes), Bashful (who hid behind the coach for three days), and my favorite Happy, who was a great comfort to me during those early days of my exile.

And, if you can count, I'm sure you figured out by now there was one missing, and yeah, it was really missing by the time we got there. Her name was Snowy, and she had actually been a kitten when my mom left which made her perhaps one of the oldest cats on record. Well, not really as I've since heard of one that made the Guinness Book of World Records. Her name was Cream Puff, and she lived to the ripe old age of thirty-eight.

But enough bird-walking; or cat-walking if you please. Back to Snowy and the strange the way her absence affected my mom who was never given to sentimentality when it came to the past. *Let bygones be bygones*, she always liked to say, and that was OK by me, especially when said bygones involved something I may have accidentally broken. Yeah *bye* to that, cuz it's *gone* now.

However the loss of Snowy was different, different enough to bring tears to mom's eyes when a neighbor insisted they hadn't seen the cat since the old lady had died over a month ago. Somehow they'd been commissioned to come over and tend to the cat house, so they should know. How they managed to take a head count of the dwarves was beyond me, but mom just took their word for it that all seven were accounted for.

"But Snowy," mom wailed. "She was my seventeenth birthday present. I almost took her with me when I moved to California."

That was mom's way of describing it, AKA her version of the truth. She *moved* to California. It sounded intentional and well thought out, and made her come off as a girl with a plan. It was like she was going off to college or had hooked a good job as a producer's assistant in LA. There was none of that business of throwing a pack out the bedroom window at two in the morning and hitching down to the bus station. Guess it's our prerogative to rewrite the past and make ourselves look as white as possible.

I just shook my head as I contemplated the image of mom accomplishing all that with a cat carrier under one arm, and if I hadn't been so traumatized by the mess that I'd found myself in, I might have even laughed. However, laughter and other positive expressions of emotion were denied to me for quite some time after our big move.

For starters, it came just as winter was closing in, and never, and I repeat NEVER, in my young life had I experienced such cold. Add to the formula that it just so happened to be one of the worst winters to assault the mid-west in decades and it becomes clear. Here I was a budding young surfer dude who refused to wear long pants, even in zero degree weather. A kid with a few rudimentary tattoos and a hair down to my skinny little waist and you get the picture, one of just how well I managed to fit into the redneck high school in which I was currently enrolled. Jeezus!!!

Talk about a fish out of water. That's right.

My woodie's outside
Covered with snow
Cold winds will blow now
New York's a lonely town
When you're the only surfer boy around.

One can only imagine just how traumatic the whole deal was for me. To say I didn't fit in would be putting it mildly and we all know how brutal high schools can be if you aren't part of the inner circle. And circle they did, like a school of sharks. After their initial assessment, during which I failed every test they placed in front of me, the in-crowd decided to do what they do best and make my life miserable. My locker was vandalized and stuffed full of old jock straps, my lunch was stolen and my homework ripped up in front of my very eyes. I was subjected to indignities like towel snaps and wedgies in gym and kick-me signs while walking down the hall. I was treated to spit-ball attacks and wet-willies, and even received a whirly once from some two hundred pound goon who'd been laying in wait for me in the bathroom.

In short, it was hell on steroids and something had to give.

"Mom!!!" I screamed at the top of my lungs one day. "I want to get some exercise equipment."

The lady in question had looked up from her Bird Keeper's magazine, where she'd been pouring over the pages of her latest passion. Apparently this was her new obsession, and I prayed to God it didn't morph into a hobby.

"Exercise equipment??"

I might have requested a trip to the moon.

"Yeah, I'm starting to get flabby sitting around here all the time."

I didn't want to say anything about the hazing I'd been getting at school. It would only make her feel bad. I knew mom suspected I might be having some problems with our little move, but I didn't want to rub it in. She was so happy, happier than I had ever seen her in my entire life and that meant something to me. Here she was a home-owner, after all those years of renting shithole apartments where the plumbing didn't work and the maintenance guy was too drunk to care. Never mind that the home was in a dipshit Ohio town which had the audacity to call itself Coolville.

Coolville, that makes it sound like a really hip place to live. OK, at least to my surfer slang ears. But remember, this is Ohio and I'll betcha the town came by its name on account of the weather because like some of its neighbors, Frost and Snowville, it was hardly a stranger to wintery events.

Yeah, good old Coolville—which was actually named for its founding father, a guy by the name of Simeon W. Cooley, who back in the eighteen hundreds probably owned stock in one of the original businesses, be it the gristmill or the sawmill. Of course, both are gone now leaving Coolville a bustling town of five hundred lost souls, a quarter of which live down the street from us in the Arcadia Nursing home.

Nope, there wasn't much in Coolville, its main point of interest being an elementary school which I was too old to attend, thus necessitating my transport by bus to Federal Hocking High School in nearby Stewart. Of course, I could still enjoy the services of a Go-Mart, a public library and a post office. But that was all, unless I wanted to hang out with the relics down at the nursing home. Yes indeed, it a real hopping place and a nightmare for a kid who was a few months shy of procuring a learner's permit in the Buckeye State. Not that I would derive much benefit from such a piece of paper since the only car in our household belonged to my mom, and there sure weren't any near-by jobs for little old me.

So I was stuck, one hundred percent at her mercy, for I knew that she wasn't going to get me a car. But maybe some exercise equipment would relieve her of some of her guilt, although what I had in mind was hardly a Nordic Track or an Elliptical trainer. No, I was shooting more for the body-building stuff. Bench presses, Gold's Gym, BoxFlex Extreme. Yeah, that ought a do the trick. That and a few YouTube videos on Wing Chun, a martial arts form I'd been getting into when I left Flagler Beach.

Well, it was a good try, I'll grant you that much. Mom acquiesced and broke out a big chunk of cash for my machines; and then, her guilt assuaged, retreated back into her bird books. I took to my workouts with a fervor and amazed even myself with my commitment to become the next Charles Atlas, and within a year, I had sufficiently beefed out to where I was a force to be reckoned with. However, the only problem with my plan was that it had been initiated too late. The damage was already done.

Daniel Rose

For those who can't remember much about High School—or who have permanently and purposefully blocked it from their memory—allow me to give you a refresher course. To begin with, High School, like war, is hell and takes no prisoners. If you don't come into it with all your guns a blazing, you are doomed; which means it helps to be born on the battle field or at least within a close proximity to it. That way, you know all the nasty little tricks your enemy will employ. You know who to stay away from and who to trust—though, like the guy in the X-files, it is probably best to trust *no one*. (And that's a little play on words for those readers who are super-astute.) So it doesn't really matter just how much heavy artillery you drag into the war zone. If you don't know the terrain, you'll be a lot like the Marines at the Chosin Reservoir. Oh, you can take your stand, and maybe even survive, but your losses will be so great you'll never ever be the same again.

All of this led to my decision to cut and run at the ripe old age of eighteen. I was in the bottom of the ninth in my senior year and though the body building had paid off to the point that the jocks had stopped picking on me, I was still an outcast, a weird looking transplant from the sweet sunny south and a stranger in a strange land. I was sick to death of it. I wanted out.

Plus I still didn't have the car mom had promised she'd buy upon my last birthday. So I couldn't even escape to nearby Athens, a really cool college town which existed in what appeared to be its own dimension. Yeah, that might have swayed my decision to hit the road. But for reasons that will always remain a mystery to me, mom had reneged on her promise of a car and instead had sunk a large amount of money into the purchase of an aviary. This menagerie now took up the entire side porch of our house, a position way too close for comfort since it could only be accessed via my bedroom. Not only did that necessitate many a unannounced visit from my mom—sometimes even in the middle of the night when she would begin to worry if the temperature was just right for her little darlings—but the noise itself prohibited any chance of ever getting a good night's sleep. I can't even begin to describe the incredible squawking. It was a true cacophony, but what do you expect when you have ten cockatiels, six parrots, two cockatoos, a handful of love birds, umpteen canaries, and a partridge in a pear tree? Thank God she drew the line at chickens, but come to think of it, at least chickens would have been useful. As it was, I could see nothing productive about any of the above and particularly hated the Green Amazon with its endless chatter. *Arriba! Arriba!* It would shout from its prominent perch, and if I'd been allowed a gun, it would have been reduced to a cloud of feathers on more than one occasion.

Needless to say, my grades began to plummet with the advent of these feathery demons and worse yet, all the cats had been shipped out including the one which had befriended me upon my arrival.

"Can't have those two species under the same roof," Mom had declared in a fit of conviction. "They mix about as well as oil and water."

However, I suspected her decision had less to do with interspecies dynamics than the sheer fact that she just didn't like the little furballs. Except for Snowy, who had never returned from her extended walk-about.

Alas, it was all too much for a cat lover. Plus, that string of red letters I'd been receiving at school was about to take its toll, a serious one that would have me repeating more than one subject if I ever intended to graduate. No way was I going to stay in that hellhole one minute past my eighteenth birthday. So when the auspicious date arrived in late March, I took matters into my own hands.

Standing in front of my mom's bedroom door, the only one in the house which actually had a lock on it, I summoned my nerve. Then I summoned the priestess of Quetzalcoatl within.

"Maw!" (My moniker for the one who bore me had changed, morphed by the redneck environment in which I'd found myself.) "Maw!" I repeated, when there was no reply. "I'm going to drop out of high school and go wwoofting."

That got her attention and, after a brief spell during which I heard cabinets closing and drawers shutting, the lady emerged looking somewhat disheveled. I knew without asking that she had been at it again, indulging in her other hobby/habit. Let's just call it a Hobbit, for good measure. Peeking within, I noticed the traces of tissue paper which littered the floor behind her.

"Got the collection out again?" I asked, and she nodded in reply.

I groaned and hoped it wasn't audible. It would appear that my mother, who had never been able to stay in one place longer than a lease allowed, was now taking full advantage of a home owner's propensity to accumulate junk. OK. So that would be putting it mildly. Accumulate was too gentle a word. Let's call a spade a spade. Though I hated to admit it, she was taking on all of the characteristics of a full blown hoarder; and like many who are afflicted with said disease, she had a specialty area.

Hers was Christmas paraphernalia, and I remember the day the disease took root in her consciousness. We'd been going through Grandma Mysterious's attic. And I might interject at this point that there may have been a family curse involved here because the attic was no easy task to tackle. The rest of the house had been doable—fairly Spartan, in fact. But the attic was another story, and Lord God Almighty, it held just about everything short of the usual bats one might expect to find in such a belfry.

"Didn't Grandma ever throw anything out?" I'd queried in disbelief as we unpacked box after box of junk. There were high school yearbooks dating back to the 1930's, letter sweaters, World War II memorabilia, wedding gowns yellowed by age, boxes of books (some even classics), beat-up guitars and fiddles sans strings, and even a large collection of silver dollars. (And those, my friends, were quickly confiscated by you know who.)

Of course, that was the good stuff. The bad encompassed a true plethora of useless junk. Gizmos destined for sale at the local Salvation Army. What-nots—same fate. Volatile, flammable fluids of an unknown nature—to be disposed of carefully. Broken old crap—toss it. Thing-a-ma-jigs—????What-cha-ma-call-its—??? Paperwork from the 1940's—incinerate it. A six-month supply of dried food—eat it, if we ever got snowed in, and a case of home-made wine—drink it if it's the end of the world. It was worse than the festerschnitzel we'd found in the freezer, an aging appliance which had the bad taste to break down shortly after the old lady's demise. Worse because this stuff actually had to be painstakingly sorted through. Whereas the festerschnitzel—my word for food that is growing a new species of mold—was merely escorted to the nearest dumpster.

But the piece de resistance, the icing on the cake, was the Christmas crap. When my mom's eyes lit up upon its discovery, I should have guessed trouble was brewing.

"The Christmas ornaments," she oozed. "I can't believe she actually saved them."

Oh, you can't. Well just look around you? OK, so those were my thoughts, and notice that I put them in italics because some words are just not meant to be spoken. So I nodded in silent assent, not knowing as I did so that I was releasing the demon from the bottle.

"Oh, we have to save these!!! Did you know that she bought me a new one for every year of my life?"

I looked at the overstuffed box. It measured a good two foot on each side. *And you're about how old? One hundred and fifty?* Once again I struggled with the impulse to verbalize my thoughts and once again held my tongue.

But mom was off and running, tearing into the box and separating each one of these archaic pieces of crap from the crinkly paper that enveloped them.

"And here's the Last Unicorn bulb, and the American Flag bulb, and even that special Swarovski crystal snowflake she picked up in a boutique in South Hills when we went over there one winter to see the lights. Gee, I wonder if that place is still in business."

And those, my friends were famous last words cuz it was all downhill from there. Alas, some people just should never come into money!

I think it's called it the culture of poverty, and I believe some lady named Ruby Payne actually wrote a book about it. Inside was a questionnaire to determine what social class you might best relate to, and it went without saying that we belonged to the lower rung of the ladder. Yes indeed, we could survive in poverty. We knew how to find the best thrift shops and locate grocery stores that have thrown-away food. We —or at one of us, after the body building and Wing Chun—could fight and defend ourselves. We could live without electricity, a checking account, a car, and a phone. We could get by when we didn't have money to pay the bills and had come up with a host of ways to put off a persistent slum lord. And when he finally caught up with us, we could move in less than a day. We knew how to access the freebies: food stamps, TANF, and medical clinics, and we were experts at bartering for the stuff the government wasn't giving away. Then, to cap it all off, Lord knows, we had our priorities, often paying our cable bill before our rent and stuffing our house full of cheap shit from the Family Squalor.

So, by now, you can see where this is leading. It's been said that rich people have less stuff, but what they have is worth some coin; whereas poor people like to fill up their space with a plethora of plastic crap they bought for a buck or less. Why, just looking at all that junk gives them comfort. It makes them think they actually own something, despite the fact that most of it either belongs in a landfill or will be languishing there within a year. That said, these were the circles in which we traveled, a road which I hate to admit was hardly the one *less* traveled in this fair country.

In fact, our recent census did not paint a pretty picture as far as poverty was concerned. According to their surveys, in 2002 (the year in which I left high school) the number of Americans living in poverty was up by 1.3 million, while the number of those without health care insurance had risen from 43.6 million to 45 million. These were scary enough statistics by themselves, but when you put them into the context of the overall population, they get worse. Loosely translated, the percentage of folks in this country who reflected this economic travesty was hanging at twelve and one-half percent. That meant that over one out of ten households were low income, and the bulk of them contained children. Good Lord! That's as bad as some third world countries.

Daniel Rose

But I digress. Back to the story at hand, or should I say, at foot because mine were getting itchy, itchy enough to cause me to divide the next five years of my life between two occupations: shit jobs and wwoofting (and some, who are ill-informed, might lump the two into one category). This would take place because they simply don't understand the fine art of wwoofting, which in my opinion is an excellent way for a young guy of modest means to see the world on a shoestring budget. If, that is, he doesn't mind shoveling a little manure and digging a few ditches. Actually, wwoofting is not all hard labor despite the fact that the word itself is an acronym for World Wide Opportunities on Organic Farms, and we all know that farm is a four-letter word. Anyway, the whole purpose of the program is to link *volunteers with organic farmers and growers to promote cultural and educational experiences based on trust and non-monetary exchange, thereby helping to build a sustainable, global community.* (And that's taken straight from the website.)

So you can sign up in either capacity, and three guess which one I chose? Why volunteer, of course, since there was no way I could convince anybody that mom's postage stamp back yard with its numerous piles of composting cat crap constituted an organic farm. At any rate, I started out small and stayed within the confines of my native country. It was a good way to get those itchy feet wet, but later after I'd learned the ropes, I quickly expanded my horizons to Mexico and then Central America. However, I never did manage to save up enough cash to explore the more exotic regions. You see, my MO was to work six months at a true blue shit job like McDonalds or Wal-Mart and then hit the WWOFT trail, and as WWofters don't get paid for their labor, I had to come up with both plane fare and enough dinero to see me through my gig.

The only glitch was wheels. I still needed some sort of transportation, and that's where those silver dollars came in handy. Guess mom felt guilty about gobbling up all the estate plums for herself and decided to share a bit of the wealth.

"Go ahead and take them," she'd indicated on that fatal day in the attic, and I was quick to comply. So take them I did, and for several months they languished in the bottom of my dresser drawer, to the point that I wondered if I, too, was falling victim to the family curse. But then, my eighteenth birthday arrived and with it a renewed interest in obtaining my own wheels. So one night, while bored out of my mind, I decide to look up their value, and… Holy Cow!!! Was I ever pleasantly surprised because no way were these babies going to the local pawn shop! Just to be on the safe side, the next time we were downtown, I double checked with an antique dealer who confirmed my initial assessment—and who, incidentally, tried to take them off my hands for a sum that was shameful considering their true value. But by that time, I was getting real good at computers, good enough to set myself up on an E-Bay auction. The results weren't as great as I'd hoped, but they did give me a good down payment on a ten year old Subaru which became my ticket to ride. With wheels, I was able to scoot on down to Athens and apply at every fast food place on the strip, and there were quite a few to choose from, it being a college town and all. Hallelujah! I was on my way to a better, though not necessarily brighter (as far as brain power goes) future.

Now things would have been easier had mom not charged me rent, a sum she had no real need for since Grandma Mysterious had apparently left her enough cash to last a lifetime—if she didn't spend it all on Christmas paraphernalia and exotic birds. But to my credit I always managed to come up with the money she required and by the first of the month at that, a feat which she herself had rarely been able to accomplish. So what's all that shit about the apple not falling too far from the tree?

Anyway, all I can say is that these were good years. I was able to achieve what we millennials do best and that's reinvent the wheel as far as employment is concerned. For half of the year—the worst half because I always left in October to return about mid-March—I was my own man, and if I had to pay for that with working for the MAN for the other six months? Well...so be it because the stuff I did while wwofting was well worth the terminal tedium of my summer jobs. I milked goats in Mexico, gathered eggs in Guatemala, butchered rabbits and tanned hides in Honduras, and even harvested coffee in Costa Rica. And I could have gone on like this forever had not the economy taken a down turn.

I was working at a small farm in Kentucky when the shit began to hit the fan. It was not my usual summer job. For starters, it was pretty far away from home, and it was pretty late in the season considering that I was generally on a plane to some banana republic by then. Plus it involved the butchering of over one hundred hogs, and though I had done such work on a small-time basis, this was a much bigger operation. Besides, the bunnies I'd butchered while down in Honduras had just about convinced me to become a complete vegetarian—or else convert to the redneck school of the Great and Wonderful Hunt. Yeah, at least that way my meat course stood a fighting chance and wasn't just being raised for slaughter.

However, there was something about the latter which really disturbed me. Doesn't it say in the good book to *Do unto Others*? Well, shouldn't that include ALL others and not just the two-legged ones? Philosophical questions, I know, but when compounded with the reality of blood and guts, it was hard not to ask them.

Nevertheless, while working my present gig, I'd shut my mouth and continued to wield my butcher knife. After all, I needed the cash if I were to reach my goal. My summer job that year hadn't been very productive. Tired of flipping burgers and delivering pizzas, I had decided to try more meaningful employment and had signed on as a peer tutor for a summer enhancement program. But I soon found out why education is a piss-poor career. God! No wonder so many of my teachers worked two jobs. I was appalled at how much had been shaved off my pay for bullshit I'd never heard of. Why so much for workman's comp and Medicare? And what the fuck was the teacher resource fund??? Lord knows, I would have quit right then and there, but by that time, it was mid-summer and most of the good shit-jobs—if such an animal truly exists—had been taken by the local kids. So I hung in there until the bitter end, only to discover that airline fares had gone through the roof over the summer, and I was about three hundred dollars shy of my goal if I were to escape another the brutal Ohio winter.

That's when one of the ladies who worked the lunch room told me about the hog farm. I'd just come in to pick up my last paycheck. It was predictably thin, and I was pissing and moaning to myself when I ran into Juanita in the hallway. Juanita was what you would have called a wetback in the old days before political correctness reared its divisive head. Her whole family had emigrated from Mexico via the Mojave Desert and little by little had worked their way north to the Tennessee River Valley. Along the way they had done it all. Harvested citrus in California, worked feed lots in Texas and chicken processing plants in Arkansas. After a spell they settled in Maggie Valley, North Carolina where they picked tomatoes and beans in the summer and apples in the fall. Then, they'd migrated further north to Cincinnati where a distant relative had set up base, and here they stayed, branching out from the slums of that fair city to work just about any job within reason. And the pig farm in Kentucky just barely fit that bill.

"Eet's hard work, gringo, but the pay is good," she'd informed me. And I'd set aside my injured pride upon being referred to by such a racial epithet—yep, this political correctness shit can work both ways—and had taken down directions. Pay? Good? That was all I heard. It was Bowling Green or Bust.

I had to admit that the place was not really what I'd expected. Even though it had all the trappings of being a bona fide operation, you got the sense there was something else going on. The whole place smacked of a smokescreen.

For starters, the proprietor, a middle–aged lady by the name of Leslie, did not seem too concerned about the production line. She only had three employees and the turnover was terrific. In fact, I was the only one who lasted the entire two weeks it took to butcher the hundred plus head of hogs. The rest were all day laborers, courtesy of Manpower, and they spoke broken English at best.

Every morning Leslie would fire up her twenty year old International travel-all and haul ass down to the local employment office. There she'd pick up whoever looked the dumbest, bring them back for a fun-filled day on the farm, and then she'd reverse the procedure in the PM. She always paid cash and was fairly generous with it (as Juanita had assured me).

How I managed to be such a favored employee was beyond me except that it might have had something to do with her crack about how I resembled a long-lost relative. To be specific: a son that she had given up for adoption at the tender age of sixteen. And yeah, there were pictures of the kid in her living room, a space which very few of her employees had ever had gained access to. And yeah, he did look a little like me though it was hard to tell because the pictures were pretty grainy, being clippings from far away newspapers, which brought to light the fact that Leslie really did NOT have any sort of real relationship with the guy, but was just participating in his life from a voyeuristic standpoint.

And that was just one of her peculiarities. Others included her sexuality. Yeah, she was distinctly of the LBGT persuasion. And she was also a card carrying medical marijuana user way before such a status existed. That is to say, she was perpetually stoned, and it didn't take long for her to sense a soul mate in that department. I wasn't there but two days before she began to offer me a few bong hits in the evening.

"Come on up to the big house, Noonnie," she'd propose and, after my initial hesitation, I was quick to comply.

Hesitation? When it came to the sacred herb? Well, to be honest my first reaction was to wonder if there would be any hanky-panky involved, and this was not an attractive proposition considering her butch haircut, floppy breasts and enormous hips. However, her overall behavior soon assured me that this was no cougar in search of a gigolo. Nope, it was more a brother-in-arms, somebody to sit around the pot-bellied stove and trade a few good stories while smoking some of the best weed I'd been treated to all summer.

The stereo would be playing old Bob Dylan tunes and we'd be singing along.

The summer is gone,
The air's turning cold,
The stars one by one they'll be folding.
My children will go as soon as they grow
Cuz there ain't nothing here now to hold them.

The fireflies had fled, and fall was not only in the air; it was in the earth and water as well. The leaves had turned their customary golden and the mists of September had morphed into the crisp dawns of October. It was perfect hog slaughtering weather, and also perfect weather for harvesting yet another cash crop. So after a week of smoking primo herb, I began to figure it all out.

"The goat barn went up fast," Leslie shared with me one night, following a fairly potent bong hit. She was referring to another building on her property, one which as yet had not attained the darkened status of weathered wood. It was a deluxe piece of architecture by dirt farm standards, having the benefits of not only electric, but running water. When she'd first shown it to me I had to wonder. All this muss and fuss for a couple of lousy goats? It was pretty weird, but then again, I'd learned during the span of my short life not to question *weird*. Come on, I had a mother who collected Christmas crap like there was no tomorrow and let's not even get into her fascination with feathered fowl. So if Leslie wanted to treat her goats to a Taj Mahal, so be it. What business was it of mine?

"Started it in October and hammered in the last board in December. Got 'er up right before the first snow." Her voice was droning on and I could tell she felt like talking. But there was something not quite right here. Suddenly, I was afraid of where this conversation was going. After all, loose lips sink ships and sometimes the less info the better. It goes with that old saying of what you don't know can't hurt you.

However, as usual, my curiosity got the better of me.

"And?" I prompted.

"Well, let's just say that's quite a speed record, especially considering the foundation took over a month. Had to call in a back hoe to dig out the hole and, boy oh boy, did I ever keep those boys down at Manpower busy!!!"

A back hoe? For an aggrandized shed. Ah ha! The plot thickens.

She must have sensed my next question because she sure enough answered it.

"That's right. The thing's got a full basement. Wanna see it?" And at this she winked before adding "You can keep a secret, can't you?"

I just stared at her. We'd only known each other a little over a week. How did she know she could trust me? But her eyes spoke a strange story, one of a shared history that went way beyond any resemblance to a long lost child. It was a odd moment for me because I'd never really dabbled in the mystic arts, being more a meat and potatoes guy when it came to my beliefs. Oh, I had toyed with all the usual suspects. Christianity with its heaven and hell. Islam with its one hundred virgin reward.(I kind of liked that one.) Eastern religions with their reincarnation. Quantum theory with its... oh, what the fuck??? But I had more or less come out the other end of the meat grinder as a born again atheist. It is what it is, I liked to say, and when it's over, it's over. We're here today, gone tomorrow... dust in the wind, as one of my favorite groups liked to put it.

Still, I could not deny the connection. There was something more here than what met the eye. Destiny had rapped at my door and Leslie had answered. She was somehow instrumental to my karma—though I groaned to use that word.

Her eyes were boring holes into my forehead, just about where that damned third eye might be, and goddamn if I wasn't tongue-tied.

"It's OK," she assured me. "I cast the cards about you, and I've got to say I haven't had such a favorable array in a long time. You may be a bit of a joker in my deck, but you check out just fine."

The cards? Surely she did not mean Poker. Or Gist or any of those other parlor games so popular amongst the bored and jaded. No, she must have been referring to the Tarot.

Suddenly visions of one of my mom's friends came into my mind, a lady in a caftan and turban. The turban actually was a cover-up for her chemo-depleted hair, but that is neither here nor there. The get-up still made her look straight out of the pages of the Mahabarata. She could have been Swami Ticklemyasswithafeather, which would have been appropriate since she'd been waving one of the cockatoo's tail feathers around as she spoke. Clearing the air of any toxic energy was the rational, but I figured it was more to cool her jets since it had been about one hundred degrees in the shade that day, making it a fine one for floor length caftans.

It was a funny image and funnier yet when I envisioned my present smoking companion in such a get-up. The only plus was that it would have concealed her none-too-attractive mounds of flesh, but I'll betcha she still would have worn those muck boots she was so fond of. Talk about a bull dyke in a China shop!!! Or in this case, a Hindu one.

It was all too much and I began to giggle. It was a tiny sound at first, a mere snicker, but it didn't take long for it to burst into a full blown guffaw, one which by its very nature was as contagious as the plague. Before long, both of us were rolling on the rug in a floor show that is surely familiar to many who smoke the sacred weed. And when we finally recovered from our attack, she showed me the magic forest.

When she'd informed me on the way over that I would be amazed, I figured she was just blowing smoke up my butt, if you'll forgive my attempt to be *punny*. But once I saw what she'd been up to, I was amazed. In fact, amazement was selling it short; it was almost beyond belief. From the initial moment when she turned the lights on to the final one when I took my last inhale of that delicious aroma, my eyes were gaga and my tongue was drooling.

Now don't get me wrong. I have been a major stoner from the time I turned eleven. Come on, get real. I grew up on the beach and dope was always a way of life with the surfer crowd. It went with the territory. We never went in for the hard stuff—the pills, both uppers and downers, and God forbid, anything with a needle attached to it. But the green herb? Now that was another story, a sacred one so to speak since some of the guys even insisted that its use was endorsed by the good book itself. Make use of every beast that walks, and every green herb that grows, or something like that. And make use we did, toking up in tandem and in triplicate beneath the pier before we paddled out to shoot the curl. So, yes, there was always a bit of Mary Jane in my life, a fair lady who ushered in the day and kissed me goodnight. But a little bit means just that: a small sum. After all, I was a poor kid with not much cash to spend on recreational drugs. So most of my turn-ons were courtesy of my beach brothers, and they were not always as generous as I would have liked.

Then, when we moved to Ohio, it got worse. In fact, it was so bad I was forced to quit for a spell, and the drought lasted until I got my wheels and my first job down in Athens. Only then was I able to locate those of like mind who were willing to sell me a nickel or a dime, which in stoner language is not a very large amount. So at any given stretch I was never in possession of more than a few joints worth, a quantity that I was forced to make last until my next paycheck.

Oh, it got better when I began my Banana Republic tours. Stoners have a way of sensing the presence of kindred spirits—as in Leslie's correct assessment of me—and it never took long for fellow wwofters of like mind to hone in on my cravings. But we always had to be careful. We were, after all, guests in a foreign country, and I emphasize **foreign**. We didn't know the ropes. Who to trust with our gringo greenbacks and who to run like the devil from. So, once again, pickings were slim.

That's why I can assure you that never—and I do mean **never**—in my short life had I ever seen such a delightful display of my favorite green goddesses. Like seductive little succubae, there they were, beaming and beckoning in all their glory. *Come here kid,* they seemed to say. *Come on out and play.* And the only problem came from trying to make a selection.

There were so many varieties there was no way I could sort it all out. In the old days all I had to chose between were Sativas and Indicas; Sativas if I wanted a more cerebral energetic high and Indicas if I wanted to fall on the couch with a bowl of popcorn. But lord love a duck!

Apparently, the fine art of cultivation was a lot more complex than I'd ever imagined. There were Afghans—for those who like high levels of THC, Northern Lights—which Leslie later informed me was a popular choice for indoor growers, Fourway and Ice—both which adapt well to hydroponics, Mazar—for an upper, Nigeria—for sweetness, Hawaii Skunk —if you like the smell of pole cats, Orange Bud—if you like the smell of citrus—and even one called Bubblegum—and three guesses what it resembles?. In short, the list was long, too long to publish in full, but then again, as Leslie insisted, a girl has to keep a few secrets.

"Like it?" she asked as she walked me through the operation, and my response was to ask if a bear shits in the woods.

She just laughed at my comment, and then went on.

"Well, the truth is that I could use a bit of help. The last guy I had over here just left for the greener pastures of Colorado, and harvest time is creeping up on me. Some of these girls have just gotta go if I'm to start the next batch. Damn, sometimes I wish I'd made this basement twice as big, but then I sit down until the mood passes. Shit, I can barely manage the business with the little I've got."

And that *little*, I was later to discover, amounted to a cash crop of over one hundred thousand a year, a tidy sum that Leslie was able to conceal from the IRS due to the wiliness of an extremely clever accountant. I now understood the smokescreen operations of the hog farm and that ridiculous jackass whose sperm she claimed to sell at over a grand a pop. Neither endeavor could have brought in enough cash to cover costs, making them more of a liability than an asset. In truth, most small farms suffer this fate as my neighbors in Ohio assured me. They often complained with a scowl that if they won the lottery, they would probably just keep on farming until the money ran out. Yeah, farming isn't much in the way of a pay off. Unless you're one of the big guys and get government subsidies for allowing your land to lay fallow. And yet people are starving on the planet. What a world.

But again I digress. For the next week, my own personal world was to consist of stripping these lovely ladies from their birthing place and clipping off all their unattractive nose hairs so that all that would remain were those delicious buds within. It was tedious work but paid well, both in terms of monetary reward and my ability to sample the wares. So to say that I remembered too much of that week would be a direct misrepresentation of the facts.

However one thing did stick in my craw. In fact, it was to herald a series of cascading events that would eventually lead me to the brink of bankruptcy. No, not bankruptcy because, at least with that unfortunate status, you get to keep some of your stuff. In my case though it would be a clear case of when you ain't got nothing, you got nothing to lose, and that's a polite way of saying that I barely got out with the shirt on my back.

It came across the newswire one bright day in early October. Leslie had moved a small TV into the bud room. (That was our designation for a tiny alcove that held nothing but a table, two chairs and an overhead light strong enough to blind you if you were stupid enough to gaze directly into its diabolical depths.) She'd commissioned me to attach the thing to the wall so that we'd have something to occupy our thoughts during the long hours we spent preparing the girls for market. It wasn't really my forte since I'd never been much of a handyman, but I somehow figured out how to mount the bracket which came with the thing and then hoist it into a position where both of us could watch. I had to admit it was a big improvement over listening to each other's steady line of bullshit which up to that point had been our only relief from the tedium of the job at hand. Oh yeah, that and the tinny radio Leslie had brought down from the big house, one which she had tuned to an oldies channel. For awhile, it had amused us with such great hits as *Gimme all your Loving* and *The Do Wa Ditty*, pathetic excuses for songs that we both clearly despised.

"Sorry," she'd apologized. "It's all that will come in down here." So we'd forced ourselves to listen until we were both ready to toss the thing into the middle of next week, and then it was back to the bullshit.

Ergo, the TV was somewhat of an improvement. And I say somewhat because it was but one step up the bullshit ladder, being corporate instead of personal. Yeah, even in those pre-fake news days it was fairly obvious that all we were getting was well-polished propaganda with a few real-time events thrown in for good measure. These events were by in large sensationalized and rarely focused on any positive developments. Hurricanes, wildfires, school shootings, nuclear saber-rattling… ah, need I repeat the litany? Anyone who has tuned into your Daily Dose of Depression gets the picture.

Of course, there was other programming. Kiddy shows, game shows, reality shows, Sitcoms, old black and white movies, and re-runs of shit from the sixties. (I particularly liked *Lost in Space* and *The Man from Uncle.*) However, no matter what else we watched, there was never any escaping the news. It began our day, showed up again at noon, and then, at six o'clock, just before quitting time, it reared its ugly head again. Finally, fully satisfied that it had accomplished just the opposite, it had the audacity to close out our viewing with a smiley face and the directive to *Have a Nice Day.* And that was all she wrote until *The Morning Show* began the pathetic process all over again.

However, on occasion, if there was something particularly juicy going down, the news would jump its banks like an unruly river and flood the airways with its vituperative vitriol. Such was the case in the fall of 2008. It actually began several weeks earlier in the year, when on September 15th, a giant Wall Street insurance company by the name of Lehman declared bankruptcy. This caused the Dow Jones average to drop over five hundred points, and began such a downward economic spiral that other companies followed suit. This resulted in the Feds announcing that they were considering a weird little financial maneuver by the name of a bail-out, one which involved using tax-payer money to prop up several banks which had been dubbed *too big to fail*. Oh happy day! The Dow responded by regaining 400 points, and it looked like the bump in the road had passed us by. Yeah, big whoop-de-do to folks like us who store their money either under the mattress or in a hole in the ground.

But it wasn't over. Since it was a Federal affair, it had to be put to the vote, and when the Senate got around to this, the result was not favorable to the economy. In other words, they nixed it, and the Dow fell again, this time 777.68 points. (Round that to 777.7 and one can only wonder if some heavy duty numerology is in play here!) Whatever the case, since this was the most the Dow had ever gone down in any single day, it was devastating, so devastating that even the global markets were affected.

By October, just about the time we peons began to tune in, Congress had changed its fickle mind and had decided to pass the bill, However, by now, the damage was done and on Monday, October 8th, the day of our viewing, the Dow shot down another 800 points, causing it to close under 10,000 for the first time since 2004. We were treated to newsreel after newsreel of panicked investors and talking heads who spouted economic jargon out of both sides of their mouths—and a few other orifices to boot, no doubt! The result was the same. We were in for a rough ride. The 'R' word was being tossed around like the hot potato it was. The only good news was that it was better than the 'D' word.

Of course, the end result of all this would not manifest until much later in the game for a little old wwofter such as myself. And as for Leslie? Well… her capital gains lay spread out in front of us in all their green glory. No, she wouldn't be hurting. In fact, it's well documented that during hard times, any sort of business which caters to a mood altering substance, be it hootch, hops, or heroin, always seems to thrive. So Leslie had nothing to worry about. Her only problem lay in hiding her assets so as to not draw unwarranted attention to her good fortune, and that's where Wil. E. Accountant came into the picture.

Daniel Rose

So we just continued to clip away at the girls and watch as the rest of the country went to hell in a hand basket. It certainly wasn't the first time I'd felt like I had a front row seat on the end of the world. Nor would it be the last.

What I didn't understand at that time in my life was the inter-connective nature of events, which meant that sooner or later the chickens would be coming home to roost in my own little coop as well. It was an oversight that would eventually lead to my demise via those damn TDA accounts, which is how I began this whole narrative and which is how I will end it. Singing a merry tune that was destined to hit a few sour notes as the singer aged and his vocal chords began to go on strike.

But for the present, I was hardly thinking that far into the future. I was still a young guy, footloose and fancy free, and I was just wrapping up a great little gig which had secured my passage to those to sweet sunny southern skies. And since, I had money to burn and time on my hands, why not take a short vacation before making my way to the nearest airport? But where to? I wasn't really familiar with the surrounding terrain despite it being but a stone's throw from my home base in Coolville. So I decided to consult the oracle, the same one who had professed to consulting the Tarot prior to hiring me for my current position.

"Leslie," I broached one morning in-between the national news and the weather, "I've been thinking…"

"A dangerous occupation…" she filled in, always being quick to complete my sentences.

"No, seriously…"

And we both broke out in a fit of laughter. Yeah, like serious was the new norm around here. Hell, the pot and the hysterics it often provoked were the only way we could get through the terminal tedium of the task on hand. But hold on a sec. I really did have a serious inquiry, and since the giggles couldn't last forever, I managed to slip it in during a short intermission during which I explained my desire to catch some of the local color on my way out of town.

Leslie's first reaction was to try to talk me into staying a bit longer. But despite her fondness for me, or maybe because of it, she soon gave up.

"Wish I could go with you," she confessed. "But this little operation needs constant attention. And, besides, I doubt if I could sit in a plane for very long anymore. Plus, I hear that they'll be soon charging folks like me double, if they aren't already. And that's just too big of an insult for a girl to bear."

I looked at her, taking in her considerable bulk, and couldn't help but flash on the old standby line of there being more to love. Yeah, to

26

bad the airlines didn't see it that way. However, I knew when to keep my mouth shut and just smiled at her little attempt to make light of our parting. Then, figuring she'd soon forget the whole conversation, I went back to saturating my fingers with that delicious aroma. True, there was a strong temptation to stick around, but a stronger urge to fly south for the winter. Gee, maybe some of the pent-up desires of maw's feathered friends had rubbed off on me. Just point me to the nearest airport. The hell with site-seeing. And, that was the end of our conversation. Or so I thought.

However, on my last day on the job, Leslie surprised me by pulling out a map of the Bluegrass State.

"Not too much in the immediate vicinity," she began. "But if you like music and the clubs, Lexington is the place for you. And, of course, there's always Churchill Downs if you're into the races and the Louisville Zoo if you like animals and the Daniel Boone National Forest if you feel like roughing it. Oh, and don't forget Mammoth Cave."

She was rattling off the list of attractions as if she was employed by the tourist bureau, and I had to stop her in mid-sentence as she extolled the virtues of everything from bourbon to baseball. The latter could be had at the Louisville Slugger Museum, just one of many oddball attractions I'd never heard of (and didn't much care if I ever did again.) There was the Shaker Village, the Muhammad Ali Center, and the Creation Museum. Then there was a place called Keeneland where I could experience the horses up close and a plethora of tobacco farms where I could work my butt off just in case I ended up blowing all my money at the races.

"Except it's getting a bit late in the season now for the tobacco harvest…" Leslie continued, and it was at that point I cut her off.

"Mammoth Cave," I stated succinctly as I pointed to its South Carolina shaped outline on the map. "It's close and on my way home." Meaning that it was right off the Interstate and easy to get to for a guy who was relying on his thumb as a means of transportation. The Sub had been left at home in sick bay awaiting a fresh input of funds from Big Daddy, AKA me. So I had to factor in ease of access when it came to planning my vacation attack. Plus it was cheap, just a little over ten bucks for a basic tour, and I could spring for that.

So Mammoth Cave it was by a default decision based on convenience and cash flow. Funny how nothing else really figured into the formula. Funny in the sense of odd because as it turned out, I would later discover just how integral that one small decision would be to my overall destiny.

Chapter 2
Lulu (AKA Stitch)
1974-2008

I have always been attracted to the deep places of the earth, the caverns and the crevices, the hollow hills of fairy lore. My fascination began young. I couldn't have been more than eight, and we were on one of those rare family outings.

We lived in Norfolk, Virginia at the time since dad was stationed at the base there. He was lowly second lieutenant in the Marine Corp back then, but well on his way to the top. But that's all another story and a sad one at that, so I'll save it for later.

Through the eyes of an eight-year old, the amount of brass a man wore on his sleeve did not matter much. All I knew on that day was that my daddy was home with us for the first time in six months, and we were finally together as a family again.

It was a bright blue day in summer. One of those days that blow in crisp and cool after a cold front has come to clear the air. The night before, it had stormed. The rain had poured down in sheets while the lightning crackled in the distance. There were even a few downed trees, but nothing so severe as to block our passage. It was the Blue Ridge or Bust, and one thing I already knew about my dad was there was no word for defeat in his vocabulary.

So we'd all climbed into the little grocery getter he kept stateside for my mom to use when he was out at sea, completing one of those mandatory cruises all Marines must endure. Then we'd gunned the poor old bucket of bolts all the way to the edge of Virginia where a camp ground awaited us just off the Parkway.

I don't remember much about the campground except that my mother hated it. Of course, that was nothing new. She hated anything to do with camping since she'd considered herself a city girl and preferred to remain that way. However, since it was one of the few cheap vacations a family of five could take on our present income, she had to make do. I think she would have preferred the Carlton Hilton or the Ritz or wherever spoiled little princesses go to play, but that was not to come until much later. For now she had to accept the fate she had signed on for.

So she kept her complaints to a minimum, and the only time she acted out was in the mornings when she refused to use the community crapper. Instead, she'd forced dad to pack a luggable loo for the purpose of her daily deposit. For those who aren't in the know, that's a portable potty, where one shits in a bucket that's been lined with a bag. What this arrangement had over the toilets at the campground was beyond me, but let's just chalk it all up to a bad case of passive aggression. For this was where dad took over, gathering the bag containing her morning achievements in his loving hands and then scooting the entire mess up to the closest latrine, an act which left us kids scratching our heads in bewilderment.

Though I could never figure it out, such was the nature of their marriage. But once again, I was eight at the time and such speculations were the furthest thing from my mind. Instead, I was more interested in the outing which had been planned for the day as it included a tour of nearby Luray Caverns. Billed as one of the most beautiful caverns in the world, Luray had cast its lure into my eight year old brain and was reeling me in. Little did I know that this was the beginning of a life-long obsession.

I had never been in a cave before but, as we were herded into its dank delicious depths, I knew at once that this would not be a one-shot deal. My eyes went wide at the sight of the stalactites and mites which up to that point had only been a difficult word in my budding vocabulary. The rooms were huge, over ten foot tall, and it was easy to compare them to cathedrals, especially since walking through them was akin to a religious experience.

For once in its babbling brook life my mouth refused to cooperate, and I became speechless. I listened in awe as our guide explained how the cave had been discovered by the town's tinsmith and his thirteen year old nephew. They had been exploring the region one day when they discovered a telltale sinkhole. After four hours of digging through mud and rocks they found an entrance to the cave through which they were lowered via a rope. Then they spent the rest of the afternoon exploring its depths with little more than candles to light their way.

What a picture that painted, and as I later contemplated their bravery, I felt a bit squeamish. You see, despite my fascination with caves, I shared a bit of my youngest brother's extreme claustrophobia. This affliction had been brought to light on an earlier trip to Shenandoah when we'd been trying to squeeze between two towering rocks while exploring the campground. I'd been half way through the gauntlet when I made the mistake of looking up. It was a mistake which forced me to back out and admit defeat. To this day, I can't begin to describe the sensation. It was somewhere between vertigo and nausea. I felt like the walls would close in and swallow me up. It would have been an outright disaster had not my little brother Davey outdone me in the Cowardly Lion department. He'd taken one look at the twin towers and refused to go one step further. So we both just stood there mortified and watched our older brother Joe slide gracefully between the behemoths.

Oh well, this was nothing new. Joe had been groomed to be a bad ass. He was the first born in a family that had been Marine Corp material for over three generations. It was his duty to keep up the family traditions. From the get-go, he knew exactly what was expected of him, to be a fine upstanding Marine. Older than me by five years he was already making plans to attend Annapolis. Dad had encouraged him at every step of the way, insisting that even if his SAT scores weren't high enough, there could always be a few strings to pull. This statement was delivered with multiple winks, ones which assured Joe that his future was secure no matter what. And what a future it turned out to be, though I'm not quite ready to get into that just yet.

As for Davey and I, the other two siblings in this miniature military? Well, our fates/futures were also pre-ordained. Since we came from a good Irish Catholic family, one of us was destined for the clergy, and that would be Davey because at the time he was the only likely candidate. It was a job that he, too, was being primed for since my mother had recently gone down to our local church and signed him up to be an altar boy.

That left me, the middle child, to dispense with. My name was Mary and by now, you are probably getting the picture. Joseph, Mary, and David. All biblical names and ones that could have been hard acts to follow had they not been about as commonplace as dog shit.

Of course, by the time I was eight, mine had been adapted to conform better to the family business. Although Mary was the one given on my birth certificate, I had gone by the nickname of Maureen as long as I could remember. Maureen. It was a play on words since it sounded so much like Marine—as in USMC—as in Marine Corps—and its advent into my life was the beginning of a long string of nicknames that seemed to define my days, changing sometimes daily as they sought to keep up with my ever-evolving personality. There was Worm for bookworm because I liked to read so much, Joanie for Joan Baez because of my fondness for that particular songbird, and then, for the last fourteen years, I had simply been known as little Mz. Black Sheep, a moniker which is self explanatory.

It wasn't supposed to be that way. I was slated for greater deeds. Since Joe was the brawn of our family and Davey the sacrificial lamb for the clergy, this left me to fill the empty spot of brains. The only problem was my head. It was far from empty, having been filled to the brim even at a young age by as many books as I could possible cram into it. Why, I was even reading college textbooks on Philosophy and Psychology when barely out of my first decade! I couldn't help myself. If it was knowledge it had one purpose—to be consumed. And consume I did, a wildfire in search of any suitable tinder that might fan my flames.

Needless to say, I became somewhat of an oddball. With my horn rim glasses and my flat as a pancake chest, I surely would never make it as a Prom Queen. Nor would I achieve the towering heights of the Academic team since that involved having a bit more pizzazz than I could ever muster. Sadly, the chatterbox propensities that I had possessed in my early years dwindled to a permanent shyness that left me stumbling over my own words whenever called upon in class. Debate Club material I simply was not.

So what was left? Not a jock since I was a one hundred pound weakling. Not a computer geek since I was a tad technophobic. Played guitar, but not well, and refused to open my vocal chords if anyone else was in the room. Wasn't into the Goth crap, or the Biker bullshit. Couldn't dance, be it ballroom or belly. Wasn't into sex, drugs, or rock and roll. In fact, I seemed to make a conscientious effort to waltz to the tune of my own drummer, who might best be defined as somewhere between a shrinking wallflower or Sylvia Plath wanna-be. Alas, how could such a weird little creature ever become the one to build the family fortunes? Not that Dad hadn't succeeded in doing this quite well, thank you. By the time of my first year in college, he had risen through the ranks to become a Captain and, according to our mother, Major was soon to follow. But build the fortunes I must since that was what was expected of me in this little pint-sized army.

That said, my first semester in college included such fascinating classes as Introduction to Business and Careers, Introduction to Computer Based Systems (where I was barely able to tread water) and

Principles of Management. Oh yeah, and don't forget the mandatory Math courses. In short, it was the kind of curriculum that sent a budding young poet in search of the nearest door, and I suppose it came as no surprise to anyone when my initial GPA was well below average.

"What happened, sweetie?" my mother inquired after perusing my transcript. "I thought you were good at this kind of stuff."

Her voice was nasal and still held a twinge of her origins. Brought up in the red clay hills of the Piedmont, she'd moved to the big city as soon as she'd graduated from High School. There she took a job which paid so little she was forced to live with an aunt and uncle. Then, when the uncle decided he wanted to extract rent from her in a nontraditional way, she quickly sought the security of a wedding ring. My dad just happened to be in the line of fire—an unfortunate circumstance that he appeared to excel at; and after a whirlwind romance, they were married in a small naval chapel. Joe arrived eight and one half months later, and thus a dynasty was born, a dynasty which I might add did not count math as a strong point.

I wanted to reply that I was just a chip off the old block. I wanted to remind her that the only reason why Joe had made it into Annapolis was on account of those strings Dad had pulled. I wanted to point out that even Davey was not destined for Rocket Science since he'd never pulled more than a D in every Math class he'd ever taken. In fact, I wanted to say a lot of things, especially about Davey because I could already tell he was in trouble. But I held my peace and managed to just smile and assure her that I would try better next time.

Then, when I went back to college, I proceeded to change my major to one of Liberal Arts and change my home address to one in Tasmania so that the Dragon Lady I called mother would never see another transcript again in her life. *Sweetie*, indeed. I knew even then that the bitch really hated my guts, though I could never understand why. At any rate, thus began my rebellion, one that was kicked into high gear two years later when my dad found the bullet which had been pursuing him down through the decades.

The year was 1993, and the place had a weird name that most Americans could neither pronounce nor locate on a map. Whatever our military was doing there was beyond me, but it went down in the history books as the battle for Mogadishu. Ostensibly—how I love that word—our government was there as part of a humanitarian effort to bring relief to a starving populace who were under the thumb of a Somali warlord. But the focus soon shifted from humanitarian to military takeover.

No, wait a minute. I meant *make-over* as let's make the world free for democracy. At any rate, it was soon determined that the warlord, a guy by the Arab sounding name of Mohamed Farrah Aidid, was the root of all the country's problems and it was high time for a regime change. That said, the USMC was assigned the task of capturing him and removing him from power.

In a mission slated to take place in little over an hour, Special Forces were sent into a burned out building where Aidid and his lieutenants were said to be meeting. Although the initial part of the mission went off without a hitch, the return trip soon spiraled out of control when the Task force was attacked by Somali troops. This resulted in two US helicopters being shot down by RPG's, an incident that I would later read about in the celebrated book *Black Hawk Down*.

It was the least I could do, reading that book. Not that my father had any direct involvement. I said he caught a bullet, but I meant so metaphorically. Yes, he was at the scene. No doubt about that. However, his demise came about in a second hand way, as the bullet was to the heart and not the head. Some might find it ironic that he shared the same fate as the warlord Aidid, who reportedly died of a heart attack three years later following surgery for a gunshot wound. But life is filled with ironies now, isn't it? Just as it is filled with sorrows, and when the men in uniform arrived at my mother's door on that crisp cold night in October, the news they brought was to become the first and −unfortunately not the last−sorrow of my sweet short life.

As I look back on it, I wonder if his heart was broken by this battle, as it was one of the few in which our military suffered a defeat. We never did restore any hope−that was the name of the operation: RESTORE HOPE−and today Somalia remains steeped in poverty and burdened with the reputation of being one of the most dangerous countries in the entire world. Beheadings, executions, pirates, terrorism, famine, suffering…it has it all, a true hell on earth. And though I had never been very political−despite coming from an extremely political family−up to that point I had always shared my father's belief that he was doing the right thing. Then came his untimely death (he was only forty-eight when he died) and a personal Waterloo. I began to question and question hard. And my questions always brought me back to the same conclusion, one which was far from pleasant.

I kept asking myself why this man's death affected me so. For starters, he was somewhat of a ghost figure in my life, always leaving for tours of duty which averaged anywhere from six to eighteen months. Do the math (a course of study that no one in my family excelled at) and you will soon see that my exposure to him had been minimal during the first two decades of life. But let's not confuse quantity with quality. One thing I will say for dad was that, during those rare times when he was around, he really did try to be the family man. That is, when his job didn't get in the way. Oh, he worked long hours, especially towards the end, but he always found time for those family outings. Hiking in Shenandoah, Quantico air shows, visits to his own family in Maine and even trail bike expeditions into the surrounding Virginia countryside.

However, that last one I was deemed too feeble to participate in. It was a guy thing. Yeah, dad always was kind of sexist. His future for me involved either a secretarial job or a marriage to a fine upstanding Marine, one which would produce the desired heir with which to perpetuate the family business.

Part of my soul searching following his demise was the realization that this *brains of the family* bullshit originated with my Mother. She was the one who wanted the security of at least one child who would bring home the big bucks. She was the one who lived in dire fear of a Marine widow's pension. Yet she was also the one who refused to work or establish her own career, feeling surely that such a move was beneath her dignity. After all, she was the wife of a Captain—soon to be a Major—and there were all those Marine Balls to shop for, and an image to be kept up, and oh yes, so many white gloves to wash.

In fact, she was so preoccupied with maintaining her reputation that I knew she would never ask twice about the absence of any more transcripts in the mail. One was enough, as it assured her that I was on the tract she'd set for me. And, if I wasn't charging out of the gate? Well, so what? I would pick up speed eventually if not for the simple reason that she had decreed it. She who was God and supreme ruler of all within her domain.

As for dad, even if he had been around to notice my college career change, he wouldn't have given a rip. His focus had never been on me. He had simply been happy that his marriage had produced two sons, an heir and a spare, so to speak. It was Joe who'd received most of his attention. Davey was merely a back-up: Plan B in case something went south with the first born.

And me? Well, for the most part, dad had struck a middle road between ignoring me and tolerating my presence. I was, after all, his seed, so I had to be worth something. And since I was such a boot licker, a true blue daddy's little girl, I am sure he'd been flattered by my attentions. I'd excelled at my role as the pipe and slippers girl, the one who brought his briefcase in the morning and his beer in the evening. Indeed, how could such an Obsessive–Compulsive guy not appreciate all that attention to detail? Why, it was more than his loving spouse ever mustered, especially the part about the beer which she watched like a hawk, always cutting him off after a few quick drinks before dinner.

"I don't want him to get like all these other guys," she'd explained, which I taken to mean her own dad and two brothers, absent members of the family who we never—and I do mean **never**—saw. Oh, we heard of their antics occasionally, usually when someone from mom's rural roots would call with a wild story about a Duke's of Hazard style car chase or some bootlegger bust high in the hills.

"Yep, John-Boy's in trouble agin. Thought he could outrun the law in that souped–up Charger of his. But, the Sherriff's got a few tricks of his own up his sleeve. Thank the good Lord the boy wasn't haulin much this time…"

This time? Wow! Just how many repeat performances did one John-Boy need? Seemed like the poor devil spent more time in jail than out of it, providing little more than on-going Grade B entertainment for the distant members of his family. His were savory stories, but they were soon swept under the rug and exiled to the dustbin of history, along with any generating from that part of the country.

It was my mother's way of breaking the fragile bonds that held her to her rustic roots, and it worked for many years. However, with the death of my father, times were changing. The glue which had held us together had come undone, and we were headed straight for the same sort of nether regions the John Boys of the world inhabited.

During the first months following my father's death, we were merely stunned, walking around like a bunch of robots on autopilot. Oh, we did the standard stuff: the military funeral at Arlington, the twenty-one gun salute, the folded flag given to a grieving widow. But then we had to go back to whatever lives we'd had before and that was the hard part, proving once and for all that postpartum depression can hit as hard after a death as it can a birth.

The shit began to hit the fan and in a big way. Joe—who was now a gunnery sergeant in the very same Corps that had claimed the life of our father—began to volunteer for the most dangerous duties he could find. Mother became obsessed with her check book, and Joey not only refused to attend Mother's church of choice, but vowed that he was taking up atheism. It made for was one hell of a Christmas, and when I went back to school in January, I hit a wall.

It was called depression, and I spiraled out of control, just like one of those Black Hawks which had come to crash and burn on the Somalian sands. I landed in my own version of hell, and unlike the hapless pilots of these ill-fated birds, there was no rescue mission planned for little old me. Like many in the battle for this planet, I was just an innocent bystander, collateral damage of a system that has ravaged the place for thousands of years. Something had to give and give in a big way.

Although practically a teetotaler, I began to go to parties where the alcohol flowed freely. There I would proceed to party until I puked, an indignity which caused me to seek a less invasive way to get high, and since it was the 1990's, a decade which was later compared to the Roaring Twenties, excess was everywhere. Not only were there the old stand-bys like Marijuana and LSD, but we now had Codeine, Ecstasy, Cocaine, Crack and Crystal Meth to contend with. Throw in a bit of Heroin for good measure and you have quite the cocktail (though, to my credit, I never got down quite that far). Mostly, it was the Cocaine and Crank that got me going because by nature I had always been somewhat phlegmatic, a bit on the slow side and reluctant to appear too excited about much of anything. Such character traits did not make me the bell of the ball. In fact, they manifested in an overwhelming shyness that had me shrinking ever further into the woodwork. But snort a little coke or crank and, boy oh boy, did I ever come out of my shell. A social butterfly, I forgot all about my fear of the marketplace or any other place for that matter and went all out, first as a dancing queen, and then, when my feet gave out from underneath me, as a self-professed know-it-all about a number of topics that I would proceed to expound upon until all hours of the night.

That was how I met Jeremy, a tall lanky townie with bad breath who suffered from a similar syndrome. However, his nemesis was not so much drugs, but more an extreme addiction to bad poetry. We hooked up for the first time in one of the many late night coffee houses that lined the streets of the little college town in the Virginia foothills where I'd been spending the last three years of my life. He'd been up at the open mike spouting off some sort of dribble which reminded me vaguely of Ferlinghetti, and we hit it off immediately. And why not? We were two frustrated poets in search of a rhyme, two dreamers in search of a dream, two lost kids in search of a home. It made for an interesting few years.

But, before I begin, let me make one thing perfectly clear. I'm just not one of those women who are seeking a man merely to spice up her life. Nor am I seeking a woman because, in essence, I am somewhat androgynous. Sex never held much of a thrill for me, which was one of the reasons why I was still a virgin when I met Jeremy. As luck would have it, so was he, and it took him a while to work up the nerve to risk exploration into that foreign country. Ergo, by the time we finally did get around to the dirty deed—an act which was so bad we both swore there would never be any repeat performances—we had already established a bond based on other interests. The main one was travel, which led to me to carve out a place for him in my life as my own personal Bobby Magee.

And if you need a reference for that, I'd advise you to check out the song by the same name. That's right, from the coal mines of Kentucky to the California sun, Jeremy shared the secrets of my soul. OK, so it was never quite that poignant. Still travel was one of our main thrills, and like many a thrill, it became addictive as one thing led to another.

Our first forays were local. Since neither of us had any wheels at the time, we had to depend on our thumbs which meant we couldn't stray too far from home. After all, I still had the illusion of classes to attend and Jeremy? Well… he was heading for Valedictorian status, so he had to show up for roll call at the local high school on Monday mornings. For these reasons we kept it simple. We hitched to nearby Shenandoah Park and hiked in the woods. We checked out a few Civil War battle sites, gazed at Jefferson's stately home of Monticello, and stood in awe before Virginia's Natural Bridge. Despite the rinky-dink nature of our explorations, it was all new and exciting to me. Despite having been in the area for over thirty-six months, I had never even attempted to set foot off campus.

But that was the old me. The new one, fueled by Coke, was itching for adventure and ready to run with the wolves, and in Jeremy, I soon discovered I'd hit the jack pot. Of all the guys I could have hooked up with, he was the perfect fit for that time of my life. Bad teeth and bad sex aside, he still possessed some excellent perks. Ironically, one was his age because, although he was a good two years younger than me—a fact which often had me feeling like a cradle robber—his youth came complete with a real prize. Let's just call it a high school graduation present for short, even though I knew that he'd done his part in manifesting this dream.

We were thumbing back from one of our little adventures when he first shared the good news with me. The rain had been pouring down in sheets and nothing was shaking in the ride department, so we had sought shelter under an overpass. Although it was a grim day further compounded by shitty weather, Jeremy was in great spirits.

"What's up with you?" I asked as he handed me the joint he'd been saving for such emergencies. "You look like the cat that's swallowed a canary."

And it was true. All day long I'd the sense he'd been sitting on a big secret. Well, it was now or never to spill the beans. Lord knows, I needed some positivity in my life about then. But he only grinned revealing once again some of the worst teeth I'd ever seen on a human being. Good gracious, why hadn't his parents stepped up to the plate with an orthodontist? Or maybe they had, only to discover that no self-respecting professional would venture anywhere near that skanky mouth.

I admit that these were not the nicest thoughts and caused me to feel more than a twinge of guilt when he delivered his response.

"Remember that old green Subaru we went to look at last weekend? The one that needed a little work?"

I nodded. Yeah, how could I forget that rusting bucket of bolts? I hadn't said so at the time, but it seemed to me as if it needed more than a *little* work.

"Well, he continued. "It's now mine and in a couple of months, God willing, it will be ready for the road. Then all we will have to do is come up with a little cash and off we go. Into the wild blue yonder. Just like we've been talking about."

OK. If it sounds too good to be true, it probably is. But I was fairly naïve at the time and, following his little speech, could only squeak a few words of appreciation. Here I had been almost ready to dump him and now this. The carrot at the end of the stick, the pot of gold at the end of the rainbow. It would more than make up for two months of enduring his bad poetry delivered by a skank mouth that never seemed to get enough cigarettes. There was actually a light at the end of the tunnel, a cure for the terminal depression which had set in following my father's death. It was the be-all cure-all of the open road, and it hardly mattered if I'd be running away from something or running to it. At least I wouldn't be at a standstill, churning my wheels while waiting tables at the local diner, catering to the very same college students who used to be my peers.

Yes, I knew what fate awaited me if I didn't get the hell out of that town. I figured there was only one more semester of guaranteed student loans before the college caught up with me. My GPA was shot, I hadn't been to a class in weeks, and the letters were already arriving about my failure to make *satisfactory academic progress*. Thank God they hadn't figured out that my home address was bogus, or I'm sure I would have been hearing from the Dragon Lady Supreme. I can't imagine her reaction when she'd found out that I had taken all the money I was supposed to spend on books and supplies and diverted it into my nose! So all that was left would be a life of indentured servitude at McJob's. After all, what else could I do? I could hardly go home, and my Liberal Arts education had left me with absolutely no marketable skills. Alas, it was either the Busy Bee Diner or California, here I come, and it didn't take a genius to figure out which way THAT wind would blow.

So I hung in there with Jeremy, despite my restlessness in the relationship. What could I say? He was the best option I had going. Let's call it any port in a storm. The only problem came when that storm turned into a terminal drizzle that just didn't want to let up. When May rolled around, the Sub still hadn't rolled out of the garage, and it looked as if our *dead*lines were leaving us dead in the water.

My finals were in two weeks and Jeremy's graduation would follow shortly thereafter, and still no wheels. Not that it was the end of the world, but I'd had my heart set on beginning our odyssey by scooting over to the rainbow festival in Kentucky.

We'd both heard of these loosely knit gatherings where old hippies spouted a universal doctrine of peace, love, and environmental awareness, and they'd sounded right down our alley. A few days with them should make the perfect introduction to life on the road. Besides, if you are looking to leave from home, sometimes it's best to have another home in mind to run away to, thus kick-starting the process.

Unfortunately though, Jeremy did not share my enthusiasm because every time I mentioned the Rainbows, he had to bring my attention back to an unfortunate incident which had occurred right next door in the Mountain State of West Virginia.

"Did you know that back in 1980 the Rainbow Festival was slated to be held just a stone's throw from here? That's right, just over the mountains in Pocahontas County, West Virginia. But, boy oh boy, did peace and love ever turn to murder and drugs. Seems like these two young girls were hitchhiking to the festival, and somebody real bad must have picked em up cuz their naked bodies were found with their throats slit."

Naked bodies? Throats slit. Well, I'm not sure it had been that graphic, but Jeremy always did like to embellish. Whatever the case, the incident had rocked the world of the Rainbows, and though resulting in multiple arrests, no one was ever convicted. It remains a mystery to this day, and one Jeremy possessed a macabre fascination with. (Though I cannot for the life of me understand why, since he must have been all of four years old at the time of the incident!)

Whatever the case, it became a struggle. I had to keep reminding him all this had happened thirteen years ago, and in the time between there had never been another problem. Not that it much mattered, since due to his inability to get the Subbie running in time, we'd never make the gathering anyway.

Now, don't get me wrong. I don't want to make it look like I'm slamming him. He surely deserved an A for effort, a quality which was becoming more and more elusive to my own drugged out brain. But his meticulous procrastination was beginning to get on my nerves. This was probably about the same time I began to notice the differences between us. Although he'd initially presented himself to me as foot loose and fancy free, another Dharma bum in search of truth and freedom, I realized that he was really singing out of a different hymnal.

For starters, he still had both parents and—wonder of all wonders—they were more than a little supportive of his wanderlust. In fact, they'd been the ones to provide him with half the start-up cash he'd needed for the Subbie project. But the remainder of the money had come from a series of after-school jobs that Jeremy had been humping away at for the past three years. Talk about an industrious little beaver, especially compared to my newly established identity as a perpetual partier.

However, I guess my real moment of reckoning came when I watched him walk across the stage to receive his high school diploma. Afterwards he'd been met by two beaming progenitors and a sullen faced little me. My reaction was more or less predictable—a big *so what?* Theirs however was typical of proud parents, all hail fellow well met and rah, rah, rah. Not that they ignored me. They were cordial enough, but their focus was mainly on their blossoming Valedictorian as well it should be.

"Well, son," his dad began. "Looks like the big day has finally arrived, the one you've been waiting for all these years. And now you've earned a little R&R. But don't forget what we agreed on."

The statement was followed by a wink, one which seemed aimed in my direction, and for the first time I wondered if all this *let's hit the road* stuff was not as spontaneous as I'd initially thought, and that maybe I was just a prop in a play that Jeremy had written years ago. Perhaps I was his bonus, just as he was mine. Because one quality we both shared was an inner loneliness, a trait which made us shy away from intimacy and the company of others. For this reason relationships were hard won and few and far between. Therefore, I am sure that Jeremy was just as delighted to find a traveling companion for his little adventure as I was to find a driver for mine.

It was an epiphany moment, that graduation, and had I listened a little closer, I could have spared myself some agony later on down the road. Just what had they agreed upon anyway? What would follow once the designated R&R time elapsed? These were serious concerns, but I was too caught up in the moment to concentrate on them. Besides, as I said before, I was running short of options.

So I just stood there and listened politely while everyone gushed on about what a fine speech he'd given, and then it was back to business as usual. For me, this involved waiting tables and living in a two bedroom flat with three other girls. I'd had to move out of the dorms at the end of the semester, and my new living arrangements put me closer to both work and play. As for Jeremy? Well, he spent every day in June working in the garage. Then, just in time for the 4th of July, the Sub emerged, a relic reborn, our chariot in waiting.

I couldn't believe what Jeremy had accomplished. Was this the same car? Oh, it still possessed the telltale chassis of a 1980 ski car, meaning that it was far from the sleek Outbacks and Legacies of today. In fact, one might call it downright boxy, but it still got you where you wanted to go and was willing to carry a ton of your gear in the process. Since it was the official car of the 1977 US ski team, I wasn't overly concerned about its ability to get us through any early snows in the Rockies. And those super heavy duty fog lights which Jeremy had installed were sure to illuminate the darkest of nights. But the crème de crème was the color, one of my favorites, a tasteful dark green that smacked of off-road jaunts into the forest primeval. Gone were all the rust spots and the Bondoed over cracks and crevices, and gone were the torn-up seats having been replaced by real leather. Why he'd even fixed the tape player and, though it would be hard to find new cassettes, he claimed to possess a prolific library already. So we'd be marching off to battle to the tune of old eighties rock.

I had to admit I was impressed and I don't impress easily. In fact, Jeremy had done such an excellent job at restoration that from this moment on he was dubbed the SubGuru. Oh, how he loved the name and wore it as proudly as one of his Boy Scout merit badges, causing me to wonder if the organization should create a new category called Grease Monkey.

Not that I was making fun of him or his pride at having attained Eagle Scout status. It was training that would come in handy more than once on our odyssey across the country, and since I hardly knew the difference between a nut and a bolt, I was not about to bad mouth my abundance. Indeed, I was glad to have found him. Who cared if we didn't make the Rainbow gathering? There would always be next year. And besides, we still might catch the tail end the celebration.

So it was final. We set off on a clear blue day in mid-July, pushing west across the Appalachian backbone until we reached the rolling blue-grass meadows of Kentucky. Here in Pulaski County we managed to locate the flotsam and jetsam of the festival, hangers on who either didn't know when to go home or had no home to go to. We also discovered that not only had the gathering taken place on an abandoned strip mine—not the most scenic location—but that it had been divided that year between Kentucky and Alabama, making it the first split gathering since the group began. So attendance had been way down.

"Looks like we didn't miss much," Jeremy sniffed.

I could tell he wasn't taken with what he saw. Too grungy, and no apparent organization. But I just shrugged and continued to pick my way through the stragglers in search of any good drugs they might be willing to share. However, drugs were in short supply by then, and all I got were directions to a nearby farm where some of the heavies of the festival were said to be still performing ceremonies.

"Blackfoot's even there," one scraggly youth insisted.

Blackfoot? Oh, right, the shaman in residence for the Rainbows. Well, I could use a little soothsaying at that time in my life. So we packed it up the next day and wandered down the road. And that my friends, is how I came to meet my personal benefactor and long lost soul sister, Leslie.

It was love at first sight when I walked into the kitchen of the small farmhouse she called home, and had I been of a different sexual persuasion—or any sexual persuasion at all for that matter—I am sure I would have abandoned Jeremy right then and there. She stood at a wood cook stove stirring some sort of messy concoction that was meant to feed the multitudes. Her hair was damp with sweat and her cotton dress clung to her corpulent frame. So it wasn't her looks that drew me in. Instead it was her aura.

Her aura!?! Come on now, did I just use that word? Previously, it had been reserved for hippy dippy new agers who claimed that everybody came in colors. But suddenly, it found its way into my vocabulary. How couldn't it when I was confronted with dancing rainbows of peacock green and gold? Later I would learn that this was heart chakra stuff. And, yes, Leslie's heart was as big as her butt, and that was pretty dang big.

"Welcome! Welcome!" she yelled. She had to raise her voice to be heard over the din from the backyard where a drum circle was in the midst of beating on everything from tin cans to hollow logs. "There's plenty for everyone... if you like gruel, that is."

Gruel??? Jeremy and I exchanged a look that would have wilted an entire bouquet of flowers before insisting that we'd just eaten. Not that it mattered. As far as I was concerned, we really weren't there for the free food. It was drugs I was after and, boy oh boy, had I come to the right place.

Later, Leslie and I sat severely stoned, reclining under an accommodating apple tree, and I blessed my good fortune. How strange to have found such a place on my very first stop. If I hadn't been so infused with the wanderlust, I'm sure I would have accepted Leslie's offer and signed on as her hired help.

"I need someone like you. Young and full of youthful energy. It's getting harder to do all this work by myself." And at that point her arm swung out to encompass the seventy surrounding acres on which her farm house sat perched, a little oasis in the midst of fields overrun by weeds and brambles.

"Oh come on," I countered. "You can't be that old. You act like you're ready for the shit pile. Looks to me like you're just getting started."

I'd already pegged my new friend for early forties, a time which, though it might seem old to a twenty year old, was now commonly considered as the prime of one's life.

"Be thirty-five my next birthday," the lady confessed. "But you know how it is. With some people, it's not the age, it's the mileage. And there's only so many times you can change the old spark plugs before you've got to break down and buy a new engine."

I smiled, then nodded in agreement, though I could hardly relate to what she really was saying. Shoot, I was barely twenty, full of piss and vinegar and dead sure I'd live forever. Plus, I already had the perfect partner if I wanted to fulfill my coast to coast dreams. So I turned down her offer that day. Not to say I permanently slammed the door shut. My understanding was that it was meant as an open-end invitation, so it became one I took advantage of anytime I was in the vicinity.

In that sense, Leslie became my Rock of Gibraltar in a world that often seemed hell bent on turning to quicksand under my feet. It was to her I returned many a time, usually with my tail between my legs, but once or twice as a conquering hero. Both surrogate mother and the sister I had never known, she became my fulcrum and pivot point, the top-dead center I came back to whenever the elliptical orbit on which I oscillated became too heavy to navigate.

Of course, all that was to transpire much later. For now I was footloose and fancy free and more than raring to go. Jeremy and I wasted no time taking off the next day. Since our journey had been postponed by more than a month, we were in a hurry to get to the other side of the Rockies before they started closing the passes for those early snows. We already knew that we wanted to spend some time in the mountains. There was so much to see, much of which we had read about beforehand and some of which we just happened to stumble upon.

Take Vedauwoo rocks for instance. Although taken from an Arapaho word that means earth, Vedauwoo has come to be better known as the Land of the Earthborn Spirit, which is somewhat a contradiction of terms. At an altitude of over eight thousand feet, it is Wyoming's high country, a place where the wind is ever present and storms of bestial proportions are spawned. For these reasons and also for the mystical presence of its massive rock formations, it was a favorite spot for vision quests. It was here amongst the hoodoos and granite outcroppings that the local Indians convened with the spirits, summoning the powers down—or up as it may be, considering the translation of the word—and it was here that I experienced my own personal bout with the spirit of the inner earth, one which became my mentor and guide forever after.

We pulled in at dusk which has got to be the strangest time in hoodoo-ville. Talk about inanimate objects springing to life. I felt like I'd stumbled into the Land of the Giants and at any moment one of them was going to come stomping over to shake my hand.

"This place is really spooky," I whispered to Jeremy, and he nodded in response before assuring me that it fit right in with the territory.

"Come on," he teased. "We just spent the day at Devil's Tower, the place made mainstream famous by *Close Encounters of the Third Kind.* Just what did you expect?"

Well, the guidebook had merely described Vedauwoo as *a rather secluded rocky oasis in southeastern Wyoming, filled with dense pine forests and aspen groves.* And yeah, it had mentioned rock climbing, but I never anticipated something like this. I stared around me into the dusky gloom, half expecting ghosts from the Permian Age to emerge from behind a two ton boulder.

Jeremy must have sensed my mood because he got downright practical and did so in a hurry. "Come on," he instructed. "We're burning daylight here. Let's get that tent up."

And so we did, and after a quick supper of tuna fish and crackers, we retired for the night. And that's when things began to get interesting.

Did you ever have one of those dreams where you fully aware you are dreaming? They call them lucid dreams, and they are highly sought after by those who focus their attention on the Dreamtime. Not that I was such a specialist at the time. Up to that moment, all my forays into the mystic had taken place via the instrument of hallucinogenic drugs. So I wasn't really prepared for what happened that night.

It started out normal enough, if indeed dreams ever follow the path of normalcy. I was arguing with my mother (predictable) about putting my dad's underwear in with hers while doing the laundry (Freudian) when suddenly this buff bronze Arapaho brave enters from stage left. *Now, what's he doing in my dream,* was my immediate reaction and from that time forward, I was awake and aware.

I look around to take in my surroundings. The air is dry and dusty, and I am standing in a pueblo village. It clings to a mesa that stands alone in a long valley. Off in the distance are volcanoes; one is quite large; all are quite active. I have been traveling on foot, but down at the bottom of the mesa I can see horses milling about in a corral. Two are outside, tied to a hitching post.

The man in front of me is thin and muscular with long black braids. We are facing each other on some sort of staircase. He looks deeply into my eyes and makes some comment about a Norwegian Indian maiden. His eyes are laughing as he holds up a mirror. I am shocked to see that I am in a different body, one with long blonde hair and clean ripe skin. My eyes sparkle like the stars on a clear night, and my dress is long and flowing. I am very beautiful.

"Come with me," he commands, and I follow.

He tells me that his name is Bear, and I can see that he is a highly regarded person in the community. A chief's son, perhaps? But if so, that does not protect us from what comes next.

The people we meet are angry that I am there. I am an outsider and my presence will lead only to destruction. They become more and more belligerent, and Bear and I realize it is time to go. We push through the mob and find the stairway that leads to freedom. At its bottom two horses await us, and we ride, knowing that we must leave here and seek shelter. We are heading for the place where Bear's father dwells, far on the outskirts of the region. Bear insists that someday soon the volcanoes will erupt, just as they have before, but that his father will provide us with safety.

We cross the valley and at its edge encounter a marsh of twisted vines and hidden bogs. We know we must abandon the horses. So we get into a saucer shaped flying machine with tiny levers for steering. We soar past pillars of rock colored violet by the setting sun. The heat from the volcanoes is almost unbearable, and it is with great relief that I find us descending into the bowels of the earth.

We are in caverns now, deep caves filled with majestic pillars of crystalline construct. The flying ship has turned into a boat which carries us down subterranean rivers. The journey is long but Bear assures me that we are almost there. We round a bend and...

Surprise! Surprise! I feel as though I have landed in as twenty-first century resort. Modern buildings abound, complete with swimming pools carved from natural rock. The people in the pools seem happy and greet us with smiles. Others are sitting at computer terminals, busily engaged in their work. I am confused. Where did all these people come from and why all this technology? But Bear assures me it is necessary and that there is no excess, that these people are only taking as much as they need.

Then a young woman leaves the group and comes towards us. She turns out to be Bear's sister, and she will accompany us on the rest of our journey. We are still not there yet. Bear's father lives at the opposite end of the lake near a sea channel. We get back into the boat and begin to travel through the strangest landscape yet. The lake is surrounded by rocky cliffs and within it are islands made of the same hard granite. Many are carved into shapes and one takes the form of a beautiful woman.

"That would be you," Bear's sister whispers to me, and I realize it is true. The resemblance is uncanny.

"He always loved that one the most," she explains and Bear smiles.

Just then we come to our destination. It looks like something designed by Frank Lloyd Wright, all rock walls and hidden halls and hexagonal shapes in gleaming metal. At its door stands the father, a man ancient beyond words. In his hands are two purple robes which we put on. Then we stand face to face in the glimmering light and...

I wake up.

A strange sound greets me. A bellowing as if some animal is in pain. I glance around in the pale morning light. Our green nylon tent has lent its color to the interior, and I am reminded of the sky before a tornado touches down.

Jeremy's eyes meet mine. He raises his finger to his lips, and I get the message.

"What in God's name is that?" I whisper.

"Just a bull," he responds.

A bull!!!??? I wanted to scream, but he was already into his damnable logical explanations, all delivered in a voice that was barely audible.

"I've already checked it out. He's on our side of the fence, probably bellowing at the cows in the next pasture. That's the bad news."

And the good????

I didn't have to say it because, if I knew Jeremy, he already had a plan.

"The good is that the fence is three feet in front of our tent. All we have to do is real quiet like unzip her and then quick as we can, get under that fence. Ready? On the count of three. One... two...

But he never got to the final number. I was over the fence before he hit *two* and staring at the blood which oozed from a deep cut in my palm. *Good Lord, I must have vaulted the thing*, I thought, an assessment which turned out to be the only possibility. Apparently, I had chosen to perform my acrobatic feat too close to the vicinity of one of the barbs in the wire. Hence, a deep puncture wound had resulted.

Jeremy took one look at it and insisted we drive to the closest doctor, who turned out to be thirty miles away. Of course, I insisted right back that we could hardly abandon our one and only tent, so after a lengthy debate, we compromised and agreed to come back for it later. Maybe by then things would have cooled down in the cow pasture.

The whole deal cost me seventy dollars of hard-earned waitress pay and a good day of travel. Not that the latter much mattered since I found myself in a time warp for days after the incident. The dream kept returning to me in Technicolor, and had I been an artist I would have been compelled to paint it. That's how strong the imagery was. To say that it ruined my little vacation is unfair. More like it kicked it into high gear, unlocking a part of me that had henceforth lain latent. From there on, every site we went to was viewed with a spiritual twist and, believe me, there are plenty to choose from when it come to our western frontier.

There was Mt. Adams in southwest Washington, home to so many UFO sightings that it came to host the ECETI ranch. (And that stands for Enlightened Contact with Extraterrestrial Intelligence.) There was the Oregon coast with its mystical fogs and odd pieces of driftwood, many of which seemed to take on a life of their own. There was Crater Lake, a deep Krishna blue gem set in the middle of an ancient caldera, complete with its own Phantom Ship Island, awarded its name due to its resemblance to a ghostly galleon. And, of course, there was Mt. Shasta, thought by many to be one of the most sacred places on earth. And it was here at this dormant volcano, where I had my second vision, and this one occurred with eyes wide open.

I'd been hiking alone up from the campground where Jeremy and I were staying. We'd pitched our little green tent close to Lake Siskiyou, and from here we were provided a ring side seat to that majestic mountain of renown. Up to that point, I hadn't given the place much thought. It was just another stop on our Odyssey, one which Jeremy had penciled in because someone had told him that it was a *Must See*. Then, on our very first day there, poor old Jeremy sprained his ankle, the one which belonged to his clutch foot, and since I couldn't drive a standard shift very well, we were committed to waiting out his recuperation. That left me with lots of time on my hands, and because I didn't really feel like lolling around the campsite, I decided to check out some of the trails in the area.

Now, mind you, I was still ignorant about the legends of Lemurians and other such enlightened beings which haunted the slopes of the mountain. So this was no self-fulfilling prophecy. Remember that Jeremy and I were both social misanthropes and didn't fraternize well with others. So unless we picked up information from a brochure or gleaned it during one of our rare conversations with our fellow campers, we were pretty much cut off from certain pertinent information. And in this case, that pertinent information involved some pretty juicy stuff.

It was ninety five degrees in the town of Mt. Shasta when I began my hike. At least that's what the radio said. But even though it wasn't quite as bad in our campground by Lake Siskiyou, I still had a pressing need to seek a higher altitude. Besides, what else do you come to a mountain for if not to scale its lofty heights? So I embarked, all on my lonesome, with little more than a rucksack and a bottle of water. I wasn't even wearing very good shoes, a pair of sneakers as I recall, which would never get me anywhere near the top. Of course, at the time I had no knowledge of the hardships that awaited me, figuring I was in for an aggrandized stroll.

Daniel Rose

I had chosen the Bunny Flats Trail, more on account of its name than anything else. Maybe I was thinking of a quote by Carlos Castaneda. *All roads lead nowhere, so choose one that has heart.* And what could have more heart than a bunch of bunnies hopping around in the snow. Yes, snow, because I was soon to discover that the snow line was a lot closer than I had expected.

At first it was hit or miss. The ground became soggy with runoff, and my sneakers began to get a run for their money. Not to be put off, I skipped the worst places on the trail the best I could and continued with my climb. However, after a half mile of dodging puddles, the snow drifts began. At first, they too were navigable, and then they began to get serious. What was initially a hardship became an outright pain in the ass, and I was just about to turn tail when I saw a figure that had stopped a few hundred yards away. The sunlight was blinding, so I couldn't really identify any distinguishing features, but I figured that, given the altitude and the pristine nature of the place, I was not about to run into Jack the Ripper.

I'll just head on up there and get a little Intel, I thought to myself and this was exactly what I did.

It took longer than I thought. The sun was in my eyes all the way, and it hid a host of obstacles. In ten short minutes I managed to fall into multiple snow drifts, the last which led to a nasty scrape on my knee. I would have given up, but something compelled me on. Call it a force of nature or just plain stubbornness, but I had to get to that guy—or girl, should that be the case.

However, when I finally achieved my goal, I was in for quite a surprise because even at close range it was real hard to determine the sex of whoever stood before me. Plus they were dressed in some mighty peculiar hiking garb. It consisted of a light tunic of some kind of translucent material that reflected the light and made it dance into a plethora of tiny prisms.

OK, so what? I'd run into oddballs before, and as long as they weren't dangerous, I saw no sense in backing off. After all, I was somewhat of an oddball myself. So in an attempt to take the situation under control, I initiated contact.

"Nice day, isn't it?" Yeah, stick to the weather. It's always a safe topic.

But my newly discovered companion just smiled an enigmatic smile before flooring me with the following words.

"We've been expecting you."

We? I looked around. You mean there are more of you spooks up here. But I knew that to inquire such would not be very polite.

"Are you lost?" He/she went on. "Because if you are, you came to the right place."

I shook my head. "No, I'm just trying to figure out if I can get to the top today."

"To the top? I think you're heading the wrong way."

Well, I wasn't about to debate the guy/girl. After all, I had just about come to the same conclusion. Let's save the mountain climbing for the mountain goats, why don't we?

Still I was puzzled.

"And what might be the right way?" I teased. Surely this was all a big joke, so I might as well join the fun.

But the answer to my question was never verbalized. At least not in the standard form because his/her lips had ceased to move. Instead I heard these words in my head.

You have been selected by the Agarthian network for pre-Event contact. We are the resistance and are centered in inner earth. If you come with me now, you will never be able to see your biological family again, but you will join with your soul family and together will work towards the liberation of this planet. However, if you are not ready, we will wait and allow you more time to prepare. Then, we will contact you once more. However, at that point should you chose to stay behind, you will never be contacted again. The choice is yours, but should you decide to come now, we must go at once.

At once??? Wow!!! That must have been some pretty heavy stuff we'd been smoking last night. Was I hallucinating? Having a flashback? Yet something about the whole deal rang true. I looked into those fathomless eyes and felt myself beginning to fall. Come hell or hell water, I was ready.

Are you sure? The words pierced my brain with their intensity and suddenly, I felt doubt.

No, wait a minute. I've got places to go, people to see and a whole whole lot of unfinished business topside. Yeah, I loved those deep dark secret places in the earth's bowels, but to live without sunlight forever more? And to leave behind…

Well, who exactly would I be leaving behind? Surely not Jeremy. Ours was a relationship based on symbiotic need. That much had been made clear to me during the past few months. And my so called biological family? Well, I sometimes wondered if I hadn't been exchanged at birth by the fairies. Excepting Joe, my oldest brother, I really didn't even like the people that much. Oh, I'd tried my best at being daddy's little girl, but where had that gotten me to? Just one dead dad, that was all… and a deep depression which had catapulted me into crisis mode.

So I wouldn't really miss out on too much as far as my personal relationships went. No real family to speak of, no friends, no fan club. Just little old me, the lonesome loner.

Still, I just didn't feel like I was ready for such a big step, and the more I focused on that thought the dimmer the light which surrounded me became until I realized the moment had passed. That was that, it had been now or never. No, not never. Hadn't he/she mentioned something about later?

I rubbed my eyes. Then, I rubbed my head which was starting to throb. Maybe it had all been a daytime dream; maybe I'd hurt more than my knee when I'd fallen. Whatever the case, it was all beginning to fade, the way dreams do when they hit the light of day.

Suddenly, I was bone tired and more than ready to hightail it back down the mountain. The return trip brought no more surprises, nor did any of my subsequent climbs during the week it took for Jeremy to recuperate. Nonetheless, my little experience—be it dream, hallucination, or visitation from a power greater than myself—had made an indelible impression upon my psyche. It was one I couldn't shake even if I'd wanted to, for whatever had happened to me up on the mountain that day was not something I wished to forget. Instead, it became somewhat of a cornerstone of my existence. A seed had been planted, but I still had more time before it would begin to sprout and grow. I felt like I'd been given a reprieve and, that said, may as well get on with the busy business of enjoying my life before it changed forever.

And so I did, at least as much as one can enjoy life when living on the road in a souped up Subaru with a born-again Boy Scout who thinks he's the reincarnation of Jack Kerouac. It didn't take long before poor old Jeremy of the wounded ankle turned into weird old Jeremy of the wanna-be writer with the over inflated ego. In fact, it pretty much began the minute we hit the Sacramento Valley. That was close enough to the Golden Gate city which had hosted his hero, and Jeremy was determined to follow in the path of his favorite Dharma bum.

"It's all about the experience," he insisted as we bent over in the strawberry fields with the real McCoy migrants. "How can I ever write about the struggles of the common man if I continue to insulate myself from them?"

But Jeremy, I wanted to say. *We really don't need the money and this here is hard work. Why don't we just mosey over to the Lost Coast and see if we can meet up with a Sasquatch?* Yeah, even that throw back to the Planet of the Apes would be preferable to all this back breaking labor.

Not that it would have done any good because the M'fer was not only the driver, but also the owner of my get-away vehicle. So I just grit my teeth and humored him until the strawberry season ended at which point, he was actually the one who made the command decision to move on.

By then it was late September and I suppose Jeremy, who had never been much further than the county line, was beginning to get a tad homesick for those green rolling hills of the Appalachians. Oh, I guess he could have graduated to the California orange groves, but that wouldn't really begin for a good three months. Besides, why bother when he could have a variation of the same experience just a few miles from home? I'm talking the apple orchards of Virginia and North Carolina, and though the work would be just as challenging—if not more so because it involved hoisting hefty ladders about all day—at least it didn't take place in a chemical swamp. Yeah, I'd read the labels on some of the Monsanto goop they were spreading out in the strawberry fields, and it was enough to make me swear I would never touch the fruit again in my life. But that was me. As for Jeremy, it was all part of the experience, one which thankfully involved visits to a number of national parks and monuments on our return trip to the East.

Yosemite, Joshua Tree, Zion, Bryce, Capitol Reef, The Arches and the Grand Canyon. We did them all in a whirlwind courtship that sometimes involved doubling up and doing two in one day. It was still hot that year for September and really tough to be strolling around in the desert at midday. So sometimes we'd camp at one spot, get up early to tour the place, and then drive around in the Subbie during the day. Its flimsy excuse for air-conditioning wasn't much, but it was still better than ninety-five degree heat.

Then, about dusk we'd pull into some other national park, pitch our tent, and sleep it all off so that we'd be ready and raring to get up and follow the same routine the very next day. I have to admit it was nice in one way as I was getting double for my money, two vistas for the price of one. However, it was such a blitzkrieg tour that it wasn't worth much. All it gave me was quick look at the places I would like to return to sometime later in life when I wasn't hampered by a peddle-to-the-medal traveling companion.

First and foremost of these was Mesa Verde, a green outcropping that rose high above the arid plain upon which it squatted. It was here the fabled Anasazi had taken their last stand only to disappear for good over the lost horizon of history. Had they too been summoned to middle earth? I couldn't help but wonder, and as we hiked the pathways that led us to eagle-eyed views of their cliff hanging dwellings, I was struck with an odd sense of déjà vu. The energy was strong here and threads of my dream at Vedauwoo came back to haunt me. The mesa was so similar to the one in my dreamscape that it could have been the same place. Yet how could I have that image in my consciousness since this was the very first time I had ever set foot here?

Oh well, maybe it was the collective unconscious, the one we are always hearing about. So I wrote it all off to coincidence and locked up any spiritual stuff deep inside my psyche. I had long since realized there was no sense sharing such thoughts with good old meat and potatoes Jeremy. His idea of a holy book was *The Boy Scout Manuel*, and as for anything that might smack of the great beyond? Well, that was all woo-woo tin-foil hat material.

It was a division that was beginning to bother me. Somehow I felt like I was on a vision quest, while he was just touring the country in his partially donated Subaru, working off some clandestine deal he had made with the devil—which in this case took the form of his two doting parents.

It wasn't until we'd finished with the apple harvest in Maggie Valley, North Carolina that the truth came out. It was now late November, and the nights were growing cold especially up in the mountains. I had already made suggestions about leaving for Florida, where we could transfer our skills to a different sort of fruit tree. I'd even ripped the designs for a small tipi out of a book I'd found in a library.

"Take a look," I suggested, proud of my heist. "We could build something like this real easy. All we need is a little canvas and a quiet place to work for a week. That abandoned tobacco barn down the road would do just fine."

Jeremy stared for a minute before answering, and then floored me with his reply.

"Did you just steal that out of a library book?"

His tone told me that this was a crime worse than infanticide in his book. In his book? I considered the bad play on words, and I couldn't help myself. I began to chuckle, and that was what sealed the deal.

He just shook his head, and I suddenly knew that nothing good would come from this conversation, at least not for me.

"Moria…" he began, then hesitated as if building up nerve.

Yes, that was my name, one chosen when I realized that this alternative form of Maureen meant not only *exceptional*, but also *bitter*. At the time I figured this was a pretty good tightrope to walk. Oh, yeah, it also translated as star *of the sea*. I liked that one a lot.

However, after checking out the look on Jeremy's face, I wondered if maybe I ought to consider changing it again. Maybe to Soolong. Soolong, as in *so long*. Get it? Right. Call me anything, but don't call me late for dinner. I waited as patiently as I could under the circumstances. Later in life I was to have this experience many a time, one in which I was waiting for the ax to fall. But it would mainly have to do with some shit job I was being let go from. Never again would it center on anything close to a romantic relationship. I would make sure of that.

It was a long moment, but I wasn't about to budge. So he was finally compelled to spit it out.

"This just isn't working," he stated.

Yeah, tell me something I don't know. I wanted to say, but bit my tongue and let him go ahead. After all, he had got the floor.

"It's not that you aren't a great gal."

Oh, how I hated it when he referred to me as such. It always reminded me of family trips to Florida when my dad would make fun of gas stations advertising **3 gals for 3 bucks.** It cheapened me and made me feel like a commodity to be traded on the New York Stock exchange. So this time I had to bite more than just my tongue. In fact, in the end I had to swallow a big chunk of my pride because the long and short of it all was that Jeremy was breaking up with me. And since he was a true blue Boy Scout underneath, he did at least possess an ounce of integrity which meant full disclosure. This demanded that the truth come out about the little deal he had done with his parents in order to secure the funds that purchased the Subbie. It appeared he had traded cash for time. That instead of beginning college right after high school he'd be given a six month reprieve during which he could fulfill one of his fondest dreams, that being to see the USA in his Chevrolet—except his choice of wheels was a Subaru. Then it was back to the books. After all, he was the valedictorian of his class and great things were expected of him, things that did not involve a union with a trash druggy drop-out such as yours truly.

"But I won't leave you high and dry," he went on, once he'd detailed his plan to dump me. "You're welcome to come back to Charlottesville with me, and I'll even loan you enough cash to get you set up."

To get me set up!!!?? I just looked at him and wanted to scream. Into what? Days of indentured servitude at the Busy Bee Diner and nights in a postage stamp apartment listening to the farts and snores of my roommates?!?After the freedom of the open road?!? No way!!! No way in hell!!

But one look at him assured me that he was as serious as he was truthful. Well, maybe there was more than one way to play this. Perhaps I could capitalize on the sense of integrity that ran so deep in his veins.

I smiled, the last thing he expected.

"How about I just take that cash right now?" I offered. (I knew for a fact that Jeremy had a good little stash left. So maybe we could share *and share alike*.)

"And what? You just walk off into the sunset?"

I could tell he was puzzled.

"That's about right," I replied. "Me and my thumb."

In the end it took a bit of convincing. I made up a story about an aunt that lived not that far away, and Jeremy even bought me a bus ticket to her fictional town, one I refunded for cash just as soon as I saw his taillights disappear down the road.

I guess I should have missed him, but too be truthful, the only emotion I was really feeling was one of extreme liberation. It was just me and the road now, and the road was an addiction that must be fed once you've developed a taste for it. However, in return it offers you the ultimate freedom as in freedom's *just another word for nothing left to lose, and nothing was all that* Jeremy *left me*. And with that little tune running through my head, I shouldered my pack, turned my back to the wind, and stuck out my thumb.

****

The first stop would be Leslie's. I wasn't a fool, and I knew that winter was coming. It happened every year in these latitudes and besides, I needed someplace to regroup. Hadn't she said to drop by anytime? Well, there was no time like the present and plus, it really wasn't that far. That said, it would provide a good trial run for my solo hitch-hiking experience. Yeah, that was for sure!

In retrospect, I had to laugh because so far my journey sure had been a trial by fire. For some reason I got them all… the crazies, the perverts, the losers and even one born again Christian family who insisted I go home with them and attend the church of THEIR choice the following morning. It had been hard to turn down the invitation since it had been late, and my previous ride had dropped me off in front of an all night drive-in where *Deep Throat* was playing.

Just what these so-called Christians were doing in such a neighborhood was not a question I cared to ask. My only interest at the time was the Sunday dinner that would surely follow the sermon, one which I'd gobbled with such relish you would have thought it was my own last supper.

What a mistake that had been since my next ride was a real weirdo who had a tooth so rotten it demanded instant extraction. And guess who got to perform that little procedure? It was an operation that had resulted in the loss of my lunch and then some, and I'd continued to have episodes of the dry heaves all the rest of the way to Leslie's farm.

Boy, had it looked good that day when I'd finally rounded the bend to behold the weathered structure of its one and only dwelling. All the rest of the shit was yet to come, but that hardly mattered as over the next thirteen years that clapboard cottage, be it so humble, would remain as the only real home I was ever to enjoy on planet earth.

****

Whoaaa!! Did I just say thirteen years? Yes, that's about right, though it's hard to believe. And just how many words had it taken to transverse almost a decade and a half? About three hundred and forty nine to be precise. Gee, that's pretty good. But that's nothing compared to the cosmic calendar. Should you scale all of time down to the size of a football field, the entirety of human history would only occupy a space about as big as a hand. Which begs the question: just how much was that thirteen years worth in the scheme of things? So how's that for perspective?

But enough of this. Back to the little microcosm at hand, one in which I'd managed to cover all of four thousand seven hundred and forty-five days with a quick click of the pen. Talk about concise. Oh, I guess I could have blown it all off with a sweep of my hand by declaring how time flies when you're having fun. And I have to admit that some of it was fun.

Take the Rainbow Festivals for instance. Gee, after a few years in attendance I almost became an honorary member of the tribe. Until, that is, the old pecuniary nerve began to act up, and I decided I needed cash if I were to fuel my dreams of future travel.

So I'd Rainbow some and then work some, establishing myself in a town close to the festival site and grunting away at some shit job until I saved up enough cash to make my next move. Then I'd either take out my trusty thumb or, if I were flush, buy a one way ticket to my next destination. And they weren't always on the Rainbow circuit.

In fact, one year I even made it down to the Yucatan for the winter. Here I toured the pyramids of Chicken Itza before dipping south to Guatemala to visit Tikal. For reasons I didn't fully understand I was drawn to these ancient sites. Oh, I knew it all had something to do with the experiences I'd had at Vedauwoo and Mt. Shasta, but I wasn't exactly sure what I was supposed to be getting out of it. To my disappointment, the great mystery that surrounded such so-called power centers just seemed a little bit out of reach. Perhaps I had grown older and lost that magical innocence of childhood. Or maybe I just wasn't doing as many drugs as I had back in my college days. Whatever the case, I never was able to reproduce the epiphanies of my earlier travels.

So I continued to drift, an aimless seed upon a restless wind, never able to put down roots. My jobs were menial and brought little satisfaction. How could they when they extended from cleaning up slop at local diners to sweeping up dust bunnies from under the beds of folks who were either too lazy or too busy to clean their own houses. Dog sitting, waitressing, telephone solicitation, yard work, I'd done it all.

Then, something changed. It all began when I was assigned a job at the local library in the small town where I'd been spending the summer. I say assigned because my presence was mandatory, meaning that I never would have ended up there had I not been arrested for public intoxication. At my trial—well, I prefer to call it a kangaroo court—I had been given the option: jail time or community service and three guesses which one I chose. So there I sat, three days a week, clipping coupons from magazines and dusting the bums who came in to get out of the rain.

Despite the manual nature of my work, it was probably the only employment that came anywhere close to professional, and I have to say that it was a productive six months. Not only was I surrounded by books, but I also became involved in a creative writing class which met once a week. All of a sudden, doors began to open in my mind out of which spilled word after word. Much of it was verbal diarrhea, stream of consciousness stuff that I would never share with anyone. But some of it showed promise, at least according to the lady who ran the class. So I continued to write, even when not at class, and soon had filled several three ring notebooks.

You know, I almost hated to leave that assignment when it ended. However, the highway was calling, and I made it a point to never winter in the same place. By the time my community service ended, I had already been in that town six months longer than I'd intended. In fact, it's a touch of irony to note that I had been celebrating my planned exodus when I'd been popped by the local gendarmes for strolling down Main Street with an open container.

Yeah, public intoxication my ass! A sentence which had both insulted and vilified me; yet also one which, oddly enough, had prompted me to pursue a new direction. First it was the creative writing class and then, after some encouragement from the library director, a foray into henceforth foreign waters.

Well, I say foreign, but the truth was that it involved a skill I had been wetting my feet with since the days of my childhood. It revolved around the one worthwhile trade I had learned at my mother's knee, the fine art of sewing.

I remember to this day how it had been introduced to me.

"Well, Maureen," my mother had said. "You may as well learn to do a few simple things around the house. With your looks no man will want you unless you can bring a few skills to the table. Take sewing for instance. What man can turn down a woman who sews her own clothes?"

And with that she had yanked me into the small room she reserved for such creations, her hobby-hole, where she proceeded to give me lesson after lesson in stitching and darning and seam ripping until my hands became sore.

You'd think it would have turned me off, but there was something about fabric which excited me in a way that no man's hands have ever been able to. The sleek feel of the satin against my skin. The sturdy wool of the yarn between my fingers. I couldn't help myself, I was hooked, and sewing became not only a favorite pastime but a possible vocation. I'd even considered a career in fashion design before it became quite apparent to me that this was not my expected role in the family.

So as my schooling progressed from the times tables to the quadratic formula, my days in the hobby-hole dwindled until they became almost nonexistent. However, I never forgot the pleasure I had experienced there, and when the library director at the joint where I was doing time suggested a sewing class at a nearby career center, I decided to give it a whirl. After all, if I was going to be stuck in this place for another five months, I may as well use my time to my advantage. Who knows? Maybe this might evolve into a whole new career.

And that it did. For starters, I discovered the skill was a lot like riding a bike, meaning that I picked right up where I left off, and in no time was churning out what can only be referred to as wearable art. That said, I skipped the preliminary stages of pattern reading and sewing machine maintenance and went straight to creation.

My instructor was at first appalled, then amazed. Never in her five years of running this little workshop had she come across anyone with so much natural talent. I didn't want to burst her bubble by telling her how hard-won my victory had been. Nope. I wasn't about to go into the hours spent at my mother's knee enduring her constant criticism and all the pin pricks and needle jabs I had suffered on my way to my present glory. So I just beamed and accepted the compliment.

Better yet, it led to financial reward because apparently my instructor had been looking for someone to help her out in her struggling business. Now, most businesses struggle because of lack of clients, but this one was the exact opposite.

"I can't keep up with it all," she wailed. "What I need is someone to take over some of the smaller projects, the alterations, the button sewing, the seam repair. You wouldn't be interested, would you?"

It was meant only as a fishing expedition, and I wasn't even sure a response was needed. There were just too many variables, the first and foremost being my restless nature. Still I assured her I would think about it, figuring this was as gracious a way as any to turn her down.

However, later that night as I lay awake in bed trying to sleep, I realized I was ready to call her up then and there and accept her offer. My resolve was strong and clear. Not only did I need the extra money—my ten hours a week at the library ate into my day job—but I was suddenly infused with a such a strong desire to hold a needle again that I could hardly wait until morning. But I held off until a more acceptable hour and then called the lady on the phone.

"Sure would," I chimed into the receiver, and though it took her a full minute to get the context, she was more than pleased.

And that's how I became known in that small community as the Alterations Girl. I have to admit there was something symbolic about the title which caused me to wonder just what was really being altered. But, for starters, let's just say my name. Because it was time to shed my old skin of Maureen/Moria once again and take up a new moniker. This time? Well, it goes without saying it had to have some reference to my new found passion. But it was a quick look at the sign above my head one evening which filled in the blank. It named the establishment as *A Stitch in Time* and that was that. I had just been reborn (again) and this time as Stitch. It was such a magnificent play on words I burst out laughing, and the days that followed made for some of the happiest since I'd taken to the road.

So you can see why it was a bit hard to leave the place. But, shoot, ever since I had seen the movie *Chocolate* with Juliet Binochet, I had identified with its leading lady. A nomad by nature, she just couldn't help herself. The same restless wind that blew down one Main Street after another infected me as well. It was a done deal. When that wind began to blow, it was time to go. And the only difference between me and Juliet—well, besides having a Johnny Depp in the picture—was her ability to support herself through a must-have occupation. Hers, of course, had been a Chocolateria, where she created such magical delicacies that even the most religious of the townsfolk were forced to forsake their Lenten vows. However, up to that point my line of work had not involved anything so romantic. Instead it was all about menial labor, and some of it was just a cut above the kind expected of the untouchable caste in India.

But suddenly I had found not one, but two vocations that were both enjoyable and productive. Well, to be honest, the writing part still required a bit of polishing, all of which could come later, maybe when I hit the next town. Surely there I would find more material, more grist for the mill. But there was always somebody who needed a button sewed on, so why not capitalize on it?

So I took advantage of my last hours in the library and talked the director into helping me design a little flyer for my up and coming business, *The Stitchworks*, and then we printed out ten or so colorful copies to post around my next port of call. Finally, we saved everything to a thumb drive, and that included all my writings up to that point. Yep, have thumb drive, will travel, and travel was the name of my game.

I left the next morning, in a late October fog. The little river town looked sad and lonely as I peered out the window of the bus which carried me off to my next great adventure. Summer was over, and all the shops catering to the tourist crowd had **Closed for the Season** signs on their doors. Soon the snow would be flying, and the drifts would be up to a giraffe's ass. Not the kind of place you wanted to be come January.

Nope, I had made my escape just in time. But maybe, just maybe I would return next spring. Oddly enough, this was the very first place to inspire me to put down roots, if only for its brief season.

However, for the present, I had bigger and better fish to fry. First and foremost was one belonging to the species of *Amblyopsidae*. This is a rare breed found only in the deep environments of caves, springs, and swamps. Since they spend the bulk of their time in the absence of light, they have adapted to the point where they lack both eyes and pigmentation. Hence, their more common name as blind fish, and ever since I had first read about them, I had been itching to lay my eyes on one. Unfortunately, I knew that such a feat might present a few problems since most of the caves I visited of the water-world variety frowned upon fishing gear. However, there was one that advertised the next best thing by offering a souvenir version of the eyeless little creatures at the local gift shop. This would be Mammoth Cave, and since it was one I had yet to cross off my list, I decided it was time to make its acquaintance.

Furthermore, it was in a direct line to my next stop which would be Leslie's farm. This was another place that was overdue a visit, and as winter was closing in, I knew it was now or never. What could I say? A little vacation village in Mexico was calling. It was a hot tourist spot and there was a lady there who sold handmade clothing to the gringos. I had already contacted her, and she'd told me to come on down and she'd see what I could do. But I already knew she'd be impressed. (Or so my recently discovered self confidence assured me. Yeah, when you're on a roll, you're on a roll!)

The bus took me to Louisville, and after a good night's sleep at a Salvation Army, I got out my trusty thumb and hitched the rest of the way. Oh I had the money to rent a car, but why dip into my winter funds? I would need them to get established south of the border. Besides why let a perfectly good thumb grow rusty from disuse?

I made it to the cave just in time to catch the last boat trip. There weren't too many people aboard, most being stragglers who had missed the previous tours. So I had a chance to check out my fellow passengers.

If you travel a lot, this is a game you get good at. In fact, at times it's more than just a game as your survival depends on it. Just like that guy Jason Bourne, it really behooves you to pay one hundred percent attention to your surroundings. Take that guy sitting next to me; does the bulge in his side pocket indicate the presence of a concealed weapon? Could be. I've been around enough preppers to know that some of those guys won't go to the crapper without taking their piece along. And that woman with the long face. She looks like she might be on oxycodone and high enough to jump overboard. Perish the thought. Yeah, call me paranoid, but it's always best to go into battle prepared.

And speaking of which, how about that kid over there, the handsome one with the buff little body? Wow! If I were still remotely interested in such shenanigans, I would be getting his number. If he even had one, and if I even had a phone. But that's a lot of ifs and compounded with the fact that he looks younger than my brother Davey, maybe I'd best back off.

So I just sat and observed like I usually do as I listened to the guide pontificate about this stalactite or that stalagmite. These caves are all alike, always having their ambience ruined by some moron who can't shut up. And why, of why do people feel like they have to assign a name to everything they see? Kind of takes the magic out of it, if you ask me.

But that was how it was in caves. I should know. I'd been in enough of them. From Penn's Cave in bucolic central Pennsylvania to Carlsbad in the wilds of New Mexico, I had seen as many as I could possibly cram into three short decades. Excepting of course, the one I was in, so I may as well sit back and enjoy the ride. And the talk, all about the eyeless fish and bats.

The following species of bats inhabit the caverns, the Indiana Bat, the gray bat, the little brown bat, the big brown bat and the eastern pipistrelle bat. All together, these and more rare bat species such as the eastern small-footed bat once had estimated populations of nine to twelve million. However, though they still abide in Mammoth Cave, their numbers are now no more than a few thousand at best. There is ongoing ecological restoration in this part of the cave, and we hope it will lead to the return of the bats. However, there are other animals which inhabit the caves including two genera of crickets, a cave salamander, and of course, our favorites: two genera of eyeless cave fish.

The Guide droned on and on, and I began to fall into a dream, one of those daytime varieties that plague me in the late afternoon more and more as the years go by. But this one was not your ordinary garden variety daydream, a little snooze/power nap to recharge the batteries. No, this one was different in a weird sort of way. For starters, I swear I heard that kid on the other side of the boat calling my name. But when I opened my eyes a slit to see if he was trying to get my attention, I realized that he, too, had dipped into daydream land.

His apparent lack of consciousness gave me an opportunity to thoroughly check him out which I did. What was it about the boy that drew me? It wasn't a sexual attraction, despite his obvious good looks. Well, then maybe it was the overwhelming odor of pot that clung to him, as if he'd just finished cleaning a summer's worth of product. Yeah, that could have been it, but still there was something more.

I flashed back to Davey, my younger brother and realized that there was a resemblance. A sort of displaced innocence, and boy, oh boy, had Davey's been displaced. What a sorry state of affairs that had been. I remember clearly the night he confided in me. I was all of sixteen and a bit unskilled in counseling, not that he cared. I was really all he had. Dad was always gone, and Joe was preparing to follow suit after completing his education at Annapolis. And mom? Well, forget it! (Though I fear I was a bit slow on the draw when it came to realizing her deficiencies.) In fact, after Davey's little confession, I was stupid enough to suggest he talk to mom and was that ever a mistake. Her reaction had been to wash his mouth out with soap while screaming that he was a little liar and no priest would ever do such a thing.

Poor Davey. It was the beginning of the end for him, the moment when his insolent rebellion began. It started with sneaking mom's cigarettes but soon accelerated to the liquor cabinet, and by the time he was due to graduate from high school, he had a full blown habit going. It didn't help that he immediately sought work in the trades as a carpenter's helper because we all know that is synonymous with picking up the beer cans the crew leaves behind. Oh, they aren't all like that, but Davey always managed to pick the ones who were lax to the max. How he managed to graduate from helper to foreman is beyond me, since his habits didn't change much, except to become more functional. This meant he didn't pop his first brew until quitting time, but then? Boy, did he ever hit it heavy.

His ability to get up the next morning was nothing short of a miracle, but maybe it's in the genes. Our granddad had always been somewhat of a functional alcoholic, and dad would have followed in his footsteps had not my mother nipped those tendencies in the bud. Of course, god only knew what he did when out at sea. Yeah, what happens in Marseille, stays in Marseille. And then there was my own rampant consumption during my university days when I was known to consume large quantities of alcohol and then show up for a midterm. Not that I always passed the thing, but at least I gave it the old college try.

Thoughts of Davey continued to play leap frog in my head while I watched the kid sleep, and I decided then and there that I'd better make one more stop before heading down to Isla Mujures for the winter, that being Thanksgiving Dinner at the old hacienda. Yep, we still maintained the tradition, one which I had honored—though for reasons unknown to me—for the past thirteen years I'd been on the road. Well, I say reasons unknown, but that's not necessarily true. I knew why I went. There were two draws, though one was beginning to fade into the haze that alcohol always manages to envelope its prisoners in. So let's just say that my primary purpose centered on seeing my other brother Joe who, despite having chosen a path in life completely opposite to mine, still remained my personal hero. For he was the guy out defending his country from a host of bad guys, the one man militia that made it safe for us little people to sleep securely at night.

Ah yes…Joe. How I worshipped my older brother. Tall, handsome and built like a rock, he was every girl's dreamboat. Then when you add in his other sterling qualities, you get someone who is almost too good to be true. Honest to a fault and with a sense of integrity to die for, his generous nature demanded his service to others. That made him the quintessential Marine's Marine, the guy you see portrayed in all the recruitment posters, the one you want by your side in a fire fight. I don't know why I put him on a pedestal the way I did because by in large I was a jaded personality, a bit cynical and hard to impress. But maybe I just had to have one icon in my life, one true blue champion.

And since I'd heard via the grapevine that he was getting ready to deploy again to the Stan, I suppose I'd better not blow off this chance to wish him a safe return. It would really be no skin off my teeth to postpone my journey. Why, I hadn't even bought the tickets yet, having planned to do so once I got to Leslie's and had access to her Internet.

Then suddenly the boat ground to a stop, and I realized we were back at the entrance to the cave. Gee, where had the time gone? I really must watch these fugue states I was falling into. They were becoming more and more frequent and were beginning to worry me. Could they be a backlash to all those drugs I did during my last year at college? Or was it some sort of early dementia. After all, most of my family did seem to march to the tune of a different drummer, one that played Looney Tunes.

Maybe I should have myself checked out, but not by any allopathic doctor. No thanks; I knew where they were coming from, all about profit and service to self. No, I'd rather go to someone like Leslie who over the years had also functioned as my friendly neighborhood soothsayer, by casting the cards and leading me to lie down beside still waters. It had always been a mixture of the mundane and the mystical with Leslie. This had been a good part of the attraction, the force that had brought me back to my old Kentucky home over and over again. And today was no exception. Suddenly I felt compelled to run as fast as I could in that direction. Something had shifted while I'd been in that cave. There was a disturbance in the force field, and I needed to find out where it might be erupting.

So without even bothering to initiate a conversation with my newly discovered interest, I exited the boat and hightailed it up to the parking lot. Surely someone would be heading my way. They always were.

Five hours later I was gazing down into the natural bowl which held Leslie's farm. I couldn't help noting how the place had changed over the years. Gone were the rusting hulks of old Internationals, their one-eyed windows winking in a setting sun. Unrecognizable was the former shot gun shack, and in its place stood a meandering mansion which could have made the centerfold for some offbeat version of *Architectural Digest*. There were outbuildings galore—one which had even sprouted up since my last visit a year before—and now the place could claim the status of a fully functional farm. The transformation was amazing, but what was even more so was the amount of cash it must have taken. One could only wonder how Leslie, a woman of meager means had accomplished all this. But Leslie was a woman who was as resourceful as she was large, so it didn't really surprise me that she had succeeded in this back to the land business where so many others had failed.

I knew for a fact that her start up cash had come from an inheritance. (Oh, would that I could ever be so lucky.) However, the rest of her spread had been built using a combination of hard work and ingenuity. Well... let's just call it heavy on the ingenuity because, given her bulk; Leslie had never been one to move too fast. Not that those in her employ were so afflicted and one of them, a little brown skinned man who probably spoke more Spanish than English was so busy cleaning out a stall that I felt guilty about stopping him to ask if the lady of the house was at home. It took all of ten seconds to realize he was clueless as to what I'd said and another ten to try to formulate the same question in his native language. However, by that time the lady in question had sailed in from somewhere out in the back forty where she'd been checking on a fence line.

Larger than life and full of piss and vinegar, she was just as I'd left her over a year ago. Oh, to be honest there may have been a few more wrinkles and grey hairs, but then that goes with the territory, the one they wrote about in that story *No Country for Old Men*.

"Hey, spring chicken. How are ya doing?" I shouted.

And the reply was one that had served us well for nigh on fifteen years.

"Still plucking, girlfriend. Still plucking."

Boy, was it ever good to be home again, if only for a short respite until I got my shit together for my winter migration. The following days were spent catching up on all that had happened in a year, and helping Leslie with the various front businesses which concealed her true enterprise. And yes, truth be told, I was more than aware of Leslie's true source of revenue. It hadn't taken a drug dog to sniff out the overwhelming odor that enveloped the place on a regular basis. But, due to the nature of her enterprise, it was imperative that such revenue be placed off the books. Hence, the need for a number of so-called cottage industries to throw the IRS off that delicious scent.

My favorite of these involved a stunning appaloosa-like Jackass named Run for the Money (though Leslie just referred to him as her cash cow). True, the guy had cost her well over ten grand, money she'd gleaned from a grant made available statewide for start-up businesses. However, he'd been worth every penny of it. Not only was his sperm worth a thousand bucks a pop, but the sale of it provided her with a legitimate income, one which covered her ass at tax time.

After all, it doesn't do to claim income from a controlled substance, the likes of which I'd never seen now that Leslie had built the new goat barn. What was once a mere twenty thousand dollar a year cash crop of sinsimila grown in a corner of her basement had expanded to reach a six figure amount. The increase in revenue came from moving the whole business into a much larger facility, one which took up most of the lower level of the structure we stood in. It was pretty impressive, and I had to admit that even though the place was only half full of a bevy of pre-pubescent beauties, the potential was overwhelming.

"Yeah, you should have seen it a week ago, before we harvested half the crop," Leslie gushed.

We'd been on our way to service the jackass when we'd become sidetracked to Leslie's magic forest. It had turned into a lengthy detour for obvious reasons since hanging out there and smoking up some of the profits was infinitely preferably to the task which Leslie so crudely referred to as *jerking the jack*.

I'd laughed when she first explained the process to me, one which involved placing a huge collection tube over the Jack's enormous dong and then gleaning the seed that fell from it during intercourse. The trick was to entice him with a jenny in heat and then slip the thing over his dick at just the right moment. You can imagine that this was no easy task and one I hadn't been looking forward too. Thank God for the Magic forest and its contents. So much better to tackle such a task when ripped to the gills!!

"Good Boy, Mr. Money," Leslie proclaimed once the product had been secured. "That's worth at least a month's groceries. No more Viagra for you for awhile. And speaking of which, did you hear about the guy who died of an overdose of that shit? Seems like they couldn't close his coffin."

It wasn't that funny, but I laughed anyway. Leslie had a way of pulling off these dumb assed sex jokes, most of which related to farming. Stuff like: why does a man need only one rooster? Because a cock a dude'll do.

It was the kind of stuff that wouldn't work coming from anyone else, but there was something about her good natured bulk that allowed her to get away with the stuff, and often in mixed company at that. Maybe it was a by-product of all the weed she smoked, or maybe it was just a way to kill time in a life that, to someone like me, would have become terminally boring.

Whatever the case, both activities did seem to make the time go by quickly. Before I knew it several weeks had passed, and it was almost time for me to hitch to the coast where the remnants of my family still resided. I was busy making the last arrangements for my flight to Cancun when it hit me. Wasn't there something I'd wanted Leslie to do for me? Now what was it? My head actually began to throb as I tried to remember, and then she walked into the room wearing one of her flowing caftans and it all came back.

"Hey, girlfriend," I began, resorting to the term of endearment she often used for me. "I have a request."

"And that would be?"

"The cards? You still read them? Right?" It had been a few years, so I figured I'd best check to make sure she hadn't moved on to bigger and better means of prophecy. Crystal balls. Runes. Casting the stones. The list of possibilities was endless, and over the course of our friendship Leslie had tried them all.

"Oh, I might have a deck lying around someplace. Why do you ask?"

Good question.

"Well," I reflected. "It's just something that came over me while I was down in Mammoth Cave. A weird feeling like …

"There was a disturbance in the force field?" she finished.

"Yeah, that's right. But how did you know?"

"Oh, the same way I knew it had been on your mind for the past few weeks, but that you'd shoved it back into the forgotten country."

This was how Leslie referred to the things we didn't want to deal with, and though I sometimes begged to differ with her, this time she was right. So I just nodded in affirmation and repeated my question.

"Could you? I mean, nothing elaborate. Just keep it simple like with that Medicine Deck you have. I just want to know if I'm on the right path. I've been feeling a shift lately, and I don't know if it's bad or good or …

"Maybe a bit of both?" She winked; proud of her ability to read my thoughts. "Oh come on," she continued, noting my discomfort. "You always knew I could read you like a book. Let's go get those cards."

And so we did.

An hour later I was still staring at the one and only medicine card I had drawn. It was number forty-two, the Bat, and given my recent excursion into the bowels of Mammoth, home to at least five species of the furry little devils, there was something a bit uncanny about my selection. However, that wasn't what got to me. It was the symbolism implied by such a selection that did it.

Rest assured that I couldn't have drawn a more appropriate card had I been given the entire deck to peruse beforehand. Why? Because the bat is the symbol for rebirth, and wasn't that exactly what I was feeling in the ethers? A trip down the old birth canal on route to bigger and better realities than the one which had me hanging around upside down in my mother's womb for nigh on nine months? Nine months? Try nine plus a few more years, for that was how long I'd been at my driftaholic lifestyle.

So, yes, in those respects the Bat card was not a bat-shit choice at all. In fact, it was pretty darn good medicine. For if Bat appeared in your cards, it pointed to a ritualistic death of some way of life which no longer suited your new growth patterns. It indicated a time to let go of old habits and assume the position that would prepare you for rebirth and in some cases even initiation into a shamanistic tradition.

Wow! What could be better? Except that initiation often equated with shamanistic death which involved a breaking down of the old *self* to make room for the new. This often entailed brutal tests of both physical strength and psychic ability and a pushing of every emotional button in the books. Sometimes it even culminated in being buried in a grave, the mouth of which was covered only by a thin blanket. This was where the initiate spent the night, totally alone, while the wild beasts that were his worst primal fears preyed close at hand. It was the ultimate test and not for the faint of heart. But in order to grow and become your future, one must die the shaman's death.

So that was the hard part, and in my case it became even harder. Not only had fortune favored me by drawing the Bat card, but I had managed to draw it upside down. This compounded matters, for when that happens, the reading takes on a slightly different meaning. Here, the birth has been compromised by a breech position. Here you have met with contrary medicine, and run the risk of struggling too long in the birth canal, the final outcome of which being death of the body. In other words, you waited too long to be born, and all those golden opportunities you once had are gone, leaving only stagnation and old age.

So Bat insists (and I quote) that it is imperative to *use your mind, courage, and strength to ensure an easy labor and quick delivery into your new state of understanding and growth. Surrender to the new life that you have created from thought and desire, and bravely greet the dawn.*

In plain speak that says to shit or get off the pot. Stop blocking yourself and ante up to your true destiny. Good advice to all and sometimes the hardest in the world to follow especially when life insists upon throwing you a bunch of fast balls.

The card both excited and disturbed me. I knew it spoke of a change that was coming. Whether I liked it or not, my misspent youth was winding down, and it was time to get serious. But what about? I had to scratch my head at that one.

I left Leslie's later that week with visions of the oracle dancing in my head, and they were no sugarplums. That feeling I had of a disturbance in the force field was growing, and was so strong by the time our customary Thanksgiving dinner rolled around that I almost cancelled out. However, in the end I was so glad I'd bellied up to that bar once more, because the drinks are always the sweetest at closing time.

Chapter 3
Noone
AKA Doe
2008-2016

Mammoth Cave was cool and I mean that to be taken not as slang, but quite literally. In fact, Mammoth was so cool I was damn close to freezing by the time we returned from our little boat trip. Oh, they'd warned everyone and told them to bring along a jacket, but you know me... always wanting to show off my buff little bod for the ladies, first and foremost of which was sitting right next to me, a stunning red head in tight designer jeans. So, my vanity once again led me down a path that was lined more with thorns than primroses.

That said, I was in a big hurry to exit the boat as soon as she docked, but not in as big a hurry as the tiny little person of dubious gender that ran up to the parking lot before me. No, that dude/chick was truly booking it like Old Nick himself was on their heels. Couldn't help but wonder just what appointment with destiny they might be in such a big hurry to keep. But all I could say was their rapid exit had suited me just fine because, sometime during the course of our tour, I'd had the uncomfortable feeling they'd been checking me out. You know what I mean. It all starts when someone seems to be giving you the surreptitious eyeball, and ends up with shivers going up and down your spine. It may have been on account of all that weed I'd smoked over at Leslie's; maybe it had made me a tad paranoid. Nevertheless, I could have sworn that he/she was up to no good. So when the creature disappeared from view all I could think was *Thank you, Lord*.

At least that was my first thought. My second was to wonder just how much longer before I was basking in the sun down in some Banana Republic because, while I'd been tooling around in the bowels of the earth, the weather up top had turned to shit.

You know the score. Late November in the forty degree parallel can be mighty fickle. I remember Thanksgivings when I was running around in my shirtsleeves and others where the snow was flying to beat the band. Yeah, sunny Belize was looking mighty good about now. But first, a more or less obligatory visit to Mom's for her customary left-in-the-oven-too-long turkey dinner.

Guess I couldn't fault the old girl too much. That ADHD stuff does seem to run in the family and many was the time when I would smell something of my own creation getting ready to set the house on fire. Good thing we followed each other around or neither one of us would have a roof over our heads.

But though I could joke about it all I wanted, I had to admit it was becoming somewhat of a matter of concern for me. Maw sure wasn't getting any younger, and as she aged those eccentricities were morphing more and more into outright weirdness, and weirdness can get dangerous. First it was that business with hoarding and the aviary, but then she began to show signs of other obsessions, one of which was a real cause for concern.

Oh, it wasn't her pot smoking. That I could deal with. In fact, to coin an old saying, it would be like the pot calling the kettle black. (And what a play on words that was!) Nor was it her politics. Since she'd gotten into the Internet, Maw had gotten hooked on all those black websites—Rense and Art Bell to name a few—and she was always spouting leftist politics and conspiracy stuff. Her favorite one centered on chemtrails, which she claimed were a government plot meant to poison us from above. Right Maw, let it rip if it makes you feel any better. Talk is cheap, and there's nothing wrong with having your own opinions.

No, these little idiosyncrasies were not what concerned me. What I found infinitely more worrisome were those stubs from leftover lottery scratch-offs that she left lying around the house. Lord knows people have lost their homes on account of these little guys, and gambling has become such an addiction that you even have billboards advertising help for those so afflicted.

I asked her about it once and got the royal brush off, some bullshit about it being a once a month indulgence, and for awhile after our little conversation, the scratch offs disappeared. Or should I say, they went into hiding. Why, the last time I'd been home, I encountered a good dozen of them, hidden away at the bottom of a trash bag, when I'd been going through the garbage looking for something I'd accidentally thrown away. Not good, I had muttered to myself. Yeah, not good.

All the more reason why I might want to start spending a little more time at the home front. As much as I hated to quit my footloose and fancy free woofter lifestyle, I might have to cut back a bit, and this business of free ranging far and wide while I was stateside would also have to end. The bottom line was that mom needed me, and who else was going to step up to the plate?

Indeed, these were noble thoughts, and it would have been nice had they come to fruition. But alas, God and Wall Street had other plans for me. Right. God and Wall Street. I had to laugh since, for to so many in this fair land, they are one and the same.

I did go to Belize that winter, but I didn't stay as long as I usually stayed, coming home in early March instead of late April. My game plan had been to beat the college rush to the shit jobs available around town. I knew it was going to be tougher than usual, a real free-for-all in fact, because I'd been following the news while out of the country and all indications were pointing towards a serious Recession. Oh well, at least it wasn't going to descend into a downright Depression. Now THAT would have put a hurt on the country, one which we may not have survived. The 'R' word, however? Well, these had come and gone and the economy had always managed to bounce back, usually stronger than ever.

Why, one might wonder if they were not engineered for that exact purpose, manipulated by a gang of big-wig psychopaths who could increase their profits one hundred fold every time they bought low and sold high. Yes, one might wonder.

However, I was not at that particular phase of my life yet, though it would come soon enough. For the present I was just a happy go lucky wwofter kid who, having returned from the land of mangos and bananas, was dead set on finding a job at the local Wally's world...or Aldis, or Krogers, or any one of those superstores where all I had to do was stand in place for an eight hour shift and ask folks if they wanted paper or plastic.

Boy, was I in for a surprise when I tooled into Athens and started to circulate my so-called resume. Apparently, things had gone even further south than I had been that winter. My first glimpse of how bad it was getting came when I was greeted by an octogenarian.

"Good Morning, and welcome to Wal-Mart," the old crone croaked, and after one look at the road map of wrinkles that covered her face, I knew I was in trouble.

Aren't you a little old for this job, I wanted to ask, but her sad eyes told it all. Of course they were in direct contradiction to her pasted-on smile. Wally's never let you show your true colors or its greeters would probably be snarling at the customers like pit bulls. Nope, Wally's was all about image, and it was one that didn't cotton to its employees advertising the fact that they weren't too happy working for minimum wage. So instead of a glib comment, I simply went on about my business of hitting up the manager for a job, and that's when it began to get serious.

"Well, son," was the reply that assaulted me. "We've got quite a few applications here, but we can sure add yours to the stack. Of course, you realize that there's a mandatory drug test now, so maybe you'd like to get that over with..." He trailed off.

Maybe the odor of the joint I'd smoked on the way over still lingered on me, or maybe it was my blood-shot eyes. Whatever the case, I knew the gig was up, at least for Wal-Mart.

"That's OK," I replied. "I have a bunch of errands to run today. I'll just come back when I have more time."

Yeah, famous last words because, as it turned out, I was destined to have quite a bit of time—more than I was going to know what to do with. For the same story repeated itself at every establishment I went into that day. Oh, it was a variation on a central theme. *Sorry, we aren't hiring right now. Come back next year. We may be hiring then, but probably not. Come back when you're straight. Come back the twelfth of never.*

It all loosely translated as *get the fuck out of here. Don't you know there's a recession going on, and jobs this good are hard to come by? Why don't you try that kennel down the road? I hear they need someone to scoop up dog poop.*

Wow! Things sure had changed in the few months I'd been gone. What was a boy to do? I even expanded my search to Parkersburg, but to no avail. Jobs were scarcer than hen's teeth, and because it was an employer's market, the employers were having a heyday. This meant they could afford to be selective and only take the guaranteed cream of the crop, which usually included displaced factory workers and retirees in need of a way to supplement their meager social security check.

Gone were the days of a good blue-collar income and a safe six percent interest on one's investments. And gone too was the security of a roof over one's head. Words like *foreclosure* and *short sales* now riddled the real estate market. In fact, there really was no real estate market, and many who made made it their business were running up enormous credit card debt just so they didn't join the swelling ranks of the homeless. Banks were failing even though they'd been dubbed TOO BIG TO FAIL, and the big players were finding themselves bailed out by truculent taxpayers who had watched their pensions disappear overnight. Seems like there was no bail-out for the little guy.

To make a long, sad story short, the economy had tanked and in its wake was threatening to drown out my generation. Summer jobs were gobbled up by desperate oldsters, as millenials were passed over in favor of those with more work experience and fewer illegal habits. It was not good, and I knew then and there that I would not be able to follow my plan to stay close to the home front that summer. Nope, I was going to have to come up with a new plan and, like it or not, it was going to have to include higher education.

It had taken a few years since I'd left high school for this simple fact to dawn on me, which was crazy because it was as plain as the nose on my face. There was an old GED ad which proclaimed that *if you don't have a high school diploma, we can't use you*, except nowadays, that high school diploma had been supplanted by a college degree. Well, I'd long ago knocked off the GED, but college had remained an unwanted goal. Mainly because all the claptrap about its value was often nothing more than that. Claptrap. The truth being that it wasn't as rosy as proclaimed.

I had seen enough of my classmates fall for this crap. They'd gone right from high school to the college of their choice where they proceeded to rack up half the national debt. Then, upon graduation, they were still unable to find gainful employment. That's because they had gone for tits on a bull degrees like History or Art. Gee, how dumb can you get in today's economy? It was fairly obvious that if you wanted a job, you had to come up with a skill that folks would kill for, and it sure had nothing to do with Civil War battles or the post-modern movement.

I took my thoughts to a park bench in downtown Athens. It was a nice park with a kid's playground, dog walk, and multiple baseball fields. Plus it provided access to a bike trail, one which I had taken advantage of on many occasions. But today I was just vegging, thinking as it were. I idly watched as some kids played ball and thought about what people needed the most besides good food, adequate shelter and clean air and water. That's when it hit me like a ton of bricks.

Computers. THAT was where it was at. Everybody had at least one of the little devils in their house, and the damn things were always breaking down. I should know as I'd spent countless hours trying to hotwire my own in any way possible. Malware Bytes was my favorite stopgap for all the fucking viruses that managed to make it past my firewalls, and when all else failed, there was always System Restore. Yet that was just the tip of the iceberg. There was so much more you could do with an IT certification these days. Web Page design, video editing, game development, cyber security, data analysis. The list was endless and growing every day.

Plus, and this was a big plus, the local Career Center just so happened to have a two year course which trained you in all of the above. I knew this because I had already looked into it during a similar down turn several years back. So all I needed to do was to run over to Tri-County CC and apply and hope that not enough of the local high school kids had the same idea. You see, it was all on a first come, first serve basis, and the high school was always allowed seniority. Of course, if that was the case, they weren't the only show in town. There were other nearby Career Centers, and surely one of them would take me in.

So, that decided, I felt free to enjoy my afternoon off from the grueling and demoralizing task of pounding the pavement in search of nonexistent jobs. It felt so good I almost felt like celebrating by lighting up what was left of the morning's joint, but sat down until the mood passed. After all, I was in a public place and despite the liberal nature of the town, it wasn't good to push my limits.

Besides, there was really no reason to celebrate just yet. I still had an entire summer to make it through before classes began in the fall, and what was a boy to do? The generosity of Leslie had seen me through the winter and then some, but I was starting to get a bit cash strapped. And speaking of Leslie's, I wondered if maybe it was anywhere near another harvest time. I was just about to initiate Plan B, which involved a trip over to Kentucky, when I spied it out of the corner of my eye.

CLASSIC MIDWAY
Carnival Rides
Food, Games, and Fun
Coming to Athens, Ohio
May 18-20, 2008

And underneath there was a contact phone number that began with area code 513.

That's a Cincinnati exchange; I said to myself and began to wonder. Well, the Lord always did work in strange ways. So, why not?

I took out my phone, gave them a call, and she answered on the first ring. Her name was Bobby Grien, and she and her husband had founded this little traveling carnival just last year. Yes, they did hail from Cincinnati and their main touring focus was relatively narrow, limited to the states of Ohio, Kentucky, and Indiana; and yes, they were looking for roustabouts for the coming season. It was all too perfect. Not only was it gainful employment, but it suited my time schedule to a tee. Plus it was close enough to home that I could check in on mom occasionally. So I began to give the lady my contact info. However, I was pleasantly surprised when she just cut me off to ask me when I could start. *Why as soon as I complete my enrollment for college in the fall*, I answered, knowing that it was always good to appear upwardly mobile in such situations.

73

To this she just laughed before informing me that most of her employees didn't even own a GED, and she sure was glad to have landed someone who could at least read above a fourth grade level.

So that was how I came to operate the Dizzy Dragons for four fun months in 2008. It was advertised as a family ride with a capacity for sixteen to twenty-four people, and parents often rode with their children. Since it was fairly low key, there wasn't much liability involved. Although there was a preliminary drug test—one which I was able to easily beat with a combination of over-hydration and a simple kit from GNC—there were no follow-ups. I suppose my recent clean cut status might have had something to do with this. I had shed my dreads for the interview at Tri-County, and had left my earrings at home. It was a new look for me and one which would be short-lived, but it served my purpose. After all, the dreads would grow back, but money doesn't grow on trees. It grows on green dragons.

I really liked working for the Greins. They had thirty years in the business, so they knew what they were doing. However, this didn't turn them into stiffs. A fun filled couple; they once had a promo shot taken aboard a carousel at Cedar Point. They ran a clean operation, one dedicated to providing safe, modern, clean equipment with friendly, well-trained operators. The last would be me, and never had I commanded such respect at the workplace unless, of course, it was over in Kentucky in the basement of Leslie's new goat barn. That, however, was a different sort of respect, one reserved for birds of a feather, and horses of a different color. The status I enjoyed working for the Greins was almost embarrassing, especially since it was meted out to someone who really wasn't me but more a persona I was putting on for the public. I almost didn't like myself for the way I doled out the *Yes, Ma'ams* and *No, Sirs.* But I figured it was high time I learned a little customer service, as most of my previous McJobs were those which had confined me to a greasy kitchen or a dingy storeroom. Yep, if I was going to start up my own Mr. Fix-it computer shop, I'd damn well better get good at kissing a little ass.

However, I got so good at it that, by the end of the summer, the role I was playing had begun to rub off on me   so much that the lines between Noone and Do had really blurred. Blurred so bad that I discovered much to my chagrin that Noone really wasn't interested in smoking as much dope as Doe used to. Yep, it was time to get back to mom's basement. It was either there or somewhere south of the border where the palm trees swayed to a rhythm of a soft sexy Salsa, and I had already made a commitment which eliminated the second possibility.

So I packed up my meager bags for the last time—my liberal schedule had allowed me many a visit to the home front over the summer months—and headed back to Coolville for what was destined to become a turning point in my life. Alas and alack, what do they say? A kid's gotta grow up sometime.

At Tri-County I found myself in good company, at least as far as the other kids were concerned. Given, few of them shared my life experiences, the only one coming close being a displaced limey from Liverpool who was so professional looking that I initially mistook him for the teacher. However, in the long run that didn't seem to matter as we were all of one mind. Call it a hive mind if you like, but it was an AI kind of bond centered on a common language. Bytes and bits, algorithms and Blobs, Java and FORTRAN, emojis and hashtags, viruses and worms and Trojan Horses, Linux and UNIX, and a whole host of terms that came under the nebulous umbrella of 1337-speak.

The later encompassed all the terms and acronyms that represent 400 level GeekSpeak. Some, like *hack* and *LOL,* are obvious and overused by the general public; whereas others are more geared towards the true denizens of Geekdom. My favorite was *PrOn* which stood in for porn since it was a good way to get around word filters. But I was also partial to *interweb* which was slang for the internet and used as a way to poke fun of folks who confused the Net with the World Wide Web. And now that I was no longer a *N00b,* or relative newcomer to all this, I felt fairly superior enough to blast others with this expression. Of course, there were other terms, ones borrowed from the military, which one hated to bandy around.

Take for instance *SNAFU* and its nasty cousin *FUBAR.* Both referred to situations and status reports that had seen better days, but *TBH* (to be honest) neither were really my problem as they were often used in conjunction with some *POS* (piece of shit) laptop that some cheap assed country boy was trying to resurrect w/o (without) breaking the bank. We got a lot of these folks, people who knew that, just like research doctors, we needed our share of guinea pigs. So they'd drop off their convulsing computers, sign a waiver, and then hope for the best. Sometimes we'd be able to fix the things, sometimes not. It all depended on the complexity of the problem. The worst case scenario often involved a trip to the recycling center. The best? Well, there was no real acronym for it. Let's just say it was now up to the consumer and any future error might be in the *CKI* (Chair Keyboard Interface), and if you can envision what connects the chair to the keyboard, you get my drift.

However if all else failed to define the problem, there was always TWAIN (technology without an interesting name). Indeed, I hadn't had so much fun with slang since my surfer days. Ours was a language which bonded us as a band of brothers, just like shooting the curl and cruising the pipeline had in my days of old.

So who cared if most of the people in my class were ten years my junior? We still had a ball and then some, and it was the *and then some* that ended up changing my life.

Up to that point, *IRL* (in real life)—meaning to say my nightly sessions in mom's basement—I was more or less a game player. Oh, I did a bit of idle surfing, checking on any new posts to FACEBOOK and downloading bootlegged music, but mostly I was into a host of computer games the like of which would have shocked my dear old mother. Some were sword and sorcery like the *Age of Conan, Hyborian Adventures* and *The Fall of the Lich King.* Some involved aliens and monsters like *Dead Space* and Call *of Duty: World at War.* (And guess who the new enemy was? Why zombies, of course). Others like *Crysis, Warhead,* and *Warhammer: Age of Reasoning* were just plain war games stuff. But regardless their individual specializations, they all possessed a common theme, one which celebrated violence and aggression.

Maybe playing them was a way to work out my anger at being dropped into a world where I felt helpless to make a difference. Or maybe I just liked the color of blood. The jury was out, but when they came back in, I knew they would find me guilty as charged. What could I say? How could I help myself? I was a product of my generation, and we'd been brought up to take such gore into our stride. No big deal if that guy's head just came off. Oops, there goes another gut shot. In a sense, watching guys (and chicks) getting blown to bits was no different than squashing an offensive bug. It was all part of the program, one that my mom with all her peacenik rhetoric would never have understood.

Of course, there was always the other side of my genes, being my dad. The jury was way out on him, so far out that it may have resulted in a *hung jury* if you know what I mean. And if you don't…well, I am playing around with the possibility that he is no longer even on the planet. Not to say it would matter much since his legacy lives on in my veins, something that mom had absolutely no control over since it always takes two to tango.

At any rate, regardless the impetus, the result was the same. There I was, playing around into the wee hours of the night, happy to be lopping off heads and setting zombies on fire, while my sweet old mother snoozed above me in her 60's styled waterbed. Thank god the thing never sprung a leak or else the deluge that followed might have put my fires out for good. Happy I was in my little self-styled escape pod where I was master of the universe and captain of the light brigade. Immersed in a heavy hitting game or two, my worries of the future subsided. I was in control for once and actually gaining ground instead of spinning my wheels in the same old, same old. It was great, no make that: I Was Great!!! Conan, the Adventurer, Luke Skywalker, and Arnold Schwarzenegger all rolled into one. (And if you note that the last name has both War and Zen in its construction, then you get the picture.)

In a way it was too bad that things could not proceed aimlessly down that path to nowhere. Oh, I could blame it all on John McKennan, but I was the one who first initiated the conversation. Later I would ask myself why. Wasn't the Geek language and its ensuing camaraderie enough? Well, apparently not, because I found myself getting edgy. Summers had always been a bit tough as the folks I shared my shit jobs with weren't always renowned for their high IQs. It's been said that the employment world wants chickens, someone who will get up early and eat shit, and nowhere was this more apparent than at Micky Dees or Wally's World. So intelligent conversation was often a bit out of the question.

However, there was always some college student working their way through a summer job or some highly intelligent and over the hill high school dropout, and these guys (and girls) provided me with the little bit of stimulation I needed. The rest came from FACEBOOK and my fantasy world in the machine. So I was a happy enough camper.

Besides, when I went wwofting, there were always people of like mind to hook up with. Why, after doing it for almost ten years, I had friends in thirty states and five different countries. The only problem was that none of them were close to home. So after my fourth week at Tri-County, I was beginning to feel a bit out of sorts—the odd man out, the red herring, the politically incorrect term in the woodpile—and I was getting so dang hungry for any kind of human interaction that didn't center on some weird-ass acronym that I was starting to talk to mom's cockatoos.

That's when I began to notice John; I mean, really notice him. Prior to that he'd just been another guy in the class, albeit a mighty quiet one. Maybe his reticence was on account of his age—he was the only guy in there whose years topped my own—or maybe it was part of his overall demeanor. Whatever the case, John was the silent one in a class of farting guffawing teens, and it went far towards separating him from the herd. Add to that his misfortunate ability to be mistaken for our teacher and you get a recipe for a real social outcast.

However, the guy did nothing, and I do mean nothing, to rectify the situation. He always showed up as if he was dressed for the office, wearing respectable tweeds and button down collars. He always carried a briefcase, one which held a ton of books. And he always spent his lunch hour reading them.

I suppose it was the books that got me going. By all appearances they were not for the faint hearted reader, as the smallest of them was a good two inches thick. Nevertheless, he would attack them as if they were *War and Peace*, and his dissertation depended on a fresh analysis. However, when I got close enough to take a peek, it was plain these were not your standard classics. I made my analysis on account of the covers alone since they featured artwork psychedelic enough to cause the toughest stoner's head to spin.

Now what on earth could he be up to? It was a question I pondered for several sleepless nights, not that it was the cause of such insomnia, mind you. It's just that a combination of the video games I played and the pot I smoked while doing so did NOT lead to a restful night's sleep. It was also a question that held no answer unless I took matters into my own hands. So after sufficient nights spent chasing sheep through hopeless pastures I realized I would just have to break the ice and ask him.

The following day gave me an excellent opportunity. Serious rains had closed the schools that fed the Career Center, and only teachers were expected to show up. However, neither John nor I got the memo, and we arrived at the sound of the first bell. Since we were in a class that was more or less based on independent projects we were allowed to come in out of the rain and pursue our higher education. And what an education that turned out to be!

"What's that you're reading?" I asked during our lunch break. I had finally got up the nerve to talk to the guy which was no easy feat since I was almost positive he might bite my head off. He'd been dressed for the job that day, sporting one of those professor type sweaters with the suede patches on the elbows, and I half expected him to take out a switch and command that I mind my own business and get to work. However, his reaction was quite the opposite when he lit up with a lop-sided smile and delivered the two words that were to change my life for good.

"David Icke."

David Icke? Never heard of him. But, once he handed me the book, this would soon change. It's title was *Children of the Matrix*, and yeah, I was hip at the time to the Matrix movies and had even considered the possibility that they might be some sort of allegory for the human experience on this planet. But wow! Icke took that sentiment to the 99th degree.

The basic premise of the book reflected on how an inter-dimensional race has controlled the world for thousands of years and still does. They are primarily reptilian—mean looking customers according to the drawing that accompany the text—and as I skimmed through the pages describing their control and manipulation of world events, I began to feel the hairs rise on the back of my head. It was some weird material; no doubt about it. And that came from a kid who played all kinds of crazy video games involving zombies and space monsters. But those were just games. This by all appearances was meant to be taken as the gospel truth, which placed it right up there with the pamphlets the Jehovah's Witnesses handed out. I was perplexed and must have shown it, for John's next words invited me to explore deeper.

"Go ahead, borrow it," he suggested. "I'm almost done with it anyway, and I've got a whole lot more like it at home."

More like it, as in this guy David Icke had written more than one of these beauties? Why this one was close to three hundred pages long which made it two hundred and fifty over the length of my average reading material. But John was *spot on*, as they say in limey speak, for David had been hard at it, having written over ten books in ten years, each one of them stranger than the last as far as mainstream thought was concerned. Warned over twenty years ago about a coming global Orwellian state where a select few would enslave humanity, David had been sounding the alarm ever since—though he had not always been such a Cassandra. At one point he was a simple soccer player turned journalist when a bout of rheumatoid arthritis ended what was meant to become a promising career in football. His former hobby had led him into newspapers, radio, and regional broadcasting and culminated when he became the national television presenter for BBC sports. Then, later, an interest in politics prompted him to join the Green Party.

However, by the late 80's he was burned out on both politics and the television world, and that was when strange things began to happen. He would feel as if someone else was in the room with him, and the feeling became so strong that at one point he begged the presence to make contact. And so it did, leading him to a particular book in a particular bookstore which was written by a particular psychic. Her name was Betty Shine, and immediately after reading her book David contacted her.

He went in cold to the interview, not expressing any of his history to the woman. But she got his number loud and clear and with a *Wow! This is Powerful!* she communicated her message from the beyond. *David was a healer. Knowledge would be put into his mind. He would face tremendous opposition, but he would communicate that knowledge. He would write five books in three years, leaving politics to pursue a new career as a writer and public speaker. One man cannot change the world. But one can deliver the message that will change the world.*

And that said, I know that he sure changed mine.

I began with *Children of the Matrix*, and then backtracked to *The Biggest Secret*, before topping it off with *Alice in Wonderland and the World Trade Center, Tales from the Time loop*, and *Infinite Love is the only Truth; Everything else is an Illusion*.

For a nonreader, all this was a monumental achievement, but well worth the effort. Icke's cosmology is complex, or should I say it's so simple it's hard. The title of the last book in line probably states it the best, that the nature of reality is that nothing is real, except for LOVE. Yeah, all you need is LOVE. However, it not all about singing Kumbaya around a campfire because his views blend New Age philosophy with conspiracy theories, some of which are to the far left of Pluto.

Consider his belief that public figures are shape-shifting reptilians, which are not only pedophiles but also into the blood sacrifice of innocent children, and you get my drift. But the funny thing about many of Icke's so called conspiracy theories is that over the years they have been proven true. Take the sad case of Jimmy Savile which would break shortly following the man's death in 2011. Turns out that Savile, a revered television personality who could do no wrong (and also a bosom buddy friend to the royals), was also a class A pervert who had been abusing hundreds of children since the 1950's. Odd, since no one gets close to the queen unless they have gone through a rigorous background check with British Intelligence. So, what gives? How was the guy allowed to get away with it? Perhaps the answer was hidden in plain sight: that Savile was procuring children for a rich and famous elite, the same ones who Icke claims are out to rule the world and shape it into their hellish image.

At any rate, I could spend hours and hours expounding on Icke's philosophy. Come on, the guy didn't stop at just five books and in the years that followed, I gobbled them up as soon as the print dried. In that way, his cosmology and politics seriously influenced mine. I came to understand the laws of intentionality (or how our collective unconscious shapes the world we live in) and those of attraction (referring to how our thoughts attract our experiences). I spouted off his problem-reaction-solution in numerous political chat rooms and tossed about his terminology (words like *sheeple* and *red dress holograms*) as if they were my own. Yet on some points I had to draw the line. Somehow I just didn't agree that the moon was an artificial construct and that space wars were going on above our heads. Call it seeing is believing, but I just needed hard evidence and so far, the only thing I'd seen falling out of the sky was a stray meteor or two.

Not that I didn't believe in ET's, mind you. I even shared Icke's belief that they had heavily infiltrated our gene pool, tinkering with the

DNA of the original species on this planet, and leaving them the fucked up mess you see now. Indeed, such explanations for the human condition were way beyond plausible. And then there was all that business with the quantum leap in technology following the Roswell incident. I mean, who couldn't connect the dots on that one? After all, I was a techie; I should know.

Maybe I was just too earthbound to consider the possibility that exopolitics affected the outcomes on this planet. My take, more or less, was that we were captains of our own ship who had been left here high and dry years ago and who now had to figure out a way to perfect warp drive so we could get off this rock. But, before we did that, we had damn well better get our shit together on this planet lest we spread our bullshit to others. In a sense, I looked upon humanity as a wayward child which needed to be whipped into shape prior to giving them the keys to the car in which to cruise the galaxy. In a sense, we were now under quarantine, and though ET's were allowed in, our species was held hostage until we cured the virus that had caused us to fuck up one perfectly good planet. Yeah, don't let it spread. We had a long way to go before we joined hands with our celestial brothers and sisters to fly the friendly skies of United.

So that was where I departed from Icke whose stance had our military working hand in hand with Dracos and the like. These Reptilians have bases throughout the solar system and under the earth, one of which is located in Antarctica which they share with a breakaway group of Nazis who fled there after the war. Icke claims that a deal was cut between these Dracos and certain elites and military insiders, and that is the primary source for our advanced technology. Such technology has allowed us to go not only to bases on the moon but also to ones on Mars. In essence, we are getting to be real solar system globe trotters. Well... at least some of us are. For the most part, the little guy doesn't even have a clue about any of this, and some are even so naïve as to believe that we are the only intelligent entities in the galaxy. Go figure it.

Of course, my stance was midway between these fools and the woo-woo tin foil hats who believed all the space war nonsense. Although I have always had a fascination for the celestial—consider my taste in video games and my previous book list which included such gems as *John Carter, Fighting Man of Mars*—I still hedged on accepting this fiction as fact. I had to admit it was a bit stubborn and tunnel-visioned of me, but there was something about the whole business which gave me the willies. My fascination was akin to that held by a reformed alcoholic for the bottle, or the son of the Son of Sam for dead bodies. And that's a really strange analogy which leads me to wonder if it's something in my genes.

Whatever, the case, it's enough of a push-pull to cause me to want to steer clear of the topic. So let's just stick with stuff that's safe which is why I entered into Icke's' old nemesis of politics in a vain attempt to try to make a difference here on planet earth. Yeah, I guess a guy has gotta put their focus somewhere, and despite my understanding and agreement with David on some of the finer points of consciousness, I chose to adhere to a rather rigid belief system in which my vote counted.

That said, my focus stayed grounded to the planet and my excursions into cyberspace were limited to those in the alternative press who were trying to find a cure for its numerous ailments. I explored various websites that seemed to offer solutions, such as THRIVE and the National Liberty Alliance. I joined local organizations that fought for the environment (and in southeast Ohio, we needed as many as we could get). Instead of spending my evenings blowing up zombies and buffing out my body on the Gold's Home Gym, I chatted with those who shared my political beliefs, which at the time of my tenure at Tri-County leaned heavily towards the left. Lord knows, we had just gotten rid of one of the worst White Houses on record, a repressive regime that had shredded our constitution by selling us a bill of goods through fear based management. Yeah, losing the Bill Of Rights was for our own good, as was the invasion of one foreign county after another because we sure did have to make the world safe for democracy. Forget the fact that we had lost the one we had at home.

At any rate, by the time the 2008 election had rolled around, everyone had been ripe for some *change you could believe in,* and it wasn't hard to sell the public on an erudite distinguished looking African American—if indeed, he was a natural born citizen, but that debate (just like the one surrounding Arnold Schwarzenegger) would come at a later date. All things considered, Obama had been our great white hope, or should I say our great black hope (at the risk of breaking the rules of political correctness). So like many other liberals at the time, I had rooted for the guy. After all, a village in the great Red state of Texas had needed of their idiot back.

Of course, at that particular juncture I hadn't yet developed my passion for politics. So, unlike some people I knew, I didn't weep when Obama won the election. Probably because at the time I'd been too busy smoking up the gleanings from Leslie's little operation down in Kentucky. Then, shortly after that I'd left the county for my annual exodus to the sweet sunny lands south of the border which had placed me out of the picture for a good six months.

So all this political stuff didn't catch up with me until I returned and hit the recession (the one engineered by the Bush cartel who were determined to leave the hen house with as many chickens in their carpetbag as *humanly* possible—if indeed, they were human. And on that note, I have always wondered about that euphemism which has to do with *blue blood*.

Alas, but wonder became a permanent state of mind once Icke infected me, and for a couple of years following my decision to enter the political arena, I actually felt pretty good about life and the direction in which our country was going because...well, let's be realistic. Anything was better than George Bush Junior.

Oh, I missed the southlands, since my commitment to Tri-County and the tech program had limited my ability to travel. But I figured it would all pay off with a six figure job, and I would be able to help my maw get out from under some of her debt. She had recently signed up for Obama's program to augment our aging electric with solar, at which point she'd be able to deduct it from her income tax. (What income!!!) However the clincher was that she would have to ante up with the start-up cash for this little home improvement, and thus far that had resulted in a bill of way over ten grand. Most of it went on a new credit card, and why they continued to give this woman the damn things was a mystery up there with the Shroud of Terrin!

No, I didn't even want to go there. All I could hope for was that the other seven credit cards were not suitably maxed out because, until I started making some money, there was no way in hell I was going to bail her out. We'd just have to starve. Guess we could always eat the birds, but something about that diet was right up there with rat. Oh, I suppose she could always continue to borrow from Peter to pay Paul, a little trick she had become adept at, but that too had its limitations. Oh well, at least the house was paid for clear and free. (Or so I thought.)

And so the days drifted by with me at school during the day learning the ropes of my new career and in the basement at night saving the world by chatting with a bunch of other trogdolites with computer tans. It never occurred to me that perhaps my time might be better spent at one of the many organic farms that were sprouting up around Athens. That would be too much like work. It was so much easier to talk about that change than to actually become it.

Then the day I had been awaiting for two whole years finally arrived. It was Senior Night at Tri-County, and I was a member of the graduating class. I looked around me at all the other little geeks, some of whom had just begun to shave. John McKennan was long gone, having dropped out after our very first term together, and as far as I could tell the guy had simply disappeared from the face of the earth. No one seemed to know anything about his whereabouts, and word had it that he had just packed up his apartment in Athens in the middle of the night and driven off into the sunrise. His absence had left me with not one, but four books by our favorite author; an oversight on his part which I felt may have been intentional. Nothing like spreading the gospel of Icke.

Maw was in the audience, many of who snuck out as soon as their kid's name had been read. Guess their hands were worn out from all that clapping. But not my Maw, she stuck it out to the bitter end and even initiated a standing ovation at the end of the whole shebang. The director loved her for that since up to that point he'd had to play the role of primary cheerleader, and I could tell that his enthusiasm was wearing thin.

And then it was all over. Twenty months and ten days of putting up with fart jokes and pubescent pimple popping. Endless hours of bits and bytes and DPS and EFS and a host of other alphabet words so numerous as to put the Department of Defense to shame. Alas, the end was not only in sight, but it had come and caught up with us. Like it or not, we were a graduating class and that meant only one thing: we now had to shit or get off the pot, a euphemistic way of saying that we had to find a job. Yes, a job…which was a three letter word turned four when I finally got around to pursuing its ambiguous reality.

I had no idea how weird the work force had become until I started checking out job descriptions. For some reason they are particularly obtuse and ridiculous when it comes to the technology sector. Maybe they figured we'd been speaking geek so long we would flounder in any other language. But really??????

- Passionate code warrior who writes highly qualified, maintainable and scalable software code leveraging best practices for test and verification?
- Deep understanding with IoT security frameworks, AWS systems, relational database systems (Redshift, Dynamo DB, PostgreSQL, S3, and Mongo)??
- Working knowledge of spectrum of leading IoT platforms highly desirable (e.g.AWS IoT, Azure IoT Suite, IBM Watson IoT)???
- Strong experience with HTML/ CSS/ Jquery/ Ajax/ AWS/ ReactJS or full stack software development????
- Experience with real time embedded systems, actuators and controllers?????
- Significant experience developing in Java, C++, Python, JavaScript. Node JS and other relevant languages, web services or API's??????

Oh, and the clincher:

> Excellent **English** communication skills, both written and oral?????!!!!?????

And did I mention that they wanted a MsC or PHD in Computer Science, Electronics Engineering, Mathematics, or related degree with a strong software engineering bias. Boy, was I ever out of my league! Maybe I should go for an entry level position. But when I did, I noticed that many of these required four to five years experience. Well now, if that were so, they wouldn't be entry level now, would they?

Something was decidedly wrong. Not only did they want all that regular experience but some demanded ten years of it be in social media. This presented a problem because social media hadn't even been around that long.

And then there were some of the job titles: Meme Librarian, Product Philosopher, Cat Cuddler, Fashion Evangelist. What the fuck!!! All I wanted to do was write code for video games. Lord knows I had enough experience as a user. I may as well put it to good use as a creator. What I did not want was a sling-shit job, which looked like an adequate description for most of what I was seeing in the want ads. These are the kind of jobs where you spend hours making up gobbley-gook in order to convince the boss that you are actually doing something creative. And they truly do require a degree (often advanced) in BS.

Case in Point: this beaut which I pulled from *The New York Times:*

Now hiring a Customer Success Director in the New York City, NY area!

Job Description

Trillium Technical currently has an opportunity available for a Customer Success Director!
Responsibilities (including, but not limited to the following)
• **Define and optimize customer journey**

> Create a vision of "FirstTimeRight experience"
> Create and/or improve templates and lifecycle processes used by the CSMs during their customer's journey
> Put in place an escalation process. Personally manage escalations to executives responsible when needed.
> Embrace change management and look for continuous improvement.

- **Value proposition for customers**
  - ➢ Coach the customers on the best practices of change management.
  - ➢ Ensure that CSMs deeply understand customers' objectives and build trustful relations with the customers.
  - ➢ Unlock any blocking issue of the customer journey through adapted solutions and/or escalations.
  - ➢ Mitigate critical situations.
  - ➢ Determine how to define, drive, and demonstrate the value (ROI) delivered.
  - ➢ Point out already delivered added-value to the customers and bring future improvement suggestions (in order to keep the account active).
- **Lead cross-functionally to drive customer success**
  - ➢ Know the implementation Partners and learn from existing experiences.
  - ➢ Clarify ownership for each part of the journey.
  - ➢ Gather feedback from other departments, including Sales, Pre-sales, Support, Product Partners and others, to improve the customer experience.
  - ➢ Advocate for changes in other departments' ways of working and collaborate with them to implement those.
  - ➢ Drive company-wide definition of ideal customer's journey.
  - ➢ Create company-wide customer feedback loop.
  - ➢ Advocate company-wide the culture of Customer Success.
- **Drive alignment with Sales**
  - ➢ Align with sales on renewal and up-sell strategy
  - ➢ Give feedback to Sales, Pre-Sales and Marketing on prospecting approach
  - ➢ Define CSM pre-involvement during sales cycle
  - ➢ Be informed regarding customers' important news.

- **Key metrics for the CS team at company level**
  - ➢ CSAT
  - ➢ NPS
  - ➢ Case studies
  - ➢ Number of used robots / number of bought robots.
  - ➢ Other KPI to come in a 2nd wave
- **Reporting**
  - ➢ Create dynamic dashboards to measure customers' health and customer success.
  - ➢ Conduct benchmarks to choose the most suitable tools for our specific activities.
  - ➢ Ensure all players involved in the customer journey have access to the concern information (inputs and outputs).
  - ➢ Perform global statistics on the CS team KPI's: CSAT, NPS, number of Case study, number of Live robots. Analyze these correlations and put in place corrective or improvement measures.
- **Recruit, mentor, inspire the team**
  - ➢ Anticipate and recruit in advance great candidates
  - ➢ Follow a rigorous interview process
  - ➢ Set expectations on performance and give feedback
  - ➢ Manage out underperformers
  - ➢ Set up training and mentoring to grow team
  - ➢ Create a customer centric culture
- **Achieve operational excellence**
  - ➢ Dispose of real time data for all customer success related metrics. Able to check, update, share these data with all the involved persons.
  - ➢ Keep all KPIs on green.
  - ➢ Define a state-of-the-art onboarding process for new CSMs and for the customer journey.
  - ➢ Identify suitable trainings for the team.
- **Empower the team and create at least a successor who could take anytime the lead.**
Apply online today!

Qualifications

• Bachelor's degree in engineering or computer science with over 15 years of work experience
• 10+ years relevant work experience in a customer-facing customer success, account management or strategic consulting organization. SaaS experience a benefit.
• Solid technical background with hands on experience in digital technologies
• Experience in technical support, project management, technical sales and consultancy
• Familiarity with software and front-end development
• Excellent verbal and written communication skills
• Strong analytical and problem-solving skills
• Self-motivated, proactive team player with innovative ideas to inspire customer loyalty and adoption.
• Strong communication and interpersonal skills. Proven experience building strong internal and external relationships.
• Proven track record in a highly-professional customer service in a dynamic, start-up environment.
• Diplomacy, tact, and poise under pressure when working through customer issues
• Ability to pass any pre-employment screenings

Yeah, I had to re-print that one in its entirety to demonstrate just how bad it's got out there. Why even Mickie D's is demanding a college education. And just to ask if you want fries with that??? Talk about slinging shit!!

However, nor did I want the opposite of a sling-shit job which for the record is known as a fling-poo job. I'd actually had one or two of these in my career and, believe me, they are the worst. Not your ordinary job, they can be very deceptive. They are usually the result of government bureaucracy and regulations that require that someone be there, whether or not there is any real work to be done; and sometimes they can get downright slow.

At first you can't believe your luck. You are getting paid to do *nada*. You don't have to hump anything: carts, merchandise, coal. The phone never rings, and you rarely see a human face. There is virtually no stress at all.

But that becomes the problem. Humans need some stress. It keeps them awake. They also need some human interaction, and eventually the job becomes a nightmare of ennui, isolation, and inactivity.

You are incarcerated alone in a small room like *The Hole* (solitary) in prison. You start to go slowly mad and eventually end up crapping in your hand and flinging it against the wall to see if it splatters, just like caged moneys do. And it may be crazy, but least you are doing something.

So what is a boy to do? The pickings were slim. The promised Recovery from the Recession was slow, slow, slow, and it was an employer's market out there, which is why they could get away with these kinds of shenanigans. Some jobs, I swear, weren't even legit, but for some reason had to be posted to fulfill some sort of quota. Maybe these were the ones that led to those government statistics claiming that we had less unemployment than this time last year. It was hard to say, but as Mark Twain pointed out, it's always been a game of lies, damn lies, and statistics. All I knew was that I was in trouble if I didn't find some way to invent the wheel. So I did what millennials are famous for and did just that.

I maxed out my own credit cards and bought some state of the art tech equipment and the software to go with it. Then, after setting up shop in my mom's basement, I printed a bunch of flyers and distributed them around the area. I also advertised in local papers, both hard copy and online, touting myself as a do-all be-all answer to everyone's tech problems. Whether it was a fragmented hard drive or a stubborn webpage, I was here to help. I even went so far as to help folks set up FACEBOOK pages (the labyrinth of FACEBOOK being one that only the foolhardy attempts to navigate without a guide).

Then I sat back and waited for the phone to ring, and tech problems being what they are in this day and age, it didn't take long. Before the month was out I had more business than I could handle, and I guess you'd say I was a success. (If you want to call living in your mom's basement with only computers and cyberspace for company a success.)

My only consolation came in getting so good at what I was doing that I attracted the attention of a guy out in California who was writing the code for a new video game, one which he needed a little help with. So for a brief moment I was allowed to follow my dream.

The name of the game was Kerbel Space Program, and it was a game where players would build spacecraft, fly them, and ultimately conquer space. It was destined to become a personal favorite of a guy Named Elon Musk since he was the CEO of a company called SpaceX whose purpose was to *revolutionize space technology, with the ultimate goal of enabling people to live on other planets.* And why I was chosen for the honor of providing this billionaire with his number one entertainment was beyond me. But never look a gift horse in the mouth was my motto and program I did, inserting weird little Easter eggs into the code as inside jokes. Like the glyphs in *Fringe* and similar Easter eggs in *Lost* these were meant to keep the viewer/player on their toes while they tried to work out their hidden meanings. It was probably the most fun I've ever had with work, and I was sorry when the project ended.

But not too sorry, because by then I was getting ready to leave for my first wwoofer assignment in over five years. This time I was going to Costa Rica to work on a small farm in the Guanacaste Region. The guy who owned it was an international, like many of the entrepreneurs in the country, and he was growing massive fields of Echinacea which would later be converted into numerous products for global distribution. He mostly employed locals, but I guess he occasionally craved the company of someone who could carry on a lengthy conversation in his native language (which just so happened to be English). And, for this reason, he usually kept at least one American wwoofer on retainer.

Since he was fairly selective about his employees, I felt privileged to finally get a foot in his door, so privileged that I came close to overstaying my visa, an oversight that had me hustling up to Nicaragua for a renewal. Nicaragua was so cool—especially my tour of its enormous lake—that I decided to put it on my bucket list for places to spend more time. But for the present, the gentle waves of Playa Hermosa and the like were calling. By this time I was on the downhill side of my winter, and had decided to skip any further wwoofing and go surfing.

It turned out to be addicting, and for the remainder of my stay in Costa Rica, I bummed up and down the beaches on the Pacific Coast, seeking the perfect wave by day and a brown skinned woman to share my bed at night. After so long in the cyber wasteland it felt really good to return to Paradise, and it was hard to tear myself away. However March winds were blowing and with them change was in the air. So after shooting the curl for one last ride, I packed my rucksack and headed for the bus station.

Here I used my minimal Spanish to book passage to San Jose where a big jet airline awaited to take me home to the states. Say goodbye to *tamarindo* and hello to local *manzanas*, the latter being apples which for reasons defying logic are one of the Tico's favorite foods despite costing an arm and a leg due to a heavy import tax. Yes, it's true. We humans always seem to want what we don't have; the grass being greener on the other side of the fence regardless of where in the world that fence might lay.

It was small facts like these which separated me from the herd of tourists that visited Central America every year, and I couldn't help feeling special as I sat in the San Jose airport and watched the Yankees flock in from numerous US college towns. It was Spring Break time, and they had all arrived for their annual week of fun in the tropical sun. Pasty white co-eds in search of a healthy tan, they'd be lucky to leave without a nasty burn or a bad case of the clap. Yeah, I knew what they were up to. What happens on Spring Break stays on Spring Break.

I caught them eyeballing me which only caused my head to swell a bit more. Sorry girls, I felt like saying. This bird is flying back north, but don't worry. There are lots and lots of surfer bums to take my place, and if you are lucky, they won't pull any social faux pas like the one I witnessed the other day. I still chuckled over the wanna-be Latin lover who asked two girls if they were German, and when they replied no, he went on to blunder that he swore they must be so because women from that country always had big butts. Needless to say, his attempt at breaking the ice only resulted in an icy reception. Yeah, try again Casanova, but polish your line a little first!

It was a long wait for my flight, and the more I allowed my ego to entertain me, the more I felt like I was returning home the conquering hero. What a great life I had made for myself. The computer degree had really paid off, so there would be no more shuffling around looking for shit jobs upon my return this time. No sir! I'd be right back in my little basement doing the thing I enjoyed most (well, besides smoking dope and surfing) and that would be hacking away at a keyboard while bringing in the bacon. I was a success story amongst my generation who had made it a point to go against the grain and invent their own wheel. We sure had outshone other age groups including the hippy dippy ones that my mom had belonged to. Merry Pranksters, indeed! All that little stunt had gotten her was banishment from the home place and fifteen years of terminal poverty. Oh, yeah, and me... because whenever I did the math, I figured that my dad must have been a member of this merry band of Greenwood dwellers.

But why chew on that cud? Dad was nothing more than another set of chromosomes to me. His blood may have run in my veins, but I was the one who had put it to good use. Yeah, I was something else, a globe-trotting world traveler who at the ripe old age of thirty had already been in forty states and two hemispheres. An entrepreneur who had created their own company, one with services so in demand that the CEO could afford to take five months off a year and still return to a thriving business. What a life I was living. At this rate I could expand my horizons to include a couple more continents for my travels, and why not? I had always wanted to surf the northern coast of Spain. Plus there was Amsterdam with its great weed; and all of it legal. Wow! I was just getting started, and all this from a surfer kid from Flagler Beach.

For some reason my inner dialogue wouldn't let up, and even for a narcissistic millennial, I was becoming a bit nauseating. Maybe I should take it down a notch because what is it they say? That pride goeth before a fall? Oh, oh, was that foreshadowing of plot I was hearing? A cat tiptoed over my grave and caused the hairs on the back of my head to rise. Oh well, ¿Diay? Or so they say in Tico—which loosely translates as: *What can be done about it?*

I looked at the clock. Still another hour and a half until boarding time. Despite the visions of grandeur that my ego was entertaining me with, boredom was setting in. Maybe I should get up and take a walk. Find an airport bar or something. Yeah, may as well have one for the road. And with that in mind, I wandered off in search of a shot of Guero, the heavy hitting Costa Rican liquor that burns a route all the way down to your toes. Of course, had I known what was coming, I might have purchased the whole bottle, and even then, it probably wouldn't have been enough.

Chapter 4
Lulu (AKA Stitch)
2008-2010

I can't say much for Thanksgiving dinner that year. I almost wish I hadn't even bothered. It was your usual for me: a *fighting with your maw, fighting with your paw, your brother had sense and he stayed away* kind of event, except that it was the paw who had sense and stayed away, mainly because he'd been long gone like turkey through the corn for over fifteen years. Not that his shadow did not continue to dominate the family table. The presence of his ghost always gave my brother Davey and me an excuse to hit the sauce heavy, just as it seemed to accentuate the rod of steel that ran up my other brother's backside. Stiff upper lip was putting it mildly as far as Joe was concerned, so much that I wondered if his face would crack if a smile ever slipped past his stony demeanor.

Yep, serious was an understatement when it came to Joe. The Marines had seen to that, especially now that he was up for promotion to Captain. Sometimes I longed for the old days when he was still approachable. Not that he hadn't always fulfilled the role of my big brother, my lord protector. It was just that now he had a whole lot more lives to watch over. But what could I say? I'd grown up in a Marine family; I knew the score.

"So where are you off to this time," I asked him as I helped myself to another glass of wine. I was trying to sound casual and also trying to sound as if I didn't already know the answer to that question.

For in 2008 a Jarhead's tour of duty was limited to one of two places, Afghanistan or Iraq, and I already knew Joe had opted for the more dangerous of the two, being the Stan. True, its lengthy name had been shortened to make it more pronounceable for the troops, but that didn't minimize the danger that lay in those convoluted hills.

"Oh, Maureen, leave Joe be," my mother's nasal voice interjected. "You know we don't discuss business at the dinner table. Here Joe, have another serving of mashed potatoes."

I just stared. That was about all you could do with my mother. Any kind of intelligent meaningful conversation was out of the question. And as for the potatoes? Well, I was surprised that the cheapskate had even sprung for them, let alone all the fixings for this lavish Thanksgiving dinner, since she'd been bitching a blue streak ever since I'd gotten home about the state of the economy.

"That market just keeps going down and down," she'd lamented, while watching the six o'clock news. "Guess that's what happens when you elect a Democrat. Boy, I don't know what people are goner do."

Goner? Yep, my mother always seemed to resort to her native hillbilly tongue whenever confronted with adversary. I came real close to correcting her, but then realized I wasn't doing too good in the Queen's English department myself. Besides, as far as my mother was concerned, there were so many other character flaws that to focus on the small change would have been petty of me, and I was trying desperately not to be petty.

The truth was there was only one person who had prompted my return home for this traditional family dinner, and he was currently trying to ward off the massive mounds of mashed potatoes my mother seemed determined to provide him with. I felt like telling him to eat up. After all, those mashed potatoes would look pretty good in another month when he was faced with nothing more than nasty MRE's to quell his hunger. Yeah, I wanted to tell him a lot of things and probably would have if my mother had allowed any of us to get a word in edgewise. But, as usual, it was all about her, so the rest of us either tended to our bottle, or in Joe's case, to the *Close Encounters of the Third Kind* mound of mashed potatoes which had been so ungraciously lumped upon his plate.

Some Last Supper, eh? Not that I knew it at the time, but all the early warning signs were there. The rain that beat relentless upon the windows. The turkey left in the oven too long. Even Davey's eighteen year old mongrel mutt who'd had an accident on the kitchen floor minutes before we sat to sit down to give thanks.

"Oh leave him be," Davey had wailed. "The poor guy's got *dogtimers.* How old is he in human years? About one hundred and twenty-five? How do you think you'll be doing when you hit that age?"

And on and on with the excuses, excuses, excuses while the real reason for the dog's little accident lay in Davey's refusal to buy doggie diapers for the poor old fellow. Guess when you spend most of your salary at the liquor store there's not much left over for Petsmart. Lucky thing he didn't chintz in the dog food department, or we wouldn't even be having this discussion. But that was one caretaking area in which Davey excelled, mixing the dog up special dinners every night from whatever table scraps maw sent him home with—and yes, although Davey had managed to untie the apron strings to some degree, he still lived but a stone's throw from our ancestral home.

I honestly didn't know what he would do when the dog finally did kick the bucket; he was that attached to the lump of fur. Just witnessing his obsession made me glad I had decided to go the solitary route. What do they say? If you ain't got nothing (nobody) then you've got nothing to lose?

Or so I thought that day as I watched through wine bleary eyes while my dysfunctional kinfolk attempted to perform one of the major family rituals in the country. In my infinite smugness, I felt so far above them, so Zen-like in my detachment. Little did I know I was setting myself up for one hell of a fall.

I stayed though Black Friday. And Why not? Even though I wasn't about to participate with the annual ritual that followed *stuff your face day* with *empty your pockets day*. No, the main reason I hung around was on account of the weather. The rain which had poured down in buckets had decided to turn to ice overnight, and all flights were cancelled until further notice. I knew I'd get an alert when my flight was back on, so I decided to stick around. World traveler that I was, I knew that even mom's house was preferable to an airport bar the day after Thanksgiving, especially when stocked with angry travelers who were in a hurry to get back to their own homes.

In a way this was good as it gave me a chance to spend a little more time with my elder brother who wasn't due back at base until the following Monday. I have to admit it was one of the better days I'd had with him in a long while. Despite the weather, we managed to slip (and hopefully not literally) out to a neighborhood bar where we spent a few good hours watching college football and devouring the hottest chicken wings I'd ever indulged in. Both choices were his, but I figured I may as well play along. After all, quality time is quality time even if the quality hinges on personal preferences.

At first, our conversation was banal, typical stuff about the teams and who might win, but later after a few rounds of Guinness, we started in on the heavy stuff, some of which was downright unexpected considering the source.

"We really aren't winning any hearts and minds over there," Joe began by way of introduction, and whoa, it was all downhill from there. He continued to expound upon the horrible losses on both sides which this war had brought about.

"Over one hundred thousand Iraqis, close to five thousand of our guys and that doesn't even include the stats for Afghanistan. But what's worse are the guys who are coming home, the ones who are stacking the beds at Walter Reed until there's standing room only. Guys with no arms, guys who will never walk again, guys with TBI's so severe that their next stop after Walter Reed is the pawn shop where they buy the gun that will blow them away. You know, it's crazy, been seven years now since 9-11 and we are still actively engaged in conflict. Where's the Operation Enduring Freedom? Freedom from what? I mean, this new guy Obama is promising us a rose garden of reduction in force, but I'll believe it when I see it. Beginning to wonder if all those peaceniks are on to something and if this just isn't all about the oil…"

He trailed off and took another sip from his beer, then sighed and changed the subject. It was almost as if he had said more than he'd wanted, but it was enough to get the drift. Although I had prided myself on being as apolitical as possible (especially considering the family I had come from) I couldn't help but get the picture. After all, I was a child of my times and 9-11 loomed on my horizon like the Jolly Roger, always ready to board my Good Ship Lollipop. You can only ignore the current events that shape your life so much before something comes along to yank your ostrich head out of the desert sands.

It happened over ten months later. That nice young black man, who had promised us *change we could believe in*, had proceeded to serve up just more of the same old shit. Shortly after his inauguration, he approved the sending of an additional seventeen thousand troops into the fray. Among these would be my brother who had probably suspected as much during the time of our little conversation. Up to that point, the Marines had not been involved in Afghanistan, something I had not known due to my preferred ignorance of such matters.

But in June of 2009, this changed and with it, my brother's destiny was sealed. Fighting intensified during the summer months, and in the fall operations began to ratchet up even more so. One of these involved an obscure village—they were all obscure to my mind—in the Kunar Province by the name of Ganjgal. It was an operation that was suspect from the first. From the get-go it had been made clear to the Team that no close air support would be made available to them.

Although in case of emergency, a helicopter could be redirected from an operation in a nearby valley. So that was the good news. The bad was that the Taliban forces were aware of the pending mission and were planning an ambush. However, this did not sway the Team who, fearing loss of the initiative, decided to proceed full speed ahead. It was not a wise decision.

The task force soon found themselves pinned down on three sides. Their initial calls for support were met with refusal due to new rules of engagement that had been put into place, rules which sought to minimize civilian casualties. Although our guys insisted they were not near a village at the time, they were still denied support. It is ironic that while they continued to take fire, they could observe women and children shuttling fresh ammo to the Taliban. So much for concern over those civilian casualties.

Forced into a retreat, the team requested smoke canisters to provide them with cover. An hour later the canisters arrived, but they were white phosphorus, not smoke. By this time three US Marines, their navy Corpsman, their Afghan interpreter, and several Afghan soldiers had been killed. My brother was among the fallen. As a final indignity, the position in which he fell was overrun by the enemy who stripped his body for his gear and weapons. Fortunately (if I can dare use such a word) all bodies were recovered after his comrades braved enemy fire to return to the location. Of course, by that time the damage was done.

There was speculation after the event that the villagers had ratted our guys out to the Taliban. There was also enough concern over the lack of requested fire and air support that an investigation was launched. Battalion leadership was blamed, and several officers were given official reprimands. It is a further point of irony that had my brother made his promotion, he may have only seen his head roll instead of his entire body. But, no...not my brother. He never would have botched an operation like this. In fact, in my eyes, he never did one wrong thing in his life. Unless, that is, you consider his decision to join the Marine Corp.

The funeral was at Arlington. Where else? It was my second one there in just under two decades, and I prayed it would be my last. Except that I knew better since my dear old mother would never have seen fit to be planted anywhere else. At least that way she could enjoy in death some of the respect she'd found wanting while amongst the living. So taken was she with the notion that she even had her dress laid out, white gloves and all. It was nauseating as was the way she stoically approached the demise of her first born. If there was a tear to be shed, it would be behind closed doors. She was that determined to keep up appearances. She was the mother of a fallen hero, by God, and they simply did not cry.

Not so with Davey and I. Together we must have brought forth a river of grief, much of which was lubricated by massive quantities of alcohol. At least as far as Davey went. As for myself, I had discovered an internal regulating device that cut me off before I became stumbling down drunk. I guess the days of wine and roses now belonged to the past. I would just have to find some other coping mechanism if I were to make it through this second dark night of the soul.

I gazed around me at the row after row of small white tombstones. They seemed to stretch out endlessly in all directions. Our fallen heroes? Sorry, but it seemed more like cannon fodder to me. I couldn't help but consider Joe's parting words about the senseless nature of war. And that from a dyed in the wool Marine? What was this world coming to? Perhaps the old paradigm was breaking down at last. One could only hope.

A grey wind grappled with the tops of the trees, bringing leaves down to a premature death upon a grass made green by too much fertilizer. But hey, why not? Nothings too good for our troops, right? Behind me a weird sculpture loomed. At first I'd thought it was there to commemorate the twin towers, but now I wasn't sure. Still those twisted pieces of steel bore the tell tale image that had been broadcast far and wide, the icon of a nation in mourning, a nation victimized by a wicked world that envied its peace and prosperity. Oh, yeah, and don't forget democracy, our crowning achievement.

Boy, was I feeling bitter—so bitter that all my grief had been transposed to anger at the system which had stolen my brother from me. My brother, my father, my sister, my lover…every single headstone marked the final resting spot of someone who had been loved, someone whose presence would be sorely missed forever more. It wasn't fair and it sure wasn't right.

The wind whipped my thin raincoat and reminded me that yes, another winter was coming and didn't that mean it was time to go south—so far south, in fact, that I might just be able to delete the past week from my life?

The bad news had found me in Cincinnati, a nice enough town on the Ohio River where I had come to roost following my stint in Isla Mujures. Things had gone so well down in Mexico the previous winter that I had considered setting up a similar business somewhere in the states. Why I chose Cincinnati was beyond me except that I'd always liked the way it rolled off the tongue. Besides rents were reasonable, and I was able to find someone who allowed me a six months lease. At that point I wasn't into committing to anything; I was just testing the waters to see if I might be able to stay afloat.

So I'd unpacked my duffle bag, leased a sewing machine and then went about the grueling business of getting the word out. This was always the hard part for me since I was more or less an introvert. But you've gotta get your butt out there if you plan on getting your business off the ground, and I was determined to give it a try.

Things had been slow at first, but by the time Joe bit the dust they were beginning to pick up. In fact, I discovered I was even able to make my rent every month by what I took in, a financial first for me. Previously, one of the main reasons for my exodus from any town was a rent payment that had fallen in arrears, and many was the time when I'd packed it up in the middle of the night to sidestep an irate landlord. But here I was, with cash to spare for the first time ever, and the longer the goldrush went on, the more I liked Cincinnati. Besides, it was really just a hop skip and a jump from Leslie's farm, a place which had become the one constant in my nomadic lifestyle. So why not *pull up a chair and sit a spell* as they say in these here parts?

Until, of course, your favorite sibling gets his head blown off in a senseless war. Yeah, that will precipitate a change and not necessarily one for the better. I could see it coming even before I left the DC area. The old restlessness was setting in, compounded by an ennui that can only come from extreme loss. Hey, better ennui than out an out depression although the two are closely related. So, it didn't surprise me that, by the time I returned to my own fair city, I was ready to pack my BIC lighter car with my meager possessions and head, once more, for those hallowed hills that housed Leslie's little farm. Once there, I could figure it out. Maybe.

At that point I didn't really know what I wanted or what Plan B might involve. All I did know was that I did not—and let me emphasize that—DID NOT want to succumb to the same demons that plagued me upon the death of my father, those being the demon rum and his friendly sidekick, the Cocaine Kid. However, I also knew that sitting around in a tiny one room apartment while bent over someone's prom dress was not going to pull me out of the black funk that was threatening to overtake my soul. No, it would have to be a bit more extreme than that, and as I navigated the short distant down to Leslie's a plan began to form in my mind.

I still had a bit of surplus cash. Right? Especially since I had just skipped out on the rent again, it having been due the very next day. Plus my mother had left a piece of paper lying around that had puzzled me, and if it referred to what I thought it might, my fortune was about to change and change in a big way. It had born reference to an insurance policy set up by my brother, and I swear I saw both my name and Davey's listed as beneficiaries. However, I hadn't time to check out the amount because, just when I was getting ready to don my reading glasses, the dragon lady had entered stage right.

"Put that down!" she'd commanded. "That's none of your business."

But I knew there was a strong possibility she was wrong (as usual) which had been one of the reasons why I'd called up Davey on the eve of my exodus from Cincinnati to inform him of my new address.

"Don't know how long I'll be staying there," I'd explained. "May be going to Peru for a while this winter. But I smell something in the wind, and I think it's best if I leave a few bread crumbs for you to follow this time."

Davey had been delighted. Well... as delighted as a dude with a half a bottle of tequila under their belt can get, and he had sloshed some sort of response.

So semi-secure that my new whereabouts would be noted, I pointed the car east towards the Piedmont. I was in need of some heavy duty nurturing from a fairy godmother, and there was only one person who fit that bill.

Leslie's was the same, except for the addition of a few new outbuildings, ones which spoke of her continued prosperity in the contraband business. Of course, the minute I got out of the car and unloaded my tale of woe (along with my belongings) she offered up the peace pipe. But the reformed me stoically declined.

"It doesn't do anything for me lately," I insisted. "Except to make me hungry, tired, and paranoid. So what's the point?"

"Wow! That's a big switch," she replied, and proceeded to shake her head in that way potheads have when confronted with a reluctant recruit. I guess she just couldn't understand how anyone could turn down her drug of choice, especially since it was part of God's green earth.

I sighed and offered her the olive branch of the bottle of wine I'd brought, explaining that my purism did not extend to tee-totaling.

A few glasses of Merlot later, we were back to where we'd always been, catching up on all that had happened in the year since I'd seen her, and it was sometime during when conversation when I remembered our final act before parting last fall.

Actually that's a lie because how can you *just remember* something which has been burned into the back of your brain in indelible ink? The truth was that the image of the Bat Card had never left my consciousness, remaining back stage like some actor preparing for their curtain call. The only part I had forgotten was the precise words delivered by the oracle. Something about being born anew via a breech birth, which we all know is not the preferred position for delivery.

Well, now… that sure had been right on target, hadn't it? It had taken awhile to manifest, having gestated ever since that weird little episode I'd experienced during the boat trip in Mammoth Cave, but it seemed as if the labor pains had finally begun. Something was getting ready to be born within me, and I could only pray I survived the process. But there was no turning back now once the water had broken. My only hope was that someone or something would part the Red Sea and set my people free. Oh, now where did such strange Biblical imagery come from? Boy, oh boy, it must really be ShowTime.

I took another sip of wine to steady myself and that's when the heart palpitations began. Actually this was another point on which I had been untrue, first to myself and then to Leslie who had dearly wished to share the gleanings from her most recent harvest. What was the excuse I had used? Some BS about how it made me hungry, tired, and paranoid? Yes, all that may be true. However, I had left out one thing, that the paranoia led to an extreme panic attack which left my heart racing and my lungs gasping for air. It was if I was a fish out of water, cast upon a foreign shore, locked in the agony of my final death throes. And this was an experience I submitted to willingly? No way! I would rather have taken a beating with a rubber hose!! Yet here I was, simply sipping a bit of wine and the shit had begun. What was going on with me? Was I doomed forevermore to a straight-laced life in the back pew of some Baptist church? Gee, can't a girl have a drink every once in a while?

Such thoughts raced right alongside my heart, and it didn't take Leslie long to catch on that something was amiss. However, her uncanny ability to read my mind spared me the usual questions of concern. She skipped the prerequisites and went right to the root of the problem. Guess she'd seen enough panic attacks to recognize the beast. Immediately she ran to the cupboard and whipped out a paper bag.

"Just breathe," she instructed, positioning the thing to cover my nose and mouth.

And I did. In and out, out and in, until the time between each inhale and exhale finally slowed down to an acceptable interval. And that's when the questions began.

"How long has this been going on?" she asked, and that did it. I began to cry and cry, my tears spilling down upon her ample breasts as she gathered me in her arms. In that moment she was the mother I had never had and the lover who had never left me abandoned by the side of the road. In short, she was my balm of Gilead, and there I go again, getting all Old Testament on myself.

Later when my paroxysm of grief had passed (and after I had submitted to her insistence to take an Adivan), I was able to find words to describe my problem.

"The doctor I went to says I'm going into atrial fibrillation. It has something to do with a quivering or irregular heartbeat, and it started bothering me just after I left here last winter. At first I figured it was just me getting old because I'd feel it when I was carrying heavy stuff up stairs or when I got up fast from bending down. But then, about the time Joe died, it got a lot worse, and I'd get really weak and nauseated, especially after drinking some of the hard stuff Davey and I were taking to anesthetize ourselves. So I tried switching to pot, and that's when the panic attacks started. I swear to God, that something is out to get me. Between this and those weird little fugue states I keep going into where I feel like I am stuck between two dimensions..." I let my words trail off, but I knew she got the drift.

"Yeah, they call it AFib for short," Leslie nodded. "I've heard of it and... girlfriend, pot's supposed to be good for it! Of course pot's supposed to be good for a lot of ailments including panic attacks. Which makes me wonder about what really is going on. Maybe it's not physical, or should I say, maybe it's just manifesting itself on the physical plane, having originated somewhere else entirely. I think you hit the nail on the head when you mentioned something was out to get you. You've heard of psychic attacks, right? When someone or something assaults your aura without your conscious permission? Well that's what it sounds like and, believe me, they can cause all kinds of problems. Fatigue, aches and pains, nightmares... plus it can result in a paranoia so strong it often mimics a panic attack."

"But who? Why?"

The whole idea didn't really make sense to me. In fact, I preferred the allopathic explanation. It was simpler and the cure was probably easier. All I would have to do was pop a few pills every day. Of course, I would have to somehow come up with the ability to purchase them, and I'm sure that, given the current state of the stranglehold Big Pharma had us in, they wouldn't be cheap. But I guess a girl's gotta do what a girl's gotta do because the alternative was unacceptable. In fact, I already had a prescription in my pocket, and one of my missions before I embarked for the winter was to find a Costco. I'd heard they had to fulfill these prescriptions at the cost they gave to their members. It was some kind of government regulation, and boy, oh boy, did I plan on cashing in on it. Quite literally.

Leslie, however, was still on the track of the psychic attack, and I let her blow for awhile as she went on about entities from the astral plane and creatures from the fourth dimension. As yet, I wasn't sure such things existed, despite several run-ins I'd had with *Fringe* type phenomenon. Let it suffice to say that whatever was itching to be born in me had merely reached the full dilation stage. The crowning would come soon enough, and then I would get to deal with the messy details of the afterbirth.

Leslie, sensing my reluctance to delve deeper into the matter, had changed course and had pulled out a piece of paper.

"Here we go, girlfriend. A little something for you to fill out just in case."

I looked at the paper she held in her hand. It was blank. Was this supposed to be a joke?

Yeah, apparently it was. However, the joke was on me. Or should I say, I was responsible for coming up with my own punch line.

"It's your application to leave the planet," she continued. "And all you have to do is answer a few simple questions. So let's get started. First of all: Destination. Check one…"

And what followed was one of the most ridiculous conversations I'd had with my favorite fat lady in the entire course of our friendship. Gee, the ganga must have been rip-roaring good this fall to precipitate such creative insanity. Too bad my panic/psychic attack had prohibited me from partaking. Oh well, I could always live vicariously through others, and so I did until, between the two of us, we created a document that had me rolling on the floor.

APPLICATION TO LEAVE PLANET

DESTINATION: Check one.
➤ The Pleiades
➤ Planet X
➤ Planet of the Apes
➤ Twilight Zone

MODE OF TRAVEL:
• Wormholes
• Tesseracts
• Babylon Candles
• Polar Express (Children Only)

REASONS FOR MOVE:
• ChemTrails
• The Illuminati and The Archonic Invasion
• Who flung Dung (Kim Jong-un)
• Ohio Drivers

PAYMENT WILL BE MADE IN:

- Chickens
- Bit-coin
- Cat Litter Futures

SOURCE OF INCOME:

- Winnings from *Hunger Games*
- The Lottery (and not the one popularized by Shirley Jackson)
- A check each month for being crazy (US Citizens only)

ID PRESENTED:

- RFID chip
- Driver's License from back pages of *Soldier of Fortune*
- Paw Print (Chimpanzees, Orangutans and porch monkeys only)

REFERENCES:

- Lady Gaga: Planet Earth
- Michael Jackson : Somewhere south of Pluto
- Beetlejuice : The Netherworld Cemetery of your Choice
- Khan: Botany Bay

And that was that. What do they say? That laughter is the best medicine? I had to admit it was working. I didn't even suffer another attack (be what it may) until I stepped off the plane in Cuzco and that one may very well have been caused by an altitude in the excess of ten thousand feet.

Nevertheless it was a doozy, and I was forced to lay low in the airport until the worst of it passed. Then, after turning down three or four small dark men who were trying to convince me that their taxi (and their taxi alone) was the answer to my teenage dreams, I settled on a guy I met outside the terminal. His rate was a bit more reasonable, even though it still topped what the guidebook had suggested by a good fifty *soles*.

Not that it mattered at this point. All I wanted to do was descend that few extra feet into the Sacred Valley where I prayed I would find some relief from my altitude sickness. I had already booked a room in advance in Pisac, and although it had also cost a bit more than I'd been prepared to dish out, I was hoping it would be worth it. In the end I was not disappointed on both accounts. My chosen taxi was both safe and clean—a real plus in that part of the world—and the driver did not race around the corners or try to cut other drivers off at the pass. Although his English was about as good as my Spanish, he did manage to communicate that he would have to leave me off at the entrance of town due to construction. But he was gracious enough to book me a mini-taxi to take me the rest of the way. This was an adventure unto itself, the min-taxi being no more than a motorcycle pulling an enclosed carriage. The only thing separating it from a rickshaw was that it was motorized and not people powered. Oh, yeah, and it cost a hell of a lot more. That said, I was beginning to wonder if my cash would last the three weeks I had allotted for this trip. Thank God I'd arranged for some of it while in the states, pre-paying at a time when I thought I had some extra money. Yeah, extra money. An oxymoron in my book.

I gazed out at the land around me. The Sacred Valley is indeed surrounded by mountains, extremely high ones, which caused me to wonder how someone had found the energy or the impetus to climb half way up their barren slopes to arrange a grouping of white stones which spelled out the name of their sweetheart. Talk about devotion. Would that I could be so lucky!

While I pondered this engineering feat, my mini-taxi pulled up at the door of my hostel. It was another pleasant surprise. The hostel was a true oasis amongst hostels, many of which are dumps, involving tiny rooms in which the inmates are packed together like sardines. Why, on one occasion, I was even asked if I minded sharing a room with a guy who I'd never met!

But this place was remarkably clean and roomy. Its colorful cubicles came complete with incense and warm alpaca quilts. Plus—and this was an enormous PLUS—my room looked out on the Urubamba River and featured a catwalk from which I could contemplate the stars. Down below on the first floor I found a meditation room complete with cushy pillows and pictures of an assortment of deities. There was something for every faith: Jesus, Krishna, Buddha, Muhammad. You name it; the entire pantheon of the planet was represented. Gazing around me, I felt as if I had come to the right place if what I was seeking was peace and a contemplative atmosphere in which to achieve it.

Parking my bags, I decided to try out the restaurant which was attached to the complex. There I found a friendly waitress who spoke fairly good English. She presented me with the menu of the day, and I chose a bowl of quinoa soup. Being somewhat of a veteran of third world countries south of the border, I knew better than to ingest anything that hadn't been well cooked. This often left me staring at a bowl of nondescript gruel; but in this case, the vegetables were recognizable and the overall concoction quite tasty. So I ate my fill and then retired to my room for a catnap. This turned into more of a bear-nap because when I awoke the sun was no longer shining, and it was so cold I could have sworn I'd slept through the entire season.

Gathering the blankets around me, I crawled out of my bed and wandered outside onto the catwalk. The stars were out in full force, yet it was impossible to find any that were familiar. This was disconcerting at first as it added to the Rip Van Winkle phenomenon I'd been experiencing, but then I remembered I was in a whole new hemisphere, and it all made sense.

At first, it was quiet on the deck, and as I had no idea what time it was, I respected the community and controlled my impulse to talk to myself. It's a bad habit I have and one that often finds me flapping my lips in the most inconvenient places. I know if people catch me at it (and I am sure they have) they probably conclude that I am a nutcase. Well, maybe they aren't too far off, but at least I have an excuse. The death of two significant people prior to one's fortieth birthday does tend to drive one over the brink.

I sat in the stillness and contemplated my life up to that point. It hadn't been an easy one by any stretch of the imagination. Still, it beat the hell out of some. I remembered the abject poverty I had witnessed in so many Latin American countries, the slums on the north side of Mexico City possibly taking the cake. The corrugated tin dwellings there which stretched from horizon to horizon didn't even classify as hovels in my book; they were barely one step up from a black plastic tent. Yeah, there but for fortune.

Then, my musings were interrupted by the sound of voices. They were soft and sweet and definitely not too familiar with the English tongue. I turned to face the source and in the starlight saw two pretty chicas emerge from around the corner. Since this was an upscale hostel and because they were the fair sex, I had no fear, despite it being what I perceived as the middle of the night. We struck up a conversation, and I soon realized that their English was better than my Spanish. The smaller one informed me that she worked as a guide and would she like me to show her the ruins in the morning?

Morning. You mean two hours from now? But oddly enough, when they set me straight, I discovered it was barely nine o'clock at night. I had forgotten that here in the tropics, the sun goes down with the chickens, leaving the Yankee tourist with twelve solid hours of daily darkness to deal with despite the season of the year. So what I had thought of as a good night's sleep had been little more than a short nap.

That established, I realized I had a good twelve hours before her proposed blast-off, and I consented to her suggestion. In the end, I was so glad I had chosen her as she showed up the next morning with a bambino in her shawl and made it perfectly clear that she intended on hiking the entire ruins with said little bundle of joy in tow. Oh great, I thought, that ought to make for some slow going. I knew it was shallow of me, but I was in a hurry to get on with my journey. I only had three weeks, and I wanted to pack in as much as possible.

However, my fears were unfounded. Miriam, my guide, managed to out walk me for the entire three hours of our tour. I'm sure her sturdy Quechan constitution had something to do with this, not to mention the fact that she'd had a lifetime to get acclimated to the altitude. Still, I was impressed, and tipped her heartily despite my reluctance to part with the cash. But I couldn't help myself. Not only was she a seamstress in her spare time, but she also had aspirations to become the next Pablo Neruda. And if that weren't enough to cause me to sense a kindred spirit, the sheer fact that her birthday was one day after mine kicked the connection into overdrive.

By noon we were back in town where she deposited me next to her husband's *tienda*. He ran a small *joyeria*, which loosely translates as a jewelry shop, and although his stuff was gorgeous, I have never been the kind of girl to display much in the way of ornamentation. So I wandered around the marketplace seeking more practical items like a corkscrew with which to open the bottle of wine that awaited me back at the hostel. Somehow the old shoe trick where you stick the bottle in a boot and then whack it against a wall just wasn't doing the trick.

However, two pairs of socks and three finger puppets later, I still hadn't found anything besides a can opener. I was about to give up and call it quits when I was approached by another gringo. A short conversation revealed that he hailed from Michigan but now considered himself an ex-pat. He'd been busy trying to hawk some magazine his friend had put together and insisted he was selling it to feed the children. What children, I wondered, since he also seemed willing to sell me some ganga and a hallucinogenic mushroom which had the same effect as peyote. A real stick-tight, he didn't want to take *no* for an answer, and it was no easy task to shake him off my trail.

"Christ," I mumbled to myself when I finally shed his company. "What is it about me that brings them in? Do I look like the kind of girl that takes drugs on a daily basis?" And at that point I managed to catch a glimpse of myself in a storefront window. Short, grubby, and skinny, with clothes that hung from me like an ill-fitting sack, I was not your average American tourist. No, I was way too Biafran for that status. Maybe I needed some fattening up. In fact, wasn't that a restaurant I was gazing into?

However, when I went inside and noticed their specialty, I almost gagged. It took a moment to put two and two together, but there it was, hidden in plain sight: A huge central oven and next to it a cage of hapless guinea pigs. Yep, that's right. Rat on a stick. Oh well, there is no accounting for cultural taste, and as far as animal rights go, well… look what we do to lobsters.

That was it. I'd had it. Time to return to the hostel and that friendly little meditation room. Maybe there, I could sort it all out. No one said that living on this planet was a breeze.

The only problem was that I found myself going straight from the frying pan into the fire because by the time I got back to the hostel I realized I was higher than a kite. Since I had been so uncomfortable with the altitude, Miriam had suggested I chew a few cocoa leaves. She had managed to extract an extra *sole* from me for their purchase, and the whole idea was to leave them as an offering at one of the shrines within the ruins. But, hey, there were quite a few in the package, so why not put the extra to good use? I had to admit it worked, enabling me to keep up with her pace as we scrambled over rocky trails, but now the chickens were coming home to roost so to speak.

An ex-coker like myself should have known better. I recognized the racing thoughts and elevated energy level right away. Just what had I been thinking? Had I really believed the guide book when it said the effect would be minuscule? Hell, I knew I was a canary in the mines, hypersensitive to any ingested substances. It was probably on account of my size, but I could hardly drink a cup of coffee after the bewitching hour of noon. And now here I was, with the tropical sun going down in less than an hour and a whole night to kill all by my lonesome. Oh dear, what's a girl to do?

Well, as it turned out, the answer to that was: more drugs.

Like a drunk who has fallen off the wagon, I went stumbling around the hostel looking for a cork screw. Maybe the contents of that bottle of wine would cure what ailed me. Nothing like a little alcohol, a known depressant, to counter-balance a cocaine buzz. I located the item in the restaurant where a late supper was in progress. The other diners stared at me and I felt, more and more, like the fish out of water I was. I sniffed under my armpits, hoping not to add *turd in a punch bowl* to my list of sins. Oh well, a little bit of vino and a trip to that great Jacuzzi I had located out in the courtyard ought to help with all that.

So my plan in place, I proceeded to activate it. An hour later, I was soaking wet under those magical stars that shone only in the southern hemisphere. I had also added alcoholic stupor to my sins of commission. What a day! And given that it was once again, barely nine in the evening, what a night I had to look forward to!

How I made it through is beyond me. Fortunately, I had brought *Clan of the Cave Bear* along on the trip, feeling it was surely long enough to last me for the entire journey. But by the time I finally snuggled in under those alpaca quilts, I was already on page two hundred and fifty-six of a book that only held four hundred and ninety-five pages. Like a box of chocolates, I had committed the cardinal sin of gorging on a treat that was meant to be doled out in increments. I knew without a doubt that I would pay for my sins in the morning which I did, awakening far too late to catch the bus to Urubamba. It had been my plan to use the town as a base from which to tour a few sites in the sacred valley before trekking on up to Ollantaytambo. From there I could catch the train to Aqua Calientes, the village that functioned as base camp to Machu Picchu. I had already booked my tickets for entry, and even though I had built some down time into my itinerary, I was worried about falling behind schedule.

However, first things first, my stomach insisted and I had no choice but to hear her out. Lunch at the café was as good as yesterday's had been, and it was then and there I realized I'd managed to skip dinner. I looked down at my diminishing frame and decided to order the special. It turned out to be the best meal I'd had yet in Peru. Chicken so well roasted it was falling off the bone and julienned vegetables complemented the standard quinoa soup and hard rolls. A steaming cup of cocoa and some sort of sugary cake topped it all off and, fully satiated, I began to make my way back to my room.

It was then that I spied it out of the corner of my eye. Being a natural born reader of everything from cereal boxes to bathroom literature, I couldn't help myself. I am the kind of person that others put up flyers for since I was sure to give them my full attention. The colorful one on the bulletin board outside the café was no exception. However, what it advertised was not something you would routinely find in the states.

EXPERIENCE AYAHUASCA

- Connect with your personal unconscious and purge yourself of past traumas
- Release limiting beliefs that lead to psychological blockages
- Connect to the higher self and access feelings of freedom, infinite awareness and unconditional love

Workshop includes two nights of journeying to meet the grandmother spirit. Meditation techniques are stressed as is proper preparation prior to ingesting the drug. Retreat is facilitated by two local shamans who work from the heart.

Experience is limited to ten participants and will take place in safe and beautiful surroundings. Inquire at café for details.

And below was a picture of a property which made the one I resided in look like a flophouse. Gee, I thought. Wonder how much that little gem would set me back and, sure that the matter was closed, I retreated to my own little workshop, one that involved a few more pages of a good book and an afternoon stroll around town. I'd decided to take it easy today so as not to jeopardize missing the bus for Urubamba again.

The first part of my laid back plan for the afternoon went off without a hitch; not so for the latter. By the time I had read another fifty pages in *The Clan of the Cave Bear* and then written a few of my own, the sun was already seriously descending into the rim of the western mountains. I would have to hurry if I was to catch what was left of the day. Donning a light jacket, I scooted out the door.

My destination was the Pisac market. Again. Actually, besides the ruins and the market, there is not a whole lot else to do in Pisac. It does not share the hopping tourist trade one would anticipate in nearby Agua Calientes or Cuzco, where there are more venues catering to the featured attractions than there are attractions. But what could I do? On account of my own lollygagging I had a whole extra day to kill in a town that serves more as a gateway to the Sacred Valley than anything else.

A gateway. At least that's all the credit I could give the place at the moment, although that was soon to change. For later I would discover that the town hosted a few hidden treasures that weren't necessarily advertised in the guide book. And shuffling around the market in the late afternoon sun, I was about to be introduced to one of them.

I probably stood in front of his *tienda* longer than was necessary, but I couldn't help myself. Although I'd never been much of a shopper, there was something about the display in the window that drew me in. Its main focus was artifacts. Most were made of clay and featured figures with weird distorted torsos and stranger heads. Everything in Pre-Columbian art seemed exaggerated to me. The ears were too long, the mouths too wide, and let's not even get into the headdresses which were so elaborate and ornate as to make me wonder if the Ancient Alien theory was correct in assuming they were space helmets.

I couldn't help myself. There was something about these little buggers that enchanted me, and I even considered buying one for my brother Davey. I figured he could surely find some sort of sacred liqueur to stash inside the ones which had been shaped into pots. I was chuckling at the thought when I realized I had attracted the attention of the proprietor.

Oh, oh! Here it comes, I thought to myself. The sales pitch that won't let up, a harangue I had come to expect from a population which made its livelihood off *dinero* from rich Yankees. But I soon found out I had committed the cardinal error of making an assumption; for all is rarely what we perceive.

The proprietor was ancient, at least eighty-five years of age, a rarity in a country whose life expectancy for males topped off ten years earlier. His snow white hair hung to his shoulders, and his face was etched with the lines that can only come from decades of expression. He was moving so slow that—had I wanted to—I could have booked out of there and avoided any further contact. However, I found myself riveted to the spot. There was something about him, something familiar, like I had met him somewhere before.

In the time it took me to get my bearings and initiate a retreat, he was upon me. I was sure that this was when it would begin. The sales pitch, followed by the inevitable haggling. But once again, I was wrong because all he said was *mira a tu corazón*, which loosely translates as *look to your heart*. At least I think it does since the only part I really got was the bit about the *corazón*, and this because he was pointing directly to that part of his anatomy.

How could I argue? He had my number; that was for sure. So all I could do was smile and point to one of the artifacts while asking *cuánto?* I really hadn't planned on picking up too many souvenirs, but I somehow felt compelled to shed my *soles* at this particular location. However, the guy just smiled with a grin that revealed the loss of a few critical teeth and mumbled something about no *para la venta*.

Well, I'll be damned I thought and turned to leave. And it was then that I saw it, the very same flyer which had confronted me at the café, except that this time, the picture given of the venue did not resemble a five star hotel. Instead, it was but one step above the hovels I had encountered on our way back from the Pisac ruins the other day. Plus there was even a cost associated with the 'experience', a mere one hundred soles which in dollars is about thirty bucks.

Gee, I could do that, I thought and then added the qualifier. *If I had time.* Yes, time was of the essence, and if I lingered any longer in this town, I was sure to miss my place in line for entry to Machu Picchu, which was the one reason why I had chosen to come to this country in the first place. And though I had a good six months grace period on my passport, for some reason I had decided to front load my visit and book my priorities first. It was almost as if I knew I might have to go back early.

I sighed and continued staring at the flyer. Perhaps he was right. Perhaps I should focus on my *corazón*. It sure had been giving me fits lately. I thought of the days ahead, blitzkrieg traveling from one attraction to another, all the while running from myself. And yes, I knew that, despite any rhetoric I had been spouting about *travel being broadening* and *flexibility being the key to survival* and *travel being the key to flexibility*, I was still the walking wounded. And those old self destructive methods of dealing with loss still rode heavy on my back, devilish little monkeys just waiting for the go-ahead. I thought back to the day before, the cocoa leaves and the empty bottle of wine, and knew it was just the beginning, that it would only get worse.

Maybe that was when I made my decision. I can't really pinpoint the exact moment. All I do know was that something about the way I was standing caught the attention of my friendly local shaman, and he returned from the shadows where he had been watching me all along.

"Estás listo ahora?" he asked, and I nodded. At which he gave me a card with an address on it.

"Manana," he instructed, and I nodded, not exactly sure what I was agreeing to, but one thing was for sure, it wouldn't be your standard tourist fare.

Manana came sooner than I had expected, mainly because I managed to clock a good ten hours on the astral plane upon my return to the hostel. Guess I was tired; either that or I was gearing up for what was coming.

The morning was a chilly one, and I was wearing enough clothes so to make my bag significantly lighter. Taking one last look about the room to make sure I hadn't forgotten anything, I was once again struck with its elegance. *Well, enjoy it while it lasts*, I commented to myself. Because I was sure that tonight's accommodations wouldn't be quite so opulent.

That said, I proceeded to make the best out of the few hours remaining of my stay, using the meditation room for the first time and enjoying the hot tub for the last. Then I packed myself full with another generous breakfast and went out in search of a cab.

The address that had been given to me was located out in the country, hidden amongst tall trees and bougainvillea vines. What it lacked in architectural charm it made up for in landscaping, which was a good thing because I soon realized that most of our 'experience' would take place outdoors.

I was greeted by a balding fiftyish guy who was distinctly North American.

"Hi, my name's Jim," he said by way of introduction. "And you must be our new recruit."

New recruit? He made it sound like I was signing up for active duty and I cringed. Such reactions are spontaneous when you grow up in a military family. The general rule drilled into me by my father was to never volunteer for anything, and here I was ready and willing to sign on the dotted line. Oh well, Joe had followed the same path.

Yeah, ana look where that got him, a niggling little voice chimed in from the back of my head. It was too much. Here I had just arrived at this so called retreat which would help purge me of my past traumas, and already two of them had jumped to the forefront. Was I in for a rough ride?

I hesitated and Jim caught my thought.

"We all come here with doubts," he explained and began to console me with the story of his life. Apparently, he would not be partaking in the sacred drink with us as his role was that of a facilitator. A by-product of his own generation, one which sought enlightenment by route of psychedelic drugs, he had come to Peru years ago looking for a more enduring high. He had found it in ayahuasca, a drug which he had taken more than one hundred times.

"Its technical name is called Dimethyltryptamine or DMT for short," he informed me. "And it's the only psychedelic which is found endogenously in the human body. That means we produce it on our own, especially at the time of birth or death or during dreaming. For that reason it's also known as the vine of death or the vine of souls since it is often known to mimic an out of the body experience."

He paused to make sure he had my full attention before going on.

"However, the vine alone doesn't do the trick. It actually acts as a catalyst, mixing with several other plants that contain DMT. When brewed together, the MOA inhibitors in the vine allow the DMT to reach our brains. Other than that the monoamine oxidase in our guts would knock it out and make it ineffective. The whole process is complex and should only be done by an experienced shaman. In fact, this retreat is one of the most authentic ones I've found in Peru. Usually you have to go deep into the Amazon Basin in order to get an experience that doesn't mimic a psychedelic Tupperware party."

"Yeah, that's right...Tupperware," he continued, sensing my shock. "Because of the colorful plastic buckets they put by your mat, conveniently located in case you undergo what is known as the purge. And you probably will."

The purge. Now that part I'd heard of, not being a stranger to drugs and their side effects. Still I couldn't help but wonder what I had gotten myself into.

But the more Jim talked, the more he convinced me I'd made the right decision despite having forfeited the good hundred dollars in American money that would have secured my entrance to Machu Picchu.

"Don't worry. We are not going to throw you to the wolves. There will be a lengthy detox period prior to your first drink, during which you will have to follow some strict dietary restrictions."

Ok, I could do that. Until, I got the details which included no salts, no sugar, no caffeine, no pork, no animal fat, no dairy products, no oil, no hot spices, no ice cold or carbonated drinks, no dried fruit, no vinegar, no spinach.

No spinach!?! The list went on…no fermented foods, no alcohol, no recreational drugs, no fluoride toothpaste, no sex, no loud music, and stay away from synthetic skin products.

Wow. It sure was a whole lot of *no's*. Still as I reviewed the taboo list in retrospect, I realized it really wasn't that hard, considering my personal situation. No sex? No brainer. And I'd been using baking soda as toothpaste forever and ever, not to mention that I didn't even bother with most of the stinky stuff women saturated their bodies with. So the only restriction I might have a little trouble with was the one about meat since I had been trying to beef up (no pun intended) my protein in a vain attempt to put on a little weight.

Still I could make it for the mandatory five day period during which I would be preparing myself for this big experience. Something told me to hang in there, that it would be worth it in the end. And it wasn't just Jim, though he certainly was a knowledgeable charmer, the kind of guy who could probably sell ice to an Eskimo.

The more I listened to his spiel, the more I liked him. Though he might have initially pushed some of my con artist buttons, I came to the realization that he was really down to earth and totally committed to the Ayahuasca experience. So committed in fact that he grew the *vine of death* in his greenhouse back home in Michigan where he worked as an ethnobotanist/ethnopharmacologist. From his home base he had conducted numerous studies on the drug and had discovered that it was highly effective in treating those with depression and alcoholism.

"I even had one girl who was a confirmed junky do a complete one hundred and eighty. She told me later that it literally saved her life. And of the hundreds who I have coached through the ceremony, I have yet to find one who didn't profess to some kind of life-changing experience."

Such words gave me courage, and I was able to fight my impulse to run as fast as I could in the opposite direction. That said, I sat back and attempted to relax while waiting out the big day. The prep time gave me an opportunity to get to know my fellow travelers. There were only four of us: a guy from Minnesota who had been practicing a Vipassana breathing meditation for the past two years, a middle aged woman from New Zealand who had just lost her husband, and a young Quechan Indian who spoke very limited English. Out of the three of them, I bonded mostly with the budding young Buddhist.

Apparently, he'd spent a few more than just five days preparing for this journey. In fact, it sounded like he'd spent the better part of the last five years. The meditation he engaged in was a relatively simple one. Just follow the breath. Or at least do it for a third of the time you intend to meditate. Then start to focus on your body parts, one at a time, concentrating on every sensation found there, be it pleasant or unpleasant.

Well, that sounded easy enough. (Did I really dare to use the term *relatively simple* to describe any meditation technique? Yeah, it's so simple, it's hard.)

I actually tried it a few times. No scratch that. I tried it quite a few since I figured that out of all of us he was the most prepared to meet the *vine of death*. However, I soon found out what a raging beast the mind can be, an incorrigible truculent terror, whose sole purpose seems to be one of distortion and distraction.

So, since the other English speaking participant only wanted to talk about her dearly departed, I decided to turn my vision inward according to my own preferences. That meant writing, gobs and gobs of words scribbled on a page, so prolific I had to send out Juanita, our chief cook and bottle washer, in search of a new tablet upon which to pour my thoughts. Indeed, if this was meant to be a purging experience, I had already gotten the ball rolling with an acute attack of verbal diarrhea.

Maybe it would benefit me in the long run, but whatever the case, it did help to pass the time. Plus I had discovered a formerly unexplored country, that of poetry and not the whacky disjointed prose that Jeremy used to spout. No, my lyrics actually rhymed and would have made for some damned fine songs if I only knew how to play an instrument. Oh, I had dinked around with a guitar a time or two, but who hasn't? And like most of us when we discover we are the next Stevie Ray Vaughn or Stanley Jordan, I had set it aside for more rewarding hobbies.

Still, I couldn't help myself, and as these lyrics continued to roll off the assembly line, I even found myself humming little snippets of tunes to accompany them. However, I was careful to do it when no one else was around, an easy task when you have a large rural estate upon which to roam, one you are sharing with only four other people.

As it were our shaman didn't show up until the night before the ceremony, and just as I had expected, it was the wizened old Indian from the tienda in town. His first action was to embrace each of us in turn, paying special attention to the young Quechan who just so happened to be his nephew. His next was to disappear into the surrounding foliage, from which he did not emerge until the following afternoon.

At that point I was almost positive we'd lost him, that he'd fallen victim to some tropical terror. But just as my mind began to race with all the endless possibilities which could have led to his demise, he emerged dressed for battle—or should I say ceremony. Barrel-chested like so many of the Quechans, he was the epitome of sturdy, despite the gravity of his years. Draped over his upper torso was a cloak of many colors, one which reflected the vibrant palette of the indigenous costumes. Crimson red met thalo blue in a marriage that could only be described as psychedelic. And the stereotype didn't end there. Around his neck was a necklace made of bone and teeth, and as a crown he wore a headdress of brilliant feathers. If I hadn't known better, I would have thought he was just putting on a show for us gringos. But, no, his was the real McCoy, not just an act thrown together for the benefit of a Hollywood documentary.

I waited with as much respect as I could muster, knowing I had thrown myself to the mercy of what was to come. Together we left the garden in which we had gathered and entered the mallocca. Here each of us was assigned a bed complete with bottles of water and a bucket to use during the *purge*. We were placed in a circle, one patterned after the cardinal points of the compass. The shaman stood in the middle where he slowly performed a cleansing ritual, offering smoke and incense up to the six directions. Then he blessed the ayahuasca and offered us our first drink.

The stuff was awful. Dark brown like coffee left in the pot too long, it tasted like someone had mashed up a bunch of herbs and then mixed them with dirt. I had to fight a gut level reaction to hurl it back up, since I'd been told that to do so within the first fifteen minutes would lead to nothing more than a stomachache, which sort of defeated the purpose.

For that reason, I followed the lead of the shaman, who after drinking, simply lay down on his blanket. By then, it was late evening in the tropics and pitch black, there being no moon. I swear they had planned it this way because the last thing I saw for some time was Jim extinguishing the candles which illuminated the mallocca.

So that was that. There we sat in total darkness awaiting the spirit of the plant. It was downright scary, and I had to give myself a firm talking to. I kept repeating the mantra. *Fear knocked at the door; faith answered and sent him away. Fear knocked at the door; faith answered and sent him away. Fear knocked at the door; faith answered and sent him away.*

I wanted to speak it out loud, but knew this was a no-no. The only sound was of the deep breathing to my left where my Buddhist friend had slipped into his meditation technique. I tried to mimic his rhythm to no avail. I was getting really spooked until the silence was broken by the shaman who began to sign his icaroos. Foreign as they were to my experience, they were also very comforting, and I began to relax.

Maybe this won't be so bad after all, I told myself. But no sooner had the words hit my head than I had to force myself not to laugh. *You signed up for it, silly,* a little voice insisted. And like a kid who has decided to go on the world famous roller coaster, I sat back to make the most of the ride.

Once my panic attack had passed, things got ultra-slow. That is to say nothing happened, and except for that initial urge to vomit, I didn't even feel sick to my stomach. But after a good half hour had passed, the nausea came on full force. As it was now safe to begin the purge, I was entertained by the sound of the slop hitting the slop bucket. It came from all around me, and never one to remain the odd man out, I joined suit. And that was when I began to get off in earnest.

Experiences such as these are hard to describe, mainly because they take place somewhere between worlds. Both time and space are warped, causing images to flood the brain so fast that it is impossible to process them. Let's call it thinking in pictures and pictures the like of which no artist could ever hope to place on canvas. Pictures of talking heads that faced each other before a series of mirrors that retreated to the vanishing point. Pictures of an enormous woman with a spiral galaxy for an eye. Visionary pictures the like of which had been attempted by many on down through the ages from Salvador Dali to William Blake. However, the bottom line is you can't paint a five dimensional picture in 3-D, nor can you paint with colors that are currently unknown to the visible spectrum.

I had to admit it was entertaining, but the speed at which I was assaulted by these images left me wishing I had paid more attention to those Vipassana breathing exercises. I could hear the guy on the mat next to me inhaling and exhaling as if his life depended on it, and once again was struck with the absolute hilarity of the thought. This time my laughter found a way out, and I began to giggle uncontrollably. I guess I might have been ashamed of myself, had not others chosen to break the silence in their own way, first the shaman with his icaroos and then the woman from New Zealand, who by this time was sobbing to beat the band. *Yeah, it could always be worse* I thought. *Better laughter than tears,* and of course, it was at that exact moment when both my father and my brother decided to make their cameo appearances.

Well, they call it medicine for just reasons. And no one said it would be a blissful journey. In fact, the general consensus was that it was more cathartic, an experience which would act as a catalyst the same way that yeast acts on bread. That said, personal growth was imminent.

I had issues. Who doesn't? And what better time to purge them from my consciousness. The visits from my own dearly departed were not angry birds, pecking at my consciousness until only the bare bones remained. Instead, they were a warm country comforter, one which would provide solace for days to come, but solace which would always come at a price due to my abject sense of loss.

What happens in the mallocca, stays in the mallocca, and no matter how much you try to bring back elements from that other dimension, they will always remain as a beautiful dream upon dawn, a little bit out of reach. And thus began my first song.

> All last night
> I dreamed to you.
> But it took some time
> Getting through
> And as the clouds boiled dry
> In a parchment sky
> And as the wind-whipped dusk
> Unleashed its load
> In the silver rain I met you
> At the crossroads.
> Well, the river she runs deep and the water she'll be rising
> And there's no turning back once you cross over
> So when I swim it in my sleep
> You know it's really no surprising
> That it flows on down through banks
> Of thistle and clover.

It was the first of many offerings. Others came by way of instructions.

I was to go to the power places of the earth.
Which ones?
Well, as many as possible.
I was to write a book.
What about?
It will come to you.

Boy, talk about cryptic. Couldn't we get any more definitive? I was getting restless, and though the slop buckets had been emptied by our facilitator, the hut still had a sour odor, brought about by a mixture of fear, sweat and the remains of last night's dinner.

I decided to get up and walk around a bit, and I groped for the small flashlight which had been left in case I needed to run for the outhouse. However as I exited the lodge I was astounded to see that dawn was breaking, and that was when the songs which had been fluttering in my throat decided to take wing.

Later the woman from New Zealand insisted that I had been her guardian angel, her only hope for survival. Apparently hers had been a rough ride, releasing more traumas than the simple death of a loved one. But I hadn't gone into this with the expectation of winning any popularity contests. The songs which had exited my throat that night had been my life raft, my only means of staying afloat on a great cosmic ocean. The other shore had been in sight, but I knew it was not yet my time to disembark. There was work to be done, and I had received my marching orders. My only doubts came from wondering just how I was going to finance them.

These were my thoughts as I sat beneath the spreading arms of a jacaranda the next day. I was feeling empty in a good way. It was as if all the crapolla of forty some years of traumatic experience on this planet had been lifted from me. I had been born again; but like a babe who has just popped out of the womb, I was in serious need of nurturing. My little family here (and yes, these bonds would never be broken) was only good for a few more days, during which we would undergo what they refer to in the military as de-briefing. Then I was on my own, and worse yet, I was a stranger in a strange land, one whose language I was able to butcher at best. How was I to get back to my comfort zone? Where was my comfort zone, anyway?

Oh hell, it was all too much and made my head hurt. I remembered the old addiction mantra. Let go and let God. Yeah, that was the ticket. However it was not until several days later that I came to appreciate the full implications of those words. Indeed they are synonymous with the Lord working in strange ways.

The first thing I did when I got back to civilization was to check into a cheap hostel, one which had Wi-Fi. Actually this wasn't really a big deal in Peru, a country that appeared to have better Internet service than many places in the states. How this technological achievement was accomplished was beyond me, though I had heard it explained on multiple occasions. Something about the country having skipped the cumbersome dial-up that we had experienced in the early days of surfing the web. Instead they had gone straight to wireless, which was not only faster, but much more efficient, thus enabling even tiny hamlets to be thoroughly connected to the global community. The ramifications of this were almost scary as we know how dependent one can get on the Net, to the point that a hard copy back-up has become a thing of the past.

However, I wasn't going to get into all that right now. The only thing that mattered at the moment was an email from Davey which was begging to be opened. You see, I had a real good idea what it said, and even if I hadn't, the subject line would have said it all. URGENT it screamed, and I responded with a quick click.

Where have you been! The first lines berated me. *I have been trying to get in touch with you for five days.* And yes, when I looked down at the rest of my inbox there was more than one email from my drunken bum of a brother. I was amazed he'd managed to pull himself away from the bottle long enough to write even one, let alone ten missives to me. But maybe I was being too harsh on him. At least that's what my recent epiphany with Grandmother Ayahuasca dictated, and as she went on to remind me that we are all one, all connected by invisible threads that transcend time and space, I set aside my judgmental attitude and proceeded to read the words Davey had sent, beginning with the earliest email and working my way up to the final one.

You were right, he began. *Joe did have a life insurance policy and guess who the recipients are?* Yeah, somehow I'd strongly suspected that, but what I didn't know was that the funds had not been evenly allocated.

Seems like he gave the bulk of it to you, Davey moaned. *The whole thing was for two hundred grand and you get one fifty of that. Guess I could be pissed, but I'm not. You're the one who can never seem to hold down a job.*

And this last reference was to the simple fact that my brother was what was known as a functional alcoholic, one who managed to bring home the bacon by day and then snarf it all up by night. Yeah, he held down a job for sure, and owned a home and a car. But everything he had was mortgaged to the hilt, and soon would come a time—as it comes to all drunken carpenters—when he would either have to lay off the sauce or suffer the consequences. I should know. I'd seen enough of his type in my travels, had even fallen into the sack with a few of the more charming ones, and they were worse bums than me. Gee, at least I was honest about being emotionally unavailable.

These guys, on the other hand, acted like all they wanted out of life was a wife and kids; but in the long run, the bottle took precedence over all else. However, it was a losing game they were playing, burning up their empire building days, just living from paycheck to paycheck while operating under the illusion that their twenty-some bodies would always be able to wield a hammer. The smart ones figured it out, cut back on the booze when they hit their forties, and since Davey was not too far behind me in pushing the big 4-0, maybe there was hope for him yet.

Nonetheless, Joe had been correct in his current assessment of Davey's inability to put money to good use. Hence the seemingly unfair split.

I, however, was a bird of another color. I was a woman on a mission, instructed by the goddess herself to seek out the power places of the earth and then write the great American novel. Boy oh boy, for someone who had just come through a life changing process, one in which the ego is traditionally diminished, I sure was full of it. Maybe I needed to tone it down. Forget about being me for a bit and focus on the great beyond.

But first there were hoops to go through. Papers to sign and loose ends to tie. My presence as Maureen Singleton, AKA Stitch was required back in the states and the sooner the better. And these last words were underscored to add emphasis. Guess one of Davey's debts was coming due, and he needed that cash ASAP.

So I did what any good heir apparent would do. I cancelled all plans for the Mer-Ka-Ba power points and hightailed it back to my hole in the wall home base in Cincinnati. Lucky for me, the landlord had not rented it out yet and was willing to give me a second chance. The fact that I promised to pay the rent for an entire year in advance may have swayed him on that matter. Not that he believed me at first. When you're a slum lord, you hear all kinds of bullshit. But the piece of paper I held in my hand was proof. I had been blessed with what most Americans might consider a nuisance fortune. However, with my well-honed skills at penny pinching, I figured it was enough to see me though a good five years.

My plan was simple. Maintain the Cincinnati apartment as a home base and then take advantage of its proximity to an international airport. From there I could go on periodic forays to exotic foreign places and still have a place to return to. During my down time, I would begin work on what was sure to win a Pulitzer Prize. It had to. The goddess had spoken. Of course, she hadn't filled me in on the details, so I had no idea what I would be writing about. At that particular juncture, I expected that my book would have to do with my travels, and would parallel those written by other great seekers of truth and knowledge. Think *Eat, Pray, Love* by Elizabeth Gilbert, *Wild* by Cheryl Strayed and *Travels* by Michael Crichton, and you get my drift.

Oh, it would be so much fun and, better yet, for the first time in my nomadic adult life, I would actually have a warm bed to return to. My God, I would be as close to stable as I'd ever been in my life. That alone was almost frightening. Yeah, there is something to be said about not having nothing, and ergo nothing to lose.

These were my thoughts on the big jet airplane which took me back to the states. I couldn't help but compare my plight to that of the homeless drifter in Early *Morning Rain*, a song I had just learned to play on my recently purchased acoustic guitar. A kid in Cuzco had it for sale cheap, and I suspected he needed the funds. Well, one man gathers what another man spills, right? So I'd taken it off his hands for a pittance and had even bought him breakfast. And why not? I'd been there, done that and knew all about the plight of being reduced to *a dollar in my hand and an aching in my heart.*

Yeah, I was a long way from home, alright. But what I just didn't understand back then was that the loved ones I was missing so much were not necessarily made of flesh and blood.

Chapter 5
NOONE (AKA Doe)
2016-2017

I stepped off the plane into what would become one of the worst snowstorms to hit the Ohio River Valley in years. Thank God it hadn't cranked up to its full potential or we might not have been able to touch down. Instead we might have been forced to fly back to lands closer to the equator, and in doing so, might have entered into the Twilight Zone. Then, like that hapless flight in *The Odyssey of Flight 33* we might have crossed over the boundaries of time and ended up in a prehistoric age, one where the dinosaurs still roamed the planet. Yeah, it could always be worse. However, as I watched my cab driver attempt to navigate the swirling snow and its ensuing build-up on the roadways, I began to think that being eaten by a Tyrannosaurus Rex might be preferable to slowly freezing to death in a Snowmageddon. It least it would be quick.

Alas, what's a surfer boy to do? Might as well just pray for the best and leave the driving to Allah, or whatever his name was. Lord, there sure had been an upswing of these middle easterners in the past five years. Must have something to do with a political agenda, one that was determined to wear down borders and with it our national identity, making it, in essence, just one more way to undermine and destabilize a the country.

But how come it was so hard to go the other way? Gee, in Costa Rica, which I'd just left, a gringo who was considering ex-pat status had to prove they possessed an income of at least a thousand dollars a month. And New Zealand, a country that I would kill to claim citizenship in, was even pickier as they wouldn't even issue a permanent retirement visa. So what is it with the US of A, that our bleeding hearts want to let anyone in, be they members of Central American gangs like MS-13 or traffickers in human beings?

Wow, was I really thinking that? Maybe I was turning into a Republican or something, and just in time since an election was looming on the horizon this coming November, one that would rock the free world. But more on that later. For now, as they say in the song, I was *Homeward Bound* at last, and despite returning as the conquering hero, boy would maw's Portuguese bean soup ever taste good.

As my salivary glands kicked into high gear, I was able to ignore the slipping and sliding of the taxi. This ride was probably going to cost me a mint. But it was a hell of a lot cheaper than it would have been to book service all the way from Cincinnati International Airport, which had originally been my final destination. At least until I'd realized that no one was coming there to pick me up. That's when I'd decided to break out my credit card and book a flight to nearby Mid-Atlantic Airport in Parkersburg. At least that way, the cab fare to the home front wouldn't break the bank.

Still I couldn't help wondering just where oh where *mi madre* had been. I swear she must have been out on some super shopping spree for the entire four hours I'd spent at the Cincinnati Airport trying to reach her. Oh, I really couldn't expect her to hang around and wait for my arrival. But she did know I was coming back sometime this week, and surely she would have taken that into consideration and not strayed too far from the phone. Plus the weather was a bitch, making it not a good day for Target or Wal-Mart.

Oh well, maybe it was my own damn fault for remaining so vague about my travel plans. Since I hadn't really known for sure just exactly when I would be returning to the States, I had left my return ticket open-ended. And lucky thing, since I had decided at the last minute to add on that little surfing safari to the Nicoya Peninsula. However, I had always assumed (erroneously) that maw would take up the slack and would be at my beck and call whenever I decided to waltz into town. In fact, our last conversation had assured me of this.

"I miss you Noonie," she'd whined, and although I was a grown guy, her voice still tore at my heart strings.

"I miss you too, maw," I'd responded. "And I'll be home as soon as I finish up a little job here."

Little job? Wow, you would have thought I was some big shot executive on an important international business trip instead of a lowly wwofter turned surfer bum. Oh well, what she didn't know, wouldn't hurt her. And so, I had hung up the phone with a perfunctory *I love you*, and had gone about my pressing business.

But now I regretted not contacting her during the time I'd been pursuing the perfect wave because it sure would have saved me a bunch of grief if I had been able to fly back into Cincinnati where she could have easily picked me up. (If you call driving the one hundred and eighty-five miles from Coolville to Cincinnati an easy task.) Oh well, maybe I was being a bit too hard on the old girl. After all, she was pushing sixty-five (or was it seventy?) Such details seemed to elude me, but whatever the case, she was no longer a spring chicken. Maybe I should take that to heart the next time I decided to go gallivanting and seek alternate means of transportation. Like Allah here, who had been more than willing to pick me up at Parkersburg Mid-Atlantic airport and drive me the thirty miles to the basement I'd called home for all these years. Yes, Allah, of the dangling Muhammad token from his dash and the broken English. Gee, what was this world coming to? Oh, don't answer that … not after serious jet lag and an even more serious ride through an ever worsening snow storm.

It was with a sigh of great relief that we finally skidded into maw's driveway. A good four inches of snow covered the pavement which made me wonder since only about half that amount had fallen since the storm began.

"Guess my maw's a bit behind on her snow removal," I joked, although I could tell by Allah's scowl that he found no humor in the situation. So I quickly paid him and wished him a safe journey back to PKB and (hopefully) more local traffic. Poor guy. I had to hand it to him. He was busting his ass to live in our fair country, a domicile that I not only took for granted, but tried to escape from on a periodic basis. Maybe I should have tipped him a little more.

Feeling like somewhat of a rat, I watched as he spun out of the driveway. Later I would come to ponder, as we often do when confronted with adversary, if my cheapness had anything to do with the punishment that would soon be inflicted upon me. It's the old bargaining stage of grief. If I do this Lord, will you grant me that? Except that I was watching it all through a time tunnel, and we all know how that goes. What's gone is gone, what's done is done and all you can do is suck it up and go on with the show.

It took me a good five minutes to get through the front door. The snow had piled up in front of it and made it really hard to open the SOB. I paused briefly to consider for the hundredth time why I'd never built that awning I'd promised to construct. That way the door would have been protected from the elements, thus saving us from a potentially life-threatening situation. After all, I had rudimentary carpentry skills, so it wouldn't have been that hard to throw something together. Anything was better than this. Why, what if maw came out to get the morning paper and slipped on the ice, thus breaking one of those hips which they say are the downfall of the elderly? God, that would be awful.

With visions of such disasters narrowly avoided dancing before my eyes, I almost stepped on her. Nothing like a touch of reality to spook a kid back to normal. No, scratch that! Nothing would ever be normal again.

"Maw?" I croaked, even though I could tell from the looks of her that she was way passed the point of answering. Good Lord! Just how long had she been lying here? For starters, she was stiff as a board with that characteristic dead man's stare that we see in movies and pray to God we will never encounter in real life. Jesus! Judging from the mail that had piled up around her, I would have to estimate at least a week. Wow! No wonder she hadn't answered my phone calls and yeah, thank God it had been cold. In fact, by all appearances, she hadn't even turned the heat up from the sixty-two degrees that she liked to keep it at during the night. Saving electric, she called it, but I knew the real reason lay in her frugality. No, let's just call a spade a spade. She was cheap on utilities so that she'd have plenty of money left over for all those little frills she so desired. The bird feed, the Christmas collection, the scratch-offs... Oh, shit, shit and double shit. What was a boy to do?

Well, call 911 for starters.

Stepping over the body that had born me a mere thirty odd years ago, I stumbled towards the phone. My eyes were clouded by tears that refused to fall. Hell, there would be plenty of time for that. Right now, I had to keep it together which was going to be tough since I had very little experience with this kind of thing. Fuck! Who was I kidding? I had absolutely NO experience with this kind of thing unless you want to include the time while kayaking when I'd rescued a kid who had gotten caught in a rip tide. At least, that had ended well. This was different. Way different. After all, you've only got one mother to find dead on the floor, dressed only in her bathrobe, the old familiar green corduroy that she'd worn for the last ten years because you'd given it to her for Christmas way back when. And that was when the tears began to fall in earnest.

The operator was Johnny on the spot. I had to grant her that much. Thank God because I was starting to fall apart by the time she came on the line.

"It's my mother," I moaned. (I'd never called her by the formal moniker before but somehow Maw seemed way too rural.) "She's had some kind of an accident and she's <u>not</u> breathing. (Nor *has she been for some time*). But I didn't add the latter as I didn't want to get into the details just yet.

"Give me your address and we'll send someone right over." A very professional voice instructed, and I did what I was told. At this point I had no other options. I was fresh out of ideas. Let the pros handle it and, boy oh boy, did they ever!

An ambulance, two squad cars, and a fire truck arrived ten minutes later. Did I mention that we were a small town and even such rudimentary matters as a kitten up a tree involved similar hoopla? Once they navigated the slippery sidewalk, they knocked on the door, where I greeted them with my best stiff upper lip. I'd moved maw out of the way so she wouldn't suffer the final indignity of having some oaf trample on her in his hurry to be the hero of the moment. I answered questions respectfully, and I guess I did a fairly good job because within moments I had removed myself from any list that may have suggested foul play. It was quite obvious that maw had slipped the surly bounds of earth at least a fortnight ago, and judging from my tan, I certainly hadn't been around when she'd done so.

"Sorry for your loss," they all mumbled to me, and I cringed. It was one of those phrases I abhorred, reeking of one's inability to come up with something more creative or heartfelt to say under the circumstances. However, I took it all in. What more could I do? The matter was out of my hands now and into the clutches of the system, an ever present army of parasitic retainers more than willing to jump on board and turn your grief into their paycheck.

Before an hour had passed, a coroner had been called and maw was officially pronounced dead. Then she was strapped onto a gurney and stuffed into the back of the ambulance, from where she would begin her final ride to the morgue. It was an unremarkable way to end what would appear to many as an unremarkable life. But for me, it was the point of no return, signifying (at last) the end of my childhood, an event I was totally unprepared for.

To begin with were the multiple forms I had to direct to the multiple addresses and offices, forms which would prove that, yes, indeed, the old lady was no longer on the planet, a news item I could have delivered for free had anyone given me half a chance. But nooooo. Not in the present day and age. That would be far too simple. Gone were the days of a good old Viking funeral. No muss, no fuss. Just a simple bonfire on a boat bound for Valhalla.

Instead, there were wills to be read, and since these were nonexistent, I had to contact the Probate Court who would determine the *intestate succession,* which was a fancy term for *who was gonna get the money*. I knew I was the only heir, so what was the big deal? But that's our culture. Sign on the dotted line, then copy in triplicate. Then there were the forms required by social security. I knew for a fact that maw got a small stipend, and I sure didn't want to be accused of stealing the government's money now that she was no longer a functioning entity. Of course, this resulted in a serious reduction of the slush fund set aside for the funeral arrangements.

Which brings us to that number one killer of next of kin: funerals. I wonder just how many loving spouses or grieving children succumb to death when they are confronted with the bill for a final exit. Today the average funeral costs between seven and ten grand which includes the funeral home, the planting and an appropriate headstone. (And let's just skip the cute little jokes about epitaphs. Like *here lies_____, here let them lie, cuz he's a peace and so am I since* I'm sure that they would include an additional cost.)

Of course, one can get off cheap with cremation which is half the price, and guess who was going that route? Nonetheless, when I started calling around, the best deal I found was one offered by Mid-Ohio Valley Cremation and that was a whopping thirteen hundred. And this is an area that catered to a low income clientele! Still, I would have to take it; cuz maw wasn't getting any younger. In fact, even if I had been able to go for the opulent full Monty funeral, it would have necessitated a closed coffin. So, what the hell? Ashes to ashes and dust to dust, it was.

That decision dispensed with, I went on to tackle the rest of the pressing paper work. There were death certificates to be sent to each and every institution that maw had any dealings with, which included utility companies, credit card agencies, her local doctor and dentist, the DMV, the IRS... and The Coolville Go-Mart.

The Coolville Go-Mart? Yep, that's right, because Maw sure did have a bunch of business going on there. In the scratch-off department. Geez... there ought to be a law, one that forbids such institutions from taking advantage of little old ladies. Because the long and short of it was—when all the dust to dust had settled—I looked at maw's bank statements and realized that at least one third of her monthly Social Security check was going to the local lottery. Oh, every so often she would strike it big, bring in a hundred bucks here or there (after having paid out thrice that amount) but mainly it was just one big financial drain coming from our state capital where a direct line had been set up to bleed such old (and young) fools dry. You could almost hear the sucking sound of money being flushed down the toilet; it was that much of a siphon on the finances of the foolhardy.

And it didn't look good. In fact, it looked so bad I was going to have to run up my credit cards just to pay for her final expenses. Not to mention the small matter of keeping the lights on. Yeah, the bills: electric, water, gas, and sewage. Small items which had never concerned me all those years I had occupied the basement apartment. Except, of course, on the odd occasion when maw would yell downstairs in the middle of the night to bitch about excessive consumption. At which point I would yell back to inform her that I was busy at work (and not just playing video games). Right. Busy at work. Well, by all accounts, I had better ratchet up the old money making machine because I was going to need some cash, or I'd soon be living in a cold dark house.

So in between trips to the bank—where I was finally allowed access to her safety deposit box and then only in the presence of a bank official—and trips to the probate lawyer to try to get a handle on what (if anything) had been left to me besides a house in serious need of repair, one beat-up old car, and a bunch of birds, I did what I could to resurrect my old business. However, it didn't take long to realize that in my absence a couple more kids had graduated from my old alma mater and they had the same idea I'd come up with. This spelled competition and competition in a town that was already glutted with computer geeks. I mean, let's get real. Most of the kids that went to Athens were no dummies when it came to tech savvy. Just like me they had been born with a silicon spoon in their mouth, and generally speaking, had several computers in their possession. So if one developed an issue, they just fired up another and did a web search on how to fix it. Yeah, it was a simple solution, but unless they had out and out problems, it usually was good enough. Plus most young people were just going to their Smart phones these days for internet access, and the Android platform had long been superior to any produced for the PC.

None of this was good news for the local computer repair guy. Business was not just slow. It had damn near fallen off a cliff, and I found myself in a real bind. I couldn't really sell anything in the house until I was cleared with probate court to become the administrator of the estate. And, of course, even when approval came, it would involve a fee. Groan, one more fee!!! My credit card was already close to maxed out and something had to give.

That's when I remembered her Christmas collection. Gee, how could I forget it when it occupied one whole closet in the spare bedroom? Now weren't there a few special items hidden away in those boxes? Stuff I could sell on EBay for some chump change? Well, it was worth a try, except I knew that I would not personally be able to complete any transactions. Therefore, I would have to look up one of my old geeky comrades from the Career Center and see if they'd be willing to do the dirty work for me. For a small share of the profit, that was. Yeah, it was a lukewarm plan, but for lack of any other way to feed my face and keep the house at a toasty sixty-five degrees, it would have to do.

Kady was her name and she'd been the only girl in the tech program, a status which had earned her more than enough attention despite being a bit hard on the eyes. Oh, I guess she may have had potential, but the jet black hair dye and multiple nose piercings had a way of interfering with her best features. And let's not even get started on her tattoos although I have to get on my soapbox a bit when it comes to ink. What is it about these girls? Do they seriously think their bodies can rival art? Shit, if so, it's more like Hieronymus Bosch than Leonardo da Vinci. And what happens fifty years down the road when all that crap starts to sag? Now don't get me wrong. I'm not opposed to a tasteful rose or unicorn here or there, but some of the stuff I've seen pushes the limits of good taste. The spider webs crisscrossing the forehead. The VIRGIN stamp that was voided. The ex's name crossed out and replaced by the current flame. And not to mention a host of booby and butt embellishments that would shame even a stripper. Yeah, the best of them all (and the most truthful) was the chick who used her back as a confessional by inking in the words surely *I have made some bad decisions.* Right, tell me about it.

However I digress. Back to Kady, who at least made up for her weird appearance by being a sweetheart (which was probably the real reason she got asked out more than a cheerleader). And the fact that she found a gracious way to fend off all these invites only added to her charm. I have to confess I'd been one of her admirers. I couldn't help myself. Red-blooded stud that I was, I had seen her as a challenge. Of course, I hadn't even made it to first base by the time the semester ended, so I gave up and settled for her phone number as consolation.

Now, almost three years later, it was a real crap shoot as to whether or not it was still a valid account. But why not give it a try? After all, the girl had been as smart as any when it came to manipulating a key board. and as I recall, she was into the EBay stuff way more than any of us. In fact, hadn't she mentioned something about an on-line store? Yeah, she was definitely the one for the job. If, that is, she was still in the neighborhood.

I went down to the basement and dug into my disorganized files where I procured an old address book. It was the one I'd kept for local contacts, and sure enough, it hosted not only her phone number, but a physical address, written out in her flowery hand. Gee, I don't know if I would have been so trusting, but who knows? Maybe she liked me more than she'd let on. Whatever the case, the address would be a real boon if the phone fizzled out since I was pretty sure she'd lived with her parents and they should be able to update me on her whereabouts. Unless, of course, they had croaked. Yeah, not a pleasant thought, but one which brought me back to my mission at hand.

What a surprise. Not only was the girl still at the same number, but also at the same locale. Our conversation revealed that like me, she had graduated from the Center to find that the job situation was bleak. So she'd decided to continue with the only job she knew which was selling shit on EBay. And I do mean shit. She laughed when she told me how she would peruse yard sales and thrift stores for worthy items and then buy them for pennies on the dollar considering what she'd make once she posted them on her store. I had to hand it to her. She knew her stuff and was just as good as Antique Roadshow.

"Will I take your mom's Christmas trinkets? Does the bear shit in the woods?"

It was the kind of question I would have expected from the old Kady of the multiple tattoos and piercings. But the girl who sat in front of me had changed. Gone were the metal and the pitch black hair, the latter having been replaced by a mousy brown. Also faded were many of the worse tats, the ones that had marred her forehead and fingers.

"I've been undergoing a procedure to get rid of them," she explained when she caught me staring. "It was just a phase, and besides, there's no way my wedding dress can hide them."

(Kady had made it plain from the get-go that she had a June wedding planned to a guy who could best be described as a born-again Baptist.) "Jeffrey's real tolerant for folks around here," she'd mused. "But he drew the lines at me having my digits numbered…"

Yeah, as if the average goon needs help counting to ten. At which point I only shook my head and congratulated her on her upcoming nuptials. Then, I got down to business. There was some serious haggling to take place, since it was best to go into such business deals with the boundaries established ahead of time.

"I want eighty percent," I began, knowing it was a highball. But what the fuck. Always best to start out reaching for the stars.

"Fifty, fifty," she countered, coming at the deal from the opposite end.

"No way!" I shouted, then reducing my voice to a whisper for the benefit of her folks upstairs I added. "Come on, cut me a break here. I just lost my mom."

Slightly softened she reduced her share to forty-five percent, to which I countered. "No more than forty." But a raise of her eyebrows and an indication that the door was over yonder forced me to mutter the inevitable.

"OK, OK, then. I'll settle for it. You can have your lousy forty-fifty. But it's highway robbery." (And its five percent less than what I'd initially set as my own bottom line! Yeah, who says that grief makes a guy generous? This was survival here that we were talking about, and survival always does inspect the profit margin with a magnifying glass.)

So, all the preliminaries dispensed with, the following day both Kady and her husband-to-be arrived at my doorstep. I took one look at the guy and muttered something about opposites attracting. Just the sheer fact that he had refused to allow her to come over un-chaperoned pegged him as a controlling bastard in my book. But that was her problem, not mine. I had problems of my own.

However, as we rooted through maw's boxes, I soon began to breathe a sigh of relief. It wasn't much, but even when I deducted Kady's fee, it would keep the wolf away from the door long enough for the estate to be settled. Then I could sell those damn birds and the old junker of a car and maybe even the house itself, which would provide me with enough cash to begin a new life somewhere else where there might be a more captive audience for my skill set. Maybe even Silicon Valley.

And why not? Perhaps it was time to finally graduate to the real world of making the big bucks. I knew I was good enough. After all, hadn't I spearheaded the design of the Kerbel Space Program game? Surely that counted for something on my resume. All I had to do rent a car and a u-haul—the Subaru having finally bit the dust and maw's car soon to follow. Then I'd pack my shit from the basement, and it was California, here I come. The Promised Land. And nobody would be stopping me at the border because I didn't have the do-re-mi!

Yeah, I was California Dreamin alright, and we all know about how quickly those dreams can go up in smoke. As in the smoke from the hundreds of wildfires that were raging in that once Golden State. I probably wouldn't have known much about them had it not been for my penchant for surfing the Internet. The mainstream media—we in the know, like to call it *lame stream*—had first sensationalized them, and then down played them, shoving them to the back-burner in favor of the big election that was taking place this fall. Big election??? Yep, I had breezed back to my country of birth just in time for a real game changer.

It began with your usual line-up as one after another, they joined the fracas that we call a caucus. The same old names on both sides, a bunch of former senators and governors, most of whom were obscure unless you were politically savvy. Oh, I recognized a few of them. Ted Cruz on the right, Bernie Sanders on the left and, oh yeah, Hillary Clinton on the corporate side.

Hey, but wait a minute? Wasn't it all corporate, a fight to the finish to see who could come up with the most bucks for their campaign? Because wasn't that what it had become in this country ever since Citizens United gave corporations carte blanch when it came to spending money on political candidates? Yes, indeed. Although they could not give money directly to campaigns, said corporations were still allowed to persuade the voting public through any and all means—including ads—and we all know how persuasive they can be in our fair land. Yet the game was on. Be it slander or support, the sky was the limit to their funding. And all on account of free speech! Can you believe it? Corporations have the right to free speech, meaning in essence that they are a viable entity, just like any flesh and blood human being.

I simply couldn't wrap my brain around this bullshit when it became public. And to call it Citizens United? What a classic example of double-speak! And yes, I was hip on my Aldous Huxley, hip enough to recognize a blowjob when I saw one. But I'm getting on my soapbox, something that is hard to avoid during an election year. Of course, what else did I have to focus on? At least all the political stuff took my mind off my own life which was basically on hold as I waited for the estate to run through probate court.

So I listened and I ranted and I raved as the candidates waged war back and forth across the battlefield like two opposing armies. I had to hand it to the Republicans. They had flooded the field with candidates, starting out with a whopping seventeen contenders. There were so many I hardly paid much attention to them. Besides, I'd always been a died-in-the-wool Democrat since I had considered them to be the people's party. However as far as this election went, the Dems weren't giving us much in the way of choice, and it soon became evident that the lines had been drawn. The choice narrowed down to either Hitlery Clinton (as the opposition referred to her) or Bernie Sanders, who may or may not be a real democrat, having just recently switched from an independent position. Lucky thing though as Independents never have won an election in our country and, more often than not, just hand votes to an opponent.

So given the choice, my allegiance went with Bernie, despite the claims that he was a socialist and even a communist by members of his own party, many of which he appeared to despise. Well, I could understand his revulsion for some of them, especially Clinton, since Bernie always ran on an anti-war, anti-capitalist platform. That said, when it came to a decision between him and Hitlary, it was a no-brainer which one would be more of a people's president.

Thus, Bernie soon became my candidate of choice. This put me in a decided majority since it seemed that, as far as my fellow party members were concerned, I had hitched myself to the winning horse. The public was sick of the same old same old, and this went double for the Bush-Clinton dynasty that had been in control of our government one way or the other for almost fifty years. The people wanted an underdog and an underdog that stood for the ninety-nine percent—which makes me wonder how in the world they would ever dream of electing Trump.

Trump, you say, as in Donald, as in the popular show *The Apprentice*. Yeah, that's right. Because just as the Democratic candidates had been narrowed down to a mere two, so had the Republican. The seventeen candidates had dropped off like flies before a can of Raid, leaving but one still standing. Indeed, the wind blew, the shit flew and there stood Trump.

At first I could not believe my eyes. However, because I try to be fair and balanced in my opinions, I did watch some of his speeches during the primaries, and I understood his appeal. Come on, the guy was charismatic with a capital 'C'. And he was giving his Republican base what they wanted, a chance to **Make America Great Again**. Of course, this involved some fairly radical steps, one which centered on the construction of a wall along our southern border. Now them's fighting words for any bleeding-heart liberal, and I must confess I was caught up in the rhetoric. However, some of the other stuff he endorsed, stuff like bringing business back to the US (they all claimed they would do that) and getting rid of Obamacare (or at least its unconstitutional mandate) were acceptable goals in my mind. Plus, although it no longer affected me personally, I agreed one hundred percent with his pledge not to decrease social security.

But, hey, Bernie's platform wasn't a whole lot different on some of these talking points, and Bernie wasn't a blowhard asshole. So, once again, there was no question as to where my allegiance would lie. Like all good members of my party, I followed the primary debates and the more I saw of Clinton, the less I liked her. It wasn't just her corporate nature and the taint of her husband's legacy (and unlike my feminist friends, I didn't feel sorry for her because she'd married a cheating rat). No, there was just something about her that wasn't on the up and up.

A typical politician, she seemed to talk out of both sides of her mouth. And then there was that business in Benghazi when four American officials as well as our ambassador had been killed in a terrorist attack. A later report by the House Select Committee confirmed that Hilary, who was our Secretary of State, refused to act on information that the place was a death trap. Isn't that just as bad as pulling the trigger?

And speaking of which, how about that strange phenomenon called Arkancide which has now morphed into Clintoncide? Call it what you may, but there sure have been a lot of suspicious deaths among people who have been in close contact with the Clintons. I think the number (including so-called suicides) is up to over seventy by now and that's a hefty amount for just plain coincidence. Yeah, I sure wouldn't want to be in bed with either one of them.

So Bernie, Bernie... he's my man. If he can't beat Trump, no one can. And by Mid-summer it looked as though the impossible had happened, this being that Donald J. Trump AKA THE DONALD would be running on the Republican ticket for the next President of the United States! Wow! Things were getting really weird, but not so weird that it wasn't obvious to me and to many members of the Democratic Party that the only way we stood a chance was to present Bernie as our chosen candidate.

The Democratic Convention took place shortly after the Republican one. It was hosted by Philadelphia, the City of Brotherly Love, and as an interesting aside, the Republican shindig was held in Cleveland, home to the Rock and Roll Hall of Fame. However, neither city lived up to their reputations when it came to the Conventions. Oh, I guess you might say that Cleveland came close. After all, wasn't The Donald somewhat of a rock star in his own right? He sure was set out to rock a few boats if his repeated promises to *drain the swamp* known as Washington, DC were to be taken seriously. But poor old Philly, the birthplace of our democracy and epitome of the loving spirit that embodied the greatest country on earth? It sure didn't deserve what it got, and it sure did have a rough time for a couple of days.

Oh, there was no fighting in the streets, no Molotov cocktails, or bands of hairy Yippies running amuck as in Democratic conventions of the past. But that did not disguise the inner struggle, one which surfaced as soon as the Convention doors opened. At this point it became painfully obvious that Bernie supporters, though in a decided majority, were going to be in for a real disappointment. Hillary, or Killary as some would insist, had garnered the most votes. However, the fact that she won all those primaries was debatable to many, including those who conducted exit polls only to find them in direct conflict to the final tally.

But it wasn't just the primaries that affected the result of the convention. It was a nasty little institution known as super-delegates. These guys can (and will) supervene in the electoral process as they are not beholden to the results of the primaries or the caucus. This means they are free to support the presidential candidate of their choice, often going against the will of their constituency. Take New Hampshire for instance, Bernie's home stomping ground. He should have won it by a landslide, and in actuality, he did. However once the super-delegates chimed in with their two cents, they effectively erased Sander's win. This kept happening over and over and in the end, the result was predictable. After receiving a 59.67% majority of delegates to Bernie's 39.16%, Hillary Clinton was chosen as the party's nomination for president.

Simple enough? Well, not really since in the week leading up to this decision, controversy reigned. And just before the convention began, it was leaked that the election results had been rigged in favor of Clinton. A group known as Election Justice USA came out with a report proving that, through all manner of monkey business, Bernie had been defrauded out of a righteous win. Their evidence consisted of emails made available by that master of the infowars himself, Julian Assange of Wikileaks fame, and the effect was so damning that the Chairwoman of the DNC herself was immediately forced to resign. Not that it stopped her career as the same conniving bitch was immediately picked up by the Clinton campaign. Funny thing about that. However, the worst moment came when poor old Bernie, despite the overwhelming support of his Party, conceded his loss and stood up and endorsed Clinton. Not one word was mentioned about the vote rigging, and the expectation was that business would continue as usual.

I watched all this in disbelief. Had it been a setup all along? Had Bernie just been planted only to gather support for Hillary? Had Trump been interjected as the wild card—and I do mean **wild**—a fascist on a power trip, a guy so crazy you'd vote for Clinton just to stop him? Had this been the plan? To divide the country? Create Chaos? And then select a known crook to act as the spokeswoman for the financial elite? Gee, it was enough to make me turn away from the polls all together. Why cast a vote when the only half-ways honest candidate was packing his bags to go back to the *Live Free or Die* State? It was a dark day in DemLand. I hung my head in shame and brought out a bottle of Old Bushnell. It seemed appropriate since it was one maw reserved for funerals.

And then, it got worse. Remember how that all the hoopla came about because some leaked emails? Well, those emails had been leaked by someone. And now the fun begins. Well… not necessarily fun for a guy by the name of Seth Rich. Seth was a young Dem from Omaha, Nebraska who was affiliated with the Convention. He'd been out late one night at his favorite bar—which just so happened to be located in one of the most highly surveillanced areas of DC—when he was attacked on the way home by thugs. It went on record as a botched robbery, yet his wallet was still on him when the police arrived and so was his watch. Since his injuries were not fatal, he was taken to a nearby hospital. However, he didn't make it through the night. No comment.

I suppose all of this would have been brushed off as another DC incident had not the DNC leaks been revealed shortly thereafter. Then, to boot, Julian Assange implied that Rich was the source of said leaks. So this is where it begins to get interesting. Add to the formula the fact that no investigation was conducted at the time and that the Police Chief resigned within one month of the shooting, leaving a new chief who insisted on keeping all information concerning this crime under wraps. This meant no ballistic reports, no video footage, no nothing; and at this point one begins to smell a rat.

Predictably the buzz grew louder. The Internet was ringing with conspiracy theories of how the so-called robbery was actually a hit, an assassination ordered to punish a whistleblower. Yeah, let that be a lesson to anyone else who might want to come forth and slam the Democratic Party. This included Seth Richard's parents who initially posted a video in appreciation to the public for expressing interest in their son's death, yet who later did a complete one hundred and eighty and threatened to sue Fox news for airing a special on it.

Indeed the plot was thickening, especially when one delved a bit deeper (as I was often inspired to do) and discovered odd little connections. Take for instance the juicy morsel of John Podesta's ex sister-in-law, who was on the DC Police Foundation Board at the time. Oh, so what...you say? What does that have to do with the price of tea in China? Well, apparently more than one would think. Because John Podesta, a long time associate of the Clintons, was also Hillary's Campaign Manager, and in early March he, too, had suffered a data breech during which thousands of his emails were stolen—allegedly by the Russians, but more on that later. (Much more, in fact.) It wouldn't have been such a big deal except that good old Julian Assange, that Commie rat, had gotten his hands on said emails and had decided to publish all twenty thousand pages of them during the two months leading up to the election.

To say they may have swayed public opinion away from Hillary is putting it mildly. As the installments were released, they offered a glimpse into the workings of the Clinton Campaign, and some were none to savory. In one, it was suggested that Hillary's attitude towards her countrymen needed a serious adjustment because she stated boldly how much she had come to hate the term *everyday Americans*. Everyday Americans? Hey, weren't they the same folks who would be putting her elitist ass in the Oval Office? Come on now, woman. Don't go and bad-mouth the hand that feeds you! At the least, just save your mud-slinging for the opposition.

But perhaps this was a suggestion they took to heart, for shortly thereafter, John Podesta came out and called Sanders a *doofus* for criticizing the Paris Climate Agreement. A doofus?!? Was this a high school kid's Facebook page we're dealing with here? OK. So what if it was? Sticks and stones, and all that. After all, it was an election year and we, the *everyday Americans* had come to expect such belittling blows from our candidates.

However, it got worse, for some of the emails were far more damning, and had less to do with simple shit-slinging and more to do with national security breaches. There was one concerning the terrorist group ISIS and how they were receiving support from Saudi Arabia and Qatar, two nation states said to be our allies. Another documented how most of the Clinton Foundation's donors were not even American. And yet another let drop that, although Clinton was wary of refugees, she had an open borders dream—which is somewhat of a contradiction. But hey, isn't that a politically correct procedure for a politician? To talk out of both sides of their mouth?

So, despite the implications of such emails, I had been far from appalled to discover their contents. You see, like many members of my generation, I had come to expect such behavior and verbiage from our elected officials. I suppose that, like the disgruntled young Seth Rich, I was somewhat jaded when it came to politics, and more than a tad disillusioned with the party of my choice, not to mention their selection for a candidate.

However, as the drama unfolded I began to discover that, not only had this woman cheated Bernie out of the nomination, but she was also receiving debate questions in advance via her DNC Chairperson Donna Brazile. That's right. Donna had been caught with her hand directly in the cookie jar. Yet she'd done nothing but deny, deny, deny. It was simply shameful. What was a guy to do? Perhaps the only solution lay in looking the other way. And indeed, I was beginning to—in the direction of Donald J. Trump.

And that's when the clincher arrived, appearing in the form of numerous emails involving a lot of strange talk about food items, specifically pizza, pasta, and ice cream. Well, maybe John and Hillary were hungry. After all, you can work up quite an appetite hoodwinking the American public, and they been hard at it for years. But speculation remains as to what else they may have been up to. Because it soon came to light that the language used in these emails was dead center for the same code used by child sex ring participants. For instance, a hotdog is a boy, a pizza is a girl, cheese is a little girl, and pasta is a little boy. Ice cream is a male prostitute, walnut a person of color, and put it all together and you have a hell of a sauce (which is code for orgy). As in a nice little spirit cooking dinner. I quote:

Dear Tony, I am so looking forward to the Spirit Cooking dinner at my place. Do you think you will be able to let me know if your brother is joining? All my love, Marina

This email had been sent from Marina Abramovic to Tony Podesta concerning his brother John's appearance at a nice little get together where some of Marina's recipes might be sampled. Many involved aphrodisiacs and were predictably weird, calling for 13,000 grams of jealousy and the mixing of fresh breast milk with fresh sperm which a person would drink only on earthquake nights. Now this is tame enough until you read on to find that the next set of directions involved cutting deeply into the middle fingers of your left hand and eating the pain; then taking fresh morning urine and sprinkling it over nightmare dreams.

On her YouTube video Marina is writing these directions on a blank white wall with a substance strongly resembling blood. Warning: this video should not be watched during or after dinner, but here is its link just in case you think I am making this stuff up.

https://www.youtube.com/watch?v=3EsJLNGVJ7E

Now the obvious question centers on just how deeply Hillary may have been involved in these shenanigans. All we know are the facts: that in an email, Hillary asks if Marina is coming to an event, and that at one time the Clinton Foundation gave $10,000 to this so-called artist. The rest of the evidence is somewhat circumstantial. Hillary had once written about conducting rituals to contact Eleanor Roosevelt and Mahatma Gandhi. Bill and Hillary took part of voodoo rituals in Haiti. Hillary had a mentor named Saul Alinski who praised Lucifer in his book. So once again, the jury is out. But it sure does whisper of guilty by association, and I know that, if I were running for office, I sure wouldn't want to claim as a friend a guy who had a deranged collection of artwork in his home, especially when its common theme appeared to be *kids I could molest and then kill*. Yeah, there's art, and then there's mental illness.

Once again, all this stuff is available on-line should you need a fact check, and it should not be hard to find. I guess a lot of the alt-press is tearing into it like a dog with a bone because Pizzagate has now morphed into Pedogate. The theme has become so commonplace that some broadcasts do nothing more than focus—almost to the point of obsession—on human trafficking, pedophilia, and worse, insisting all the while that the *Truth is about to be Unsealed*.

And well it might be, but in *truth*, I simply had more pressing matters to attend to. All the mail ever brought was a constant flow of bills, bills, bills. I had no idea one woman could have that many credit cards, and all were about as close as you could get to maxed out. I tried to do some research on line as to what I should do with all this debt.

Since she was dead, would it be forgiven? No, probably not. They would just come after the estate, if and when it was ever settled. And then there was the curious matter of some of the more official looking letters, one which bore the title: **Notice of Default**. Now what was that all about?

Assuming that it had to do with one of the credit cards, I just tossed it in the ever expanding pile of bills to pay at a later date and went on about my business. I have to confess that running a household was not really my forte. Maw had always taken care of all that stuff and now that she was gone, I found I was clueless. Oh, I got the important stuff together, the monthly payments to South Central Power, Southeastern Oil and Gas, and of course, Frontier, the telephone and Internet provider. Yeah, the last was a must, cuz what's a boy to do without the NET?

I wouldn't be able to follow all those alternative news sites, the ones I had become hopelessly addicted to because, even though I professed to have better things to do with my time, the truth was quite the opposite. Besides, it made for some pretty interesting entertainment for a guy who was just spinning his wheels while sitting around waiting for his ship to come in. So I stayed with the election news right up to the bitter end, and yes it was pretty bitter for any flag waving member of the Donkey Kong party. Because one night in early November the unspeakable happened, and Trump (AKA The Donald) won the election. Like the rest of the country, I was shocked, though perhaps not as shocked as the editors of TIME magazine who already had their next issue set to go to the presses, an issue which celebrated our first female president. Pretty strange, huh? Did they have a crystal ball, or was some serious rigging going on at the polls?

Oh, but wait a minute. The Dems didn't cheat. In fact, according to the mainstream news, they had never done one wrong thing. That honor went to The Donald, who by all appearances could do nothing right. If he said it was white, they screamed back *black*. If he tried to compromise with a neutral grey, they criticized him for not taking a stand.

And, no way did he ever win that election fair and square. Remember that little data breech that affected Hillary's campaign manager, John Podesta? Well, I said we'd get back to it. Because it was—and here I have to use a string of noteworthy adverbs—ostensibly and allegedly instigated by none other than the Russians. That's right. The Ruskies, those Commie rats who have been our enemy ever since the days of the Cold War. Well, not everyone's enemy. For there were certain liberals back in the McCarthy era who got really steamed up about Socialism and how much better it would be for the people in general.

But that was then, this is now. Communism bad; Capitalism good. And never the twain shall meet, and never, never, never should those Ruskies interfere in one of our wonderful elections, because they might just sully the waters of this impeccably squeaky clean land. Yeah, like we never got our hands dirty. Why even on our own soil, we'd been caught dipping into more than one dubious cookie jar. Think the 2000 election and the hanging chads deal, and you get the picture. Not to mention all those Diebold voting machines which were supposed to fix the fraud problem, but which only led to worse since they could be controlled remotely by someone with an eighth grade science education. And let's not get into our far from subtle influence in elections around the world, especially those taking place in Banana Republics where we had more than a vested interest. Yes, the US has had a long history of meddling with elections, at least eighty-five of them since 1945. So maybe this is the pot calling the kettle black.

Whatever the case, they (meaning the lamestream media) were all over Trump like flies on shit. (And yes, that is probably an appropriate metaphor.) It was Russian Collusion every time you turned on the tube. In a case so convoluted that you needed a mile long time line to keep up with it, they tried over and over again to prove beyond a shadow of a doubt that the guy had put the Russians up to it. There was a special council appointed which was headed by a guy named Robert Mueller, whose name had all my liberal associates sporting tee-shirts declaring that it was Mueller *Time*. There were hirings and firings galore; there was talk of impeachment. There were a whole bunch of indictments (which include thirty-two people and three Russian companies). There were a few guilty pleas and then a few plea deals. And, oh yes, there was a whole lot of taxpayer money spent, twenty-five million to be precise, which beggars belief. When is enough, enough?

Yet the weirdest thing about all this came from a simple oversight on the part of our so-called free press. You see, at no point had there ever been any mention of a number of emails implementing the Dems favorite daughter, Ms. Hillary Clinton herself, in the sale of Uranium 1 resources to one of our main adversaries. And who might that be? You guessed it. The Russians. Of course, if you try to fact check that with anything other than alternative news sites, all you will get was that it was *a complex conspiracy theory.*

Yeah, for this boy, enough was enough. I was shaking my head in disbelief, at least the part of it that wasn't spinning out of control. I really needed to give this stuff a rest. It was all lies and disinformation and impossible to separate the truth from the bullshit. What happened to the good old days of real investigative journalism? Boy, did I need a break, something else to focus my attention on.

And given that one should take care what they wish for, the universe in all its splendor delivered the goods. Because just about the time I was really starting to burn the midnight oil in the chat rooms, I received a foreclosure notice from the bank.

A foreclosure notice???? For a house I had lived in close to fifteen summers and one that (to the best of my knowledge) had been paid off years ago by a cranky old lady who didn't believe in debt.

Didn't believe in debt? Why that's almost un-American. I should know since I'd been living off of credit ever since mom had passed, only paying the minimum amount on my cards with whatever money I could spare from the chump change Kady was giving me for the sale of maw's Christmas crap. It was a little gig that was getting old, especially since my priorities were more about keeping the lights on, and every penny I gave to Chase Bank was one I had to rob from the South Central Power Company.

I'd even had to resort to pawning off a bunch of my techie equipment, figuring I could always get it out of hock when things turned around. What a life!!! It already had me wishing for a magic bullet, a quick and easy way to get all this debt forgiven, and that was before I realized that yet another bank wanted close to one hundred grand if I were to maintain a roof over my head.

One hundred grand!!!! Now where was I supposed to come up with that kind of cash? And come to think of it, how the hell did I even owe it in the first place? Could it be the previous owner of the house, AKA me mum, had run up a gambling debt? Does, as Katy was so quick to utter, a bear truly shit in the woods? Was it possible that maw had really refinanced the house to play at Scratch-Off?

Now I'd heard of gambling addictions, but that one took the cake. It didn't even have any pizzazz, like betting on the horses or the Super Bowl. Just lowly scratch-offs, the kind you encounter at any convenience store, the kind the poor line up to purchase in hopes they will win their first million—which by the way, has been proven to be gone in less than a year, the poor being piss-poor at managing money.

Oh maw, what have you done???? My lamentations were so loud you probably could have heard me screaming in the next county—or at least as far as Kady's because, oddly enough, the girl called me the very next day and out of the blue at that. Up to this point our correspondence had been limited to the small amounts which showed up periodically in my PayPal account. I had given her the bulk of *Christmas Past* when we'd first agreed on our business arrangement. This had suited me just fine on account of her creepy fiancé. Truth be told, I didn't much care if she darkened my door again since it was apparent that where she went, he was sure to follow.

That's why I was a bit surprised to hear her voice. Surely she hadn't sold all that shit yet. There had been so much of it, and the only way to make a profit involved parceling it out one piece at a time. So by my reckoning, we had at least a couple more months worth before I had to dig around and find something else to fob off on the American public. But I was even more surprised when I understood the purpose behind her call.

"I'm only telling you about this because I always had a secret crush on you."

Well, no shit. But I guess it's not secret anymore.

"Plus, I know you're having a hard time with all this…"

And by *all this*, you are referring to the fact that my maw went belly up and left me so deep in debt that it will take me centuries to crawl out? Yes, that may be one hundred percent true. But just how…?

My random thoughts went without saying. Had she been cyber-spying on me? Hacking onto my email to find my rousing correspondence with the brain dead corporate zombies over at Chase Bank? If so, all she really would have found was a string of explicatives, ones I had wanted to scream into the phone to silence their awful MUSACK whenever they put me on hold. It was a classic case of letters you'd written, never meaning to send, knowing they would serve absolutely no purpose other than to enrage the already out of control beast. Nope! There was no arguing with the central banks. They held all the cards, and it was their way or the…

"The foreclosure," she began, answering my unspoken question. "My dad works down at United Bank, and every so often he brings work home from the office, and I just so happened to see it lying around on his desk and… well, you know."

Yeah, I knew. Once a hacker, always a hacker. Old habits are hard to break. But that wasn't the point. The nitty-gritty of the matter was that she'd called, not to provide a shoulder to cry on, but to offer a possible solution. For hadn't she said something about *only telling me something because she had a secret crush on me*? If so, what was that little something? Well, it surely wouldn't hurt to ask.

However, the answer I received was about as ambiguous as the rest of the phone call.

"I really need to come over and show you," she muttered in a low tone, one which I found a tad too conspiratorial for my taste. What could she have to say that should not be repeated to the NSA? Was she about to give me the code for the bank vault where her dad was employed? I had to admit that my curiosity was pumping, and it felt good, the first ray of sunshine in an otherwise grim season.

"OK," I muttered. And then as an afterthought. "But is HE coming too?" (Meaning her controlling redneck husband, for surely they had tied the knot by now.)

"Oh, don't worry about that. We split up and I'm now dating this cute little guy who I met at a club in Columbus, place called Kahoots."

Kahoots? Wasn't that a strip club?

My pause indicated my confusion and she picked up on it.

"Yeah, a bunch of us girls went up there last June for my bachelorette party, and there he was in all his glory. Talk about buns of steel! I mean… wow!!!!"

Yeah, *wow* indeed, girlfriend, was all I could think. Talk about an identity crisis. It was all I could do not to laugh out loud—or LOL as they so succinctly said in the cyber-circles.

"Well…" I stammered. "Yeah, come right over. I'm all ears." And that was putting it mildly. I had to say I was intrigued by this girl and, although not necessarily attracted to her, she possessed a certain mystic that surrounds the truly weird. Her rapid fire changes were enough to make a head spin, and it was hard not to want to just sit back and enjoy the ride. However, for the present, there was work to be done, or so she had indicated. So let that show begin. At least I could rest assured that she would not be trying to extract payment via a pound of flesh. By all appearances, she had that angle pretty well covered.

We spent the better part of the afternoon perusing Internet sites which involved an obscure entity called the **I-UV I AM Power Love Absolute.** It was hard for both of us to get a handle on it because a lot was written in legalese, and what wasn't belonged in a category which can best be described as Hopium.

The basic principal is that the countries we think we are living in are actually corporations, where our rights and privileges are determined only by a very small group of the Elite. And if one doesn't want to accept that, check out the NY stock exchange where all said countries of the world are listed. However, in 2013 a woman by the name of Heather Tucci Jaraf decided to go up against this system by filing foreclosure on this corrupt system. Since she came from a banking background, she was able to wade through the legalese and using Uniform Code registrations, she served notices on a host of banks and corporate governments. In these she stated that they were *lawfully and legally duly canceled and foreclosed upon by their own free will choice not to remedy the damage they had caused.* These documents also determined that *these entities had no legal standing or authority between individuals and their creator.*

Now, in order to refute these claims, the trustees of these organizations needed to file a rebuttal. However, she had them by the balls, because if they did so they would have revealed that they had knowingly, *willingly, and intentionally committed treason by owning, operating, aiding, and abetting private money systems and operating slavery Systems used against citizens without their knowing, willing, or intentional consent.*

I had to admit that, despite the little I understood about law, it seemed a perfect coup d'état. She had them checkmated. They were damned if they did, damned if they didn't. And it was enough to compel me to wade on. As I did so I was informed that henceforth *there were no more laws on earth and that the only jurisdiction that still counts is yours alone. In short: All people are free of debt certified,* and all one needs to do is take back *possession of Be'ing by simply Do'ing.* This involves the sending of something called a Courtesy Notice along with Invoices (if needed) to the appropriate debt collector. As far as I could tell, said Courtesy Notices were a bit of a fuck-you-a-gram, but one that was delivered in a respectful way.

Shaking my head, I had to confess to Kady that I had a few reservations. If all debts had truly been cancelled on March 13th, 2013, why hadn't we heard of this before? And where were all the success stories that I-UV had requested from their followers? The so-called Freedom Stories contained more questions than answers, and one girl even decried her own stupidity and asked for someone to walk her through the site.

"I don't know, Kady. This seems like pissing in the wind to me," I began.

"But wait, here's one where Chase agreed to retract a loan in the amount of $99,692.21. And then there's my friend Tara over in Zanesville who literally had a $5000 hospital fee forgiven."

Oh yeah, I had heard all about Tara today and the book that some rebel without a clause had written about her. And as I recall it didn't really end too favorably. However, I also figured that the Courtesy Notices might provide me with a hiatus. Though a crap shot, they were a good way to stall for time, to shove the same legal shit back at the almighty banks that they had been dishing out for years. Stuff like:

I am the sole lawful and legal REGISTERED owner, custodian, and trustee of my BE'ing, any and all creations therefrom, and property thereof, UCC Doc. File No.'s 2012127810, 2012127854, 2012127907, 2012127914, restated and incorporated here by reference as if set forth in full, original notice of DECLARATION OF FACTS by public registration made and given by the One People's Public Trust, hereafter "OPPT". I have and do knowingly, willingly, and intentionally adopt, reconfirm, and ratify said DECLARATION OF FACTS as my own duly verified due DECLARATION OF FACTS, nunc pro tunc praeterea preterea, unrebutted as a matter of law, as matter of fact, and as a matter of public policy, hereafter "Proponent".

> Yeah, take that and stick it in your pie hole.
> "OK, let's do this," I said. After all, what did I have to lose?

In retrospect, those would become famous last words, but this would not be revealed until much later. In the meanwhile, it seemed like a good enough plan and something to combat the terminal tedium I'd been experiencing for over a year now. Here I was ready to get on with my life, and there was that damn bank throwing a monkey wrench in the works. The nerve of them! It was true; they were the ones who deserved to be foreclosed on.

So while I sat around waiting to see if the courtesy notices I had sent out had any effect whatsoever on the evil minions who run this planet, I decided to do something I'd been putting off ever since the old lady had been placed into an urn. It involved going through her personal effects. I had rationalized that up to this point it hadn't been allowed because it was all part of the estate and heavens to Betsy, I might find a winning lottery ticket in one of her pockets. But I was done playing Mr. Nice Guy with these bastards. If I did find anything of value, I would do my best to make sure they didn't get their greedy little hands on it. That said, I started with the closets that held her clothes. After all, one never knows. Right?

An hour later I sat amidst a pile of ugly old lady clothes—maw never had an ounce of taste—with a tear in my eye and empty pockets (both hers and mine.)

"I really need to bag up all this shit and take it down to the thrift store," I stated out loud, and the sound of my own voice was enough to propel me out of my sadness and into a path of action. I rustled up some trash bags (extra large ones) and stuffed the crap inside. Out of sight, out of mind and all that.

Then, feeling a little better I got into some deep exploration involving a bunch of boxes stacked at the back of the closet. The first were just more Christmas stuff. Must have been specialty items, and I made a mental note to shuffle these over to Kady ASAP since I needed all the help I could get. But a dusty box residing far back in the corner was the one which led to my biggest surprise of the day. No, make that of the decade, or maybe even of my life. For the contents were solely letters and every single one bore a return address from a prison in California.

"Now what the fuck!" I muttered out loud. "What on earth had maw been up to?"

However, as it turned out. It had nothing to do with earth.

The architect of the letters was a guy named Captain John McCumbers, who purported to be a member of a Secret Space Program. Apparently the Captain had been locked up for a murder he did not commit so that he would lose all credibility should he decide to become a whistleblower.

Well, judging from the contents of the letters I didn't feel like he had too much to worry about since *in*credible was way beyond an adequate description for his major talking points. According to this guy, who supposedly served off planet for a number of years, our solar system is a very desirable area and highly contested by a number of ET races. He went on to enumerate the major players. First there were the eight foot tall Raptors, a group which considers the earth as their personal property, but who are still our allies—at least when they can refrain from their impulse to eat us. Then there were the Reptilians, who also wanted earth for their own (which is why we have allied ourselves with the Raptors, so we can defeat them) and the Dracos, who have a hard time with our atmosphere and who are constantly transforming it to suit their physiognomy. (Think Fukushima and you get the picture.) And finally there are the Greys, who are mostly clones and therefore at the beck and call of the Reptilians. There were also cat-like beings and super-tall Nordic beings from Aldeberon, and even the Telos People from inside Mt. Shasta. Plus there were a group of off-planet peace keepers and watch dogs called the Confederation or Ashtar Command.

Now our military has known about all these guys forever, forming alliances with some and battling with others. Their advanced technology has been gifted in return for allowing them to experiment on our citizens. Because of this we humans already possess warp drive tech. So we have bases all over the place. On the moon. On Jupiter and Saturn. And in the far reaches of the galaxy. In fact we are even capable of time travel and can use something called our Merkaba or light force to move between centuries and millenniums.

However the preferred means of transport are our fleet of ships which we built in the 1950's, one of which this guy claims to have captained prior to his incarceration by evil forces of our shadow government. This guy's ship, by the name of Minerva, was a sentient AI being who considered humans an irritant but still allowed them to fly her via a mind melt. This our illustrious Captain accomplished, courtesy his extreme psychic abilities. Apparently, he was quite the guy, a super-soldier, who had been augmented like many members of the SSP. But wait a minute! It wasn't all about the genes. It would seem that

Chemtrails had made said augmentation easier since they not only poisoned people and made them more docile, but possessed the added advantage of turning them into super-soldier material.

Poisoned people? Yet had an *added advantage*??? Wasn't that somewhat of a contradiction in terms? And Chemtrails at that, me maw's favorite conspiracy theory! Well I'll be a monkey's uncle. Yeah, that was about as plausible as any of the stuff I'd been reading through. Oh, it made for some entertaining reading material for a rainy afternoon... but really, maw!? And who was this a guy anyway? A long lost relative? Nope, at least not anyone I'd ever heard of. Well then, was he a romantic interest?

Nope again, because a quick search revealed that he was already married—and predictably to a woman whom he'd met while in prison. Oh you poor sweet ladies! Why, oh why, do you fall for this shit? Boy, oh boy, are there a lot of lonely people out there. And a lot of suckers.

Because the Captain's bio intrigued me enough to conduct a quick fact check, and many of his so-called assertions just didn't survive the test. For instance, both his father and grandfather were said to be friendly with Tesla, and the father even worked with him. Yet these are undocumented claims with no facts to substantiate them. Then there is the Captain himself who claimed to be a Rhodes Scholar, although nowhere was he listed in their database. In fact, his rank of Captain was also suspect, especially when one considers that he claimed to have been on active duty from the ripe old age of thirteen. Then he somehow managed to switch from being a Captain in the Army to one in the Navy, a complicated process that takes years.

But the weirdest contradictions were those surrounding the case of the murder for which the Captain was (allegedly) framed. First of all, the victim was his best friend, and the motive was money. Now who kills a best friend to get a little cash? Well, perhaps the same guy who enlisted the help of two teens who he had convinced would be elevated to the exalted positions of dukes and earls in a new kingdom that was coming to Marin County. It went by the name of Pendragon, and three guesses who would be its king?

Sound familiar? A bunch of poppycock from a con man who was once described by a classmate as possessing a silver tongue. Yeah, and it only gets piled deeper since there was no way the Captain could have been involved in this brutal murder since he was off planet at the time—though he was quick to return and purchase a boat with some of the money that had been stolen. Oh, and those items which had belonged to his friend? The ones that ended up in his possession? Well... duh...

OK, I'd read enough. Hadn't I bitched at maw over and over again, telling her to do her homework? Not that it's easy anymore with everybody working the room with a scam. And everybody—and I do mean *every*body—has their own agenda, including the people who compiled the data which condemned to perdition every single claim the Captain made. So I guess someone needs to fact-check the fact-checkers, too!

However, my gut level reaction was to dismiss all of the Captain's claims as the ranting of a madman, albeit a very charismatic one, which may have been what drew my mother in. Or was it something else? A niggling little thought kept returning for days after I'd taken this small detour into this dark corner of cyberspace, and it was one I refused to allow to enter the light of day. However, the age was right, and even though the guy had been married, it was his second time around, and who's to say what the sly fellow may have been up to prior his first walk down the aisle. Could he be...? After all, the Merry Pranksters attracted a plethora of nutcases, some of which have turned out to be CIA plants.

Oh well, let's not go there today. Come on now, we have so many other interesting matters to attend to. There are those Courtesy Notices and the Russian Collusion fiasco and the Stormy Daniels affair and... Oh, the list was endless. Making me wish for the good old days of digging latrines down in some Banana Republic. At least there, the shit had been real.

And so my days went, the Courtesy Notices bringing about as much fruition as all of the varied attempts to impeach our President. Boy, were they going after this guy. I had never seen such a bunch of vicious attack dogs, and it caused me to take one of my old theories out of the closet for a good dusting and cleaning. It went like this. When they are really afraid of you, because you are really on to something, then they try like hell to get rid of you. They don't bother with minor players like the politically active rock stars who never made it or the centerfold dolls who never had sweet secrets whispered in their ears during some pillow talk.

No, these folks aren't worth their time. You have to be a big shot, someone capable of rocking their boat and rocking it good. Somebody like John Lennon, or Martin Luther King, or the Kennedys. Then you may as well paint a target on your back. And yes, according to the alt news, there had already been more than one attempt on Trump's life. They were just never publicized. So whether or not they really happened becomes debatable. But one thing I did know was that the mainstream media was bound and determined to rip him a new one meaning that, if my theory was correct, he truly was out to drain the swamp.

Yeah, mine was an interesting theory and one born not so much from personal experience but more from a study of history. The minor players never did make it to the front page news, for they were but annoying gadflies in the eyes of the faction which ran the planet. Instead, it was the real rabble rousers, the ones who had some clout one way or the other, who were either demonized out of existence or just plain reduced to ashes. Of course, they could always find themselves behind a locked door whose key seemed to have magically disappeared, which was a fate worse than death to someone who has been a freedom fighter and light warrior.

I thought back to Captain John. Who knows? Maybe he had been barking up the right tree. But that had been so long ago that his impact today was about as effective as a rusty nail. By now, there were probably sharper adversaries to the system, and God help them if they were not *too big to fail* (or *fall*, as it were.)

It was a strange thought and one that stayed with me for the better part of June. Perhaps it was a foreshadowing of plot, the kind of prescience we occasionally experience within the passion play of our days. Or perhaps, I was just about to get some first-hand experience that would put my theory to the test.

Sometime in mid-summer the phone rang and it was Kady. She was more excited than usual, and that's saying something for a girl whose every other word was *awesome!*

"I need to come over. Right now!" she nearly shouted into the receiver. And I prayed this had nothing to do with her breaking up with Mr. Chippendale because that meant I might be next in line for her experimental forays into the world of relationships.

But, no, her and Chip were still an item and should her new scheme pan out, they'd be honeymooning in Bali by the end of the summer.

Wow! Bali? That had to be a high ticket item as far as honeymoons went. So, my ears perked up, and in the end, I had to feel sorry for them.

Her spiel began with a hot little item called the Strawman Account. OK, so this was something I'd heard mentioned a time or two in the Internet chatrooms which I frequented. Apparently everyone who walks the surface of the earth has a STRAWMAN, and I put that in CAPS so as not to confuse such an entity with its flesh and blood counterpart, which would be you or me.

The whole notion of the Strawman came about back in the 1930's with an effort to save the financial system by issuing Birth Certificate bonds. Up to that point all births were recorded in the family

Bible. However, once the government found a way to hone in on the commodity of its citizens, it did so with a passion. Following a move away from the gold standard, they came up with this novel idea of pledging their own citizens as collateral so they could borrow money against their projected productivity. First they demanded that birth information be collected by hospitals and then turned over to the Department of Commerce. Then, using your real name, now elevated to all CAPS, they created a legal document called the Birth Certificate. This they traded shamelessly on the stock market.

Everyone had one of these accounts, known as a Treasury Direct Account, and everyone was worth millions, some more than others depending on just how much revenue the system figured you'd generate in this lifetime. Now bear in mind that this revenue was not just your income but all the taxes you would pay from the moment you were born until you went belly up. (And I won't even get into that incredible amount as it beggars belief).

At any rate, since these accounts were known to exist and since they were in your name and tied to your social security number, what was to stop a bloke from accessing their funds? And this is exactly what several sovereign citizens had attempted to do. The first bore a name already known to me. Heather Tucci Jariff of OPPT fame.

"Oh no, not again," I groaned as Kady gushed over the news she'd been sharing with me. "Wasn't that the same gal that gave us the Courtesy Notices, none of which has born one ounce of fruition I might add?"

"Yeah, but this is different. And don't bad mouth the OPPT. They did a lot of good work. The world just wasn't ready for them. There just wasn't enough strength in numbers. Besides this is different. In this case, you actually see cash and goods arrive at your door, whereas with the other, you were just sitting round wading through legalese while some big financial institution decided whether or not to forgive your debt. Anyway, check out what happened with this dude, Randall Keith Beane. Guess he was up to his neck in debt when he saw the video on Heather's FACEBOOK page. Following the instructions given, Randy used his accounts to create three million dollars worth of CD's at several banks. From these he was able to withdraw two million and place an order for a half-million dollar mobile home!"

A half a million? Well, Beane sure wasn't messing around now, was he? Apparently it must have been a real deluxe model; and indeed it was, complete with marble floors and two bathrooms Hell, my humble abode only boasted one such throne room!!! It was beginning to sound better and better.

"And he'll be picking the thing up in a couple of weeks. So there you go. The proof of the pudding and all that. Come on," Kady concluded. "What have you got to lose?"

Indeed. There it was again. The same old question with the same old obvious answer, immortalized by such greats as Kris Kristofferson and Bob Dylan. Think *freedom's just another word for nothing left to lose* and *when you ain't got nothing, you got nothing to lose* and you get my drift.

I looked around me. Here I was living in a house the bank was getting ready to foreclose on. I'd hocked most of the stuff of any value within it and now all that was left was some shabby 1950's style furniture. Oh yeah, and those damned birds which for some reason the estate had prohibited the sale of until they were properly assessed. Now just how do you **ass**ess something that doesn't even have a righteous ass, at least not one you can find for all those fucking feathers!!!

I chuckled at my own little play on words and Kady must have taken it as a sign of consent because she quickly went to her thumb drive and accessed a file by the name of Factualized Trust. It was a six page piece of legalese courtesy the IAm Folks, and I didn't understand a word of it.

"You'll need this though," Kady explained. "Because it takes the power back into your hands in case anything ever goes to court."

Goes to court. Hey, wait a minute. I thought this was supposed to be foolproof. I raised my eyebrows and started to speak. But she was already typing my name into the allotted spaces.

"I'll print it off and you can sign it later," she noted once she'd finished. "And now on to the fun stuff."

Which involved the actual accessing of the funds themselves. Fortunately there were detailed directions on-line as to how to accomplish this feat. So after watching a couple of videos, and reading through some tutorials, we felt confident to begin.

First of all I had to find the branch of the Federal Reserve Bank where my TDA was currently held. These were scattered about the country, and the location of your particular account was designated by a letter on the back of your social security card.

My social security card had something special on the back? Well, that was news to me. But there it was. A letter followed by a string of numbers.

"Well, I'll be jiggered," I shouted. This was starting to get exciting. A game of hide and go seek with the government. But did it really have any significance? However, when Kady directed me to the webpage where all the codes were itemized, it made sense because my letter corresponded to the Deep South where I had been born and included the cities of Miami, New Orleans, Birmingham, Nashville and yes, my home town of Jacksonville, Florida.

This accomplished, we went to another website where we were able to type in the routing number of the bank. There were two given. The first was used for setting up a transfer of funds and was designated with the letters FedACH. This would simply transfer money from my TDA account to my local bank. The second was a wire transfer number should I want to wire money to pay for large ticket items such as cars, real estate, etc. I decided not to go this route yet, but to start out small and see what happened.

The truth was that I did not one hundred percent trust Kady. I suspected that she was in a bit of debt herself and using me as a guinea pig to see how this whole TDA stuff went. Then if I got the green light, she would proceed to pass GO.

Well, our first few forays into the account went OK. I transferred some money and then used it to pay a couple of outstanding bills. A week later, there had been no repercussions. As far as I could tell the bills had been taken care of since the lights were still. And better yet, I still had the luxury of both phone and water; despite my having already received a FINAL NOTICE of shut off should I fail to comply with a deadline.

Emboldened by my success, I turned my attention to the Fed Wire numbers. Hey, if Randy Beane could go for an entire motor home, I could at least outfit myself with a more modest version, something that would transport me and my meager belongings out west to where I could begin my new life in Silicon Valley. So one morning when I was feeling particularly lucky, I drove Maw's old clunker down to Irvine's Camper Sales in Marietta and picked out a nice little number for my upcoming travels. It was used, but still in great shape, a sleek thirty-one footer attached to a Toyota Tundra. The previous owner had taken it out once or twice before succumbing to a heart attack at the tender age of sixty-seven.

"Now we don't usually sell these fifth wheelers with the tow vehicle attached, but we're doing it as a special favor to the guy's widow who's a personal friend of the owner. Not too much she can do with it since she doesn't even have a driver's license. Lucky for her she lives two blocks up from the Senior Center and all. Sad about her hubby though. Poor guy had just retired from thirty-five years at the grind. Had big plans to sell everything and become a rubber tramp. That's what he called it, anyway. Guess that's somebody who vagabonds around in style. There's lots of hobo camps for these old folks, except maybe hobo is the wrong word because these campgrounds are far from free. Why, I've heard some spaces cost a pretty penny, more than you'd even pay to rent a nice two bedroom apartment. Guess it depends on where you're traveling to though."

The salesman had been going a mile a minute but clammed up when he suspected his pitch was having the opposite effect of what he'd intended. After all, it doesn't help to scare the fish out of the water with talk of hefty bills to come. Let people figure it out for themselves. What country did they think they were living in anyway? The days of the free lunch were long over in this one, and everything was on a pay as you go basis. And by the looks of the kid who stood in front of him, this was not a high roller. Jeez, would he even be able to afford toilet paper for the rig?

However, appearances can be deceiving because the threadbare scarecrow who'd been listening to Big Bob, salesman of the year for Irvine's, was quick to say *I'll take it* and even quicker to provide a routing number so as to cough up the necessary funds.

So, everyone shook hands and went home. The deal was sealed, or so everyone thought. It was just a matter of waiting for some paperwork to go through, and then this little scarecrow would be the proud owner of his own little rubber tramp castle.

Boy, oh boy, I could hardly wait and went home to pack my bags, what little there were of them.

My first inkling of trouble came when I returned to the house to find a letter from Birch Telecom. At first, I just figured it was a follow-up to the earlier letter they had sent informing me that my balance had been reduced to zero. However, this one was a bit different. The balance was back and even larger this time. So what the fuck? Puzzled, I simply paid the bill again using the same routing number because nowhere in the paperwork from Birch was any record of the Federal Reserve refusing to honor my account. Then, satisfied that I had safely navigated this little bump in the road, I sat back to wait out the arrival of the fifth wheeler into my life.

But the plot soon thickened—or sickened as it were—for several days later I got a phone call from Birch. Some lady was on the other end, and after confirming that I was who I said I was, she informed me that the account I'd used to pay my bill was one of limited participation only.

So what did that mean? I inquired, but was unable to get a straight answer. All I could deduce from the call was that the account had been paid and that was that. OK. No problem, or so I thought. Until later that night when I received an emergency text from Kady.

You need to get in touch with me, like now!!!! it shouted.

Like now? Was she serious?? It was three in the morning, not a good time to be banging on doors. ___

Whtaz up? I typed back, cuz I sure wasn't about to follow her suggestion and run right over. But whatever it was, she was not about to spill the beans on cyberspace. So all I could do was put on a pot of coffee and wait for her arrival since it was definitely going to be my place, not hers.

I heard her tires screech as she pulled into the driveway, and prayed that old man Helmick hadn't fallen asleep with his hearing aids attached again. He'd already threatened to call the cops if Kady pulled that Mario Andretti routine one more time, and I sure didn't need any trouble. However, from the look on Kady's face, I was about to get a king sized helping.

"Who died?" I asked, trying to be light-hearted.

But there would be no flirtatious banter here today. The serious look on her face said it all. Something was definitely up, and I didn't like the looks of it.

She dove right in.

"You're going to have to get out of Dodge. And quick..."

"Moi?? You mean me?" I said pointing towards my chest, but she just countered the move by raising it up a few feet to indicate a slice to the neck. It was the universal symbol for *off with their heads*, and it was not a good sign.

"Randy's been busted," she began. "Went down to pick up his motor home—had the engine running and was getting ready to drive off into the sunset—when the FBI showed up. It happened a couple of days ago and yet no one posted anything until Heather got involved.

Randy? You mean the guy who ordered the 2012 Entegra Cornerstone? I was mentally patting myself on the back for my new-found knowledge of RVs. But my little ego moment was short-lived, for the next thought to enter my four in the morning brain fog was that I, too, had purchased a similar vehicle, and although it may not have come with quite the exorbitant price tag, it was still hefty enough to attract the attention of the FBI. Maybe I shouldn't have tried to up the ante so fast. Maybe I should have stuck to paying off rinky-dink phone bills. Oh me, oh my. I guess I had not learned the lesson that many a good crook swears by, and that is to never take more than the traffic will allow.

Kady must have interpreted my pause for confusion and, assuming that I needed further clarity, she began to fill me in.

"Yeah, he told the goons to contact Heather, that she was his lawyer, and it didn't take long for them to write her up as an accomplice. Guess she'd already been involved. Had pressured some veteran's financial group into accepting the withdrawals that Beane used to buy the motor home. Anyway, now there's a warrant out for Heather's arrest, but I understand that she decided not to run. Instead she's down in DC right now demanding a meeting with President Trump. The fool!!! It's just a matter of time before they toss her in the slammer, right next to Randy. Oh crap! Why did I ever get involved in this shit in the first place?"

"You...involved in this shit?" I gave Kady my hardest look. "Well, unless there is something you aren't telling me, it sounds like you're just the penny-ante thief, whereas I'm going down for grand larceny."

She lowered her eyes. "Well, I..."

She didn't need to complete the sentence. I got the drift. My suspicions about her had just been confirmed. I was her test drive, her trial run. And now that her little experiment was backfiring, there was no way in hell she'd be joining me at the precinct. Nope, I was on my own and had no choice but to do what Heather had been either too stupid or too honorable to do and that was TO RUN. And I say that in all caps, because wasn't that where all this started in the first place? With the strawman account of one NOONE _____. (And this is where I begin to protect my true identity.) Yeah, if I just stick to my first name from here on in, no one and I do mean NO ONE will be any the wiser. Or better yet, maybe I should consider changing my name to Doe, which is short for Dope, and you can read that anyway you like. Had the pot really made me that stupid? Or had the cart truly preceded the horse?

I shook my head in disbelief and went down to my bedroom of fifteen plus years to pack. It wasn't difficult. Most of my electronic gadgetry had been long pawned, and I never had owned much in the way of clothes. Kady, made shy by guilt, quietly exited out the back door, and just as quietly drove out of my life. No wheelies or donuts accompanied her exit. Guess she figured it was best to keep a low profile from here on in. It was hard not to bear her any malice. However, every time my inner dialogue cranked up with accusations, I sat it down for a good talking to.

No one held a gun to your head, I reminded myself and then laughed because, in truth, NOONE had held a gun to my head, metaphorically speaking. Ah, for a sense of humor. I prayed to God that when all this material crap was gone from my life, at least I would be left with the ability to have a good laugh.

I hoisted my rucksack and headed out to the garage where maw's trusty rusty Ford Fiesta stood waiting to carry me away. I knew I wouldn't be able to keep it for long; it was too easy to track. But it would get me to the nearest carnival where, hopefully, I could resume my illustrious career as a roustabout. There I would sell what was left of the car to the highest bidder before moving on to the next town... and the next... and the next. What do they say? That a moving target is hard to hit.

I chuckled again at the image of me on the run. It was neither poetic nor pathetic. It just was. Then, as a parting shot I remembered them. The birds. They were still cooped up in those shitty, and I do mean shitty cages, just as they had been for over a decade, and it was way past time for a prison break. Yeah, it was now or never.

Turning on my heel, I went back into the house and opened all the windows. Then, I opened all the cages and, satisfied that I had succeeded in parting the Red Sea, I watched as one by one they made their exodus. It would be a free-for-all for the bird watchers, but I didn't plan on sticking around to read about it in the morning news. I had bigger fish to fry and Ferris wheels to fly. Let's see, where might the Griens be about now? Oh, it hardly mattered. This time of year every little bum fuck town in the Midwest had a carnival to entertain them. I just had to get as far away from here as possible before I started to put in applications.

Ha! Applications! Like it was some sort of fancy-shamancy high rolling company where I was seeking employment. Hell, all those carnie folks cared about was if you could walk and chew gum. Why, most of them didn't even bother with a drug test. Oh well, it would be a means to an end. If I could possibly save up enough from a couple months of Dizzy Dragoning and add it to the cash from the sale of the Fiesta, I just might be able to get out of the country before my name went out over the wires. And if all else failed, there was always illegal immigration. I had visions of myself going the opposite direction of thousands of Mexicans down at our southern border; all of them taunting me about not knowing which way was north.

Yeah, well maybe I didn't know what end was up. But a plan is a plan, and at least I had one. Of course, I should have known better because what's that old saying? Oh yeah. *Man Plans, and God Laughs.*

Chapter 6
Lulu (AKA Stitch)
2011-2018

Seven years. It's amazing how quickly they can tick off the clock. For starters, the bulk of the first one was spent spinning my wheels as I waited for my ship to come in. Whoever said that insurance policies are easy to cash in never had one underwritten by the military. Yeah, the military, quick to receive, but reluctant to pay out. It was frustrating, but all I could do was make the best of it, researching places on my spiritual quest bucket list and then scratching off the ones that screamed NO WAY IN HELL. Places like Taklamaken in China—known as The Desert of Death; Rapa Nui in the South Pacific—which was over a thousand miles from the nearest land; and Mt. Kailesh in the high Himalayas. Now don't get me wrong. It wasn't for lack of interest. Both Easter Island and Mt. Kailesh in the Himalayas had long called to me. However, when I considered the cost of the airfare to get there, I had to sit down till the mood passed.

It was definitely more prudent to stick to the more doable venues. Some were underwater, so I wrote them off immediately. Others, like Mt. Shasta, I had already visited. Stonehenge was a must and Lourdes a possibility (though its underlying Catholicism made it somewhat of a turn-off). Then there was Giza—I had always wanted to see the Pyramids—and the big island of Hawaii and a number of South American destinations including one I had already been to—Ollantaytambo—which was about as close as you could get to where it all started.

All this was from a website which hosted the seven Merkaba centers and their corresponding power places. Like most of the stuff on the Internet, I found it confusing. You see, unlike many in my generation, I had never joined the lemming march into the sea of cyberspace, and I used technology only when I had to or when I was really bored (which was my unfortunate state while waiting for Joe's parting gift to show up in my bank account).

So I proceeded to peruse various web pages in an attempt to stitch together a travel plan. I figured on taking several years to work my way down my list and then retire to some remote location where I could live dirt cheap. There I would write that book which the Ayahuasca spirit had dictated and self-publish the thing. Because I had total undying faith in the source of my creativity, it was sure to become a best seller, thus providing me with royalties for the rest of my life.

It was a wonderful game plan. Travel, travel, and travel some more and then write until my little fingers bled, before retiring to a peaceful life of clipping coupons while I dinked around with all my other creative endeavors. Yes, like many who had gone before me, I had it all figured out. The only thing I didn't take into consideration was the rapid fire rate at which one can burn through one hundred and fifty grand, especially if one has no money management skills whatsoever.

In retrospect, perhaps I should have done what Joe intended for me to do with the money and gone back to school. Then, after a couple of years I would have had some kind of degree, one good enough to land me a job shelving books at some small town library. From there, I could have worked my way up the corporate ladder until I was the head honcho, small town libraries not being too particular about demanding higher degrees from their staff.

Yes, in the end, it may have lead to a drab colorless life, but there were always the books, number one of which would be my best seller—because I could still follow the spirit's directive to write, write, write. Indeed it was an alternative reality and one which might have been more suitable in the long run. However, at the tender age of thirty-eight, I was hardly an adult, having managed to side-step most of the rituals which define adulthood in our culture. Nevertheless, I was getting ready to enter into my mid-life crisis period, a time when one rolls back the clock and attempts to recapture their ill spent youth. Indeed, with both factors coming into play, I was surely heading for a collision course and was hardly about to make the most prudent decisions. Oh well, that sad realization would come later. For the present I was busy with travel plans.

Then it finally happened. The long awaited travel funds came through, and I found myself on a big jet airliner heading for the city of London. I had decided to combine several of the sites into one big trip that would last quite a few months. First, I would do England and its famous Stonehenge. After that, I would scoot over to Egypt to take in the Pyramids—and here I had chosen to take a tour due to pressing political factors. Then, finally—and only if I had enough time—I would meander back to France and check out Lourdes. The last destination was not one which called to me. It brought to mind too many visions of humble peasant girls fabricating the Virgin Mary so they could achieve their ten minute sound bite of fame. This imagery came to me courtesy of my mother, who insisted on wearing a pendant inscribed with said Virgin's image. Yeah, dream on, lady, as if somehow by osmosis some of that goodness might rub off on you.

At any rate, it would be one step at a time. Except for the tour, which I had to set up stateside, nothing was written in stone. I had left a lot open-ended, penciling in more than ample time in England just in case I got sidetracked by one of my other passions—AKA English literature. So if I didn't end up with enough days left over to do Lourdes properly? Well… so be it. There was always another year.

Oh, how I loved this line of thinking which was easy enough to indulge in at the front end of my so-called vision quest. The money was fresh in my bank account, my heart had settled down into more predictable rhythms, and the world waited at my feet.

Chapter 7
Lulu (AKA Stitch)
Summer 2012
England

The trip across the Atlantic was unremarkable, despite it being my first. I wasn't used to traveling in an easterly direction, especially one that set the clock ahead by so many hours. So when it started to get dark one hour into my journey, I began to get spooked. In an attempt to inject some sense of normality into the flight, I did the usual, indulging in movie after movie, until I sickened with other people's drama. Then I scribbled in my notebook—chaotic, incoherent thoughts, brought about by flying too high and too long through too many time zones. Later I tried to sleep, but it was useless. I was way too wound up for my own good.

So it was a very red-eyed and jet-lagged specimen that landed in Heathrow airport. Thank God I had decided not to rent a car right off the bat, but to tour the city of London first. Somehow I made my way onto the tube, and found my stop at Paddington Station. Once there, it was a quick walk to my hotel which had the nerve to advertise itself as The *NEW* Atlantic, new meaning that it was built sometime in this century.

What a joke! The paint was peeling, the rugs were threadbare, and the windows covered with grime, which was probably to my advantage since a group of college kids on the floor above mine appeared to be engaged in some sort of barfing contest, entertaining me with the sweet sounds of regurgitation. So at least I didn't have to bear witness to the graphics associated with such a display. Exhausted, I fell into my little bed, the one whose sideboards had been etched with what surely must be every sexually explicate epithet in the world. Alas, tomorrow was another day.

However London did not impress me, and if I had structured this trip to include more time to explore its dubious charms, I would have been sorely disappointed. As it was though, I had only devoted a couple of days, during which I did the standard tourista stuff, first and foremost being recovery from that wicked jet-lag. I was so tired I even fell asleep on the River Thames tour, and all I could remember of it afterwards was the cheesy music. Likewise, Big Ben, Trafalgar Square, The Houses of Parliament, and Westminster Cathedral all passed by in a blur.

The only thing noteworthy was those weird dragons which seemed to define the boundaries of the city. There were close to twelve of them, all cast iron statues and all painted silver save for their wings and tongues. These were done up in a crimson vermilion which was way too close to the color of blood. Looking at them did not give one the warm fuzzies despite my knowledge of the dragon motif in English mythology. The Pendragon was one thing, but there was something about these creatures which did not reflect the good King Arthur. In fact, they were about as far from the Round Table as one could get, and their infernal presence was just one more reason why I was not at all disappointed to see the fair city disappear out the rear window of a train.

I was speeding back out towards the airport where I would pick up my rental, and as I did so I passed mile after mile of sprawling suburbs. The rain which seemed ubiquitous to this climate did nothing to add to the ambiance, and the whole scene was hardly my cup of tea. Yeah, cup of tea. When in England, do as the English.

I have to admit that the countryside was way more charming. My first stop was Salisbury, home to both a famous cathedral and Thomas Hardy of *Far from the Madding Crowd* renown. This last tidbit of information came to me as I stalked the streets of the town in search of tea and crumpets. Leave it to me to hone in on any and all literary references that might come my way. I couldn't help myself. It was all that excessive reading I'd done as a young adult, my escape vehicle from a family which provided me with little or no stimulation.

So it was predictable that much of this trip found a focal point in one English author or the other. This became so extreme I found myself stalking the French Lieutenant's woman on a windswept Cobb in Lyme Regis and pursuing Heathcliff across the misty moors. Neither brought much in the way of fruition as far as my mission of the spirit was concerned. However, neither did the trip to Stonehenge.

What a horrible disappointment! For some reason I thought I'd be able to walk close enough to the stones to feel the energy streaming from them. Fat chance! The whole site had been roped off so that hoards of visitors could not completely destroy it. And given the traffic, destruction was inevitable. I watched in horror as busload upon busload of tourists disembarked to snap photos and chatter in foreign tongues. Most were dressed to the nines which reflected the exorbitant cost of entry and none seemed too spiritually inclined. You could tell the sum total of their involvement with this sacred place centered on photos to brag about and souvenirs to waste money on.

I left the stones feeling as though I'd missed the boat. Years ago a guy I'd hooked up with briefly had entertained me with a story of how he'd hitchhiked around England and, being in need of a cheap flop, had been able to sleep amongst these monoliths. The guy had been pretty old, at least fifteen years my senior, so it must have been during my looking for a daddy replacement stage. At any rate, those days sure are a thing of the past. Lucky him! Shit end of the stick for me.

This pattern repeated itself at many of the other Meccas I had planned for this island. These places—Glastonbury and Avebury specifically—weren't necessarily on the Power Place list, but they still had significance as far as I was concerned. The first, Glastonbury Tor had come to my attention during my Marion Zimmerman Bradley phase. (Didn't I warn you about the possibility of this becoming a literary tour?) Well, Bradley may not qualify as a famous English Author—in truth, I believe she hails from America—but she sure did write a hell of a rendition of the Arthurian legend, one told through the eyes of the women and one which did not necessarily patronize the patriarchy of the Roman Catholic Church. I gobbled up her work in my late teens, and I have to say it provided some intense bibliotherapy. At the time I was struggling with my sexual identity and needed—no **demanded**—strong women role models and an alternative to **HIS**-story. Bradley dished up both on a silver platter, and ever since she'd cast Glastonbury as the mythical Avalon, I had longed to see it, praying that the good goddess might find me worthy of penetrating the mists and traveling back to that sacred isle.

However all I got out of Glastonbury was a dose of the crabs. Oh, it could have come from any one of the youth hostels I'd been flopping in, but the Backpacker's Hostel, an ultra-sleezy little hole-in-the-wall establishment was a likely culprit. I should have known better when I first pulled into town and found it crawling with human vermin in the form of new–agey dirtballs. They were everywhere, spilling out the shops that sold (yes, SOLD) spiritual paraphernalia and the bars where one went to suck up magic elixirs which were sure to transport you to fairyland—but which probably just hosted cheap vodka as their main ingredient.

However, I had no choice. The Backpackers was the only place in town, and if I wanted to make it up the Tor first thing in the morning, I would have to share my space with the like of such ungodly specimens. So I checked into my tiny room, painted a garish purple to complement the overall overkill, and I waited out the dawn.

Needless to say, I didn't get a lot of sleep since everyone in town seemed bent on partying like it was 1999, but the plus side was that I was one of the first out of the gate in the morning. Climbing the hill as the sun peeped out over the horizon, I was full of promise. This was what I had come for. Surely this was where the ayahuasca spirit would speak to me again. It was a struggle to get to the top, and I had to remind myself that the path is never easy. Words came to me, snips of a song I would later write about how the path may be stony and drear, but the wind and stars would guide me home, and my love would be so very near. It was enough poetry to compel me forward until, huffing and puffing, I finally achieved my goal.

Pity because nothing changed. The mists did not part to reveal the sacred isle of my soul sisters, and the only revelation came from words inscribed in a storyboard, words which told the history of this special place. As I read, I discovered that the last abbot of Glastonbury had been hung here, ostensibly **before** he was drawn and quartered. Needless to say, this was not a pleasant image, and my descent from the Tor took half the time it had taken to scale its dubious heights.

Next stop was Avebury where my disappointment mushroomed. Indeed, Avebury was worse. To begin with, I could not find the place and tooled around on the A roads, scrapping the sides of my rental on cantankerous hedgerows, until I was about to give up. Then, finally, I achieved my goal and pulled into town just in time for lunch. That in itself was a mistake as the only pub, a thatched roof relic appropriately named The Red Lion, hosted standing room only. Just like Glastonbury —and Stonehenge and Bath, and every other tourist hot spot on the island— it had been discovered and there they were, lined up in triplicate at the front door, so that even if all one wanted was a simple cup of tea , it would surely be a two hour wait. To make matters worse, most of them appeared to be bikers, grungy looking guys with lots of leather and greasy hair.

Now don't get me wrong. I've got nothing against those who ride a steal horse and in many respects admire their sense of independence and freedom. But they belong on a desert highway, not crowding the view of a megalithic monument.

I shook my head and turned to face the stones. They were huge in girth and hard to miss, having run a rugged circle around the entire town. In fact, there wasn't much to the town except the pub and the stones, meaning that my guidebook was right and there would surely be no room at the inn. Maybe in a sense this was a good thing. At least it would keep out the hordes of new age pilgrims who seemed to be drifting from one sacred site to another.

I had run into them on more than one occasion as I'd toured the wilds of Cornwall. Tintagel had also been a bust, and like Glastonbury, the only way I'd been allowed a private view of Arthur's birthplace was by jumping out of bed during the wee hours in an attempt to beat the crowds. This in itself had not been such a colossal feat since the nearby hostel I'd been staying at had been within spitting distance of the site. Plus I'd been in a big hurry to exit it because my room had been about the size of a Harry Potter closet, and the hostel itself had been carved from an old slate quarry, providing surrounding views which were far from scenic (unless you were a miner).

Oh, I had to admit that it was a novel idea. In fact, one of the selling points of my tour of England had been these International Youth Hostels, aka IYH. Some were true dumps, remodeled barns and places so rustic the sheep rubbed against the walls at night and the doors accidently locked, imprisoning you in your room. But others were close to four star hotels, with opulent stained glass windows and sweeping staircases which made you feel like landed gentry.

However, one thing they all had in common was the spirit of camaraderie that flowed through their clientele like holy water at Sunday Mass. It was over shared breakfasts and hasty conversations that I received much of my real Intel about where to go on the island. This was where I got my best tips of which roads to travel and which towns to avoid. Information flowed freely and was always delivered with a nod and a smile which made me wonder if the donor had inside information on the nature of my quest. Like the woman who ran the deluxe Blue Dolphin in Penzance, a hostel with cozy little garret rooms that boasted their own bath and shower.

"Now deary, if you want a true taste of Cornwall, you should pay a visit to Madron's Well," she offered over scones and marmalade. "There's an ancient Celtic chapel there where many go to pray. But then, if you are looking for some of that old time religion, there is always the Merry Maidens. They'll be sure to set you straight."

Madron's Well? The Merry Maidens? Neither had made my guide book which was (unfortunately) geared more towards the three star traveler than the Dharma bum.

So I followed her advice and was not disappointed, especially by the former. I found it by following a muddy path lined by hawthorn bushes and at first wondered if I had come to the right place since it featured little more than a small grotto with ruins of the chapel in the background. However it was not the building which drew me in but the myriad colorful ribbons that had been tied to the branches of a tree close to the well. They called it the wishing tree and for good reason, for each scrap of paper bore a prayer for peace. Somehow as I read them, the good intent of all the scribes flooded the place with a light of its own. I thought back to the screaming sexual comments engraved into my headboard at the Barf Hotel in London, and could not help but appreciate the juxtaposition. It was as if I had finally found my spot.

I stayed there for some time, during which I was mostly alone—a real treat after the assault to my senses delivered by some of the more popular sites. And as I sat in contemplation, I realized that perhaps the spirit does not require a sacred venue through which to speak. Perhaps the best revelations come while centered in the quiet of nature. And it was with this thought in mind that I decided to follow the advice of one of the other hostelers and head for the wilds of Wales and the poetry of the Lake District. Both were purported to be more sparsely populated areas, well off the tourist path—although the Lake District did enjoy some notoriety on account of Wordsworth and Coleridge. But what can I say? Once a literary buff, always a literary buff, and the spirit had never insisted I forsake all other deities.

Wales was wild and wonderful and reminded me a lot of the state of West Virginia back home. The only difference was the ever-present sea which was never more than a quick drive from any one of the weirdly named towns. Most were unpronounceable to me—with names like Llansantffraid and Pontrhydfendigaid—and I didn't even try to ask for directions, but just blindly navigated my way to a hostel on the outskirts of nowhere that possessed a similar ambience to Tintagel. I had chosen the place because of its remoteness and abundance of walking trails, and I ended up spending a good week there scouring the countryside in search of wildflowers to identify and ponies to befriend.

Then, when I wasn't out walking, I was touring the roads in search of Camelot, a project assisted by the Welsh who were determined to assign this distinction to every pile of rubble in the entire region. It was amazing; the place didn't even have to bear any resemblance to a castle to achieve this honor. And so many of them! Why Arthur and his knights must owned quite a bit of real estate. It was somewhat overwhelming, and in the end I simply bought a coffee mug bearing the red dragon motif of good King Arthur. I figured it would serve to remind me that some legends are best left to lie, and that some places are better viewed through the window of one's imagination.

In keeping with my need for solitude, I motored up to the Lake District where I hoped to avoid the crowds which had plagued me in the south. Maybe it had been a bad call to visit so many popular sites during the peak of the season, but what had I expected? They call the area west of London the Summer Country for a reason and as far as the excess of quasi-spirituality went... Well, I could have picked a better year. After all, it was the summer of 2012, and we humans were gearing up for the big one.

Would the world truly end on the eve of the solstice as the Maya and other doomsayers had predicted? No, probably not. It would just be—in the words of a Mayan lady I had once questioned of the matter—*different*. Yes, different. I liked the ring of that, and prayed it would be different in a good way. In the meantime, there were peaks to scale and pyramids to gawk at. So I'd best get on with my itinerary, and make some hay while the sun was still shining on this gem of a planet.

It took the rest of the summer, but in the end I felt as though I'd overturned more than a few English rocks searching for my own private Holy Grail. I had witnessed spectacular sunsets from lofty mountains in the Lake District and walked the prehistoric paths of the Ridgeway, an ancient walkway in southern England that travels for one hundred miles across the island. Following the east west migration of thousands who came before me, I explored the roots of my DNA before turning my attention to my other passion, that of English literature. I traced the route of the hound of the Baskervilles across Dartmoor and   marveled over the tiny shoes belonging to Emily Bronte which were displayed in the Haywood Museum. I watched small houseboats navigate the locks on the Avon before touring Ann Hathaway's Dove Cottage. Then I scurried on over to Oxford where I hobnobbed with intellectual snobs before stopping for a pint at an inn frequented by Oscar Wilde. It was an aggressive itinerary, but I covered as many of my old friends as I could. Lord Byron, Keats, and Shelley; Daphne Du Maurier, James Herriot, and Kenneth Graham; Beatrix Potter and Jane Austen; C.S. Lewis, Tolkien, Thomas Hardy, and Virginia Wolfe...

Oh, the list was endless, a true smorgasbord for the English literature buff, and so deeply did I immerse myself in such dusty tomes that I almost forgot the other part of my mission to this misty isle. For I, too, was to write a great novel. Yet at the moment, I had no clue as to where to begin.

Then, the revelation came to me. It was my very last day before I headed for the continent, and I had decided to journey south and take in the fabled Cliffs of Dover. However, Dover had been too far for the time I had allotted, so I ended up at a nearer cliff by the name of Beachy Head.

I walked the short distance down to the sea and stood there on the windswept beach gazing across the English Channel. At my back rose the chalky cliffs of Beachy Head and the Seven Sisters in all their glory. For centuries, these forty foot escarpments had presented the weary westward traveler with their first view of merry old England. However, for me, these breathtaking precipices would be my last hurrah. Other ports of call beckoned. Maybe they held the answer. But for the present, I could only sum up my English holiday using the words of yet another famous English poet.

I have climbed highest mountain
I have run through the fields
Only to be with you
Only to be with you

I have run
I have crawled
I have scaled these city walls
These city walls
Only to be with you
I believe in the kingdom come
Then all the colors will bleed into one
Bleed into one
Well yes I'm still running

But I still haven't found what I'm looking for
But I still haven't found what I'm looking for

Chapter 8
Lulu (AKA Stitch)
Autumn 2012
Egypt
Gabriella Rossini Interlude

It's long been said to watch what you wish for because the universe has an uncanny ability of dishing it up in triplicate. No, make that quadruplicate in this case.

I had my doubts about the trip to Egypt. For starters, I wasn't really a tour group kind of girl. I had always traveled alone and always on the cheap. But, in the case of Egypt, circumstances conspired which forced me to change my MO. To begin with, this was 2012, and let's just say the political climate in Egypt left a lot to be desired if you were an American, especially a young female traveling alone. The Arab Spring which had swept this part of the world in the early part of the decade had not overlooked the Nile Valley. There had been bloody protests, regime changes and military takeovers which resulted in the kind of political unrest that puts a country on the Travel Advisory list, and although there had been no direct attacks on US citizens, our government still instructed travelers to proceed with caution.

Since caution did not seem to equate with backpack and a footloose and fancy free attitude, I decided for once to follow protocol and hook up with a group, one that would watch my back and would provide me with safety in numbers. It was hard to find one that suited me. I wanted small and I wanted cheap, and I really don't think those two qualities mix when it comes to tour groups. But after a whole lot of Internet searching at the local library—a practice in which I do not excel—I was able to narrow down my possibilities to three. All were going my way—down the Nile—and all cost about the same, close to three grand for a ten day journey. Three grand! I cringed at the dollar amount as I watched it whittle down that beautiful lump sum that had recently been deposited in my account. But what could I do? Egypt was a must as far as those power places went and besides, I would already be in the vicinity, which meant I wouldn't have to ante up any more expensive airfare. So I looked over the details one last time and finally settled on one named Intrepid Tours, mainly because it boasted the most intimate numbers.

Yeah, you can say that again. Intimate numbers. Because despite suiting me with its overall head count, there was still that little clause about double occupancy. So since a single room was not an option with this company, I would be forced to room with a stranger. Now, this was a new first for me and would take a bit of getting used to. However, if I wanted the deal, I would have to play the game according to the rules.

I had groaned upon hitting the **Pay Now** button on their website, hoping as always that my personal info was not falling into the hands of identity thieves. Then I'd bit my xenophobic bullet and said a little prayer that they wouldn't pair me with a total nut case.

Well, all I could say was that Gabriella Cummings was not complete nutty butter. However, she was definitely a few pecans short of a fruitcake as they like to say. But since this is all about travel, let's stick to a more suitable metaphor and say that her suitcase certainly fell a few items short of a standard packing list. Not that she didn't seem to have quite a bit of baggage in said suitcase, most of which appeared to be dirty laundry.

I should have known I was in for trouble when she first walked into our cramped quarters. One look at her assured me that Mutt and Jeff we were not; in fact, it was more like the odd couple. Whoever had paired us at the travel agency had no doubt done so out of desperation since we were the only two singles to sign up. Either that or they had a severely twisted sense of humor. At least six foot tall (I topped the charts at five foot two) she had the ability to take out low hanging light bulbs if she wasn't careful. However, most animate and inanimate objects would probably do as I did and shrink away from her overwhelming beauty. Stunning was not the word for it; and even stone cold gorgeous fell short. So like many before me, my jaw dropped in deference to her splendor. In a word, I was speechless.

However, not to be put off by groveling subjects, the queen merely introduced herself.

"Hi," she began in a sultry voice. "I'm Gabriella, and I guess you must be..." and here she scrutinized the placement list given to her by the agency. "Uh, Mureen?"

I looked up. Really **up** in this case.

"Maureen," I corrected. "Though you can call me Stitch." I had discovered long ago that when confronted with royalty it was always best to come off as casual as possible. After all, as far as I was concerned, we were all in the same boat down here on Planet Earth, and if indeed the waters were rising as they said they were, then we'd best all row together.

"Marine?" she queried in a diminished tone. And it was then and there I realized she was neither stupid nor blind, but simply not a natural born citizen. And that may been the only thing I got right about her for the entire duration of the trip.

Not that she didn't try to fill me in on all the salient details. Nope. They hadn't nicknamed her Gabby for nothing. In fact, once she warmed to her narrative, she just about wore out my ear at night when we were bunkered down nursing our sore feet and trying to beat the heat with whatever tiny AC at our disposal. And in the end, though Cairo and Aswan and Luxor held untold mysteries and scenery galore, the one and only thing that ever came to my mind about the entire trip to Egypt was the stately Scheherazade who put me to sleep each night.

All the stories began in the same way.

"I was born in Croatia before the war."

"What war?" I always wanted to ask, not being much of a historian when it came to the more current events. However, I never had to because she would always fill me in on the gory events about how the Serbs came to her village and killed her parents right in front of her and then...

"...some men came and we were shipped out of the country. All girls, all young. Nobody was over the age of sixteen. Oh, they dressed us up to look like we were early twenties. Lipstick and eye shadow and padded bras. Not that the men really cared. They were there to meet the baby doll of their dreams. And probably the younger the better."

At which point she would always pause as if for emphasis before going on.

"Except for my Jay that is. He was good man and really loved me. Loved me so much I was sure he'd be leaving his wife and babies for me. But, hell, what did I know about your dirty politics at that time? He had money. That was for sure. But he wasn't no Donald Trump who could afford to buy his way from one woman to the next whenever the mood hit him."

Oh, no, not Trump again! I learned the hard way, after several nights of her monologues, that The Donald was one of her favorite American icons. She followed the tabloids as if they were *The Washington Post* or *The New York Times* and could spit out names of the stars quicker than those of our founding fathers. In short, she was exactly what she'd been groomed to be: a girl toy for the rich politicians and potential sex bait for any who did not vote as they were told.

Her paramour, one Jay Cummings was a name known even to me. Despite my apolitical leanings you can hardly ignore the guy who might be your next Vice-President. A super rich fuck from old old money, he came to the political altar complete with such sterling recommendations that one could only wonder how they had missed the cankerous sore of a kept mistress. But the Illuminati always did take care of their own, so the secret had been buried deep.

"No, my Jay. He love me, but he still wasn't able to toss away his blueblood wife for a girl of barely twenty. So he set me up in a pretty little townhouse in Georgetown and came to visit me every other week on Wednesday. And sure enough, after awhile, I am to bear his child. Oh, oh…big problem now for him, but not for me. Give me lots of bargaining chips at that table. You see my momma and poppa, they were what you call diplomats back in Croatia, and they teach me a few things. I learn to document, that is take pictures, and my Jay is all over my camera and when I ask for computer? Well, no problem. Jay knows I am bored and lonely and figures I only want to Facebook a bit. Yeah, I see your eyes rolling, but you get the picture."

Yes, I had to confess. Her narrative did have that effect, but since it was always hard to get a word in edgewise, I always allowed her free rein.

"Well, they fix my wagon. No baby. I have what you call an accident, and I live but baby goes bye-bye. I think then that it is all over. Goodbye Jay. Goodbye nice little townhouse. So I have to lay a few of my cards on table. Let Jay know that I have pictures, and that they are in safety deposit boxes in what you call a trust and the only people who can get at 'em are the editors of *National Enquirer* and, of course, me. But if I go away and don't come back? Well, guess what? They go straight to the presses."

Blackmail. Was this airhead princess capable of such a ploy? I had to admit I was beginning to question her narrative. There were too many holes in the plot. How does an undocumented illegal get access to a safety deposit account anyway? And why had her so-called diplomat parents schooled her in espionage. It all read like something out of a bad spy novel or Made for TV show. Wherever had she done her research? Netflix?

And then, it began to change. Just small details, but enough for me to realize that she was either making this up as she went along or else —and here the plot really thickens—she was smart enough to realize that loose lips sink ships. So she had attempted to cloud the waters with so much horse manure that I wouldn't be able to see my hand in front of my face. Or then, there was that last possibility, the one that simply held her to be a pathological liar with a flair for drama that would have sent those tabloids she loved so well flocking to her door for fresh turds to publish.

In one version of her story she'd been an Olympic trainee in Croatia and when nabbed had been shipped first to England. However, she'd literally jumped ship in the middle of the English Channel and had swum to shore, washing up near the same Beachy Head I had recently visited. This little detail had caused me to wonder if she hadn't been dipping into my diary when I was asleep, because who the hell has ever heard of Beachy Head? Unless of course you have been there, done that. Yet she seemed to have first hand Intel on this neck of the woods and even described the little pub where I had sat to devour my final fish and chips before leaving the country. Now, there was no way she could have come up with that detail from my journal because it simply hadn't made it to the presses. At any rate, it was here that, dripping wet and suffering from hypothermia, she had met a young couple from Scotland and...

"The poor dears! They had just lost their daughter a year before and so sad, so sad. So when I show up, they decide to adopt me. But they know there'll be all kinds of red tape, so they just pass me off as their daughter instead. You see, they just moved to a really remote island where nobody knows anything about them. So it's easy-peasy..."

Easy-peasy?? Yeah, fraud always is. But it was getting to be high-waders time since something about this plot line reminded me of a book I had just read about a lighthouse keeper and his wife down in Australia. Oh well, why not let her finish? It was just getting interesting.

"And when I grow up, they send me to Georgetown to school, and it was there I meet my Jay."

Yeah, back to Jay. At least there were a few consistencies to her story and he was one. Sometimes he'd be a Navy officer who'd been in Croatia to quell the political unrest. (Had we sent any troops? And, if so, had Cummings ever been in the Navy? I was compelled to look all this stuff up, but had no way to do so.) Other times they'd met while on a tour of Italy. (Can you say *Roman Holiday*?) But they always hooked up somehow and, good years or bad, stayed together for over a decade, at which point, he managed to conveniently croak and leave her with a shitload of money.

Yeah, the money was a given because this tour wasn't cheap. Nor were the last three she'd been on, one to Tuscany, one to Portugal and the Azores, and finally one to Dubrovnik where she allegedly tried to look up long lost relatives.

I had to admit, she was entertaining, if not just a little bit scary. My mind kept returning to a multiple of scenarios, all of which generated extreme paranoia on my part. What if she was telling the truth, and by listening to her, I was painting a target on my back? Because a good bit of her rap was all about human trafficking and sex slavery, and she wasn't shy about dropping a few household names, people important enough to have little people like me silenced for good.

So it was with a sigh of relief that we parted ways at the end of the tour. She promised to write, but I prudently gave her a fake address. Then, confident in my ability to be a moving target and ergo one that is hard to hit, I shouldered my backpack and issued my parting benediction.

"Maybe you should write a book," I suggested. "You definitely have some pretty interesting material."

And that's when it hit me that I was really talking to myself, or should I say the Spirit of the Ayahuasca was talking through me. Because wasn't this what I was supposed to be doing? And what better subject to write about than a familiar one. Indeed I, too, had a story to tell, and at least mine was true. So why not write it all down? What did I have to lose?

Well, in the end...a lot. But we'll get to that later, much later. For this was yet a seed thought that would take some time to sprout and mature into a full blown dissertation. And like that guy before me who stopped in his own snowy woods, I had promises to keep and miles to go before I slept.

Chapter 9
Lulu (AKA Stitch)
Late Autumn-Winter 2012
Half way Around the World
Lourdes to Hawaii

By the time I got to Lourdes, the die was pretty much cast. I was to write about my family, using both my father and Joe as linchpins. This impulse was so strong it prompted me to visit a place which up to this point I had shown little or no interest in, writing it off as religious claptrap that only the gullible would fall for.

The story of Lourdes is well-known, especially if you were brought up in a Catholic family. A young peasant girl is out gathering firewood one day when she comes across a strange and wondrous apparition. Because she has been heavily steeped in Catholicism all her life, she assumes it must be the Virgin Mary. This suspicion is confirmed when she brings the story back to the local priest and throws around terms like the Immaculate Conception, a concept which had only been defined four years prior. Since there was no way in hell such an ignorant peasant could ever come up with this stuff on her own, the church decided she must be genuine. The apparition had instructed Bernadette to dig and drink, and when she did, lo and behold, a spring came forth. Although small, it was easily diverted into pools where the ill and infirm came to bath.

Miracles took place. The sick were healed, the blind could see again and what eventually sprang up (no pun intended) led Lourdes to become one of the biggest tourist attractions in France. Although it hosts only a handful of these bathing pools—six for men and eleven for women—it boasts the greatest number of hotels per square kilometer of any other location in the country. That said, it would be easy to get a room, but not so simple to gain access to the bathing pools.

Not that I needed to. It would be better for humanity to save that honor for those who really had problems, and at the moment I was only in my third decade and not troubled by much except a slight arrhythmia of the heart. However, I could still view the place and why not, since it was located in one of my favorite geological formations, a cave.

Now this cave was not really much too write home about in comparison to some. It lacked the stalactites and mites that so often went with the territory, and as far as size went, it was a flea on the back of the big guys like Carlsbad and Mammoth. More like a grotto, it was open in the front and only about thirty feet deep. Inside were three irregularly shaped rooms which held the baths. The water came from a spring towards the back, its origin covered by bullet proof glass.

Yeah, bullet proof glass. I had to laugh when I saw that. What a world we had made. I wonder what Bernadette would have thought. Too bad the waters had never healed her afflictions, but she'd had a rough beginning and an even rougher end. Word had it she died in agony at the age of thirty-five and after a long illness at that. Long illness? And well before her fortieth birthday? That sure hadn't given her time to do much other than discover this spring. But if that had been her life's purpose, it sure had improved the lives of many to come.

It was a point to ponder, and as I stood reverently in front of these healing waters, I was determined to find my own way to leave my mark. The idea for a book, which had begun as a simple biography, was morphing into much more. It would be designed in such a way as to be Balm of Gilead, healing essence for those who are sick of soul and hurting in the heart. If done correctly, it could my opus, my swan song; and the beauty of it all was that I had both the time and the money to implement my plan—which, in itself, was yet another miracle.

I left Lourdes not necessarily a convert, but more of a believer. You know those kitschy little plaques that implore the viewer to BELIEVE—although they never specify exactly what one should believe in? Well, that was me. But what the hell? Sometimes it's better to follow in blind faith, because it sure cuts through a lot of the crap. After all, aren't most belief systems mainly about the blind leading the blind?

No, I wasn't about to adopt my mother's religion, any more than I was about to shave my head and chant Hari Krishna down at the corner market. But what I could do was offer an olive branch to any who might be out there who felt as I did—that it was high time the waters receded to reveal a New Earth. Yes, it was time to release a dove.

Dove. How strange that that is one of the few words in the English language that rhymes with love.

So I gathered up the tools of my trade—alliteration, metaphor, and rhyme—and readied myself for my next port of call. My plan was to return to the states for a brief respite and then, since it was getting on towards winter, avoid the bulk of the bad weather by transporting myself to a tropical isle. And I had just the place in mind. For hadn't my sources informed me that our fiftieth state shared the honor as one of Gaia's power places?

And hallelujah! I would be showing up there just in time for the Winter Solstice, AKA 12/21/12. Now how's that for some heavy numerology? I always was fascinated by palindromes, and this one took the cake—or so the Ascension cult maintained.

Of course, they might be a bit off in their predictions. So just in case, I had come up with a plan B. If by chance we all did not experience some sort of apocalyptic rapture on the eve of the winter solstice, I would sit out the rest of a wicked Ohio winter basking on balmy beaches and preparing a rough draft of what was sure to be the next *War and Peace*. Then I would return to the states again before embarking on yet another pilgrimage, this time to the South American pulse points, one of which I had already visited. However, it was important to remember that, despite the pearls of wisdom flowing from my pen, I was still on a mission with four doable power points down and four more to go.

Oh, maybe I was a tad full of myself, but a bulging bank account will do that to a girl who up to this point had been subsisting on hand to mouth peanuts. I guess you might say that I, too, was partying like it was 1999 (or December 20, 2012).

A month later I was on my way to Kauai, better known as the Garden Island which should have given me a clue as to how much rain to expect there. My plan was to hike its lush trails for about three weeks, just long enough to see me through the apocalypse—should it really decide to grace our presence—and then head over to the Big Island to do some serious writing. In order to initiate this plan effectively, I had purchased a small pup tent, a large back pack, and an assortment of gear which filled it to the brim. It was heavy enough that, when I walked, it made me look like SpongeBob, Square Pants, all boxy and top heavy. The only thing lacking was his indelible grin, because carrying all that weight sure didn't make for a happy camper. Oh well, it was only temporary as I had booked a bona fide roof over my head for my time on the Big Isle. I figured that, by then, I would surely appreciate the modern conveniences, and boy, oh boy, had I figured right.

However, all this would be seen through the hindsight that is well known for its 20/20 vision. For the present I was merely contemplating my journey, having just passed over the patchwork quilt of Kansas and the barren expanse of Nevada. It wasn't much of a view, but as I was flying TWA—AKA Tight Wad Airlines—and I really didn't have too much else to do. Unless you wanted to count paying five bucks for bad movies and mediocre music; and for some reason, despite my recent windfall, I was already starting to pinch pennies. There were a lot of Merkaba sights left to see, and so far I hadn't even started chapter one of the book I was set to write. Hence, my decision to camp on Kauai, which would be the best budget way to see the island.

So I settled into the thirteen hour flight. Thus far it had been my longest journey, and my body, though much younger than many who occupied the cabin, was not relishing the prospect of sitting in a tin can for all those hours. Take Sally, for instance. She sat beside me, and though not much of a talker, was still able to give me a brief rundown on the purpose of her visit to our fiftieth state.

"I'm a retired school teacher," she explained, "And this is my retirement trip. A group of us decide that we needed to see the USA a bit without our hubbies in tow."

Hubbies? That term of endearment sure dated her, but I didn't comment and fiddled with my earplugs instead as if to signal that I wasn't in the mood for a thirteen hour conversation.

But apparently, neither was she because she got out a book, predictably Daniele Steele, and proceeded to enter into a marathon read. So I went back to my inspection of the view outside the window and didn't pay her much mind again until we landed at Honolulu airport.

And that was when I experienced my first twinge of the loneliness which was to accompany me for the duration of my walkabout on the Garden Isle. For Sally, my mostly silent seat mate, and her bevy of blue haired companions were the first off the plane, and as I watched them exit the airport concourse, I couldn't help but notice the brouhaha that met them. Young coffee skinned men with ready smiles and fragrant leis awaited, and did that ever cause a few old school teachers to crack a smile. You almost expected their faces to break in two. It had probably been a long time since they'd been allowed to show any real emotion, having adopted what is known in the profession as a stern no-nonsense look. It was one which had frozen their faces in place over a thirty year career and one that every kid learns to respect, then hate. I didn't know whether to laugh or cry. Where was my lei? My brown skinned man?

Oh well, another place, another time. And trying not to feel too sorry for myself, I hoisted my fifty pound pack and shuffled over to the inter-island flight that would take me to Kauai.

The island was quick to live up to its name. Beautiful is way too tame for the Maxfield Parrish painting that greeted me upon arrival. But a Garden Island depends on water, so it's understandable that Kauai would get its fair share of rain. Now, I had planned my trip accordingly, arriving in what was supposed to be the dry season. But note that I used the adverb *supposedly* to clarify this statement, and we all know about adverbs in writing—that they are considered weak and reflect the author's inability to find a more suitable word.

OK, so let's try out a few. Precipitation just doesn't cut it. Let's try tropical downpour, torrent, and even deluge for starters; then hope we don't graduate to an out and out flood. Not being fair, you say? Well then, I guess I'll stop at showery, drizzly and damp with an occasional raining cats and dogs thrown in for good measure. But I assure you that I experienced all of the above during the three weeks that I trod the soggy trails of this Pacific gem.

I started with an unscheduled stop. Since I was only going to be on the island for less than a month, during which most of my travel would take place on foot, I had spared myself the expense of a rental car. However, this meant I would be dependent on the kindness of strangers in order to haul both my skinny ass and my oversized pack around. My first ride almost caused me to reconsider this decision.

"Sure, hop on board. But we're heading over to Mile marker 14 first, before we go up the Canyon," they informed me.

And since the Canyon—Waimea to be exact—was my first destination, I was happy to comply. So what if there were a few side trips? Wasn't that what it's all about? Going with the flow? Allowing the experience to find you?

Well, not necessarily, especially when the experience involved stripping off all one's clothes and walking butt naked across an expanse of sand where huge waves threatened to gobble you up and spit your bones back upon the shore. Since this was not for the faint of heart —meaning yours truly—I opted out and remained back at the parking lot, fully clothed and feeling a bit out of sorts. But what could I say? A ride's, a ride, and sometimes you have to take the flies with the horse.

Thank God that was our only detour, and the happy couple who I'd hitched a ride with was quick to deposit me at the head of the canyon, which by the way, has earned its reputation as a second Grand Canyon. Though nowhere near the grandeur of the one that straddles the southwest, it still is a pretty good runner-up. The lack of vegetation on much of its acreage testifies to its location on the leeward side of the island. Therefore, it was *supposed* to be spared the brunt of the weather which marched across the Pacific. But there's that word again—*supposed*—and in this case it does hold water. Lots of it because this was just one of those unusual years where previous predictions were thrown out the window. Alas, the rainy season had been extended, or else had come in early. Or maybe it had just known I was on my way because it sure had greeted me with a big bang. Lucky me to have chosen such a year to walk the paths of this natural wonder of the world. But walk them I did, often wearing an improvised raincoat made from a trash bag. I tried them all, the Piheau Trail with its hard-won lookout, the Nualolo and Awaawaapuhi trails which offered such spectacular views of the Pacific I swore I would request my ashes to be tossed from their lofty peaks, and even the infamous Alaki Swamp trail (and the word swamp explains why this was my shortest hike of all).

My world became a hodgepodge of images. Macadamia nuts from a Chinese flavored Wal-Mart, scary strolls across razor edged ridges which dropped twenty five hundred feet on either side, scimitar shaped koa leaves, fellow hikers clad only in bikinis (one who was accompanied by a gorgeous specimen of a man who wore a red flower in his hair), the feel of the red clay dirt beneath my feet, and always the blue blue horizon below. Because although the rain was excessive for this time of year, it fell mainly at night, or else graced us with those brief, yet powerful, downpours the tropics are so famous for.

So though it was challenging, I probably got my money's worth (or at least what little I was paying to camp in such adverse conditions). I started out at Kokee campground at the head of the canyon and later relocated four miles inland to Kawaikea campground which was much better in the sense that it actually had a sheltered picnic table. This meant I was no longer confined to my tiny pup tent at night, listening to the steady drip on the plastic I had so wisely purchased to cover its flimsy frame. Within its musty confines I had tried unsuccessfully to find a channel on the radio which did NOT call for more rain in the forecast. I guess it could have been worse as on more than one occasion I was assured there was flooding down below.

So, I made the best of it. Despite the dampness, there were moments of extreme wonder. Incredible tropical foliage surrounded me as I passed though enchanted groves of Jurassic ferns and Pilo Trees. Birds of another feather sang to me from the treetops, and I did my best to warble back a sisterly greeting. As my days and nights were mainly spent in solitude, my feathered friends often provided my only interaction.

Not that I was as xenophobic as one guy. He had been living at the end of a trail, which afforded me a stunning view of the canyon. I chanced upon his hobo camp one day while hiking the ridge out to

Kokua vista and concluded that he must have really liked the view because he sure didn't have much else going on. A rumpled sleeping bag, a poncho, a black plastic tent, and a can of Sterno reflected his only belongings. Talk about getting it down to a deck of cards. I didn't know whether to envy his Zen-like simplicity or pity him. But as his little camp gave me the creeps, I decided on the latter and turned a quick tail.

Darkness was coming, and I had a ridge to run before nightfall crept in on its six o'clock feet. Then it would be time would to retire to my own little cave. Here I would listen to the Hawaiian radio stations which, when not bemoaning the recent bout of bad weather, would play endless songs of love and redemption. Listening to them caused me to ponder what beautiful sweet people these Hawaiians are. The love they speak of is not always your garden variety involving man and woman but more LOVE taken to its highest order. Song after song featured words of peace, harmony and unity, making for real easy listening.

I was reminded of the Hawaiian concept of Ho'ponopono. This is easily summarized by four simple statements—I'm sorry; please forgive me; thank you; I love you—all which can be addressed to either oneself or others. Spoken from the heart, they pretty much cover all the bases, making them a very useful meditation for the healing of emotional wounds. And speaking of which, it was during these long nights when I began to summarize some of what I wanted to say about my family.

So far I had been scratching out notes using a three ring binder divided into five sections, one for each member of the family. The ones pertaining to my father and Joe had the most notations, but nearly all were mere peristalsis charts, stuff like dates when they entered service and battles they had fought in. However, it was with my mother and Davey that I really got going, and it was here I realized I would have to tone it down a bit. After all, I was not shooting for a Tell-All expose. Even Pat Conroy of *Great Santini* fame had enough sense to change the names to protect the guilty.

So then, what was I shooting for? Whatever it was, the military factored deeply into the picture. How could it not when two members had been actively engaged in four major conflicts, spanning almost fifty years of our nation's history. With my father, it had been Korea, then Vietnam. That had been bad enough. But then Joe, despite having grown up in a post-Nam era, had managed to enlist in an institution which had become famous for nasty little wars. I attributed his recklessness to several factors, the first and foremost being testosterone. However, the violent video games he'd been spoon fed at a tender age did little to curb his high levels of the hormone. In fact, one couldn't help but wonder if it had been part of the agenda all along, a way to draw the average eighteen year old into a life that would be perceived dangerous and exciting. Yeah, forget the danger, as the heads that rolled were never your own. Until that is, you hit the mine field and watched your best buddy blow up right in front of your eyes. Then no matter how much you'd been desensitized to violence, suddenly it was all real.

What was amazing was that Davey had never fallen for the same line. But Davey had fought his own battles very early in life, battles brought about by his cherub-like good looks and ones which may have caused him to question his ability to exist in an all male environment. So he'd stuck to cultivating a macho image back home, as a hard-drinking tradesman and slayer of every female barfly he could find. Alas, Dave's image of women had focused on only one aspect of a good Catholic boy's ideal. Out of virgin or whore, he had definitely chosen the latter. Women were mountains to conquer and then bulldoze into oblivion. He never had been able to maintain a long term relationship. Hell, he'd never been able to maintain a relationship that lasted longer than a week.

The way he collected pubic scalps could have given us reason to wonder. But not all of us. I knew why. So did our illustrious mother who had threatened to wash his mouth out with soap if he ever said one more word about that good Father McCory. Yeah, denial runs deep when you're a devote Catholic. I couldn't help but wonder how the old ostrich was taking the breaking news about the rampant rash of pedophilia in the Church. Must be hard to finally face the truth after all these years. Too bad it had left so many broken beyond repair—or FUBR as they like to say in the military.

At any rate, I would have to be careful how I presented this information. It was shame and scandal to the max and there was really no way to deal with it delicately. Maybe I should just leave it out. After all, wasn't that the way I'd been trained? To sweep the gory details under the rug? Of course, I could just treat the book as if it were a fictional account. This way no one would be any the wiser, unless they were a personal friend of the family and, believe me, when you were as high up in the military hierarchy as my dad had been, there were quite a few friends of the family. Indeed, it was a dilemma, a *damned if I did, damned if I didn't* sort of deal.

I mean, how can you write about stuff unless you've had first-hand experience? You need to have some kind of working knowledge about your material, which is why most writers focus on some version of themselves. But do you ever really know yourself? Doesn't the story keep changing with your perception of the events? Yeah, maybe that's why Pat Conroy got five or six stories out of his fucked up family, all just variations on a central theme.

Oh well, it would come. I knew it would. I just had to have faith and believe. So with those final thoughts in mind I would lie down on my hard little bed and listen to the steady dripping of the rain off the Sugi Pines until the inevitable happened and I fell into a deep dreamless sleep. Then the next day would be a repeat performance of the day before. There wasn't much stress. Just eating and hiking and reading and writing, and before I knew it my time at Kawaikea had ended. I had applied for a permit for only two weeks, and I was on day fourteen. This meant I would have to break camp (in the morning drizzle) and hike back to Kokee. There, with any luck, I would be able to catch a ride back to the coast where a state park awaited me.

The state parks differed from the national ones in that you didn't have to have a permit, and could camp for free, which sounded like a really good deal for the itinerant vagabond. But there was a hitch. There always is. In order to discourage permanent guests, the authorities had ruled that one day a week all the campgrounds would be closed for cleaning. In other words, dusting the bums. Now this might seem harsh as it forced many a homeless family to evacuate on a weekly basis. So in order to take the sting out, these same authorities decreed that each state campground would designate different days of the week for cleaning. That way at least one would be open at all times, thus assuring a free roof over one's head on any given day.

I had timed my exit so that I would (hopefully) arrive at the state park of my choice to find it squeaky clean. That way I would be first in line for my pick of campsites. However, I had not factored one little detail into my plan, that being the infamous 12-21-12. Oh, my gosh! Was it really so late in the month? And did I really want to be that close to population on such an auspicious date? Maybe I should wait another day before I crawled out of the woods. Give the smoke a chance to clear, so to speak. But it wouldn't do to stay here. The rangers came by every night to check on the place, and they damn sure had memorized the expiration date on my permit. No, I had no choice but to evacuate. But it didn't mean that I would have to go all the way down the canyon. There was more than one way to skin this cat.

Oh, I did pack it up, but left most of it well concealed in a patch of tree ferns and wild ginger. Then, with only a skeleton pack on my back —my trusty little Jansport to be precise—I hot footed it down the very same trail where I'd found the hobo camp. My hope was that the guy had either moved on, or if not, wouldn't mind sharing his space for a night. His had been a perfect location for the end of the world, and that said, I hit the trail in search of a suitable place to wait out the apocalypse.

It was a dumb move, and I knew it; and I guess I was lucky to find the camp deserted. What would I have done had some surly Charles Manson awaited me? Would I have merely smiled and ask him to join me for a delicious dinner of Top Ramen? Perhaps shared his sleeping bag in a last ditch attempt to achieve that ultimate orgasm?

It's hard to tell. I wasn't too big on foresight back then, and I'm not so sure I'm any better now. Let it suffice to say that the Lord looks after drunks and young children, and thank you lord, because my decision to go AWOL from the National Park Police resulted in one of my best nights on the island.

For starters, the scenery was astounding, a long languid bird's eye view of the red clay convolutions of the canyon, made even more stunning as the deep colors of evening set in. I stayed at the edge as long as humanly possible. Then, fearing that one minute more and I would join the birds which rode the thermals, I forced myself back to my borrowed camp. There was no picnic table under a pavilion to greet me, no tent save some flimsy plastic I had draped over a tree. Still I felt more peace and comfort than I had since my time in Peru and later fell into the deep sleep of a newborn, confident in the ability of the planet to refresh itself one more time while the universe looked after its own.

Sure enough, I opened my eyes to a new morning. No black hole had swallowed us in the middle of the night. No smoke and brimstone had rained down from the heavens. The only subtle difference came from the sun which was actually peeping through the clouds for a change. It was rising in the east (as it always had) and as I gazed down the canyon, I realized it was signaling my next destination. The little state park on the coast was calling and with it would come fresh fruit and drier weather, as well as an increased interaction with my fellow man. I had to admit I was ready and impressed even myself with how fast I made tracks down the canyon that morning.

I didn't even stop for coffee and sweet rolls at Kokee Lodge. I was in that big of a hurry and lucky thing because had I waited I would have missed one of the few rides heading in my direction. It came in the form of a bright yellow school bus, whose driver had just deposited his load at the Kokee Discovery Center. Apparently, such field trips were part of the curriculum on this little island, making me wonder if maybe I should go back to school and get a teaching certificate. That was what Joe would have wanted when he left me all that money. It was a shadow thought that rained a bit on my parade that morning but only as far as Salt Pond State Park where, just as I had suspected, I was able to cherry pick the perfect campsite.

It had both sun and shade and was but a stone's throw to one of the sweetest strands of water I had ever seen. It was a perfect place for a morning, noonday or evening swim, and I planned on taking advantage of all three. Plus it was within walking distance to Hanapepe, a small yet prosperous town which featured an abundance of restaurants and mom and pop stores. There were even a few art galleries thrown in for good measure, and I was sure a walk around the place would make me feel like a civilized person once again. Besides, it might be a good way to ease me back into the presence of other people on the planet, some of which were already setting up camp nearby.

So I did what I had done best for so many days and set out for a stroll. I was not disappointed. Not only did I find a great Chinese restaurant which filled me up with enough take home to last several days, but I discovered a cheap little thrift store where I splurged on a few Hawaiian shirts. I figured on one for myself and one for Davey, who would probably never wear it being a jeans and black tee shirt kind of guy. But what the hell? It's the thought that counts. Then, take-out and fresh fruit in hand, I returned to Salt Pond just in time to catch a rainbow illuminating the hills above the town. I could tell from my view of the mountains that it was still raining up above and was grateful for the sun on my back and the wind on my cheek.

Town had also given me an opportunity to oil my rusty vocal chords which was a good thing because as soon as I got back to camp, I realized there was a party going on. Some Hawaiians had assembled at the public pavilion and were playing music. Their leader turned out to be a guy named Tony who was presently the camp caretaker. However, he too had come from a place of solitude, having been born on Nihua, the forbidden isle.

"I left there when I was only fourteen," he explained to me. "And I never went back. It's sad. The community there is falling apart. The young people…" And at this, he shook his head.

Yes, I understood, for I'd heard tales of Nihua, a community of about two hundred souls who lived without electricity and roads. It made me think of that song, *King of the Road.* No cars, no pools, no pets, ain't got no cigarettes.

"Guess it's hard to keep 'em down on the farm once they've seen Parree," I relied, and he winked at me and pointed in the direction of some recently arrived Germans.

"Crazy people," he chortled. "Bunch of them started taking their showers in the buff. Had to get Sammy to go over there and tell them to put their clothes back on." And he sighed which was understandable considering the dimensions of some of the tall Valkyries that graced the group.

I laughed. Boy, was this a far cry from last night. And though I had really relished my solitary retreat and the possibility of a pending accession, I was grateful the delicious diversity of the human race had been spared to party yet another day.

Daniel Rose

However, that thought was put to the test the next morning when, instead of awakening to the sound of twittering birds, I was jarred from my sleep my raucous laughter. As I emerged from my tent I realized that sometime during the night an entire family of Hawaiians had set up camp within ten feet of my tent. Although I felt as if my space had been violated, there wasn't much I could do about it. So I just ate the rest of my Chinese food, knowing it would not live to see another day. It was my game plan to digest a little, then write a little, and then go for a long swim. Of course, when there are other people around it is so easy to become distracted.

She caught my attention right away. I don't know which of us had a red light flashing on their forehead, but as like often attract like, she came to me like an exotic bird in search of a Hibiscus flower, except that such a metaphor is way too gracious when you are describing two Dharma bums. I could tell from the look of her that she'd been on the road about as long as I had, maybe longer. Her hair, though washed clean by the Pacific, was in sore need of a trim, and her clothes had seen better days. I immediately pegged her as one of the semi-homeless the state parks catered to, and figuring she was after a bite to eat, I began to offer up some lo mein. However, as soon as she opened her mouth, I realized, once again, what a great deceiver one's appearance can be.

"Hi, I'm Iynet," she offered, and with her delivery I knew this not her real name, and that she certainly wasn't from around here. I was right on both accounts, although only one was verified by our conversation. As it turned out she was what I would refer to as a JAP, or Jewish American Princess, brought up in all the right neighborhoods and educated at all the best schools. However, like my upbringing, something had gone array, far enough array to lead her to be living in her car on a faraway beach.

"When I came here, I was writing a piece on the native Hawaiians," she confessed, "And that's when I met him. Eokepa. He was truly one of the most gorgeous men I'd ever seen, but that wasn't what set the hook. He's a messiah, you know. A true believer in the prophecy that the Hawaiian people will rise again."

And at this, she must have caught my look of skepticism.

"After the second coming, of course," she continued, even though, just like me, she must have realized that one potential date for such a blessed event had just passed. Not that this mattered much to her. She chattered on, mostly about Eokepa, who had just left her to go on an extended walkabout which as far as I could tell had been standard operating procedure for the duration of their stormy relationship.

I don't know why, but I liked the woman. She was a high powered rifle, as far as her non-stop monologue went, but at least it was articulate and **consistent**. I couldn't help but flash back on my last parasite, the one who had attached herself to me during my tour of Egypt, and gave thanks for that much.

However, after twenty-some minutes of her prattle, I was ready for that morning swim. But when I suggested as such, she had a better idea.

"I know a great hike, but it's about five miles from here."

OK, now she was talking my language, even though I could read between the lines. Five miles meant we needed a car to get there. She had a car, but it was probably low on gas. So for a slight stipend, she'd be glad to accommodate me. It was your classic case of *you scratch my back, I'll scratch yours*. And I had to admit she sure was good at getting my number because she knew just where that little itch was beginning to form.

"Sure," I found myself agreeing, and that's how I managed to hike one of the loveliest trails on the island. Verdant green mountains gave way to razorback ridges which, once navigated, gave birth to long languishing views of the sea. All the while Iynet entertained me with tales of Eokepa, to the point that I was sure she must be trying to conjure up his spirit.

It was spooky thought and spookier still when, upon our return trip, we were cruising down the streets of Lihue in search of the perfect smoothie and encountered the man of the moment instead. He was all she had described, tall, bronze, and gorgeous and emitting a certain mysterious air which forced one to believe he did indeed talk to the spirits of his ancestors.

Of course, we braked for such a specimen, and of course Iynet convinced him, once again, to come in off the range where he'd been roping metaphorical stars. Yes, desperado, you've been out mending fences for way too long.

The way she catered to him was both frightening and enlightening and made me really glad that, ever since Jeremy, I had not succumbed to the call of the guru. As I watched their interaction, it became obvious he had bound her in the stickiest sort of glue, her desire for all things spiritual, and I realized that there but for fortune (and a reduced sex drive) would go I. Fortunately though, I had come to the conclusion long ago that   messiahs do not make good husbands, if indeed, it was a husband I sought. I shook my head and listened to his tales of how he had once buried himself in the sands at Polikale, an alien landscape of high waves and enormous black cliffs. Here the grandmothers had spoken to him of a reef that runs all the way to Nihua, the forbidden isle. It used to be that you could walk straight there without swimming through shark infested waters, but now the old ways are forgotten. He'd gone from this tale to an extensive rap about names. (I never did find out either his or Iynet's Christian one—if indeed, they even could even be considered Christians, being more of a pagan persuasion than anything else.)

"You need to find your name," he instructed me in a tone which indicated he was used to respect. And I shook my head again.

He was right. Who was I anyway? Mary? Maureen? Moira? Stitch? All of the above or none of the above? Was it time to dump them all and branch out into new territory? Not that I was about to fall victim to this guy's line of BS. In one sense, I prayed his world did come to pass. We needed to return to the old ways of the indigenous people. We had lost so much when we bulldozed them into oblivion, and one could not help but wonder if that had not been the plan all along

However, another part of me prayed that those who fell prey to his lines were able to walk away when necessary. This included my new found friend Iynet. May she discover a way to straighten her world out with or without him.

But I never stayed in Salt Pond or even Kauai long enough to see the end of their particular passion play. Other destinations were calling, as was my own life's purpose. That book wasn't going to write itself and besides, a little Airbnb in Honoka'a was waiting. I had booked it in advance for the remainder of the winter, figuring it would be as good a place as any to begin my masterpiece, and I hoped it would not disappoint me. However, it wasn't a bad idea to check out the competition to make sure I had found the best spot for my purpose. So, after disembarking in Kona, the Big Island's airport, I decided to rent a car and do a little touring.

As soon as I stepped off the plane, I was acutely aware that diversity was the name of the game here. First off, the place was yang to Kauai's lush yin—very spartan and male, and the youngest island in the chain. Stark lava lands stretched out in all directions forming a rugged lunar landscape that would have been considered bleak by many. The locals had done what they could to counteract the effects of such monotony by taking white coral and arranging it into a host of messages for all to see. There were your usual peace signs and *Joe loves Sally* and one which proclaimed that *Jesus is Love*, but mostly it was just weird graffiti that bore meaning only to its creator. I tried not to be distracted as I steered my car towards town.

But distraction is something that is hard to avoid when it comes to Hawaii. Circumnavigation of the Big Island convinced me of one thing, that if I didn't like the scenery (or the weather) I should wait five minutes because, by then, it would be entirely different. In the span of twenty miles, I went from lava beds to green valleys and from sea level to a little over thirty-five hundred feet. There were high pastures aplenty, with rolling fields and contented cattle. There were windswept beaches, many of them composed of the famous black sand. There were waterfalls rushing down to the sea and cliffs rising up to meet the heavens. There was flora and fauna too abundant to name, and just when you were about to give up trying, you would round a bend and begin to head back towards the volcanoes.

A tour of that part of the island was like visiting the seven concentric circles of hell complete with   sulfur, steam, fire and brimstone. It looked like the world's largest slag heap and would only appeal to a geologist or a follower of the cult of KaliYuga. Stupidly, I chose to navigate the Chain of Craters road which involved a steady drop from four thousand feet to sea level. Lava flowed on both sides of the highway, looming like powerful monoliths to some ancient god. The landscape on both sides reflected the powerful urge the earth has to renew herself. Through the numerous cracks left by the lava peeked tiny ferns and Lehua trees that were struggling to find a toe-hold. Some would survive the fiery fury of Pele's eruptions, and in another six million years or so, this island would resemble Kauai, with red clay hills and supercharged soil. It was all in the power of evolution, the ever present, ever constant flow of life on this planet to its ultimate end; and watching just this minor demonstration of its force made me feel small indeed.

It was a humbling experience and one that would be repeated every time I decided to crawl out of my bungalow and wander around the island. But for now, I had internal affairs to attend to. With a slight feeling of regret, I turned the car around and headed back towards Honoka'a. On the way I passed Waipio Lookout where I decided to undertake my last detour for awhile. I would descend into the valley below, one which had been made famous by its abject remoteness.

Its isolation was a quality which appealed to the wanna-be writer in me, and at one point I had considered staying there for the duration of my retreat. However, as I walked the increasingly steep mile down into the depths of the valley, I thanked the good Lord I had sat down until this mood had passed. It was the kind of terrain even a goat would find challenging, a twenty-five percent grade which swallowed any car not in possession of four wheel drive. When I finally attained the bottom there were a few rusting cars scattered about that had been unable to make the return trip, and even the working vehicles looked exhausted, making me wonder how their owners managed with   simple tasks like returning books to the library. It certainly wasn't the kind of place where you ran out at regular intervals to pick up some beer or (God Forbid!) a pack of smokes, and a quick look around assured me I had made a wise decision to stay clear. Isolation was one thing, but inaccessibility was another.

As if to punctuate my thought, the journey back to the main road proved even more difficult than the downhill run. At times I really had to watch my step so as to avoid sliding backwards, and it was with a sigh of relief that I reached the welcoming seat of my rental car. Yeah, some places just weren't for the faint of heart, and by the looks of things, Hawaii had more than its share.

So I called it a day and pointed the car towards the quaint yet navigable town which I would call home for the remainder of the winter. My quarters had once been part of a hostel, at least until the turn of the century. Before that the building had served as a haven for gamblers, a place where folks sat down on long tropical evenings to fritter away their pay. But now it was merely a series of converted rooms with adjoining baths, all of which shared a common kitchen. My wing was home to a retired widow—a septuagenarian by the looks of her skin—who fed a total of five semi-feral cats. Right off the bat, I tried to befriend them, but was rewarded only with scratches.

So I retired to my self-imposed solitude and began the project which had been gnawing at me for so long. I had pages and pages of notes, most of which were semi-legible and disorderly. It would take the better part of a month to sort them all out, and then I would begin the true task, that of transcribing them into some sort of marketable manuscript. In order to expedite the job, I had purchased a small laptop, even though I rebelled against anything that had to do with technology. But gone were the Jack Kerouac days when you wrote it all out in long hand on one continuous roll of paper. So like it or not, I would have to play the game according to the new rules.

The winter was long and tedious at times. My quarters were cramped, and I often felt like I was in a tomb. The widow next door preferred the company of her feral felines to my smiling face, and the locals seemed preoccupied with their own lives. So I stuck to myself, emerging occasionally for walks about town. Its wooden structures were fun to explore, and its bakery provided me with ample goodies for those days when I didn't feel like cooking. It wasn't much of a life, but then again, I wasn't there for the bar scene. If I wanted the big city, I should have stayed home.

However, sometimes I would get terminally bored or come down with a bad attack of writer's cramp. At that point, I would call up the nearest Enterprise and have them deliver a car so I could scoot around the island in search of the perfect picture. There were so many interesting sites it would have taken a lifetime to explore them all, especially since many were remote enough that only a Sherpa could gain access to them.

But others were more doable, like Hilo with its famous fish market and spooky tsunami museum. Or Hakuna Beach, where Mauna Loa could be seen in the distance at sunset, a reigning queen amongst the blue green hills. Sometimes I felt like I was in a dream. Tropical islands are like that, which is why they are so hard to leave. But time waits for no one and marches on, a relentless stream of army ants, devouring all in its path.

So one day the inevitable happened, and I found myself once again at Kona airport boarding an inter-island flight for the big city of Honolulu. My suitcase was a bit heavier this time as it sported at least two hundred pages of my manuscript. But my heart? Well, it was a little lighter for having gotten so much out on paper.

I guess you could call it exorcismic writing. That's my word for it anyway, and it has quite the cathartic effect, packing a punch that can send you to your knees if you don't watch out. In retrospect, I should have been more mindful, for these things need to be done carefully and often require the assistance of a priest. In short, beware of rubbing that bottle too hard; you never know what sort of genii you might release.

Chapter 10
Lulu (AKA Stitch)
Summer 2013 to Summer 2014
Cincinnati to the Azores

I first started having problems on the way back home, but wrote it off to jet lag and travel travails. Bear in mind that up to this point, I had never been too much of a jet setter. So a thirteen hour flight, no matter how many layovers, is still a bit of a stretch. I looked around me at my fellow passengers in coach. Many were much better prepared with fancy headrests, sleep masks, and their own library of down-loaded movies. Sighing, I turned my attention back to the headache that was forming behind my left eye, not that it had been easy to ignore.

Headaches had always been my bane, but this one was different, a real ball-buster, and made me regret once again that I had forgotten to buy some gum back at the airport. It had been another oversight, a little detail that was so obvious to the well-traveled but easily forgotten by the novice. Oh, I had been warned about the extreme changes in cabin pressure common on international flights. But this was the first time in my travels that I had experience their crippling effect, and the only reason I could fathom for my discomfort arose from what appeared to be a really steep descent into the St. Louis airport. It was the first and last of my layovers before I hit my home turf, and as I white knuckled the seat, I prayed that relief would come soon. My only consolation came from the realization that at least it was a controlled descent, and we were not simply falling out of the sky. However, if this had been the case, all the surrounding passengers would have been screaming or clutching rosaries and instead they all seemed peacefully engaged in those little tasks which signal the end to a long flight, stuff like stowing their laptops and hitting the head for once last leak.

Somehow I must have caught the attention of a stewardess because, as she issued the customary instructions about tray tables and seat positions, she stopped to inquire if I was alright. My gray around the gills look said it all, but at that point the damage had been done.

"Try yawning," she suggested, before moving on down the aisle, and I knew that, once again, I was on my own. Not a pleasant thought when you are experiencing pain right up there with childbirth.

Thank God, it ended once we hit the tarmac, and along with everyone else, I shuffled out to meet my connecting flight. It was four in the morning, and I had just traversed through six time zones, so I was a bit disoriented. However, it was nothing that a strong cup of coffee and Danish couldn't fix. So I mustered my bravado and set my sights on the nearest Starbucks.

It remains to be seen as to whether or not this little episode was a contributing factor to what came next, but I'm sure it didn't help matters any. My true troubles began shortly after landing in Cincinnati, after a painless enough flight that had afforded me an excellent view of the sunrise. I'd taken my bird's eye view of this daily spectacle to be an omen and was feeling full of promise.

The universe was giving me the A-OK. I would be unpacking my bags just long enough to reconnoiter before setting off on a new adventure, one that would take me to the hidden rain forests and ruins of our southern neighbor. For this sojourn, I had earmarked three of the power places, beginning with the enchanted Galapagos Islands and ending back where it had all begun in the high Andes with Tiuhuanaco and Ollantaytambo. And this time, I was bound and determined to make it to Machu Picchu.

Then, with my batteries fully recharged I would return once again to Cincinnati before embarking on the final length of my journey—yet another winter retreat. However, this time, it would find me in the middle of the Atlantic instead of the Pacific. It was a great plan, and we all know how they go and how vulnerable they are to the secret whims of the Almighty.

My little apartment was just as I had left it. My agreement with the landlord to have someone come in once a month and do a little dusting had paid off. But the fresh flowers in a vase? Well, that was above and beyond.

"Guess he sure appreciates a tenant who pays a year in advance," I murmured to myself before collapsing in the turned down bed, and my last thought before reaching a delightful dreamless sleep was that I must be sure to thank him.

However, by the time my eyes popped open twelve hours later, the landlord was the furthest thing from my mind. Instead, I was trying to figure out just why in hell the world didn't look right. Squinting, I realized the problem centered on my left eye. The right eye seemed fine, but when I transferred my vision to the other side, I was appalled to see that the lower part of my vision was obscured, just as if someone had drawn a veil across the room. It was a hard phenomenon to describe, and all I could come up with was to compare it to a classical migraine.

This sort of migraine is centered on optical disturbances. It begins in the center of your vision with a hole that can best be described as shattered glass. Then the hole slowly begins to expand into a bull's-eye, creeping steadily towards the edges of one's vision. Now, note that I am using terms which may suggest an optical phenomenon, but not so. Because upon closing one's eyes, the show goes on. This points to a neurological problem, and it may have something to do with the optic nerve.

It is a malady I have shared with many others, some great, some small. It is said that Picasso suffered from the same syndrome, causing him to invent Cubism. Would that I could be so lucky as to turn such a lemon into lemonade. In my case, it just translated into a weird half hour out of my life, during which time I could only wait out the inevitable return to normal. At this point, the flashing lights and broken glass would have receded over the far horizon of my peripheral vision, and I would be able to proceed about my business.

But not so with the issue assailing me that morning. It was as if the visual disturbance had refused to leave, and in its determination to stay stuck at the edge of my vision, it was wreaking havoc on my ability to do much of anything involving sight. Plus, there was still a slight headache, reminiscent of the one I had experienced during our downward descent into St. Louis, but nowhere near as strong. So what was I to do?

Well, one thing was for certain. I wasn't going to be doing any heavy duty editing until it cleared up. And clear up it must, for I was an eternal optimist when it came to health related matters. Yeah, right. Who was I kidding? The truth was that said optimism was actually founded in a deep rooted fear and loathing of anything to do with the medical profession, which meant I would go out of my way to avoid them at all costs.

Now if I weren't such a Luddite, I would have realized that this classified as a medical emergency. But I was too stupid or too stubborn to admit I was up against something that Vitamin C or a hot bowl of chicken soup couldn't resolve.

So I waited, not one, not two, but a good five days before I finally got the picture. Or should I say, I DIDN"T get the picture because the problem just wasn't going away on its own. And it was then, and only then, that I finally bit the bullet and called up the nearest eye doctor. That was when the fun began. The first guy immediately put me on hold with a polite message explaining that *my time was valuable to him.* Then, when I finally did get a warm body, I was informed that the good doctor was booked through the end of the month. So I tried another and then another, before finally locating an up and coming young whippersnapper who was trying desperately to build a business in an area that didn't take kindly to upstarts. The news that Dr. Lucky will be glad to see me tomorrow was music to my ears. It had to be because my eyes sure weren't allowing for much input.

Well, the long and short of it was that, after multiple glimpses into the inner workings of my eyeballs, Dr. Lucky was able to ascertain that I wasn't very lucky. In fact, according to him I had some sort of high falooting long-as-your-arm disease which involved the swelling of the optic nerve.

"Funny about that," he murmured as he delivered the bad news. "We usually don't see this in people your age. Or if we do, it's because they are overweight smokers with high cholesterol. How is your cholesterol, anyway?"

And when I told him I had no idea, you would have thought I had just threatened to assassinate the Pope.

"You mean to say you haven't had any blood work done in years!" he shrieked, using a tone that should condemn me to hellfire.

And when I nodded meekly, he quickly set me up at the local pin-pricker where I was instructed to bare my arm and give blood. OK, so I never would have made a good junky. Despite all my druggy abuse, I had never taken to the needle. Thank God for that, considering the havoc it is now wrecking on the population. So this was a difficult directive to follow. But I submitted, figuring that, since I had committed to this plan of attack, I may as well pursue it to its bitter end.

And it was bitter, that was for sure. Two weeks later, I had not only given a sample of my precious fluids to the vampires, but had been coerced into releasing several vials. This was done per request of the retinal specialist Dr. Lucky referred me to. He was a guy who operated out of a big office downtown, which just so happened to have sister offices all over the state of Ohio. So you can probably get the picture, one that resulted in him rarely being at his desk. For that reason, most of his paperwork was handled by a nurse, who depending on her mood or time of the month was capable of the work load assigned to her. I don't think I was very lucky in this department either because I sure got the run around when the blood work came back in. If I'd been more tech savvy, I would have demanded a copy. However I erroneously figured that the doctors had it under control, so why bother? In the end, this was a colossal mistake,

Well, let's be fair. At least they didn't get my blood work mixed up with a chimpanzee. However, they did manage to get it mixed up with someone who had cats in their life because the only thing they could find in my system which may have precipitated such a weird optical reaction was a little known bacteria by the name of Bartonella Henselae.

OK… I know. That's like legalese and needs a translation. So here goes. Are you ready? I feel like I should be setting up a drum roll for this one because Bartonella Henselae is really a fancy term for Cat Scratch Fever.

Cat Scratch fever?? Wasn't that a song by George Thurgood? Or was it Ted Nuget? Oh, who knows? And who cares? The devil may usually dwell in the details, but in this case, he had unleashed a whole army of demons into my bloodstream. When they finally did get all my tests results back, including those from an extremely traumatic and outrageously expensive MRI, they barraged me with questions.

"Are you sure you were never around any cats? And what about the recent illness you described, the one you described as a bad bout of the flu?"

And that's when I remembered. Gee, I guess in all my jet-setting I was getting a bit foggy, a condition that was allowing one time zone to bleed into another and causing me to forget the little details of each port of call. Between that and a rich inner life reinforced by the book I was constructing, I may have been getting a bit of tunnel-vision. For hadn't that old lady who lived next to me all winter been somewhat of a cat person? Yeah, maybe she'd been able to handle those she-devils, but they sure hadn't taken a shine to me. Alas, I cringed to remember the multiple times the little monsters had drawn my blood while I was trying to cajole them with tidbits of fresh mahi-mahi. What had I been thinking? Any sane person would have stopped after the first incident, so why had I come back for repeat performances? Guess I was lonely, and we all know that such a state does not always equate with rational thought.

And as for the flu? Well… yes, come to think of it, I was down for about a week in early March with some nasty little bug that had me aching all over like a son of a bitch. But since my immune system had never been one to brag about, I hadn't paid much attention to it, even when I developed night sweats and a temperature of well over one hundred and two. Like most illnesses, I figured it would run its course, which it did. But now I saw that the nefarious foreign bug which had invaded my body had really just been warming up for a marathon.

With a sheepish look, I acknowledged all this to the good doctor, who immediately wrote me a prescription for some sort of babycillin. That's what I call the weaker members of the pharmaceutical arsenal. Not that it much mattered. I would take the shit anyway. By now it had been a good three weeks since my eye had gone on the warpath, and I was getting concerned. My next date of departure was looming and there was no way I would be leaving the country in the condition I was in. The antibiotics would take at least two weeks to kick in, and even then there was no guarantee my symptoms would abate.

"How long am I looking at, Doc?" I implore, and his answer of six to eight more weeks minimum was far from music to my ears. More like the crap George Thurgood (or whoever he was) would have written. Cat Scratch Fever, indeed!

So there I sat in my home base of Cincinnati, watching the plane as it took off without me and wondering if I would ever slip those surly bonds of earth again. And that's when I discovered there was more than one way to travel.

I will never know whether it was a by-product of the issue with my optic nerve, but I do know it was one of the strangest things that ever happened to me. It occurred in the middle of the night. (When else?) At the true time of the witching hour, which despite popular belief clocks in at somewhere between two and four AM in the morning, a time when our PSI fields are said to be at their lowest. This means we are ripe for the picking, be it a psychic attack or a visitation from angels or aliens. In my case, it may have been a perfect storm of all three.

All though the night sweats had passed, I was still running hot, and for that reason had left several windows open in my bedroom while sleeping. These windows faced east, and I loved them for the brilliant sunshine they afforded under certain conditions. On a sunny day, they acted as a natural alarm clock, blaring the bugle horn that implored me to rise up and seize the moment. Add a couple of morning song birds and you have the perfect reason to climb out of bed and get moving. Even though I couldn't jump on a plane and travel to exotic locations, life was still good, especially on the days when sunlight poured into that room like molten honey.

It was enough to give a girl a positive attitude. I would recover from the Bartonella bump in the road. I would get my eyesight back again. I would finish the great American novel. I would become a world renowned author and... Oh yeah, was I still dreaming? Because that sun sure was bright for this time of day.

Day? Yes, I must be dreaming because, come to think of it, the cock had not even crowed once. Yet the sun was already ablaze, illuminating everything in its path, causing all the objects in the room to morph into one big ball of light. This was downright odd.

But it got stranger when I realized everything outside held the same luminescence, a brilliance which made it seem as though a nuclear bomb had gone off. Right. You've seen the video footage of those early test sites in Nevada where there's just a big flash and then nothing. Well, that's as close as I can come to describing this phenomenon, except that it all happened in slow motion, and though I wasn't paying much attention to the clock—since it seemed like time had stood still—I could have sworn my world basked in this glow for a good five minutes. Long enough for me to realize there was an auditory side to this illusion—if indeed it were but a figment of my imagination—which manifested in a roaring in my ears. No, make that more like a thump thump roaring, the kind a big machine makes or maybe even a helicopter. Or maybe even an alien spacecraft.

Yeah, I had read the reports. Who hadn't? And I had even known people who swore they had been abducted, and they all described the same thing. A roaring sound accompanied by bright lights. An inability to move as if one was frozen in place. A sense of every hair on your head standing at attention...OK, need we go further?

So this is what's going on, I concluded. Which was all well and good because, after all, what do they say about a known evil? However, there was still that pragmatic sliver of doubt in my mind, and I needed to put the whole business to the test.

If it is external, I knew I wouldn't be able to hear it with a pillow over my head. So overcoming my fears, I forced myself to move and burrowed deep into the bedding. And alas, it never let up—that infernal thumping which soon revealed itself to be none other than the pumping of the blood through my veins. Well, so much for that.

But what about the light which had now receded to reflect only the muted shadows of the hour of the wolf? Was that also a by-product of a body gone astray? Had I experienced some sort of aneurysm, a stroke to the brain perhaps? Well, if so, wouldn't there be other symptoms? Limbs that won't raise, words that won't form, eyes that don't see. No scratch that last one because the eye thing was already a given.

I had to admit I was puzzled. But I was also tired as the entire incident had worn me out. Gee, maybe I had been off planet, enduring a number of demeaning and debilitating tests. If so, a girl needs their beauty sleep. So despite any latent fears I might still be experiencing, I just rolled over on my side and went back to dream land. And what a dream it was!

I am in a beautiful sanctuary. One by one, I am flying people to this place. Except I think that they are really cats, not people at all. Whatever the case, they need to come here, to experience this heavenly haven. It is a combination Grecian grotto and eighteenth century log cabin complete with a walk-in fire place. One of the 'cats' tries to claim this spot as his own, but no one is allowed preference in this place of equality. No one can monopolize or take more than their share. I begin to read from a book. I am teaching now and the sound of my voice fills the room just as the light had filled my own and I wake up, a dream within a dream.

This time it was merely a gray day in April. The rains had come and, with them, those infernal showers. I felt slightly depressed. The way you feel when you wake up from a really good dream only to realize you are back in the same old game. Nothing had changed overnight. No miracle had taken place. My eye was still clouded, and my joints still ached. I had been told that both were by-products of the Bartonella, that nasty little bug I had picked up from some feral cat half-way across the world.

Cats! Who would have thunk it? Hadn't they been worshipped in ancient Egypt? At least that's what our guide had said as he narrated our way down the Nile. Yes, venerated to the point that it was a sin to harm one, the killing of a cat being grounds for execution. Gee, the world sure had changed. Now the poor things were lucky to find a full bowl of Friskies and a warm cat crapper in which to leave their deposits. And a complete and total moron to read to them in her dreams. Yeah, don't forget that!!!

Wow! Had the Bartonella invaded my brain? Was I losing it? But let's not go there because I really had so many more interesting ports of call in mind. Yes, Peru would have to be put on the back-burner again. But there would be more time for travel once the book made the best seller list, so now it needed to be all about the book. It was my number one priority, and if all I could do was churn out one page a day? Well, that went for three hundred and sixty more pages between now and next April, and I would surely not need that many to finish saying what I wanted to say. In fact, another hundred or so should do quite nicely. That said, all I needed to do was plod along with the task at hand until the fall, at which point I had optimistically booked a flight to the Azores. It was there I would reside for the next six months, polishing and editing, and voila! When spring came again, my book would be ready for publication.

It was the best plan I could come up with under the circumstances. It was a plan born by a dreamer of cats, a species which have certainly fallen from grace on this planet. Alas, if any symbolism were intended by that remark, maybe it would have caused me to drag my heels a bit when it came to implementing said plan. But the lemming in me could not help herself. For once I have plotted a course of action, I always seem hell-bent to follow it through. Yeah, hell bent and high water. They always did seem to go together, which is why my trip to the Azores culminated in the storm of my century.

Ok, let's be fair. On a global scale, it was more like a tropical depression, and one so localized it only affected a handful of the population. Due to its size, the weather people managed to ignore this event, so unless I take matters into my own hands, it will go down in history as nameless. And that is simply NOT acceptable. Therefore, it's up to me to choose a name, and in keeping with decades of misogynists, I will stick to the feminine persuasion. For indeed what better name than that of the one who spawned it.

Trixie. Yes, Tropical Storm Trixie. What great alliteration. I really liked the way it rolled off the tongue, and for the first time in my entire sweet life, I could actually say that my mother's birth name was put to good use. In the past, it had always been gentrified to Tricia, which she claimed was short for Patricia, a very patrician sounding name.

But let's call a spade a spade here, for my mother was a far cry from any privileged bloodlines. Instead her roots were found in the red clay hills of the foothills, marginal tobacco and cotton country, the sort of soil that only yields a reluctant pittance while extracting its revenge in toil and trouble.

She spent her entire life trying to put her humble beginnings behind her, and her birth name was one which was rarely uttered in our household. But I knew it to be so from the occasional phone call we would receive from some well-meaning relative. When this happened, I would pick up the phone, only to be greeted by a nasal tone at the other end of the line inquiring as to whether or not Trixie was home. At which point it was my responsibility to inform the caller that no Trixie lived there, but I would be glad to call Tricia to the phone. These were my mother's words, not mine, and I found them remarkably cruel. But when you are a kid of ten, you do what you are told.

However, I stopped being a kid the day my father died, and now it became my turn to be cruel. Oh, it never started out that way. I never really intended the story of our family to be anything more than some dry military history. But, of course, it morphed into more. How could it not? It's a common phenomenon. Consider a mirror. When you are too close, your reflection is distorted, and it's only when you back up that the world comes into focus.

Well... I thought I had backed up far enough. I was wrong. Given a few more decades to ripen, I might have been able to pull it off, but at the tender age of forty, I was hardly seasoned. Oh, I thought I was. But that's because I was infused with the hubris and bravado of youth, two characteristics which translated to a belief that my shit did not stink. As far as I was concerned, my book was a masterpiece, albeit one complete with too many adverbs and uses of the word *that.*

Granted, it probably had its moments, but was still seriously in need an editor—which I could not afford. And as for the overall content? Well, I had to concede that it was more an exorcism than a novel. In truth, I had just used the military careers of both my father and brother as a way to get on my soapbox and spout some anti-war rhetoric. Then I filled in the blanks (of which there were many) with what I perceived to be witty and scandalous stories about the other members of my family. I left no stone unturned...the many moves, the heart rendering absences due to those infernal tours of duty, the arguments upon return, the drunken brawls, the long silences, the classic passive aggression as a means of retaliation. It was all there and so thinly disguised as literature that, in short, the book amounted to little more than a good shit; and though it may have provided the author with a deep sense of relief, it left the reader searching for high waders and a nose plug.

However, don't even try to make me fess up to all this for at least twenty more years. It would probably take that long to climb down off the high horse I was on and admit I had just laid a literary bomb. Please remember that despite the little setback of my eye—which had improved enough by the time I hit the Azores to allow me several hours a day behind a computer—I was still on a roll. It was a roll that allowed me to winter in a place that most of my hard working countrymen would give their eye teeth to even visit. It was a place of extreme beauty and mystery, and one which will call to me long after the last wave washes ashore. In essence, I felt like I'd spent most of my life trying to get there and will spend the remainder trying to return.

It didn't take long to realize I was in a paradise, and one distinctly different from the one I'd left on the other side of the world. For this was a paradise that was off the beaten track, and for that reason it gave me the impression it had reserved its pristine splendor for my eyes only.

As soon as I stepped off the plane I felt it—the sensation that I had been there before. Of all the Merkaba power places, it had the strongest pull. Maybe because it was one of the rumored sites of the fabled Atlantis. After all, it made sense. For if that mythical continent had gone down in a cataclysm of smoke and water, what better place to rest its bones but way down below the ocean. Of course, there would always be a few volcanic peaks sticking up. Hence the islands of the Azorean archipelago.

There were approximately nine of them and they were divided up by region into three geographic groups. I chose the largest on which to set up camp since I figured I would be spending the bulk of my time there. It would have been nice to tour some of the other islands, but I had to be practical. My funds were running thin, and I still had to budget enough money to last me through the process of publication. So Sao Miguel it would be, a whopper of an island that ran about sixty-five kilometers in length and only fourteen in breadth. Yet despite its scanty surface area, it still boasted the largest population in the region.

Not that I would be fraternizing with too many of them. As usual, I had chosen an out of the way spot in which to lock myself away for the winter. It was a small apartment on the north shore of the island, and it sat within walking distance of a remarkable beach. I call it remarkable for two reasons, the first and foremost being that the front porch of my apartment looked down upon it, creating a spectacular view that back in the states would have brought in a pretty penny. But because this was the Azores, I was getting the whole place for six months at a bargain price, a deal which became even better when I realized the scarcity of such beaches on the island. Indeed there were very few places where one could access the ocean, the main part of the coastline being rugged cliffs that plunged to the sea. It was so steep that every time I saw a tractor working near the edge, my heart would jump to my throat, and I would utter a prayer for the poor farmer who sat precariously perched in its seat. It must have taken a lot of skill to run machinery in that kind of terrain. Skill and guts.

It was hard to believe the way these people had managed to eke a living out of these islands. Sure there had been some tremendous raw material, the soil being of a rich volcanic origin and the climate stabilizing at agreeable temperatures which remained consistent year round. That meant there was no harsh winter, no brutal tropical summer, just a temperate sub-tropical paradise where sun would give way to showers and rainbows at any time of the day or night, thus assuring enough rainfall to support a variety of crops. The place was probably close to sustainable in the vegetable and fish department, and the land managed to produce enough beef and dairy products for export. Toss in the development of the hot springs that always came with a volcanic territory, and you have enough geothermal to almost wean the place from the petrodollar. On the surface, it looked like it might be paradise on earth, and had I been younger and more of a back-to-the-lander, I might have learned Portuguese and settled down with some nice farmer to work the fields and milk the cows.

But such was not my mission this time around, so I was content to merely observe. And from the moment I stepped off the plane, observe I did. How could I help myself when confronted with the proliferation of hues there were to greet me at the airport? Flowers were everywhere, a riot of color despite the fact that it was autumn where I had just come from.

"Shouldn't all this be shutting down? Don't you guys have a winter here?"

These were my questions to the cab driver as he navigated the steep roads of the north shore. But he just winked and replied that I should wait until I saw the place in spring.

So I sat back to enjoy the ride and not for the first time wondered if maybe I had chosen the wrong artistic endeavor to pursue. Perhaps film would have been a better medium for expression considering the perfect photo ops that lay around ever turn of the road. Or maybe I should have traded in my pen for a paintbrush. Oh well, that die had already been cast and there was no changing horses in mid-stream.

And then, I had seen my apartment, which up to this point I had only been allowed on-line access to, and considering my tech skills, it was a marvel I had managed to find the place at all. But the Ayahuasca spirit must have still been strong in guiding me because it had led me to the perfect place for my purpose—so perfect it took several days of sitting on that porch and gaping over the view before I was finally able to get down to business.

The days began to drift into a blur. I would get up early and walk down to the little town for coffee at a local café. Then I would check to see if the green grocery truck had shown up on schedule. If it was parked nearby, I would load up on provender and head back my room with a view. There I would sit on its idyllic porch for the better part of the afternoon, churning out page after page and ripping up half as much as I produced. Whoever said that writing is not hard work never attempted the task, and there were times when I wished I had opted for a simpler means of expression. Especially in consideration of this particular story, which I had approached from its bitter end and proceeded to write in reverse. In this sense it was somewhat like a fish that had already been laid upon the table, making it my business to pick amongst the bones for the tender meat, cautiously savoring each bite until only the skeletal framework remained.

To be fair and give credit where credit is due, I probably got this analogy from too many dinners down at Mare' Cheia, the restaurant down the road which always allowed you to inspect the fish before ordering dinner. Then, once it arrived, it came complete with head and tail and enough bones to choke a person who was in a hurry. Yeah, hurry was not a word common to the vocabulary of most Azoreans. Why be in a rush to enter into the next moment when the one you are in is about as close to heaven as you'll get this side of Jordan? Hence the reason why one moment seemed to blend into the next with the perfection of a dancer executing a well choreographed dance.

However, there were times when multiple walks on the beach and hikes on the nearby trails—some which were poorly maintained and downright scary—were just not enough. So when terminal tedium began to set in, the terminally bored got going. Fortunately, the island was quick to cooperate. For despite its small size, Sao Miguel was home to many splendid attractions.

One was a must see given my other purpose (that of accessing as many Merkaba points as humanly possible) and this was Sete Cidades, the volcano which dominated the landscape on the western end of the island. According to geologists, it had been erupting since time immemorial, exploding and then collapsing to form geographic features so stunning they were well advertised in every guide book.

However, accessing them was not always possible. I had been forewarned that one was rarely allowed the privilege of viewing the miradores on this part of the island as they were often shrouded in fog. Therefore, the only way to beat the odds was to get an early start. So I had taken a taxi to Ponto Delgado and spent the night just so I could get a jump on the following day. Then, after renting my own transportation, I hightailed it up the mountain at first light.

I was bleary eyed and groggy, and relieved at the absence of traffic. Apparently, the early hour had afforded me an open highway, if you wanted to honor this twisty rugged track by such a misnomer. Even though I had now been on the island for over a month and was getting used to the wild rides its roads afforded, I had never been called upon to drive them myself. So this was a new first, and as fortune favors the brave, it was not meant to be a new *last* as well.

Following my guidebook, I made my way to a location well off the beaten path. It took me down a narrow unpaved road which led to a car park, resplendent with picnic tables and barbecues. But this was not my ultimate destination. From the car park there was what was described as a fifteen minute walk to a view billed as one of the finest in all the Azores, a truly stunning vista of the two Sete Cidades lakes, which are as strange and fascinating as those dog breeds which sport one blue eye and one brown. For such is the case of what has become known as the Lakes of Tears.

Lakes of Tears? That's right. Of course, it would have something to do with romance. It always does, and the romance never ends well. A princess, a shepherd boy and a disapproving father. Need I say more? Because we all know where this one ends. In a puddle of tears. Green for boys this time, and blue for girls. (I guess pink would have been out of the question.)

Yeah, whatever. Like I'm supposed to believe in such fairytales? Reject the science that calls for millions of years of geological upheaval in the formation of such a place? Call a covey of distinguished geologists a bunch of liars?

Right. Tell me another one. Come on! We all know these islands are all that is left of Atlantis, and it went down in a colossal cataclysm. Why, they'd even found pyramids in the nearby waters.

Indeed. So let the folklorists and geologists have their day because I was having mine. And why not? There was plenty of mystery to go around. But just for the record, Sete Cidades does translate as Seven Cities, a fact which leans seriously in the direction of the Atlantis explanation. Yeah. *Way down beneath the ocean, that's where I wanna be...*

Seriously? Well, what can I say? The view was so stunning it had annihilated any sort of activity in the left hemisphere of my brain. All I knew was this was one of the finest vistas I had ever gazed upon—even though there was a good bit of the world yet to explore. Whatever the case, I felt privileged indeed and suitably in awe. It had all been worth waking up at 4:44 AM.

And yes, that's a repeating number, and I'm sure it has some significance. It must because it kept showing up at odd intervals, be it day or night. I would catch it out of the corner of my eye on the way into the apartment. I would awaken in the middle of the night to find it flashing an early warning signal that another dawn was approaching. However, it wasn't until much later that its mystery was revealed to me.

This happened during one of my rare flings, and it was a sure sign it was spring and ergo just about time for my expulsion from paradise. So, why not go out with a bang, quite literally?

I met him on the beach. Where else? He, too, was on a fling, a little jaunt to celebrate his pending graduation in August, and judging from the lack of crows-feet around his eyes, I would wager he was probably in his last year of college. No, let's make that grad school, so that I am allowed to keep a shred of my dignity. The last thing I ever wanted to be called was a cougar, a term I found quite demeaning when ascribed to the feminine persuasion. But, hey, it takes two to tango, and apparently he was just as open to the horizontal boogey as I was.

He was most assuredly Ivy League, which meant he was out of my league. But I got the impression he was one of those landed gentry blue-blood inbreeds who are so highly intelligent and over the brink that even their own kind have little to do with them. So perhaps he was seeking solace amongst the lower class where with any luck he could *slum a few bars and fake it*. Whatever the case, he got more than what he bargained for with me, an intellectual equal and fellow member of the out crowd. Because even though his name has been conveniently forgotten, some of our conversations have become indelible, lingering in my brain like precious metals confined to bedrock. In fact, I'd venture to say that it was his words and not his looks which drew me into his arms—all esoteric stuff which made me feel like I was back in Peru again.

His opening line was a dead giveaway that there was more to come. I guess he'd been striking out with the girls in string bikinis because by the time he got around to me, he wasn't pulling any punches. He sidled up to my blanket and mumbled some under-the-breath comment about *these kids today*. I took one look at him and felt like saying something about how he should talk. But then our eyes met and some sort of invisible spark flew, the kind which alerts you that a kindred spirit has quietly entered stage right.

He smiled. "Did you know that a 2012 survey revealed that one in four Americans believes that the sun orbits the earth? God, no wonder they say that stupidity is the 5th Horseman."

They say that? Well, I never... But it was enough to whet my appetite. Why not play this game and see where it leads?

"That's why the good and the wise lead quiet lives," I responded. It was one of my favorite tests to gauge just how deep the river might run in someone's veins.

And he passed it without missing a beat by uttering a single word—*Euripides*—and I knew the game was on.

What followed was an elaborate fencing match with the two of us employing our full arsenal to see who could impress the other the most. However he won when he began to spout off about Antarctica, a place which had been on my list of must-see power points, but only in a dream-on sort of way.

"You won't believe what they found hidden beneath the ice," he began. "Yeah, all those big shots had to go down there to see for themselves. Obama, Putin, Kerry, Prince Harry and Royal Family, King Carlos of Spain, even the Russian Orthodox Patriarch, who went there immediately following an audience with the Pope! Roosevelt knew about it. Oh yeah, and old Buzz Aldrin went, too. You remember him?"

I didn't, but nodded anyway.

"Well he was one of the Apollo 11 astronauts, and guess what he tweeted after his little visit?"

Again I was clueless, but sure didn't want to betray my ignorance.

"Something like *we are all in danger. It is evil itself.* Now what on earth could he have been referring to? Unless, of course, it wasn't on earth. Whatever the case, they've known about it for some time because Roosevelt sent Admiral Byrd down there in 1946 for what was supposed to be a scientific expedition—although Byrd swore it was military in nature. But whatever the reason, it was one big deal. They covered over twenty thousand kilometers and took close to four times that many photos; and then, in a blink of an eye, Byrd gets called off.

"So the question that comes to mind is, why? Yes, why spend all that time and money just to drop it like a hot potato? Well, later it was leaked that Byrd had been under attack, that there had been an assault on the expedition by some sort of flying saucers which surfaced out of the water and pursued them at high speeds. Lives were lost, and so was equipment. Enough was enough. Byrd was definitely out gunned, and it was time to cut and run.

"Of course, the next question that comes to mind involves the identity of his pursuers. And don't think our government didn't try to unravel that mystery, but do so in such a way as not to attract the attention of the masses.

"Now, it's no secret that Hitler was also interested in Antarctica Did you know there was a mystical side to the Third Reich? Yeah, that's right. They actually believed the earth was hollow and inhabited by a race they called the Hyperboreans."

And at this point, my ears perked up. But my mouth remained shut. I knew better than to interrupt just when the juiciest morsels were about to be dropped onto my plate. So I listened as he went on.

"The Hyperboreans were advanced both socially and technologically and originally had their home in what is now the North Sea. But events conspired against them. There was either a pole shift or some such global catastrophe which caused the seas to rise. Whatever happened though didn't take place overnight. They had time to prepare by digging tunnels to other parts of the world. First they went to the Himalayas where they resettled, but it didn't take them long to branch out to a multitude of bases. Under the Sahara, in the jungles of Brazil and the Yucatan…Mt. Shasta."

And wow, did I ever do an up periscope on that last one!

"The Aghartians," I mumbled, and he smiled.

"Yeah, that's right, so you are familiar with all this? How this ancient civilization, and I do <u>mean</u> ancient—like millions of years old—may have taken up residency on what is now a frozen wasteland, but what was once—and this is well documented—a tropical paradise. And perhaps they live there still, though deep underground. And those vast rivers and caverns which we've found under the ice are simply their thoroughfares, gates to the upper regions. Of course, they could have just been a convenient place to hide a u-Boat.

"But that doesn't explain the many sightings of UFOs near the South Pole, especially near the Beardmore Glacier. In fact, two whistleblowers just came forth to describe a massive octagonal shaped structure that is buried fifty feet under the ice in what has been dubbed a no-fly zone. According to them, these things are huge with twenty foot ceilings and doors of basalt so strong that bullets bounce of them, and they extend way down into the interior. So once again, is it a case for the hollow earth, or just a bunch of bullshit?"

And at this he winked, and I knew I was in trouble. It was a whirlwind courtship, one constructed mostly around sentences. On opening day, he had given me a small sample of the amazing thoughts which   proliferated in his mind. And as the days unfolded, so did the incredible flower of his unusual intellect. We'd be lying on the beach soaking up those quintessential subtropical rays when he'd rise up on one arm, look deep into my eyes and proceed to spout off

"The greatest lie," he would begin, "is that we are all separate. When, in truth, everything is connected."

Then he'd follow that pearl of wisdom with the second greatest lie *which is that we are powerless, pawns in a game and victims of a capricious god.*

"But meditation will set you free," he insisted. "It's a lot like those 3D Magic-Eye books. The longer you mediate, the more of the total picture emerges from seemingly random dots."

Yeah, he was fun, that was for sure, and if you get the impression that our short sweet relationship consisted more of mental gymnastics than any other kind? Well, then, I'll have to give you an **A** for being so astute.   Yeah, let's just say it was different kind of coupling, more of a mind-fuck that anything else. He was the kind of guy you revealed your dreams to right off the bat, and in retrospect, I know he didn't just randomly appear in my life. It was more like he was sent into it as a combination shaman, guide, and interpreter, firing off round after round of witticisms and philosophical truism. But his parting shot was his best, for he was the one who taught me the meaning of 4:44.

It was his last day on the island, and I had finally allowed him access to my inner sanctuary, my room with a view apartment. Prior to this, we had always gone to his place which was actually several miles away in another town. This had been an arrangement which suited me fine as it protected my privacy. Besides, he was the one with the car, a little perk I confess to have taken full advantage of during his stay. But the clock was ticking as far as this little love affair went, and soon he would be on a plane, winging his way back to the Ivy League school which had spawned him. So what was the harm in allowing him to cross my threshold?

It had been a magical day, the kind you reserve for a grand finale. We'd started off with a tour of the Northeastern part of the island, riding a fine highway all the way to Nordeste (where else). It was road resplendent with not one, but two superior miradores, both which housed little picnic parks where one could dine amongst the blooming hydrangeas and hibiscus. Flowers bloomed in abundance, it now being almost June and peak of the season. It was hard not to succumb to the heady aroma of azaleas and roses that lined the walkways, and the odors coming from the stone barbeque pits had reminded us that lunch time was nigh. So we poked around at every tiny town we came upon trying to find the perfect restaurant. But the ones we were able to locate were either closed or severely lacking as far as a menu was concerned. However, one shopkeeper directed us towards the town of Provocao on the southern coast, insisting it would be worth the trip. And that, my friends, turned out to be the understatement of the century.

It was one of those wonderful events which occur only through happenstance, meaning that we couldn't have planned it any better had we tried. At first it was just the four star restaurant on the square that drew us in, but after lunch when we decided to take a spin around town, we realized we had arrived just in time for a major festival. They call it Corpus Christi which loosely translates as the body of Christ, and though we would miss the procession, the preparation was worth every minute.

I have never seen anything like it and probably never will again. It was enough to bring out the latent Catholic in me, and I caught myself muttering a host of Hail Mary's under my breath. Talk about opulent, but in a way that celebrates nature over any man-made construct. Yeah, these Catholics sure knew how to throw a party.

They had laid wooden templates on the streets running through the entire town. Into these they had arranged various small colorful flowers to form geometric patterns, the colors of which were kept in separate shapes via the templates. Some also held vibrant wood shavings and the soft tipped branches of a local conifer. But whatever the medium, the effect was profound, and as we walked entranced through this stunning display, I was given the impression I had died and gone to heaven.

"It doesn't get any better than this," my companion asserted and I'd nodded in agreement.

And then it did.

We almost didn't make it out of town that day, our car being centrally parked in the middle of a square which functioned as the bull's eye for the festival. But a friendly cop helped us navigate the bustling streets, and we made it all the way to Furnas where we'd heard tell of a fantastic hot springs—another understatement. Words fail when describing the place, the Poca de Dona Beija pools being about as close as you can get to heaven this side of Jordan. The sight of all those happy humans bathing in healing waters amidst abundant sunshine and vegetation made me wonder if I had traveled back in time to antediluvian days. Needless to say, we spent several hours languishing in the staircase of pools which made up the baths—each one labeled by temperature so that you could choose the perfect spot. I tried out all of them, even the one closest to the small mountain stream which fed the entire place, before reluctantly agreeing that it was time to head back over the mountain. My friend was set for an early morning flight and needed to drop me off before returning to Ponta Delgado where he had rented a room for the night.

"I wish I could stay," he ventured with a sheepish look, as I turned to key to my apartment. And then he saw the view and decided to postpone the inevitable just a little bit longer. We sat on the veranda and looked out upon the beach where we'd met less than a week ago. The apartment had displayed its typical mess, festooned with scattered scraps of paper and moldy banana peels. The trash was taking on a characteristic odor of compost, and the whole place needed a good cleaning. I could tell from his reaction that the only saving grace was the view and the drink I had stuffed in his hand. Yeah, nothing kills a romance like a few moments in the lair of your lover, especially if she belongs to the Church of the Latter Day Slobs.

"It's been… well… I guess you'd say…fun. Maybe we can…" he started, and then shook his head. There was no reason to go on. We both knew that this was it. There would repeat performances.

"Your book?" he asked, pointing to the unruly pack of papers which lay scattered about on various tabletops, and I nodded. I had alluded to it only briefly during the course of our friendship and was in no mood to share. I was too busy noting the time on the clock.

"4:44," I muttered, and he looked to where I was pointing.

"The damn thing must be set on that time," I explained. "Because it's the only one I ever seem to see."

"Ah, yes, a repeating number," he noted. "Did you know that four is the number of home and family? And that can be soul family as well as earthly. Anyway, when it's repeated, the universe wants to let you know you are not alone, and that the path of awakening you are on is fully supported by those in the higher realms. Pretty heavy stuff, huh? But then again, it might just be happening because you're on this island, and the clock is picking up on its vibrations. Did you know the very last eruption of any significance occurred in 1444?

"Anyway, I guess there are multiple interpretations, depending on just how deep you want to go. But the main significance to me is more mundane. You see, I have to get this car back by six o'clock, and it's a good hour to the airport. So I guess you know what that means?"

Yeah, I knew. No problem. These things never ended well for me, making me wonder why I indulged in them at all. I really needed to give this kind of stuff up for Lent. No, Lent had already passed for this year. So how about I just gave it up for good? That would be much better.

I showed him the door, gave him a peck on the cheek as a parting shot and went back in to mull over those pages. I had taken too long of a break, and it was time to get to that magical moment where THE END appeared on the page. Next week it would be my time to board that big jet airplane. I needed to finish what I had come here to do. And, that said, I stayed awake half the night, scribbling and typing and deleting and typing some more until I finally passed out on the couch.

Oh yeah. The last thing to grace my eyes before I surrendered to the astral plane? Why that infernal clock of course reading 4:44 again. What else? Unless, you hit the shift key. And then it's $:$$ and that's more like it. Right. If you can't make love, you may as well make money.

Chapter 11
NOONE (AKA Doe)
End of summer 2017 to Spring 2018
Aniel: An interlude

Yeah, man plans and god laughs. When did I   last say those words? Seems like an eternity ago, so that wise old patriarch should be rolling on the floor about now.

After walking out of Coolville that day… No, wait a minute. Let's not mince words. After *running* as fast as my little feet could carry me out of Coolville, I had hit one bump in the road after another.

The first came when an internet search at a discreet library pulled up the Grien's schedule, only to discover that their last date for touring had already come and gone. Golly, was it that late into the summer already? Or were the Grien's just getting old and henceforth deciding to cut back on their work load. However, a search for similar carnivals at which to hide had produced the same result, unless of course, I wanted to head for Florida. It was a thought, but one soon cancelled once I got back into mom's untrusty Fiesta.

"What's that smell?" I muttered when I fired up the engine. Yeah, fired up was an appropriate verb to use since smoke and fire always did seem to go together.

My next words being *oh, shit … what now?* I had no choice but to limp over to the nearest garage. The prognosis, though not as grim as terminal cancer, was pretty bad.

"It's your rings, buddy," the grease-covered cigar-smoking mechanic informed me. "And you're gonna need a complete overhaul before too long."

I looked at the guy, and then I looked in my wallet. Gee, it sure was thin these days.

"And how much is that gonna cost," I asked, even though I knew the answer would   send me over the brink of despair—which it did, leaving me no recourse but to head for the closest port in a storm.

It would not be Florida or bust. That was for sure. I would be lucky to make to Cincinnati where I just happened to have an address which might lead me to some well-needed assistance.

"I know you're done for the season..." I began.

I was sitting in Bobby Grien's living room, and yes, she had taken me in as if I were a long lost relative. She was really putting on the dog, lemonade and all, and I felt a tad guilty.

For our entire relationship, I had really been a class A phony. It had all been *yes ma'am* and *no sir*, giving everyone the impression that I was just a good old middle class college boy, working his way through school. The real me, the dope smoking basement dwelling conspiracy theorist, was unknown to her. All she'd ever seen was the son she'd never had, and this meant he could do no wrong in a mother's eyes. Ah, for such unconditional love, which in my case had now been reduced to ashes. It was enough to choke me up, but best skip the tears since I was on a mission. So I plunged right in with my tail of woe.

I gave her the short version, taking care to leave out the part about the TDA accounts. However, the little I told her was enough to gain not only her sympathy, but her assistance. Of course there wasn't much she could do for me by way of employment. They were indeed done for the season, having knocked off a bit early so her husband could have minor surgery. But she still had connections with similar carnivals and even knew a few folks in some of the small traveling circuses that were tooling around the country. The best thing about these guys was that some of them operated almost year round.

"There's this new one called UniverSoul Circus. It just started up a few years ago, and it's just wonderful. I took my granddaughter to it when they came to Cincinnati and you wouldn't believe..." And at this point she began to gush, describing in detail a number of the acts and her granddaughter's enthusiasm upon witnessing them.

It was a bit too much for a kid who had recently lost his mother. Still I had no choice but to hear her out, and when she was done, I had to admit I would have been intrigued even if I weren't so desperate.

"So where did you say they were camped out?" I asked, interrupting her for the third time. I was trying not to be too aggressive, but I needed shelter from the storm, and I needed it yesterday.

However, if I was bordering on rude, she forgave me, and finally paused in her monologue about Kitty and Me—Kitty being her granddaughter's nickname—and scribbled the name of a town in Kentucky on a piece of paper. It was an odd name, and later I was glad she had written it down, since I might have been lost without it.

As it was I still found myself lost when, a few days later, I tried to find this bumbuckville. I kept asking and asking at every convenience store I encountered, but no one seemed to know the place. Either that or it went by a different name.

"But surely you'd know if a circus had come to town…" I was close to screaming at this point and seriously considering dropping in on my old friend Leslie. Maybe she could fix me up for a spell. Who knows? There was probably a crop down in her basement which needed some serious attention and…

OK, that wasn't such a good idea, especially I had any lingering love for such an old friend, because the last thing I wanted to do was lead the cops into that den of iniquity. No, I would have to proceed with Plan A, which had me passing the same crossroad for what must have been the fifth time that morning.

And that's when I saw it. Hidden on a telephone pole in faded letters, it surely wasn't the work of an operation that sought business. It was so yellowed with age I figured it must have come over on the Mayflower, and when I stopped the car to get a closer look, I realized why.

"Jesus," I swore under my breath. "This was last years. So where are they now?"

I looked at the name of town. It was a bit more familiar, and a close scrutiny of my map placed it at only fifty miles away. So why not check and see if maybe, just maybe, they decided to keep the same schedule?

"We can do this," I said to Uncle Fester, that being my nickname for mom's scary Fiesta, and the old girl responded with a fresh plume of smoke.

"Yeah, we'd better be able to do this," I muttered. "Because next stop for you is probably gonna be the junkyard."

And that said Uncle Fester and I roared on down the road into what surely would become known as my own personal Twilight Zone.

It started out slow with a gut level feeling that I had stumbled into a scene way out of my element. Pietre Miklanovich was one of the strangest looking dudes I had ever encountered, and I had encountered quite a few. Come on now. I'd worked the carnivals for Christ's sake, and they were well known for trolling the deep in search of the finest bottom dwellers.

But Pietre was no bottom dweller. Instead, he went the other way, with an aura that almost caused him to shine. Call it a halo effect brought about by a head of the whitest hair I had ever seen on a young dude—and the guy surely wasn't much past his fourth decade—or write it off to just plain personal charisma. But all I could say was the man seemed to shimmer like a star.

Mine was not the standard job interview. I never had to explain to him where I planned to be in five years, nor tell him what animal I could best relate to. Instead, he merely popped out of his trailer, white hair trailing like an after-thought, and asked me if I believed in magic.

Thinking he must belong to the old school, the real old one, since that little ditty about believing in magic had been one of mom's favorites, I simply began to crank up the tune. Now I'm really not much of a crooner, and god only knows why I burst into song at that particular moment. I guess I just couldn't help myself, as it seemed the reasonable thing to do.

Jesus, Doe, I chided myself as the final refrain wafted into the distance. *You've done it now. The guy will think you're a real fruit cake and send you packing down that oil-splattered road.* I hung my head, somewhat shamefaced, and was surprised when the apparition in front of me let out a long belly-roll laugh.

"That should suffice," he said as soon as his outburst subsided. "You can start with cleaning up Dolly's trailer."

As you might expect, I was overjoyed until I realized that Dolly was the aging camel I'd seen on all the circus flyers. She bore the dubious honor of chief honcho at the petting zoo which the circus featured. I soon found out that if I had been expecting elephants and tigers, I had come to the wrong place. For The UniverSoul only catered to domestic animals, the camel being the only species that pushed the limit. There were dogs and cats and pigs and chickens and one equally geriatric pony who was housed in the same trailer as Dolly. Together, the two of them must have generated enough shit to fertilize the entire county, a fact I soon discovered much to my chagrin.

Alas, there would be no Dizzy Dragons to entertain me here as my job description soon became defined as Chief Shit Shoveler/ Jack of all Trades. If there was a stake to pound or a dog to walk, I was expected to be Johnny-on-the-spot. My day began at six o'clock and didn't end until Pietre called it quitting time. Some might say he was a tough taskmaster, but in all fairness he gave me the best deal I could hope for under the circumstances. Besides, I was somewhat at his mercy since the Fiesta was pronounced dead shortly after my arrival. As this left me with nowhere to sleep or stash what little remained of my worldly possessions, I had no choice but to take whatever shit was dealt out. (And Dolly and her crapping little side-kick made sure I was never in short supply.)

"You can move in with Jorge," Pietre directed, once he understood my predicament, and I'd sighed and grabbed my rucksack. Jorge was the only other roustabout for the entire operation, and I got the impression he was about as down and out as I was. His worldly possessions included a statue of the Virgin Mary and a moth eaten old poncho. Add to that a change of clothes and some denture paste and you just about have it. Jeez, the guy must have been as old as the two super-shitters in the adjoining trailer, despite his tattoos being of a contemporary nature.

I had to comment, especially on the Celtic stuff which seemed way too millennial for an old geezer like Jorge. Certainly my generation had cornered the market on cool. Never before had I seen Celtic knots on an anciano (Spanish word for old fart).

"My grandson, he give me big idea..." he stumbled over the English, and at that point I realized there would be no long fireside chats with this one. Oh well, at least bunking with him should be peaceful, if I could ignore the cacophony of squawks and grunts from the nearby trailers and the olfactory aromas from the one which housed my other two friends.

Friends? Yes, it was a sad truth that I just didn't fit in with this crowd and ergo would not be adding any names to my Christmas list this year. But what did I expect? These were circus people—a rare breed in itself and one I had little experience with. So, despite my carnie walk on the wild side, I was simply out of my element. For starters, half of them spoke other languages whenever off duty. As I made my rounds about camp at night I heard so many tongues spoken I could have sworn I was at the United Nations. Some, like Spanish, Russian, and Chinese, I recognized. But others were more obscure, and one I even came to understand as Romany, the official lingo of the gypsy race. Yeah, mom would be proud of me. I had finally made it as a linguist. Add that to my growing number of new talents like slopping hogs and stapling up circus flyers, and you've got a real college graduate.

I had to console myself with the belief that all this was just a means to an end, and after a couple months I should have achieved my goal of enough dinero to see me through a winter south of the border. After that, who knows? There were plenty of places in the jungles of

Central America where a gringo on the run could hide. So maybe I'd just stay down there for whatever remained of my life, swinging from the trees while I dined on bananas and coconuts.

As you could see, I really didn't have much of a plan at the moment. I was still in the same state of shock which had compelled me into flight mode. Plus, so much had been lost in the last year of my life that I was probably still experiencing PTSD, and for that reason, establishing myself as a fine upstanding member of the UniverSoul Circus was probably the last thing on my mind. Alas, there would be no juggling acts or plate spinning for me. No walking on stilts, balancing on unicycles or topping off the human pyramid. No spangled tights or death defying feats. Nope, not for little old me. I would simply smoke my cigarettes (a bad habit I had picked up from the clowns) and bide my time while familiarizing myself with Jorge's tattoos, many of which features bodacious beauties. It wasn't much of a life, but I had approached a real lull and maybe it was way past time for a *lull*abye.

And then I saw her and everything changed. Now, don't get me wrong. In addition to Jorge's beauties, this little circus was home to more than one devastating beauty. But they all belonged to some muscular trampoline artist or lithe acrobat. Indeed, circus folk seemed to come in twos, with many a husband and wife team on board; and since I really wasn't the kind of guy to ogle other men's possessions, I pretty much ignored the parade of pulchritude that passed by me on a daily basis. Besides, even if I had been an indiscreet ho-dog, the size of their husband's muscles and the glare in their foreign eyes would have been enough to set me back.

But she was different. I sensed it from the very beginning when I saw her disembark alone from a yellow cab and then signal the driver with a wave of her hand to *get my bags, Jeeves*. Yeah, she had an aura of royalty about her, that was for sure, and it didn't take long for me to figure out why.

By that time, I had been traveling with UniverSoul for about two weeks, and even though the acts were stunning and the act-robots a visual feast, there always seemed to be something missing. Had I paid attention to any of those flyers I'd been stapling up I would have known why. However, I'd been too busy lamenting the loss of my old life to focus on what was right under my nose.

But remember when I said that circus folk seemed to travel in tandem? Except, of course, for the contortionist who was either a true blue fag or so nimble that he did not require the services of another to find his pleasure. Well, anyway, here was the missing piece, and by all appearances, the *piece de resistance*.

I should have guessed when I first saw the head of white hair that emerged from the interior of the cab. And as for royalty? Well, there was only one ringmaster, and this surely was his cohort.

Shit, I thought to myself. Why do I always go after the unattainable as far as women are concerned? Chalk it up to a human tendency to hanker after what we can't have, or call it just plain stupidity, but it never failed to amaze me the way I would set myself up for such an inevitable fall. However, an alley cat could ogle a Bengal tigress, and that, unfortunately, was a metaphor which would stick as far as my present obsession was concerned. It was love at first bite, and once bitten there was no turning back. I was in thrall, a slave to powers greater than my own.

I followed her that day; I had to, and I can only pray that discretion had been the better part of my valor. All I needed was to get booted for an uncontrollable case of the hots for Pietre's significant other. And it was on account of my initial stalking that I was able to find one glimmer of hope in an otherwise dismal swamp.

She hoisted her rucksack, a bright red blunderbuss that must have weighed a ton, as if it were nothing.

"Ah, strong," I murmured. Yes, strong as well as beautiful. What a deadly combination.

Then she strode nonchalantly over to Pietre's trailer. Where else?

I tried to pretend that there was some stray dog shit over there which needed attending to. It was best to look busy when your real intention is one of downright voyeurism. I mucked around on the ground below an open window searching for troublesome turds, and listened in. But instead of the warm welcome I would have expected from a breeding couple, all I heard was business. I could only pick up scraps of the conversation but it was enough to bring a sigh of relief to my lips.

"Ah, sister, you are back..."

Sister? Why, yes, of course. I had always heard that couples began to resemble each other after a number of years, but these two were way too young to have achieved that status. So sister it was. Yeah, I should have guessed. Who else but a sibling could match that alabaster china look—alabaster which a touch of iron, that is. The unicorn mane should have been a dead giveaway. Oh happy day! This meant I still maintained the same chances as a snowball had in hell, but what did it matter? When you're a lemming plummeting willy-nilly over the nearest abyss, you don't stop to consider such odds.

I continued to listen. There was something about command central, whatever that was and the Alliance Group. Gee, these circus folk were more organized than I'd originally thought. But enough was enough. It appeared the conference was over, giving me pause to wonder if it weren't more like a debriefing than a happy reunion. I stepped away from the window, empty pooper-scooper in hand. I had no excuse to linger, and I sure didn't want to be branded as an eavesdropper. If I had learned one thing during my brief association with the circus, it was that these people were very private and did not take kindly to anyone who sought to dig too deep into their personal affairs. In a sense, this made it the perfect place for me to hide. No one even questioned my lack of a last name or the strangeness of my first. For I was strictly Doe now, having shed the Noone during the high noon of my shoot-out with the Feds. It gave me just a touch of glamour, being a wanted man as it were, and it provided me with the chutzpah I needed to pursue the unattainable. Not that I wouldn't have gone for the golden ring at the top of this merry go-round anyway. The first time I saw her in action sent me over the brink. I knew at that moment I was doomed.

Her name was Aniel, and her official act with UniverSoul was one that I had never seen before. It goes by the name of aerial silks and has only been around since 1995, hence my ignorance as to its existence. It was originally invented by a member of Cirque du Soleil as a means to find original and imaginative ways to captivate an audience, but captivate is far too mild of a word to use in this context. More like mesmerize, enthrall, or bewitch. Yes, bewitch, for she was most assuredly a white witch of the aerial regions when she took to the silks.

Call it aerial contortion, yoga a la air, fabric, ribbon, or just plain *tissu*, but the main point (as the name of the game suggests) is that the artist employs the use of one or two long strips of fabric in their performance. Wrapping the fabric around their bodies, they suspend themselves in mid-air without the use of any safety lines. Then they drop, swing and spiral in and out of incredible positions while the mesmerized public oohs and ahhs at their elegant tricks. The athletic prowess involved in this act was way beyond my own body-building experience, and let's not even get into the sheer nerve it must take to drop close to six feet from a height of sixty. But it wasn't just her courage and stamina that roped me in; it was the overwhelming grace with which she performed. Even though I had never seen such a performance before, I strongly suspected that she was top of the line in her league. At times it seemed as though she was almost flying up there, weightless as an astronaut in deep space. Add to her mystique an assortment of intensely beautiful costumes—and she averaged two an night, one for each act. Then toss it together with a pulsating light show and the overall aura of magic which permeated the UniverSoul, and you have a recipe for one totally mystified boy.

Every time I watched her it was right up there with a religious experience, and by the time a month had passed I was one hundred percent converted. However, I might also add that within this span of time, said princess of the aerial regions had probably uttered a total of ten words to me, most of which were centered on one command or another.

"Did FedEx deliver that roll of Nylon I ordered?"

"Did you pick up Dolly's meds yet?"

And worst of all: "That commode is stopped up again. Could you take a look at it?"

The commode? Oh, right. Her word for toilet—AKA shitter—and though I don't recall it being on the fritz before, she must be referring to the one in the trailer she shared with Pietre. Alas, what a way to pop a guy's bubble. My princess did indeed excrete, which meant she was slave to the same bodily functions as the rest of the human race. This came as quite the revelation because, believe me, after a month of watching her soar the aerial ethers, I was beginning to have my doubts. And for that reason, I was more delighted to process her latest request than I should have been.

Plumber's tool box in hand, I sauntered over to the trailer in question. Would she be within? No, probably not since I had just seen her talking with Lola, whose specialty centered on training a fleet of Salukis. Apparently one of the Salukis had eaten too much and had a bad case of the runs, which meant that my services would soon be required elsewhere. But what the heck? Might as well deal with one shit storm at a time. At least the one generated by the humans would allow me access to my beloved's inner sanctuary.

Suspecting that Pietre would be within, I knocked on the door. But there was no answer which presented somewhat of a dilemma. Was I to enter unbidden? After all, I was on a mission and not a pleasant one at that. Call it the epitome of the dirty job that someone's got to do. But then again, I can't remember ever seeing anyone enter through that door unless either Pietre or Aniel was there to greet them.

Oh well, what's the harm? That toilet wasn't about to pull rank on me. Nor was it about to require a written invitation. So I might as well risk a good chewing out, and with that, I opened the door and entered within.

The first thing that came to my attention was the smell, something like heady incense, and surely not the odor one might have expected from a ten by fifteen dwelling with faulty plumbing.

"Guess they were trying make a silk purse out of a sow's ear," I mumbled as I passed the small table that served as both kitchen and command central. On it were scattered a ton of papers as well as the remains of last night's dinner. Why I paused there was beyond me. Let's just say that something was just not right, and it niggled my brain.

Some of the paperwork was predictable, payments due and bills pending, and I could tell by the coffee stains on both that the UniverSoul was in sore need of a secretary.

Jeez, I muttered. *It's a wonder they can pay my salary.* But then come to think of it, they were already two weeks behind on that little detail. Oh well, there were always all those intrinsic rewards which came from working such a gig. Anonymity for one, and Aniel for the rest. Right, Aniel, which brought me back to the task at hand.

Until, that is, I saw something out of the corner of my eye. It stood out like a red herring in a sea of green—all the rest being items which pertained to financial matters—and at first my brain didn't want to let go of the notion that it must have something to do with the business end of things. But, guess again, since business doesn't usually involve the detailed configurations of solar systems (unless, of course, it's involved with off-world trade).

Off-world? Gee, Doe, I swore. *You big dope. Why don't you just smoke another one?*

However, it was too late. My curiosity, once aroused, was worse than my dick, meaning that it became hell-bent on satisfaction. I couldn't help myself and lifted the pile to get a closer look, and that's when I really got a shock. Because what lay before me was no familiar solar system. Gone were the old standbys of Jupiter and Mars, and even though I hadn't really paid much attention when we'd turned to the astronomy section of the textbooks, I was hip enough to realize that the stars on this chart were none-too-familiar. In fact, the names of them seemed to be written in a different language, one which if I had to guess lay somewhere between Chinese and ancient Sanskrit. Determined to make some sense of it all, I fell into studying the document in front of me and became so hypnotized I didn't even hear the door open. But, boy, I sure did hear his voice.

"Just what are you doing in here?" he demanded, and the tone given was surely not one a lowly flunky wished to hear uttered by his boss.

I whipped around, dropping the document back into the pile from which it came. I had to think quick or I knew that my expulsion from the UniverSoul would be so sudden it would take two weeks for my underwear to catch up with me. Thank God, I had developed a flare for lying.

"Looking for a something to write on," I blundered. "Aniel sent me over here to check on the plumbing in the bathroom, and I need…"

Thank god, he interrupted me because I had no idea what I needed, having never gotten that far in the little story I'd been concocting. Hell, I hadn't even made it as far as the water closet, so how did I know what I would need to fix it?

However, he conveniently, filled in the blanks.

"You need to do an about face. There's nothing wrong with our plumbing here. She must have meant to send you to Lola's trailer. Jorge was just over there last week, and the place is a nightmare. So gather you gear and get going."

OK, OK, no problem. I can do that. And trembling a bit because the star chart still showed signs of recent tampering, I did exactly as I was told. After all, there was no room for argument. That said, I hightailed it out of there feeling as though I had dodged a major bullet.

It was a good feeling, and one which stayed with me halfway to Lola's. However, at which point the second revelation of the day hit me like a ton of bricks. It had been Jorge who had executed the earlier repairs. Jorge, of the thousand tattoos and bad breathe. Not Slim Jim sleek and studly little surfer boy me. Which could only mean one thing. That in her mind, we were one and the same. No diff. Just two down and out roustabouts whose sole purpose in life was to follow the orders of our masters and follow them to a tee, an act which often involved the fine art of mind reading.

Wow! Talk about a buzz kill! To say it was a real blow to the old ego was putting it mildly, and it would have stopped most guys dead in their tracks. But remember what I said about my old periscope? That once it went up, it seemed to get permanently stuck in the ON position until someone came to lubricate it? Well, that should explain why it was so hard to turn my tail and run as fast as I could in the opposite direction. Lord knows I had every reason to. There is nothing worse than unrequited lust, and it's gotten more than one bloke in a heap of trouble. Combine this with a growing certainly that there were strange forces at work in the immediate neighborhood, and you have a real recipe for disaster.

But did I heed the voice of reason? Nope, you guessed it. That would have been much too simple. Instead, I allowed said forces to continue to play with me in their capricious little will-o-the-wisp way, similar to the method a cat employs with a mouse. Cats, the only species on the planet, save mankind, that kills just for sport.

The months wore on, until we were deep into winter. By that time, we had migrated south to the border states of Arizona and New Mexico. I should have been ecstatic, finding myself that close to my purposed escape route. All I needed to do now was grab the cool five hundred that was still owed to me and slip across to Mexico in the middle of the night. It seemed like an easy enough plan, but one I kept postponing. Yeah, if the will is strong enough, one can always find a way; if not, one can always find an excuse.

I had to hand it to myself. I had more excuses than Carter had little red pills. I needed more money; my grubstake was too grubby. (A partial truth.) I enjoyed circus life. (A lie.) I was making new friends. (A boldfaced lie.) I was learning a new skill. (Out and out bullshit! What's so skillful about cleaning up after a geriatric camel?) Oh, the list went on and on, but it always came back to its starting point. Aniel.

Her name had become somewhat of an anthem to me. You would have thought I'd be saluting with hand to heart every time I witnessed her soaring through the air in her star spangled leotard. But instead, I was just trying hard not to cream my jeans. Yeah, me and every other red blooded American boy in the audience. The only difference between them and me was that they could go home and sleep it off. Then, after awhile, the vision of her would recede into a mere memory, a pleasant one at that, and not be the raw wound I had to deal with on a daily basis.

Boy, did it hurt. So much so that I began to question my sanity. I began having wild fantasies. I'd be working up a sweat in the heat and she would pass me by. *You look so hot,* she'd murmur, and I would request a cool down by asking her if she'd pour water over me. But not before I stripped off all my clothes and stood in front of her, my buff body sending out streams of irresistible hormones.

Oh, I know; it was just awful. So awful I should have quit the whole business and joined a monastery, the kind where you got to wear a hair shirt and flagellate yourself regularly with a cat-o-nine tails. Call me a masochist, but anything would be preferable to the agony I was experiencing by remaining in her presence. I just didn't see how I could possibly go on this way much longer.

And then life, with its usual aplomb, managed to come along and issue me an exit plan, and given that it was a one way ticket, there was no chance of turning back.

We were parked in the Carson National Forest in New Mexico, taking a much needed break from our busy touring schedule. The place was famous for hosting some of the finest mountain scenery in the southwest. There were lakes filled with fish, forests of conifer and aspen, and trails which lead to unique geographical features. These could be reached by horse, mountain bike, or just plain foot travel, and I was making it a point to take in as many as possible since it gave me a reason to get away from camp and the constant allure of one of its principal inhabitants.

However, on that particular occasion I have to confess that I had succumbed to her charms once again and…OK, let's call a spade a spade. To be blunt, I was stalking her.

It was evening and there had been talk of a hot springs which wasn't far off. Some of the members of the troupe had already sampled its healing waters and had nothing but praise for the experience. So it came as no surprise when I overheard Aniel speak of her intention to follow suit.

"I'll be going alone," she stated, and I knew this meant business. When Aniel made statements like that, the entire camp had best stand at attention.

Yet I still couldn't help myself. I was in love, remember? Yeah, OK… Call it what you may, but them was fighting words for you know which part of my anatomy. Alone? In a beautiful remote location where soothing waters relaxed all inhibitions, so much so that they had become famous for their clothing-optional status? Alone? Yeah, we'll see about that!

I followed her through the forest that evening. Thank god there was a rising moon big enough to read by, or I would have lost my way. Oh, I guess I could have followed her scent; I'd become that adapt at separating it from all others. But the moon was a real plus, especially since it and only it would guide my way home.

The path was long, at least a mile hike from camp, and led through whispering pines and aspens. It was probably twice as beautiful by day, but that hardly mattered to me since I was in pursuit of a different sort of beauty, one which I was struggling to keep up with. Wow, could that girl set a pace, but then what did else did I expect from a world class athlete?

Then, just when I was beginning to wonder if we would ever achieve our goal, I heard the rush of water. At this, I dropped back, not wishing to blow my cover, but not before a series of pools came into view, all laid out like a string of pearls under the moonlight. The steam which poured off them was a dead giveaway that I had reached my destination. The only problem came when I realized that, in my attempt to remain incognito, I had lost sight of my prey. Which way did she go? Upstream to the cave which fed the pools? For there the waters would surely be hottest, and you could sit inside and get about as close to a sauna as nature could provide. Or did she venture downstream to where a picturesque waterfall was rumored to spill into a pool deep enough for a righteous swim?

It was a difficult dilemma, but in the end, my vision of her as a slippery fish led me to pursue the downstream path, and it did not disappoint me. As I came around the final bend before the waterfall, I heard her splashing and knew I had made the right decision. But I'd best not advertise my presence yet—or maybe not at all. Best do what I had come to do and merely watch. After all, just how could I explain my presence, especially when she had made it so clear she preferred solitude to the company of others?

"But, wait a minute!" my dick insisted. *"Who is running this show anyway?"* Boy was the MF'er screaming, so loud I was sure she could hear his complaining above the roar of the waterfall. What a struggle—the old spirit is willing, but flesh is weak routine—and I swore the spirit was losing the argument.

But just when the flesh was zeroing in for the kill, something strange happened. The moon was swallowed by a cloud, and the whole scene became shrouded in darkness. The whole scene that is, except the pool in which my lady frolicked. It was on fire, the fire of a phosphorescent tide, bubbling and boiling in a rainbow of colors which streamed from her naked body like the molten magic of a Jamaican sunset. It defied all logic, and my brain gave up trying to find a rhyme or reason for the data my optic nerve was feeding it. Let's just say it was other worldly and leave it at that since words fail when it comes to describing certain experiences. But weirder yet was the aftermath of all this hoopla, because no sooner did the moon peek back from its resting spot, than my eyes beheld an even stranger sight—an empty pool,

Empty? As in no one around? Yes, Noone, that's true, unless you want to count yourself, which once again comes up to a big No One, you big dope!

"Well, I'll be damned," I muttered, and then not entirely sure I wanted to condemn myself to such hellfire, I amended that to read *well, I'll be a monkey's uncle,* because that was more like it. For whatever she was, she had certainly made a monkey out of me

Stymied as to what to do next, I stood on the shore for at least five minutes, hoping that maybe she had just ducked down under the water to cavort with her brethren within. Then, fully satisfied no living person could hold their breath that long, I decided to pursue the only practical path left to me; and stripping off my clothes, I entered the pool. My mind was still racing, and my brain continued to pump out the fantasies which had kept me going for the past few months. Who knows, maybe it was a magical pool and I, too, would disappear, only to emerge in some other dimension. It might even be the fifth dimension of Internet fame, that marvelous place of ascension which transcends all earthly delights. Yeah, farewell to all that worldly bullshit. No more eating and shitting and fucking and breathing. Just pure unadulterated essence of being in which me and my lady had finally merged into one big ball of love. Oh, happy day! Oh, Kallabunga!

Yeah, it was a nice thought and a nicer try. Jeez! Were those waters ever cold, so cold my balls sought instant solace in the cradle of my groin. Now, how the hell could there be hot springs less than a quarter of a mile away? Had I dreamed that, too? Just like I had conjured up the rainbow of colors that had engulfed my pretty little nymph? I looked down at my arms and legs and noted with some chagrin that they remained invisible under the water. Alas, there would be no more light shows for this boy tonight.

I hung my head and that's when one of the most intense feelings I have ever had washed over me. It was like a tidal wave in its strength and just about as destructive, for when it departed, it left me feeling totally devastated. In one way this was good, for it had sucked all the lust right out of me. No longer would I ever look at a pretty girl the way I had since puberty had come and conquered me. Now, some might say this is a good thing—if, that is, they are a monk living on top a mountain somewhere. But for a red blooded boy, it was almost a death sentence. At least the monk had some sense of universal love to fill the gap. Me? All I had was a hollow spot, a lonely itch somewhere in the middle of my back in a place that defied scratching. It was hell, sheer hell, this sense of longing for a love I had never known, and I knew right then and there I would be spending the rest of my days on this planet in search of the unattainable.

I guess that was when it began—my journey of a thousand miles. Everything up to that point had just been a trial run. Now began the real McCoy.

I swam to the shore and slipped back into my clothes. May as well not face eternity naked. It was bad enough that my soul seemed to have been stripped bare, leaving me a motherless child lost in the wilderness.

Well… not exactly lost, because I somehow managed to find my way back to camp or at least where I thought camp should be. It was dawn by now, not that this helped matters because empty means empty. I blinked my eyes and turned around several times, searching the horizon for any sign of a dozen trailers and their inhabitants, both human and otherwise. However, the view remained the same, blending right in with the rest of the terrain, nothing but rocks and trees. The latter seemed to whisper amongst themselves, and I swear they were talking about me—how it served me right, since I had broken a taboo, and hadn't I been warned, and who did I think I was?

It made the hairs on the back of my neck stand up to think such thoughts. They were right, of course. But wasn't the punishment a bit harsh. All I had done was... OK, there I go again, making excuses for myself. I bent down to pick up a flyer, hoping it would provide a clue. Perhaps they had simply moved on in the middle of the night, or maybe the ranger had come and evicted them. Hell, they were well known for side-stepping authority and the fees it often imposed. Yeah, and speaking of which, hadn't they just waltzed off with five hundred big ones that belonged to little old me as well as what little remained of my earthly possessions? Thank God, I still had my phone. Yeah, at least they'd left me that much. Following the siren song of my generation, I fallen into the habit of taking it with me at all times, even to places where all I could hope to pick up was Pluto. But as for the loss of the money and all my stuff? Now, THAT was harsh!!!

I sat down on a stump, my head between my knees, and then took a peek at the flyer. From its depths she glared back at me. I was reminded of scriptural references to the Holy Grail and how it would turn the unshriven into dust. Wow! If that was so, I had dodged a major bullet, because I still remained flesh and blood. I guess.

I pinched myself to make sure I wasn't still asleep. Had I slept at all during that endless night? I think not, but Rip Van Winkle had probably suffered from the same affliction, and his inability to stay on task had cost him twenty some years. Had I come back an old man? I felt my face. It was still the smooth shaven silk of an android's butt. I had kept it clean so as to impress my lady whose perfectly waxed skin reflected an aversion to bodily hair.

I sighed. My lady. What a joke. And then, because I had no other recourse, I got up and began to walk. At least I had the clothes on my back. She could have taken them too, and then I would have had a hell of a time catching a ride to God knows where.

And speaking of which, where was I going? It came as no revelation that I was clueless. And that's when a strange memory popped into my head. It centered on a roly-poly lady who lived by nefarious means. We'd just finished cleaning up some of the best sinsemilla I had ever sampled. The stuff had been so fine it had been hard not to smoke up all the profits. However, there had also been so much of it this was virtually impossible. Just a field of voluptuous green buds languishing on a table beckoning to me to *come and get it, big boy.*

Yeah, those had been the days, the happy-go-lucky hop-along-sassily days of my misspent youth. But that had also been some time ago, at least a decade. Still her words had echoed down the years only to bounce back like an anthem to my sore ears.

It had been the words to a song, a popular one in my mom's day, but one now demoted to the jukeboxes in redneck bars. Something about finding out that the whole world was smoldering, but if you get lost? Well, just come on home to Green River.

Yeah, that was it. Green River…and by the process of association it all flooded back. Leslie's *little big woman* spread in the foothills of the Appalachians. The days well spent butchering hogs. OK, then, not so well spent. But they sure did morph into something much bigger and more down my alley when I realized the hogs had just been a front for the farm's true source of revenue.

Ah yes, Green River indeed where the emerald hued marijuana flowed freely downstream to where it was converted into a different shade of green—as in greenbacks. So if she hadn't gone belly up or been busted by the Feds, good old Leslie would still be in business; and since she'd always been a woman of her word, I figured her offer still stood. Just in time, too. Because boy, oh boy, did I need to cash in on a piece of that cash cow.

If you get lost? Was that supposed to be some kind of joke? If so, I was the walking punch line. And though I had every reason not to, I smiled and strode off in the direction of the rising sun.

Chapter 12
Lulu (AKA Stitch)
Summer 2014 to Spring 2018

They say that pride goeth before a fall, but that's selling it short. You see, it's never that easy to sum up human behavior in such simple terms, so I have amended that statement to fit the circumstances. How about mouth *opens before a fall*? Especially if you've managed to stick your foot in it, and had I ever! It all came back to my book, where else? I was so convinced it would be another War *and Peace* that I was completely incapable of separating the two.

War and peace. Two opposing entities and about as far from each other as you can get. Indeed, there is no peace in war, as anyone who has left home and hearth to fight in foreign soil will assure you, and the more I wrote about my first hand experience in a military family, the more obvious this became. That said, I found myself straying further and further from my original intentions.

The book was meant to be a simple biography, but I was way too close to the topic to allow it to remain in such didactic status. If I had, all I would have written was three hundred pages which stated over and over again that both my father and brother were outstanding Marines. Exciting stuff and exactly what they want you to say. You are never supposed to depart into the dark waters of interpersonal relationships, and heaven forbid should you ever completely go off the reservation and flounder in the quagmire of anti-war sentiment.

In self-defense, I never meant for this to happen. It just did, making it a crime of passion versus one of premeditative murder. You see, writers need to write about what they have experienced personally, and all the books I read on Korea, Vietnam, and Afghanistan became nothing more than military history, a skeleton framework upon which to hang my own dirty laundry and air my own personal opinions. I know this now, but there's another popular saying which states that hindsight is 20/20, a revelation that comes way too late. But I'm getting ahead of myself again, so let's back-track and fill in the blanks with all the gory details.

The Azores was meant to be the apogee of my orbit, and as I began to descend from its dizzying heights, I started to wonder if I would ever again achieve such a high. It goes without saying that after six months in a subtropical paradise, the bleak streets of Cincinnati held little charm. Oh, it wasn't as though I hadn't done this routine before. Why, only last year I had returned from a similar scene, albeit one on the opposite side of the globe. Yes, life after Hawaii had also been a bit of an adjustment. However, back then I was still on my walkabout, so Cincinnati was nothing more than just a station break. But now my travels were officially over, and it was time to buckle down and roll up my sleeves, not an easy thing to do when you have spent the last four years of your life flitting around the world, searching for one Holy Grail after another.

But there was no getting around it. The simple fact that funds were getting short was enough to prohibit any more jet setting. Besides, I had been assigned this mission, and it would be a slap in the face of the Ayahuasca spirit to quit in mid-stream. So I did what any intrepid traveler might do once they realized their ship had set sail without them and won't be returning for awhile, and I sat down to take stock of the situation.

The first item on the agenda involved a serious examination of my financial picture. I knew the past few years had cost more than originally intended, but just how much more came as a shock. Gee, maybe I should have been examining those bank statements all along instead of tossing them in the nearest circular file, if there had even been one nearby. During the times when I had arranged for long term accommodations, I had attempted to have my more important mail forwarded to me. However, it's easy for said paper trail to get broken when we are talking distances of thousands of miles. So there had been more than a few gaps in my correspondence with my bank. My attitude at the time had been one of *what the heck*, and I guess this had been somewhat irresponsible of me. But there had been a reason why I had switched from a major in Accounting to one in Liberal Arts, as numbers simply weren't my forte. I was much more comfortable in the nebulous clouds of classical literature or Renaissance Art—and even more so in the fine art of crafting my own words upon the page.

Which brings us back to square one. My book, that is. It was a rambling manuscript of well over four hundred pages now, and I still hadn't reached its glorious conclusion, though I had to give myself credit in that department as I was close.

But close wasn't going cut it. Close wouldn't pay the bills for very long. Besides, the appearance of those two wonderful on the page—the ones signaling THE END—did not necessarily equate with a finished product. No, it was really then that the fun began. First would come the editing, and then the proofreading, both laborious processes in themselves, yet nothing close to the final labor which would involve finding someone to take on the publication process.

Publication. I groaned. It had been a word I had pushed to the back of my brain for years now. I had been so caught up in the creation of my novel that I had purposefully ignored the bottom line of the entire writing process. It was the one dictating that, unless the author wanted their manuscript to be for their eyes only, they'd best find a way to make it public. However, making it public was so much easier said than done.

I thought on all the scare stories I had heard of writers who could paper their entire walls with rejection letters. I pondered on the people skills that would be necessary to court the publishing world. The phone calls (I hated to talk on the phone). The emails (I hated computers and only used one for the writing process). The interviews (if I ever got so lucky). The...oh, you know. The list is endless.

Wow! Had I ever dreamed it would be this difficult? And this time consuming? And time was money and both were running out. I knew I needed to do something and fast. There was always my old trade to fall back on. The Stitchworks had paid the rent once, and if I took it out of the closet and dusted it off, it could probably do so again. But it had been a long time since I'd held a needle to fabric, long enough to lose most of my clients. So the process of resurrecting my business would be just about as painstaking as trying to find a publisher. Plus there was at least a year of grunt work to accomplish before I even began my search for the latter, grunt work that would take hours out of my day. So where would I ever find time to sew on buttons and take up hems, tasks that seemed easy enough until you realized how many of them added up to a week's worth of groceries. No, I needed something more permanent, yet definitely not full-time, and that kind of gig could only be found in the established work world, not the dubious one of entrepreneurship.

However, for the time being, I would have to make do with the resources available to me. So the Stitchworks it would be—at least until I found something better—and with that in mind, I set off towards a small local library to make a few copies of my old flyer.

Now it's funny the way life seems to come around again, so that you find yourself running in circles which are a variation on a central theme. Years back, I had been forced to work at a library as a payback for crimes against the state. Community service was what they had called it, but I'd called it a blow job—until that is, it paid off in a big way by leading me to the flyer I now held in my hand. I had owed my break to the head librarian, an aging matriarch who had befriended me for reasons I never fully understood. Whatever the case, it had been my lucky day.

So why did it surprise me when the old revolving door of the library came around to smack me on the ass with yet another opportunity. Except this time, the details were reversed, and instead of ramping up my arsenal to work outside its doors, the library provided me with an inside job.

It helped that I was no stranger to the place. They knew me well from the past few years in which I'd taken up semi-permanent residence in this fair city. In fact, I had even dropped in on their writer's group a time or two, a fact which had really ingratiated me to the head honcho, another aging matriarch by the name of Miss McClure. I think it was hard for her to find interested parties for all the little add-ons the library sponsored, just as it was imperative for the library to expand itself from the stereotype of a place devoted only to dusty tomes. For today's libraries need to be so much more if they are going to continue to receive the funding that keeps their doors open. Hence all the little crafty crap which was held for the kiddies on weekends, and the book signings, and bake sales, and poetry slams. Yeah, libraries sure do rock a whole lot harder than the days of my youth when all they featured were books, books and more books and a strict overseer who implored you to remain silent at all times or suffer the consequences.

Enter one Miss McClure who, though somewhat stereotypical with her horn-rimmed glasses and unattractive hairdo—can you say a bun—was still one of the coolest people I had ever met. In truth, she never ceased to amaze me. She had every reason to be a grumpy old biddy since a childhood affliction had left her with a considerable limp, one which greatly impeded her ability to move around on the planet and which even confined her to a wheel chair at times. However, this never held her back. Rain or shine, sitting or standing, she often stood at the door welcoming all who entered and smiling like a Wal-Mart greeter. This routine sure beat the hell out of most head librarians who preferred to remain in an office buried deep in the stacks somewhere, and it was one which found many customers returning to this little hole in the wall excuse for a library again and again. I was no exception.

"You're back," she noted and her face broke out in an even deeper smile, one which made me feel special. She had that effect on people. It was as if she was going the extra mile just for your benefit.

"Yeah, home is the sailor..." I responded in my best old-salt-on-shore-leave tone of voice. I had always tried to perpetuate the image of a world traveler and therefore not just another bookish matron in need of a good Danielle Steele read. But the truth was that libraries were one of the few places on the planet I called home, regardless of where in the world they might be. There was something about those cloistered stacks of books which was holy to me, and sometimes I would just stop into one to inhale the musty odor of the printed page. So Danielle Steele or Leo Tolstoy, it hardly mattered. I was usually just there to soak up the ambience.

Today, however, was a different matter. Today I was on a mission, as the grubby piece of paper in my hand insisted. So I got right down to business. I figured I'd better before she got into the second part of her routine which was to name by heart new arrivals to the library. How she kept them all straight was beyond me. She must have taken a list home every night and memorized it.

"Just here to use the copy machine," I began, and that was the moment my life changed in a big way.

"Oh, I'm so sorry..." She looked disappointed. "Yesterday was Amanda's last day, and I'm no good with that machine."

Amanda was the girl who usually assisted with any copying the library did, arguing with the antiquated machine when it refused to spit out its required pages and repairing it with duct tape and rubber bands and *Grimoire's Book of Spells* whenever the thing broke down completely. However, this was not the only item on her resume. She was also chief book shelver, and toilet scrubber, and plant waterer, and just about any other sort of menial task the library required. And for her efforts I am sure she received the monthly stipend mandated by the state agency which funded the place.

Now, I'm no genius when it comes to fixing machines. However I can push buttons, and if by chance today was one of the copier's better days, I might be in luck. I sensed an opportunity here, one which might lead to bigger and better things than The Stitchworks.

"Oh, that's no problem," I assured her. "If you don't mind, I can do it myself." And as it turned out, this was just the exact attitude Miss McClure was looking for.

Later, when it became apparent—and I made sure it did—that I was copying material in order to resurrect my old business, my friend was quick to catch on.

"So you're looking for work?" she asked.

And that's when I made it known I needed something part-time so I could continue to work on my manuscript.

Well, that sealed the deal.

What followed was a gentlewoman's agreement, a shaking of hands, which assured me that—yes, indeed—I had found a pot of gold at the end of the rainbow. And if all it amounted to was mopping up around another pot of gold, the one in the library's cubbyhole bathroom? Well, at least I was assured a steady paycheck for my efforts.

The gig lasted a good two years. To say it was the most exciting time in my life would be a boldfaced lie, but it served its purpose and then some. Within several months of my employment, I saw those magical words appear at the end of my manuscript. By then, I had been firmly reinstalled in the writer's group which gave me ample opportunity to receive feedback as I labored over the editing process. Of course, this was slow going since the group only met once a month. But my mentor, Ms. McClure, had seen fit to take me under her wing and provide me with a crash course in the finer points of grammar.

Every time you see the word THAT in your writing, cross it out!
Comma splices. Seek and Destroy.
Don't name an emotion, express it through action.
Get rid of all nonessential words.
Don't use an explanation point unless you plan on shouting.
That's passive voice. Remove it!
You have too many adjectives there.
Watch those adverbs!

Oh, the list went on and on and I have to say that, though she was a strict taskmaster, she was good. I guess that's what a Master's Degree in Journalism will do for you. Or is it *to* you? There's a subtle distinction, you know.

Whatever the case, by the time two years had gone by, I had not only achieved a polished manuscript, but had also been steered towards a way to see it in print. This, too, was a by-product of my association with the writers group.

It all began the day we discovered a new face among our participants. Since our group was very small—so small it often amounted to only McClure and me—this was a significant development. That said,

McClure fell all over herself trying to impress the newcomer. Little Debby cakes were rolled out from their turn of the century hiding place, and the coffee water was set to boil. However, all the hoopla quieted down once introductions were made and that inevitable question answered.

"So what are you are working on right now?" McClure asked the newcomer, and the response was not one that sat right with old-stick-to-the books.

"Well..." the guy drawled (and one look at him suggested a Faulkner wanna-be, fake accent an all)..."I'm kinda in the middle of editin' a couple of my books that I published on LULU."

Published on LULU? My ears perked up, but any reaction I may have demonstrated was quickly upstaged by McClure's. You could almost sense the steam rising from her boiling blood, and I feared that any minute now it would burst forth from her mouth in a stream of expletives, the kind that are completely unacceptable when uttered by an aging library matriarch. How she kept it under wraps was beyond me, as was any reason for her reaction.

However, the mystery was soon solved when she went on to politely denounce the self-publishing business. You see, in McClure's mind, such a shortcut was cheating. It was absolutely essential that one suffered the many stages of the cross if they were to ever see their name in print. Call it old school, but this was her take on it all and no amount of rhetoric on the part of the Faulkner wanna-be could convince her otherwise.

What followed was a lively discussion, or should I say an argument amongst friends—not that I ever felt McClure and Faux-Faulkner would ever reach such an enlightened status. I tried to remain an impartial observer as they both held viable talking points, but in the end I couldn't help but take sides. Hell, my life depended on it. I had neither the money nor the patience to pursue the stereotypical route offered by McClure. I was in a hurry, you see. Funds were running low and unless I wanted to be doomed to the tether of a full-time position at the library—and McClure had made sure I was up for promotion—I had better get this ball rolling.

So afterwards I waylaid the guy in the parking lot. I knew from his reaction to her reaction that he would not be coming back which made this my only chance to pump him for more information.

"How about a cup of coffee on me," I offered, even though we'd already drunk enough of the black brew to float a boat, and his smile broadened. It became my green light, and I proceeded full speed ahead.

Over coffee he gave me the run down on LULU. In essence, it was an on-line self-publishing house which eliminated a hell of a lot of middlemen, namely the uppity elitist snobs who called themselves editors and publishers.

"You got no idear just how many of these clowns I've sent my manuscript out to," the Faulkner informed me. "Why if I had a nickel for every rejection notice those sons of a bitches sent to me, I'd be a rich man. But that was in the bad ole days, before the Internet came along and changed the publishing world for good. Now anybody can find a soapbox to stand on, and the best part is that it's almost free. All you gotta do is send your manuscript up there, and they do all the rest."

"Meaning?" My eyebrows rose to emphasis my question.

"Meaning they publish on demand on, and in less than two weeks you are lookin at a shiny new copy of your precious work which only costs you, the author, about ten bucks. Yeah, ten bucks to see your name in print. Of course, the rest is all up to you because, until someone else comes along and orders your book, that copy could very well be the only paper one in existence. But who cares? That's what I say. Cuz at least you've gone and done it!

"Now I researched a bunch of these on-line guys. They've been springing up like mushrooms in a hayfield over the past ten years, but LULU was the one that stood out. For one thing, they've been around longer than most and for another..."

Well, I didn't want to interrupt his monologue to insert that his analogy was a bit off. The only mushrooms I knew to inhabit a hayfield grew on cow manure and were of the psilocybin variety, and that brought forth the image of a pipe dream, which I sincerely hoped was not his intention. No, I was done with chasing rainbows. I needed that pot of gold at the end of one.

"So," I interrupted. "Just how do you go about doing all this if you aren't too good with computers?"

And that's when I hit my first stumbling block. Apparently one had to be pretty sharp with Microsoft Word in order to wade through the formatting process required to upload a manuscript to the site. However, my new friend had a solution to that.

"I've been at this for awhile, ma'am," he explained. "In fact, I'm on my fourth novel right now. So I've got it down to a science with all that there formattin'. So if you want, I could send you a blank start- up file, one with the headers and footers already embedded into it."

Start-up file? Headers and footers? Oh crap! I was quickly careening out of my element here. Basic Word I could master, but not all the fancy stuff that went with it. In fact, to most, my manuscript would probably resemble one big long rambling paragraph. Oh, McClure had helped, but there was still a lot of polishing to do. So maybe it was time to call in the heavy artillery.

"Sorry," I began. "You're not really talking my language here. I'm going to need a little help getting started with all this. I don't suppose you know anyone who would be willing to work with me. But it can't cost an arm and a leg, cuz I'm getting a little low on funds and..."

I trailed off. No need to plague a perfect stranger with my financial woes. Besides, being a self-published Faulkner wanna-be, I'm sure he was on a first name basis with the wolf at the door.

"Well, little lady," he smiled. (And at that, I cringed as no one had ever had the balls to call me out on account of my pint-sized frame. However, I cut him some slack since I figured it was all part of his show.)

He paused, as if catching my distress, then went on.

"I just might have a person in mind. Happens to be a niece of mine who lives over by Athens. Graduated from a local tech school with a geek squad certificate, but can't seem to do much more with it than sell crap on EBay. However, I know she'd be more than happy to take on your little project for a slight fee. She's a good girl and probably wouldn't charge you much. Want me to hook you two up?"

Not that he needed a reply. The desperation in my eyes said it all.

It was a crisp fall day when I met Kady, Faulkner's niece. She lived out in the country a good two hour's drive from Cincinnati, so I had to rent a car for the day in order to take my files over to her. No way was I about to send such precious material through the hackable vacuum of cyberspace. Plus she wanted to establish an account for me on LULU and needed me present so I could help her develop an online presence on the site. So I bite the bullet and broke out my credit card for the car rental.

I had to admit it was a nice drive, despite the landscape being despoiled by a plethora of political signs advertising the upcoming election. Those for TRUMP decidedly outnumbered those for his opponent, one Hitlary Clinton as the TRUMPETS liked to call her. However, I called her just another politician, which meant that:

Number 1: She didn't give a rat's ass about the people and

Number 2: She was probably as crooked as Horseshoe Bend down in Leavenworth, Indiana.

And, come to think of it, wasn't there a major prison there? Oh who cares? For today my mind was not on the best place to house politicians, but on my own little political dissertation which just so happened to be riding along with me via thumbdrive, securely hidden in a secret compartment in my small backpack.

Yeah, I must have known, even then, that my writing was inflammatory to the point of needing special protections just to cross the county line. Or maybe I was just being paranoid, but I kept on looking over at the backpack to make sure I hadn't left it at the last pit stop. The file inside was, after all, the only copy I had except for the one on my laptop. And who knows, maybe at this very moment someone was rifling through my personal effects back home. Well, that would soon change. Soon it would be available for the entire world to read, and would it ever be a game changer and eye opener! That said, it was sure to become a best seller, meaning I would have to get over my aversion to the spotlight and get out there and go to press conferences and writer's conventions and trade shows… and…

Wow, was my mind ever going a mile a minute. So fast I almost missed the turn-off to Kady's driveway, a lane that led to a Levittown like dwelling in a small subdivision. *Doesn't seem like the kind of place a computer whiz would live*, I thought to myself. However, since Faulkner had already prepped me for the fact that Kady, like many of her generation, still lived at home, I should have known what to expect.

On the other hand, Kady threw me for a loop. I had anticipated the orange hair and wall-to-wall tattoos that many millennials sported, but the only concession this girl seemed to make to her age group were some faded tattoos. Other than that her appearance was about as normal as you can get with mousy brown hair, standard issue American garb (jeans and a tee-shirt) and not one bit of metal to be found. Jeez, she could have been working at a library, like me.

I tried not to stare as she introduced herself. Funny how automatic that response is when you are expecting one thing and get another. But if she found my gaze disconcerting, she blew it off and we quickly got down to business.

It didn't take long. Just a few simple questions and, if I hadn't been so obsessed with maintaining what little privacy is left to us by our cyber–world, they could have easily been answered over the phone or via email. However, when it got down to the title, that became a different story.

The title? Well, you might have thought the title would have been one of the first things I'd come up with, for isn't it standard operating procedure to put the horse before the cart? Yeah, but not for me. I always did have to go about things bass-ackwards. Not that I hadn't contemplated and dismissed plenty of candidates. Biblical shit like *The Sins of the Fathers*. (Way too harsh.) Plays on words like *Many are Called, but Few are Chosin*. (OK if I'd just been writing about my dad, but this was a duet involving both my father and brother.) English lit spin-offs like *The Rhyme of the Ancient Mariner: Part Two*. (Copyright issues?) Alas, the list of rejects was endless, and I was just about ready to throw out my current baby with the bathwater when I got a big idea.

It arrived as many big ideas do, born out of happenstance, because my biggest stumbling block with this most recent title was its sheer redundancy. After all who is going to take a book seriously which bears the name A *Mariner's Marine* by *Maureen* Singleton? I mean, that's way too much alliteration even for me!

Yet I still could not bring myself to complete rejection of this title, for it said it all. You see, the Marine Corps is an institution which prides itself on being made up of the elite amongst the elite. Therefore the term a *Marine's Marine* refers to the best of the best, and wasn't that a proper way of referring to these two guys. Why, either one of the them should have won that contest the Corp sponsors every April during which they compare two Marine Corps legends in the categories of service, legacy, and motivation and then vote to see which one wins the award for the year. And the fact that it would be a posthumous award made their case all the stronger. Yes, *A Marine's Marine* was a hell of a good title for a book about two outstanding members of the Corps.

But not when the author bore a name like Maureen. It had been one which had quickly replaced my birth name of Mary, when my overzealous father insisted that *we've always had a Marine in the family and aren't about to stop now.* I guess he was setting me up for back-up, just in case something happened to either one of my brothers or, perish the thought, they decided not to follow the family tradition and join the Corps. Yeah, at least in the worst case scenario there would still be a Marine (Maureen) to carry on the family tradition.

Until, that is, I reached adulthood and developed enough sense of autonomy to ditch the first name for one of my own liking. Stitch it was, and Stitch it remained. Not that Stitch Singleton bore any more clout than its predecessor as far as a good stage name went. Besides, I had always wanted the book to be published under a pseudonym just in case of....

Well, you know. The old paranoia ran deep. Let's just say that not only did I not like my birth name, but the whole idea of the book had been to write a bunch of my personal history out of existence. So why own up to it now?

Indeed my rational for wanting to remain anonymous was a bit weak and would probably not be understood by many. However I remained stalwart in my determination to find a pen name. Here again, I had been through many—and I do mean MANY—possibilities, all of which had bit the dust for one reason or another. Lonestar, Lee Starlone, Danielle Rose, Rose Daniels. Oh, I could go on and on, but why bother as all of them now lay festering in the bone pile, leaving me back at square one, trying to make a round peg fit in a square hole.

I had to admit I was stumped, but as Kady continued to ply me with questions that day for my LULU author page, it suddenly came to me. She'd just questioned me as to who I wanted to use as a publisher.

"Most people choose themselves," she stated.

Oh no, I groaned. Back to that again. Just who was I going to be? And that's when the lights went on.

"Isn't LULU really the publisher?" I asked.

"Well, technically," she replied. "But the bottom line is this is your creation, and you are free to peddle it anywhere you want. This means that LULU reserves no rights and has no strings attached."

"Well in that case, it shouldn't matter what name I use here, as long as I can prove that it's me. Right?"

Kady rolled her eyes. I think she was getting tired of my obtuse questions, just as I was getting tired of asking them.

"Oh hell," I spat out. "Just make it Lulu. In fact, you may as well make Lulu the author, too."

And why not? I liked the name. If it was good enough for a hot shot on-line publishing house, it was good enough for me. But wait, I would still need a surname. Well, what was wrong with Singleton? It was, after all, my birth name, and since this book was about two blood relatives, I might as well stick to the point.

I looked over at Kady to check her reaction, but she was busy typing. I could tell her patience was wearing thin and the pittance I was paying her for this was not worth her time away from Ebay. I think she was only doing it on her uncle's behalf. Whatever the case, I sensed that our interview was coming to a close.

So Lulu Singleton it would be. And it was not until way later when I realized what a terrible mistake it had been to name any names at all.

By early December my manuscript had been formatted and uploaded to LULU. It had been a painless procedure for me, as Kady did all the grunt work. My only other input had been to find suitable photos for the cover, at which point I made my second serious faux pas of the century by providing her with one from my father's obituary and another from my brother's. Initially, I'd planned to put dad in the cover slot, with Joe bringing up the rear. But later I decided to simply post a picture I'd taken at Joe's funeral of those white tombstones in Arlington, stretching out unto the vanishing point. If a picture was worth a thousand words, that one would surely do.

"Yeah," I instructed Kady. "Just put my dad and Joe's photos on the back cover, where you'd normally insert the author's."

It was a command decision that killed two dogs with the same stone. No, scratch that! What a horrible comparison! Let's just say it featured the main players while down-playing any involvement I might have in this expose.

In fact, I'd kept my author bio simple, real simple. As in *Lulu Singleton has been writing for several years and this is her first novel.* Yeah, that ought to sell my first ten thousand copies. Boy, did I have a lot to learn about advertising.

And that wasn't all, for it would seem that some of life's harder lessons were just beginning.

Since the book rolled off the presses just in time for Christmas, I decided to present it to my two remaining relatives. It would be a gift, one I would place directly into their hot little hands, which meant my presence was required to deliver the goods. This was a bad idea for many reasons, but I was too blinded by pride to see the wider picture. Or to be blunt, my head was so high up in the clouds I didn't realize it had arrived there via my ass.

Oh, to be fair, my intentions were honorable. It was their story, and they needed to be the first to read this twenty-first century version of *War and Peace.* To say I was a bit full of myself was putting it mildly. However, my moment of reckoning was coming, for I was soon to feel the full force of an old saying which maintains that *the road to hell is paved with good intentions.*

I hadn't been home since Joe died, so my presence there was going to be weird to say the least. Traditionally, I had only showed up for Thanksgiving or Christmas, but never both in the same year. However, for some time now I had been on my vision quest and a good two thousand miles away during the Holidays. So I'd managed to avoid the annual agony in all its glitzy grandeur. It wasn't the best excuse, but it held water—usually a lot of it, composed of the miles and miles of ocean which lay between us. Ergo, my absence from the festivities hadn't been up for debate.

Then, when I took the job at the library I had an even better reason for a no-show. "Gotta work the whole week again," I would lament over the phone to my mother, who as far as I could tell was just as glad as I'd been to avoid my presence at her table. I knew Joe's money had deepened the rift between us, and she sure hadn't approved of my spend-down of said funds.

"You should have gone back and got yourself a sensible degree, Maureen," she had chided. "Something that will land you a much better job than at some rinky-dink library. Accounting or engineering are good fields to get into, and you always were good with numbers."

Oh, yeah. In what reality? I wanted to spit back, but as usual with the Dragon Lady, I held my tongue. She just didn't get it. That was for sure.

So the question that begs answering is just why in hell I thought she would GET my book. And since we're talking about realities, in just what alternative existence would she be gushing over said pages and extolling their virtue? Good Lord! I had never received any praise from the woman for anything I'd ever done, so why did I expect any now? And especially for the project she opened on that fatal Christmas morning.

As it tumbled from its festive Santa Claus wrapping paper, it was anything but a welcome guest. I should have sensed the vibe immediately when, upon gazing at the cover with its celebrated scene of Arlington Cemetery, she exclaimed something to the effect of *now what on earth is this?*

"It's a book, mom," I explained, reporting the obvious. "And I wrote it."

And that was all the explanation necessary.

"Oh," she uttered, and quickly dismissed the bundle as if it were a petrified turd, before moving on to a bigger and better package from Davey, one which held a coveted brand of cologne.

About that time, Davey was unwrapping his little bundle of joy, and I have to hand it to my younger brother. At least he had the good manners to thank me, though I'm not sure that thanks would be in order in the long run.

Sadly, it's all about hindsight. Had I read the manuscript over as an impartial observer, I might have seen it for what it was. But unfortunately, I was gazing into its murky depths through the prism of my own pain. Or was it the prison of my own pain?

Who knows? Who cares? Whatever the case, its contents shouldn't never been shared with my closest relatives. And since I'd chosen to send it out into the public domain, I should have used a little more common sense and changed the names to protect the guilty. At least that way when the finger of blame was pointed, I could have blithely referred the reader to that old disclaimer which insists *that any resemblance to any actual person living or dead is purely coincidental.*

But on all accounts I remain guilty as charged. However, if my crime is merely one of stupidity, it is nowhere near a hanging offense. If so, most of the people on the planet would be swinging from a rope.

Not that this defense swayed the dragon lady. Her mind was made up the minute she read the first page. Hell, it was probably made up long before that since I hadn't been able to do anything which met with her approval for decades.

The fallout began several days after Christmas. By that time, I had flown home to my little garret room in Cincinnati where I was spending what was left of my Christmas Break tending to my plants and the stray tomcat who had allowed me the privilege of feeding him expensive cat food. It might not have been the best way to spend a vacation, but it beat my mother's house with its antiseptic walls and immaculate furniture. Worse yet, she'd taken to replacing dad's version of entertainment—which was 24/7 reporting from CNN—with a vapid music that filled the house with the most insipid Christmas music in existence.

Oh, I could have stayed with Davey. If, that is, I wanted to switch to the Sports Channel in every room, or dirty dishes piled high in the sink, just waiting on some sympathetic barmaid to come along and give them a perfunctory swipe. But neither place won any awards in my book, so I had conveniently insisted that I had to open the library in two days flat as McClure was out of town and, oh my fur and whiskers, I best not be one minute late…

It was a pathetic excuse, but they fell for it. In fact, they probably relished it as neither one enjoyed my company enough to apply for status as bosom buddy. So, in a sense, I got a one-way ticket out of Dodge before the bullets began to fly. I call it one-way because, once the shit hit the fan, I realized in all probability this would be my very last Christmas at *home*.

I'd been back in Cincinnati about two weeks and had fallen into my usual routine. This meant Saturdays were shopping days, so I had just returned from the store with my hands full of groceries. The phone was ringing, and I was dead sure it had to be LULU calling to inform me that my book had just topped their sales charts. So I dumped the groceries and ran to get the call before its final ring. However, when I picked it up there was no professional sounding voice at the other end of the line offering me a Pulitzer Prize. Instead it was just the drawl of my brother Davey.

"Hey, give me a minute," I implored. "I just walked in the door."

"Yeah, well, you'd better sit down then," came a drunken slur, and that was my first suspicion I was in trouble. Drunk already and only two o'clock in the afternoon? Hey, I knew my brother. Though he may have been a total lush, at least he had his standards, which somewhat paralleled those of our dad. No booze before Happy Hour, and then it was bottoms up straight on through until bedtime or morning–or whichever came first.

"Have you been drinking?" I asked. It was a stupid question. Not only was it none of my business, but confronting Davey with the monkey which sat on his back was never a good idea.

"Have I been drinking?????" he mouthed, answering a question with a question. "Have I been DRINKING?" And this time the activity in question was emphasized to the point that I could almost taste the alcoholic fumes through the phone lines.

"Jeez, Louise, Maureen! Who wouldn't be drinking after reading that piece of shit book you gave us for Christmas! Not that it bothered me that much. But mom? You know how she is."

(Did I?)

"Lord God Almighty! Whatever were you thinking, girl? She's just about ready to call in a team of lawyers. Says she's going to sue the pants of you. But once I told her you probably only own one pair, she backed down a little and decide that ruining you would be enough. Ruining, yeah, those were her exact words. Though I don't really know how she plans on pulling that one off. Seems to me that you're already destined for skid row...."

There was a pause in the tirade when I heard the ice clinking in his glass. Then there was a loud slurp and he went on.

"Better not darken her door for a while. That's for sure. The old witch is really on a broomstick roll this time."

His final words assured me that he was at least partially on my side. His opinion of our mother was only slightly higher than my own, and the only reason he hung around her at all was to pick up the occasional crumbs she would send his way. OK, maybe not so *occasional* because I knew for a fact she had bankrolled him entirely several times when he had been looking for work.

Nevertheless, I was stunned. I had never expected such a reaction to this book. In my mind it was a simple family archive set on the backdrop of my father and brother's military careers. This meant a great deal of it was basic military history, a boring enough topic if you weren't on the front lines. But we were, so to speak. So maybe this was what had set everyone off.

"She thinks that you are going to go public with it..." he continued.

Well, I had planned to. But at the moment it had been chucked into a category that LULU called PRIVATE, meaning it was not available to anyone unless I chose to allow them access.

I tried to explain this to Davey, but the alcohol was taking its toll and he just kept repeating that *I was in trouble now*. So, after a promise that we could talk about it in the morning, I finally gave up and said goodnight. However as I was removing the phone from my ear, I heard him mumble something about tomorrow being too late.

Several days later her letter arrived. In the interim I had sat on this shit storm and done nothing, hoping maybe it would all blow over. However hurricanes rarely pass through without inflicting some sort of damage, and even though this was no Cat 5, it was also no exception. Later I would come to refer to it as Tropical Storm Trixie, after my mother's unfortunate nickname. It was my neatsy-cutsey attempt to blow off all the ill-will it had caused, but it failed miserably. The damage was irreversible, and my mother's letter said it all.

The first part of it was nothing more than a tongue-lashing concerning details. I had them all wrong. She hadn't been born in a shack in the foothills of the Appalachians; she hadn't worn the same pair of shoes all winter; her brothers weren't a bunch of drunken bums who ran moonshine when times got tough. I skimmed through it all aghast, not believing my eyes. Had I possibly stumbled into someone else's family history? Why, I was sure I'd heard the antics of my uncles discussed over the dinner table on multiple occasions. Oh, it was true. My mother certainly wasn't proud of her roots, but nonetheless, she had chosen to marry into a culture that exonerated the imbibing of spirits, so she may as well contribute a few drinking stories of her own.

However, if her attack had just stopped there, with what she perceived as misrepresentations, it might have been OK. We may have been able to salvage what little relationship we had as mother and daughter. But nooooo…. She had to go for the jugular, and in the rest of the letter she proceeded on her merry way to rip me a new asshole. Everything I'd ever done was wrong, starting with my birth. I was supposed to be a boy. All she ever wanted was an heir and a spare, and her gun-totting spouse demanded that all offspring be male. So she was forced into pregnancy number three all because I'd refused to come out of her womb sporting a dick! How dare I??? And what I did to her figure? Why it took her three years to return to her size thirty waist, before Davey came along and forced her to start all over again.

But that wasn't all; for I'd gone on to embarrass the family by being an out and out oddball. All those books! And those stupid horn-rimmed glasses! My God! The least I could have done was to blossom into a Georgia Peach, the way she had. Then she could have found a suitable Lieutenant or Colonel to mate me with.

However, when it became obvious that this ugly duckling was never going to morph into a swan, she had shipped me away to college in hopes I could redeem myself through higher education. I had been slated for a career in finances, something dear to my mother's heart, and she was sure I would excel in the field chosen for me and make her a millionaire by the time she reached sixty. That way, if her husband succumbed to the inevitability of the battlefield, she would not have to rely upon a widow's pension to see her through the rest of her life.

Well, I'd blown that one too, by shredding my GPA to pieces and then taking off across the country with that bum... *what was his name?... oh, it hardly mattered. You couldn't even make that one work out, Maureen. You are nothing but a loser, and by what you have done here, you have sealed your fate. From this day on, you are on your own* (When had I not been?) *and though Davey may chose to love you, I most certainly DO NOT!!!!*

And Davey had the gall to say my words had been too harsh?? I was stunned. I stood there reading the letter over and over, trying and failing to find that glimmer of hope in the bottom of Pandora's Box. But there was no silver lining to be found. I knew my mother. She was as stubborn as the old mules of her childhood, and when she made up her mind about something, that was that. I asked myself why I cared. We'd never had much to do with each other anyway. There had been those perfunctory Holiday dinners and a few conversations scattered around the year. But other than that, I'd been on my own for some time.

Maybe it had something to do with my very nature. Yes, I was a loner, and probably a loser to boot—at least in the eyes of the world. And yes, I had a face only a mother could love (and at that I almost chuckled.) Not that this was any laughing matter. It cut deep. I knew I should just dismiss it all, but with my father and brother both committed to the ground, I had only two living relatives. One was a drunken bum who could barely remember his own birthday, let alone mine. And the other? Well, if it was parental approval I had sought in this life, I was tilting at windmills. It just wasn't going to happen. And forget all that business about a mother's love being the only unconditional one you will never know.

Yes, I was on my own alright. She'd nailed that one. And like any cub left to fend for themselves, I had developed somewhat of a surly attitude. I didn't make friends easily, romantic liaisons were even rarer, and for the most part I walked a lonely road.

It was a realization that did not sit well, despite it being no revelation, and for the first time in a very long time, I began to experience the classic symptoms of a panic attack. Oh no, not this again! The last major assault had taken place shortly after Joe's death, and that was close to seven years ago. At the time it had been diagnosed as a complication of atrial fibrillation and since then, I had been taking my pills regularly. They'd worked so well treating the symptoms, that I was sure they'd cured the disease. Why just think of all the stressful situations I'd been in over the years! None of them had triggered this kind of a reaction.

As I struggled to find my breath, I tried to remember the last time this had happened. That's right. I'd been at Leslie's, and she'd been trying to coax me to smoke some of her premium product. I'd declined, claiming some BS story about how it didn't sit right with me anymore. But the truth had been that it often led to the affliction that was raging in my veins at the moment. Leslie, being sharp, had figured it all out and had placated me with some deep breathing into a paper bag. This had eased the symptoms long enough for me to begin a coherent discussion as to just what exactly the problem was, which I figured would be the end of it. However, Leslie hadn't stopped there, but had proceeded to dig deeper into the realm of unseen forces.

At the time she'd suggested that the roots of my problem may lie in something known as a psychic attack. I'd been skeptical then, but that had been before ayahuasca had changed my perceptions for good and I had become a true believer in things that go bump in the dark. However, back in those days, I had not been able to name my attacker. Now I knew. She had both a face and a name, and hadn't she said she was out to ruin me? Hadn't those been her exact words? Pretty melodramatic, but then Trixie always had a flair for the theatrical.

I shivered. It was all that was left of the panic attack, but it wasn't fooling me. I knew it would be back again, zooming out of apparent nowhere to incite a riot in my susceptible cells. That said, I had better find a way to combat it, and the only way I knew was to rise above all this and spring forth from the ashes like a good little Phoenix.

Fuck her! I would market the book despite what I'd said. It was a good book—a hell of a lot better than the crap that lined most library shelves—and it was sure to make it to the top. I would make it happen by marketing it aggressively; I would have faith and believe; I would prime that pump and the waters of life would spring forth and nurture me for all my remaining days. And best yet, I would prove her wrong!!!

Yeah, dream on, for when I made this command decision I had little idea just how difficult it would be to see it to fruition. For as it turned out, the perspiration necessary to commit my inspiration to paper was but a drop in the bucket compared to what it would take to gain the best sellers list. For starters, I didn't know where to begin. Oh, there are reams of paper out there promoting the process. In fact, some enterprising authors have given up on their masterpiece and have settled on writing a book for other authors containing detailed instructions on how to get famous. Three guesses which one hits the big time.

However, in the beginning of my campaign, I read all these *Complete Idiot Guides* and took them to heart. Or should I say, I tried since many of the suggestions therein involved computer skills that were far beyond my expertise. Get a Twitter Account. Set up a Website and a Facebook Page. Write a blog. Make videos and post them to YouTube. Send Instagrams and mass emails.

For heaven's sakes! Why, there was social media I had never heard of! Snapchat. LinkedIn. Pinterest. MeWe (which claimed to be an alternative to Facebook). And let's not get into the myriad of on-line book clubs, many which featured over fifty thousand members.

It was mind-boggling, especially for a semi-Luddite, and all I could think was that I needed to employ the services of Kady full-time. It was an idea I seriously considered until I checked the balance in my bank account. At which point I'd groaned. Now where did all that money go?

Then to make matters worse, the panic attacks were growing more frequent and were interfering with my ability to stay employed. Yeah, employed. If you wanted to call eighteen hours a week a high-powered job which delivered six figures annually. Gosh! Who was I kidding? The gig at the library barely paid my rent, and now it looked like my head might be on the chipping block there due to circumstances beyond my control. Let's face it. My body was in a full scale rebellion. First it had been the panic attacks, and later another old nemesis had reared its ugly head, that being a bad case of the Papilledema. Sounds like something out of a Grade B sci-fi, but it was an actual medical condition, the same one that had brought me to my knees prior to my escape to the Azores. It involved the swelling of the optic nerve and on bad days, which were most days, my vision was severely compromised.

At the time of the initial onslaught, my eye doctor had warned me that it may be reoccurring, and that I should take care to limit my time behind any device with a blue screen. Blue screen? This meant computers. And guess who had been burning the midnight oil for the past year with their little Toshiba laptop? Then, to add insult to injury, McClure had decided I was too valuable of an employee to waste on menial tasks like Johnny-mopping and book-dusting, and after a brief tutorial on the library software, had positioned me behind the circulation desk. Now what part of my pop-bottle glasses did she not understand?

Needless to say, I failed miserably at this job, and after the one hundredth fuck-up even McClure, despite her affection for me, was ready to show me the door. Oh, she didn't say anything, but I could tell my days were numbered. Lord knows I'd been canned enough over the course of my life to read the signs. Yeah, I knew the score with these shit jobs. You're just another warm body, disposable and replaceable, no one special. And when you get too old or too sick to work the line? Well, then, you get the shaft. Yeah, some of us get the elevator, others get the shaft. Alas, there would be no golden parachute for this girl as I was neither wall street mogul nor silicon valley CEO. Instead I was a simple W-2 employ, trying to subsist on a meager salary while waiting for my ship to come in.

What pained me the most was knowing this was the exact lifestyle I had deplored for years and years, a lifestyle I had gone out of my way to avoid at all costs. But this was before I had developed a host of afflictions which made each day a challenge. Indeed, that was putting it mildly because the truth was I never knew from one day to the next just how compromised I would be. Some days were better than others, but most were pretty damn bad, so bad that I was forced to go along with Leslie's pronouncement that I was under a psychic attack. It was as valid an explanation as any for the downturn my health had taken, a downturn which was destined to release a detrimental domino effect in my life.

That said, the inevitable happened, and it came in the form of a pink slip. It was McClure's gentle way of informing me that my services would no longer be required. She could have been brutal and simply fired me. Lord knows, I was hardly the employee of the year. But her heart must have won out because she simply downsized me out of the budget.

"I'm sorry, Lulu," she began. (She'd come to referring to me by penname) "But they just didn't pass the levy this year and that's where a good deal of our funding comes from."

The levy? I thought that was something that held back the floodwaters. That's how little I knew about local politics. However, symbolically, this wasn't far from the mark because the funds from the levy were what kept me and a host of other nonessential personnel in our Wheaties. Guess the dam was about to break, and soon we'd be cast adrift in the deluge, either to sink or swim, come what may.

I looked up from where I was struggling to remedy the mess I had made of the circulation software and sighed. I knew what was coming next.

"So today is going to be your last day. Of course, I'll be glad to provide you with a good reference, and you are always welcome at the writers group."

Her face bore a trace of sorrow, yet she had forced it into the classic mold of the impartial administrator. No, it wouldn't do to let one's emotions play into the efficient running of a small branch library, especially when it was at risk of closing its doors for good.

If she hadn't appeared so serious, I might have laughed in her face. Yeah, a reference to work another shit job that barely paid the rent? And oh yeah… the writer's group, a big whoop which totaled three members on a good day.

But instead, I just mouthed the usual bullshit about how I understood and how much I would miss the place and on and on until I was sure my nose had grown by ten inches. Yeah, Pinocchio had nothing on me.

So that was that. My last day at a job which to its credit had outlasted any other of my feeble attempts to join the world of the working stiff. Why, the only reason I had hung around so long was because of the atmosphere. Maybe I figured that through the simple process of osmosis I would hit the big time. Surely spending all those hours in the presence of published authors would rub off on little old me.

But noooo… I was set adrift to make my own way in the vicious world of wanna–be famous. It wasn't going to be easy, especially with my meager means, but I would give it a try. After all, what else was I doing? Might as well join the rest of the modern day guns for hire. That's right. Have thumb-drive, will travel.

Still I could not control the demoralization which was setting in, a relentless fog that refused to lift. I'm sure it clung to me with wispy tentacles that smelled of defeat, and every time I walked into a local bookstore in search of a sucker who might be willing to display my books (or at least offer me a book-signing opportunity), it advertised its presence with a capital **L**. Right, **L** for loser, and no one wants a loser around because in this day of go-getters, one can never be too careful. That loser stuff just might prove contagious.

It didn't take me long to exhaust the nearby bookstores, and as for all the libraries which shared the same umbrella as McClure's? Well, they had a waiting list for their book signings that went way up into the fall. Hell, by then those eviction notices my landlord was threatening to serve would have overtaken what was left of my back account. So if I wanted to continue to peddle my wares, I would either have to become real computer literate or take it all on the road. I chose the latter, mainly because I would soon be deprived of any roof over my head, a place to return to and lick my wounds when I received those inevitable rejection notices. Besides, we all knew just how good I was with cyber-marketing.

Fortunately, the days of stuffing one hundred copies of your darling manuscript into the back of a station wagon had become passé. Good thing, since I didn't own a station wagon or any other wheels for that matter. But I did have the thumb-drive, and a couple of hard copies of my book. Plus McClure had helped me order some business cards and a shiny brochure which featured a print-out of my author page on LULU. The page was a bit scarce as far as a bio went, but we'd done the best we could to make a silk purse out of a sow's ear. After all, nowadays no one wants to patronize an author whose life resembles that of a Bowery Bum. No, folks today look for stability and a sterling resume with lots of MFA's. It's almost to the point that you have to bury them in bullshit before they'll even take a look at you. So we'd beefed up my bio to make me look like a world traveler who came from a long line of military-style heroes. In a sense it was the truth, albeit a bit exaggerated. But, hopefully, it would be enough to get my foot in the door.

However, that business with the foot was my own responsibility. During my last days on the job I had compiled a long list of independent bookstores around the country, realizing I would have to branch out from my local area if I were to get my book anywhere near a willing market. Then I'd proceeded to do a mass mailing and see how many interested parties might be out there. To my chagrin there weren't many replies, but I was able to find about a dozen or so who were willing to take my book on a consignment basis. Since all my sales would be conducted electronically, I didn't even have to show up at their door with a book in hand. All I had to do was send the addresses to LULU and have them mail out an advance copy. Then, once sold, it could automatically be replaced with another, using part of the royalties to restock the shelves.

It seemed like a simple plan, too simple in fact. And if I'd known anything about publishing on demand, I would have seen its obvious snag. The flaw lay in the word *automatically*.

Automatically? In what universe? Who was going to step up to the plate and conduct an inventory of sales? Who was going to notify LULU when replacements were necessary? Gee, just because it was an electronic age didn't necessarily mean the computers would do it all. There still had to be a driving force behind the machine, someone to instruct it what to do and when. Just what was I thinking?

However, by that time my focus had become so narrow. Its focus was on one thing and one thing alone. Money. This most assuredly would now grow on trees—specifically the money trees that were obscuring my view of the deep dark forest. Yeah, money. It would solve all these little problems, iron out the wrinkles, unravel the snags. Why, I'd be making so much moola, I could easily afford to employ an army of retainers to keep up with sales. That way, I could go gallivanting around the countryside at will, in pursuit of my next holy grail.

Indeed, it seemed like a workable business plan. The only thing it didn't take into account was a little matter called the start-*up phase*, a time when most good CEOs had to work overtime in order to get the ball rolling. Simply put, at this vulnerable juncture there would be no time (or money) for fun and games. I was chief cook and bottle-washer. There would be no one else to clean up the mess I was already making of my accounting. No army of retainers to do the dirty work for me. And no way in hell could I ever push the task off on technology, to those spinning computers at LULU press which would *automatically* do my biding. Hell, with my tech skills, I couldn't have even managed the task if there had been an algorithm written for it.

However, all this fell under the banner of lessons yet to be learned. I suppose, like all good dreamers, I would have to find out the hard way that perspiration is nine-tenths of inspiration. Alas, to say my head wasn't screwed on quite tight was putting it mildly. To be fair, it's hard to think straight when your heart is running the show, especially when one's heart and head have set up camp as long-standing rivals.

So, despite its obvious potholes, I continued to preserver on my present path, convincing myself that those royalty checks would just be flooding my mailbox, reproducing on a level akin to rabbits on a roll. This, of course, presented me with a new angle to snaggle, one which centered on just how this blessed event would take place. Because, in order to receive said checks, I would need a physical address, a given which was going to prove a bit difficult when the present roof over my head was collapsing.

Oh well, no matter, never mind. I would just do what I always did when I was on the move, drifting from place to place, meaning that I would establish a semi-permanent address via a PO Box. I had always used them before and still had a string of keys from old expired boxes. In fact, I had recently taken to wearing these as a necklace around my neck. They went well with my new tattoo.

New tattoo? Or should I say: one and only tattoo. That's right. I had finally decided to join the millennials in their passion for ink and had commissioned a local tattoo artist to circle my neck with a rope resembling a hangman's noose. Somehow it seemed appropriate. For hadn't my mother acted as though my little transgression was a crime worthy of capital punishment? So I might as well look the part. Then maybe when they found my body lying in a ditch one day, she'd feel sorry for all the grief she'd caused me.

In truth this was the one thing about her reaction which had really bothered me. Her abject self-absorption. Though I shouldn't have expected any different since it had always been all about her.

Where were my feelings in all this? Was I some sort of AI robot incapable of human emotion? Come on, now! For better or worse, she and Joey were the only family I had. And yet she comes out with that loving statement about wanting to ruin me? Well, she should be happy. No family, no job, diminishing funds, and my health in the toilet. I sure was getting closer and closer to the gallows. So I might as well sport the insignia.

These were dark days indeed, and it's a miracle I managed to shuffle from one part of the chessboard to the next. But I wasn't checkmated yet. Demoralized as I was, I still had a few moves left in me. I began by setting up a couple of PO boxes. The first would be in Cincinnati which I'd check whenever I was nearby. This was where all my forwarded mail would come during the following year. However, I needed something permanent for my royalty checks, and for this, I paid in advance for two years, choosing a small town in New Mexico for my *permanent* address. At that point I really didn't know where I might end up. But hell, winter was closing in, and I'd better make sure I wasn't caught with my pants down in some frozen town high in the Rockies. Yeah, that would lead to frostbite of the ass cheeks for sure, and I certainly didn't need to add insult to injury by deep freezing yet another part of my anatomy. It was bad enough that my heart had succumbed to the Blizzard of 2017.

Then, the mission of forwarding my mail accomplished, I set about breaking camp. Fortunately, my worldly possessions didn't amount to much. Despite the fact I had rented my apartment for nine years, half of the time had been spent abroad, spending down my brother's life insurance policy and *painting my masterpiece* so to speak. So my tenure in this river town had always been viewed as temporary, a simple resting spot in between Stations of the Cross. I guess I'd known I'd be moving on someday and therefore had collected little of any worth.

There was a bunch of old furniture, most of which had either come from the local thrift store or had been picked up on the curb when neighbors moved on. Cheap apartments are like that. We tenants beg, borrow, and sometimes even steal from each other. This was why it was simple enough just to pack the few items I truly cared about in my rucksack, one of which was my newly purchased slim and sexy laptop. I didn't know what I'd be getting into, but one thing was for sure, it was certain to involve more writing. The craft is like that. Once it gets into your blood, it's there to stay, a persistent little hitchhiker who refuses to take **no** for an answer.

So, my major possessions now shouldered my back and my guitar case in one hand, I simply walked out the door, leaving it wide open for any and all scavengers who wanted to pick the bones remaining therein.

I wasn't sure where I was going, but I had a pretty good idea. She'd always been somewhat of a second mother to me, and in the absent of my biological kin, I sure was in need of some motherly love. So I wasn't surprised when my first ride asked me where I was going, and I simply replied "Kentucky."

It had been awhile. That was for sure. Though we had seen fit to keep our relationship alive through snail mail and an occasional phone call. Still I was a bit shocked when Leslie came to the door.

What happened to you? I wanted to say, but I held my tongue for I knew the sad and bitter truth. It's called old age, and it sure isn't for sissies.

Leslie's hair, which had been sporting a few white threads years ago, was now entirely covered in frost. The lines on her face had deepened in direct relation to the size of her midriff. In short, she was fat, grey and wizened, a true Appalachian archetype, the kind that has been popularized by the stereotypical imaginations of Hollywood. Think *The Beverly Hillbillies* and you get my drift. Pretty when they're young, but boy oh boy, they sure don't age well. Must be the lifestyle, one of hard work and scant beauty parlors and spas. Oh, I guess I could have gone on and on with the excuses for her descent into antiquity, but then I caught a look at my own reflection in the full length mirror that hung in her hallway.

The phrase which came to mind was *rode hard and put away wet*, but I preferred to make that *road* hard. At least that gave me an excuse to look ten years older than my birth date. However, any musings I may have had were soon eclipsed by one of the biggest smiles a wayward daughter could hope for.

"Well looky what the cat drug in!" she exclaimed. "At least you could have given me some advanced warning. I would have cleaned up a bit."

And then, as she scrutinized me from head to toe, she added, "Not that you're necessarily dressed for dinner yourself. Come in, come in! Let's wash some of that road dust off your face. And fix you a hot meal. Sure looks like you could use a bit of fattening up. And what's with that weird new tattoo around your neck?"

And that's when I broke down in tears.

My paroxysm of grief lasted too long by my standards. Remember, I had been brought up in a military family where keeping a stiff upper lip was the rule of the day. However, after it was all over, I had to admit I felt better. Somehow by sharing my tale of woe I had minimized its impact, especially when Leslie offered her customary words of wisdom.

"Oh don't fret over it all too much," she'd directed. "This kind of stuff always happens in families, especially after someone dies. Why I recall my sister pulled the same shit on me. Didn't talk to me for ten full years after our mom and dad passed away. And then one day out of the blue, she calls me. And now we're back to where we were before it all started. Yeah, death is hard on families; that's for sure. But they always recover."

At which point I'd nodded in agreement. With Leslie, there weren't too many other options. I didn't want to get into the gory details concerning my family. They were all there in the book should she chose to read it. And that was when I began to get the first of many reality checks about my masterpiece because at no time during the spilling of all my beans did she step up to the plate and offer to buy ten copies. The revenue sure would have helped at this point, but what the heck? Maybe she just wasn't much of a reader, unless you wanted to count all those scholarly manuals on animal husbandry… and, of yeah, let's not forget High *Times*.

And speaking of which, wasn't that a huge joint she was rolling?

I groaned.

"Hope you don't expect me to help you smoke that shit," I began. I had planned on going into a long rap about how I had transcended psychedelics following my Ayahuasca experience in Peru. But fortunately she stopped me before I had a chance to get on my self-righteous soapbox.

"Nah… I know better. Though I still think it would be good for your Afib. And probably for that eye thing you've got going on as well. But no sense trying to change the spots on a leopard."

And with that she disappeared into her customary cloud of smoke which left me to conclude that it was the end of the interview.

So it went for nigh on two months. Leslie was hardly demanding, and required very little of me. She was in between crops so there was nothing to do down in the basement of the goat barn. I moped around the house and went for long walks in the woods that surrounded the property. I helped out with menial tasks like dishes and vacuuming just to feel as though I was earning my keep. But I knew in the long run this was a temporary gig. I simply wasn't far enough into the main source of the farm's revenue to make it my life's purpose. Besides, I had another life purpose, that being my writing. However, my last venture into the dubious waters of self-publishing had left me rocked to my center, and I wasn't sure a repeat performance was going to remedy anything.

Nonetheless, I got my laptop out every morning and stared at a blank screen for over an hour, hoping my next project would materialize in front of my wondering eyes. Oh, but that was another issue, that of my wandering eyes, because staring at the blue screen light of the laptop was about the worst thing I could have done for my eye condition. So after a month of this non-productive activity, I was forced to limit my time in the wicked world of writer's block to a mere ten minutes a day. In that my efforts were akin to a victim of constipation, I concluded that if nothing had happened by said amount of time, no amount of straining was going to bring forth the desired result.

Needless to say, the frustration was growing in me. I needed a new mountain to climb, a new excuse to take up space on the planet. I felt empty inside, drained of any creative juices, and all I could hope for was that something or someone would come along to inject the proper dose of get *up and go* into my system. And then it arrived as many catalysts do, out of the blue and into the mystic.

It was my birthday, January 4th, and I would be turning forty-four. Ever since I'd returned from the Azores, I had been anticipating this day. Somehow I had decided it held significance to me. It all hinged on the last major eruption on San Miguel which had taken place in 1444. Using that as a springboard, I had played around with the numbers and come to the conclusion that my forty-fourth birthday would be a special one, as it took place on the fourth day of the first month. Ergo on 1/4, I would turn 44. It was all about the numbers, and surely they never lied.

Nonetheless, birthday or not, it was a day like any other, meaning to say a predictably boring day in early winter. A light snow had fallen overnight and then turned to rain, causing the trails around the farm to morph into a slurry of slush and mud. After checking out the weather conditions, I realized there would be no way I would manage my daily constitutional. So I was doomed to a long day of cabin fever.

Leslie, who never didn't cotton too much to celebrations unless they were of a Wiccan nature, had gone to town in search of supplies. The next round of ass-kicking sinsemilla was sprouting in the basement, and soon she would be too busy to have time to run out even for a roll of toilet paper. So she'd taken the horse trailer and set off in the general direction of the nearest Sam's Club.

I knew the routine, one that would take an entire day of loading up palettes of supplies into the back of the trailer. Leslie never did like shopping and always managed to save it up for one big expedition which occurred several times a year. It was a task I was happy to bow out of, pleading a bad heart day. Yeah, I liked the sound of that. What a wonderful excuse for shirking one's responsibilities.

However, it wasn't far from the truth. The old Afib was acting up again, leaving me tired and breathless, so there was no sense aggravating it by visiting a host of Big Box Marts. I always had found the places confusing to say the least, a marathon shopper's delight whereby one got to work off at least ten pounds while marching endless aisles in search of the best deals.

So I was alone for the first time since I'd arrived at the farm. Alone and bored enough to pick up any stray reading material within arm's reach and lose myself in the fine print. Hell, I would have settled for a cereal box at that point, Leslie's library consisting primarily of Merke Manuals and farm bulletins. Oh yeah, and a few crisp National Geographics and Smithsonians, two mags that some enterprising neighbor kid had talked her into purchasing, claiming it was for a good cause—a senior trip or something like that. Whatever the case, they had provided the only source of reading material in the house which I deemed digestible, and I'd found myself anxiously awaiting their newest monthly installment.

Knowing they usually showed up about the first of the month, I decided to brave the elements and slog down to the mailbox at the end of the lane. It was a short walk and at least the road was graveled, unlike the trails I usually took on my daily walks. Still it was tough going and my heart was pounding by the time I got to the mailbox. I looked inside, a kid perusing the bottom branches of a Christmas tree and Eureka! What was that in the back but a shiny new Smithsonian! Ah, thank God for the educated elite who made this available to the masses! I was in hog heaven and on a hog farm at that!

Clutching my prize in my hand, along with a few circulars for local stores, I waltzed back up the lane. I was ready now, prepared for whatever boredom the rest of the day decided to throw at me, because I had a good day's reading at my fingertips. I knew the Smithsonian. It would take me at least until dark to polish off its contents, and by then, my eye would be bitching too bad for any further frolicking through its pages. Oh well, there was always Netflix, a little addiction I refused to allow myself to indulge in until just shy of bed-time. Yeah, some life, but it could always be worse.

So that was that. Time to settle in for some serious delving into American History or medieval art or museums or mammals or... oh, da da dada... You get the picture; it would be whatever the Smithsonian had decided to throw at me for this month's entertainment.

But wait. What was this? A long and colorful article about—of all things—hobos? That's right. Hobos. The guys who ride the rails and catch the westbound. An itinerant worker and not to be confused with a tramp who travels, but doesn't work much, or a bum who travels and doesn't work at all. Yes, there are clear distinctions amongst the traveling kind, and as I read on, I realized I most closely resembled the hobo in nature. For hadn't I, too, drifted from town to town, working a wide variety of odd jobs? Short gigs which provided me with just enough to get by on until I decided to move down the road?

The only difference lay in the fact that I was paying for my transportation, whereas the hobo acquired his for free. Well, not necessarily for free since the life of the true-blue hobo was a harsh one, dangerous and even deadly at times. Plus the ability to simply hop a train had been vastly reduced since 9-11 had come along and damn near eradicated anyone who chose a lifestyle of freedom over mainstream mediocrity. Not that hobos didn't still try, braving the elements and the railroad *bulls* as they coaxed aging bodies to perform a feat that many twenty-year olds would find challenging.

I looked over the pictures again, and saw myself as I'd pulled into Leslie's a few months back. How had I described myself? *Road* hard? Hell, what a joke. I couldn't hold a candle to these folks. Why I still had all my teeth. And my disabilities, though crippling to me, were invisible to others, making me a suitable candidate for the label of bum.

Yet here were these guys, flaunting their lifestyle in all its dubious glory, convening in some little town in Iowa once a year to select a king and queen from amongst their unwashed masses. The criterion for coronation was far from your standard beauty contest. No high heels or swim suits for these gals; no studly physiques for their male counterparts. Instead, it seemed like a race to the bottom where one's merits were counted in terms of tattoos, scars, and missing teeth. Not that they weren't colorful, and some were downright spotless, especially the women. But *odd* was too weak an adjective to use when describing their over-all demeanor. And odder yet was their philosophy, one which paralleled my own to a tee.

In a society of consumers, to have nothing, to own nothing by choice, might be the most radical politics of all. That's what the article said, and if I were still a drinking girl, I'd drink to that!

Except that in all fairness, I had to admit I had never gotten down to my last nickel; whereas I'm sure many of these folks had. Plus I'd always had the back-up of my mother's money—for whatever it was worth—and then, most recently, one hell of an inheritance to spend down. So I guess that made me a hobo wanna-be, an outsider looking in, a gawky kid who wanted to grow up to be a prom queen.

However, I did have one other characteristic in common with some of these rail riders. In fact, it was a characteristic I excelled at. For, like James Michener and Louis L'Amour and Jack London, I, too, was a writer. So maybe I should capitalize on this claim to fame.

It started as a kernel of thought, as many big ideas do. However, as I continued to read on about various authors who had explored the hobo life only to publish an award-winning expose of their findings, a light began to glow in my brain and with it came a nagging little voice I recognized so well.

Why not? it implored. *After all, you wrote one book about a subject you were totally familiar with, and your mother had the brazen gall to insist that it was all lies. So why not write about something you know jack shit about? Maybe that would get you more credibility.*

Yeah, the world is like that, a bass-awkward place where leaders don't lead, and teachers' don't teach and doctor's don't heal, and writers? Well, check out the majority of the books that line the shelves of a local bookstore and you'll see where I'm going with this!

The thought was but dry kindling. All it needed now was a spark to turn it into a raging conflagration, and as I turned the page to one of the final pictures, there it was. Or should I say, there he was, in all his kind-eyed glory—the man of my dreams. It was a sentiment most women would not agree with, but then again, I was hardly one to fit into that *broad* category.

He shared the photo op with two others, a girl who looked young enough to be his granddaughter and her nine year old son. Her moniker was Crash and his was Dutch, and together they would reign as the new king and queen of the hobo tribe. It wasn't the best picture. Other hobos received much better footage, but it was enough for me. Despite his rugged appearance, his crows-feet and grey beard, his eyes were a magnet to my soul. Deep blue and bright even in the grainy photo; there was just something about them, ancient and ephemeral at the same time. He stood there, king of the road, selected primarily on the basis of a speech he'd given which caused the crowd to go crazy.

In it he explained his name away, of how he'd always been in *dutch* as a youth, so much so that his father finally chased him out of the house. What followed was close to fifty years of riding trains, interspersed with brief gigs as an electrician. Everything he owned and everything he wanted fit in his knapsack. *Anything that doesn't fit in my pack, I can't carry with me. I don't want it. I can't have it. It all gets left behind. It makes me a different kind of person. It's given me something special in life. I'm not attached to anything. I wander the winds...*

Yeah, the Flying Dutchman. Just as all hobos have nicknames, ranging from weird stuff like 4 Winds and Bookworm to locale descriptors such as Minnesota Jim and IoWeGian, Dutch was no exception. It was an easy way to divorce yourself from your past with a dissociation so complete you may not see a living relative for thirty odd years, and it sure sounded good to me.

Americans are proud of being what they call 'free'. You ain't free until your backpack is full and your pockets are empty.

Both Buddha and Jesus would certainly agree. Empty your pockets. Empty you hearts. Don't take anymore than what you can carry on your back.

It was a philosophy that would make most folks downright uncomfortable. Why even many of the so-called hobos had permanent winter addresses, especially the older ones. But here was this old guy of sixty summers, a guy who *owned the boxcar* so to speak, claiming that the heaviest stuff he carried were his memories.

He had me at 'hello'. The article was way too short. I was entranced and had to find out more, and in the middle of Kentucky, cabin fevered into a corner of a house whose primary reason for existence was the *hog farm* it presided over, there was only one option for exploring the outside world.

I groaned. That's right. The Internet. A rabid web of what I considered to be mostly bullshit and propaganda. At least that's what I told myself in a sour grapes sort of way. It was my feeble attempt to gloss over the truth—that the towering internet wave was so intimidating I'd rather take a beating with a rubber hose than surf its massive swells. Oh, I knew it was supposed to be easy. All you did was type a name or place into the search bar and some huge computer would grind into action and supply you with an infinite amount of hits concerning your subject. But that was where it lost me. Those infinite amounts of hits. Because how did I know which of the 1,234,567 references to my desired search were the most relevant? Oh, I knew they were supposed to be present on the first page, but did I trust the great computer in the sky? Was it really capable of sorting the information I desired and placing the cream of the crop at the top of the search heap? What about those other 1,234,557 hits? Maybe they contained something of value too.

It was thought out like a true victim of autism, and I had always suspected I was somewhere on the spectrum. Whatever the case, the overwhelming amount of information presented by one simple search was enough to send me running for the nearest Skinner Box. It was just too much for an over-stimulated brain to process. However, if I was ever to find out anything more about this fascinating man, I knew I would have to bite the bullet and hit the keys.

I groaned again and then, a moth to a flame, slipped into Leslie's office. Fortunately, she'd left the thing running so I didn't have to bungle a password and send it into a deep freeze. I looked at the squat little machine Leslie used for the business end of the farm, then sat down and began my search.

First I tried *Dutch*, but that just yielded way too many results. So I decided to get more specific with my parameters and typed in *Flying Dutchman hobo king Iowa*. I figured this should do it, and indeed it did because that's when I received the second lightning bolt to my brain for the day.

For he was there alright, in what I assumed to be newspaper articles. However, when I clicked on the links they were actually videos, the kind that are produced for local TV stations. This did not surprise me since Dutch's coronation was a nine day wonder and surely filler for the six o'clock news. But what got me going was that every single video was the same and produced by the same group. And their company name? Well, here's where the drum roll comes in.

Stich.

Yes, that's right. You heard me the first time, but I'll say it again once the hairs at the top of my head recede to their normal position.

STITCH.

Now who or what STITCH might be was hardly relevant. I wasn't about to exhaust my Internet patience by pursuing that particular thread. The name alone was enough of a coincidence to cause me to realize that strong forces were at work here. I began to listen to a voice belonging to my man of the moment.

"In America there are ghosts, people who live in the shadows. But they aren't bad people," he began.

And then he went on to elaborate about how people are enamored with this lifestyle and bring kids to the hobo convention to help them understand that if someone needs help, you should help them. His speech was short, a true sixty second sound bite, but it was powerful–especially to me. His explanation of a concept known as far *lust*, which is the opposite of home sickness, cut to my bone. I could relate. For I, too, was one of those folks who found it hard to stay in a house somewhere. I, too, had to hit the road periodically in search of that elusive dream.

"You have to go do something," he concluded. "It can't be stopped." And his words dwindled into the dust of a thousand roads I had never set foot on, a hundred trains I had yet to catch.

I sat there in a trance staring at the now blue screen. It could have been moments; it could have been hours. Whatever the case, my path was now clear. I had to meet this guy. He was my destiny, and although he didn't know it yet, we were flipsides of the same coin.

Leslie found me in the same position when she returned from her shopping spree. Thank God she needed help unloading all that crap she'd stocked up on, or I might have truly slipped into a catatonic state.

"Snap out of it," she bellowed from the doorway. "I've got six months worth of TP that needs carted to the upstairs bathroom."

Yeah, well if that didn't bring a girl in off the open range, I don't know what would. By now the blue screen saver had turned to black. The computer was back into its sleep mode, so I didn't have any explaining to do. At least not until the next morning when she powered up again to find the video clips of Dutch front and center on her monitor.

"Now what on earth have you been up to while I've been gone," she inquired. And when I explained, she only shook her head.

"Sounds like a rough life to me. Plus really dangerous."

Leslie, who by this time was probably approaching what most would consider retirement age, had developed little interest in thrill seeking. I guess the bomb waiting to explode in the basement of the goat barn was enough to keep her on edge. There would be no fast trains for this gal, until of course, she caught the westbound—a euphemistic way of saying she would no longer be on the planet.

I sighed. It was hard to explain my wanderlust to this woman who had spent the last thirty-five years of her life in a place she harbored no desire to leave. Indeed, her quarterly trips to the Big Box marts were almost too much of an adventure. So I gave up and kept my plans to myself until the inevitable day came when we had THAT particular conversation.

"Well, Stitch," she drawled one morning over coffee. "It's been a few months now, and I was wondering if you'd come up with any sort of game plan."

I understood. I had, after all, remained at guest status, and we all know what happens to fish and guests after three days have elapsed. There was no doubt about it; I had been pushing the envelope on her good graces.

I cleared my throat, a bit hesitant to speak the words that had been on my mind since I'd met the Flying Dutchman in cyberspace. It had been my intention all along to head west in search of this guy. With the blind faith of a true zealot, I was sure our paths would cross. Of course, I knew that in order to better my odds, I would have to meet him on his own terms. Yeah, I doubted if I would find him in any of my own haunts, like the local library or bookstore. So I would have to frequent his stomping grounds which might involve hopping a few trains of my own.

Leslie listened in disbelief. The notion of my hitching around the country was bad enough. In the good old days, I'd most always had enough cash for a bus ticket. But riding the rails?!?

"Good Lord, girlfriend! Do you have any idea how dangerous that is? Why, right out of the horse's mouth you heard that it's a good way to get killed, and an even tougher call now that they've cracked down on national security. And yet you're seriously considering this cockamamie scheme. All because you went and got a bad case of mid-life crisis hots for some aging bum?"

"He's a hobo, not a bum," I muttered, sure that I had shared the distinction with her. "Plus it has nothing to do with the hots, or whatever you want to call it."

"So what does it have to do with?" Leslie persisted, and I was just about to counter with some spiritual gobbly-gook that she would never understand, when our eyes met.

It was a Mexican stand-off. We both knew we had just come about as close to having our first real argument in twenty some years of friendship. It wasn't worth it. She knew me too well. She knew that once I made up my mind to do something, there was no stopping. My disabilities be damned, it was always full speed ahead as far as the Stitch Train was concerned.

"Guess you're determined," she sighed, and turned to walk out of the room. But once she reached the threshold she paused, throwing her final words over her shoulder.

"But promise me you'll at least allow me to do a bit of research on-line for you before you take off. I've heard there's a newer generation of gutter punks out there that like to hop trains just for fun. Maybe they can give you a few tips. Might save you a whole lot of grief."

It was her subtle way of getting under my skin. Guess she figured that, once I'd read about their tales from the crypt, I would back down and reconsider my *cockamamie scheme*. No way.

But I smiled and nodded my head, for I'd always asserted that the best tack to take with others was passive agreement. After all, what they didn't know couldn't hurt them.

And so a few more weeks went by, with Leslie firing up her computer and printing me out whatever she could find about rail punks, all of which I gobbled up like candy before taking it to heart. Most of her info came from a multitude of sites, none of them very complete as far as instructions went. Some of it was lofty rhetoric.

The best place to catch-out a train was out west. There the trains rolled for hundreds of miles at a time without stopping, as they transversed the wide open spaces of the plains with a grace that must have had every rail rider feeling like they were bound for glory.

Others held the obvious stuff.

Watch out for railroad security. ___

Take care in winter.

Be selective about who you talk to.

Take a cell phone. (Take a cell phone???) Also waterproof clothing, good footwear, a flashlight, sleeping bag, and some food. (Jeez... it made it sound like a walk in the woods!!!)

Be careful with Plug Door cars. They can lock you in.

The safest are the open boxcars. But they're not that comfy. You'll be sleeping on metal floors and exposed to wind, dust, and noise.

Avoid any loaded car where cargo could shift.

Try not to hop a moving boxcar. It's a good way to crush a femur.

If you have to hop, hop the train just as it is coming out of the yard, just past where security can see it. And only hop a train if you can clearly make out each bolt on its spinning wheels.

But it's even better to case out the train yard. Learn the schedules and sneak aboard a stopped train.

There are these unmanned engines in the back known as Distributed Power Units, DPU's for short. Some are real swank and come complete with refrigerators and a toilet.

Go on-line. There you can trade train schedules with others for goods and services. (Yeah, in what world? Not everyone is a computer geek millennial.)

And that's when the reality set in. Apparently, there was a whole new breed of hobos out there. Gone were the days of *Mice and Men*. Gone were the four and one-half million souls who rode the rails during the depression in search of work and a hot meal. Instead, they'd been replaced mostly by kids a good fifteen years my junior who sought a life of adventure and freedom. These kids, a hodge-podge of lost souls who looked upon train-hopping as the ultimate in independence, were often into cheap booze and street drugs. Alienated from their birth families, they had bonded together to form a brotherhood complete with its own rules and code signs.

They were best captured in action by a guy named Mike Brodie who had left home at the ripe old age of seventeen to ride the rails. Brodie had done over fifty thousand miles, seen forty-six states, and hopped one hundred and seventy different trains. It was quite the track record. However, to my misfortune, his log came mainly in the form of a photo essay. The guy had been obsessed with recording in celluloid the daily lives of the dirty kids he'd encountered, and his pictures were so good they had attracted the attention of publisher. They were now available in a glossy anthology entitled *A Period of Juvenile Prosperity*, a book which Leslie promptly ordered for me, hoping that its pictures of grime covered stowaways would sway me from my chosen path.

But it only wet my appetite all the more. One look was all it took. Ripped clothing, multiple tattoos, painful piercings, and dreadlocks that were home to a host of wildlife… These were the drop-outs, outcasts, vagabonds, and anarchists; and my heart went out to them. They needed a voice, not just a photo shoot.

However, it would be hard to hold a torch to Brodie. A picture, after all, is worth a thousand words. So I was going to have to come up with a new spin, especially if I were to catch the attention of one Flying Dutchman, AKA Dutch. It was my intention to win queen status at the hobo convention as soon as my new book came out, one which would be an instruction manual for this newest generation of rail hoppers. I was sure these kids needed not only a voice, but more than a few words from the wise. Oh, there were suggestions here and there as to how to live this life without risking its multiple hazards. Fights, Muggings, even murder were way too common, as were the old standbys of dismemberment and death by rail. So maybe if they had a guide book to follow, somewhat of a Train-Hopping 101, they could avoid a multitude of pitfalls.

Yes, I could see myself now, up in front of the crowd in Britt, Iowa, extolling the virtues of my newest book, giving a short two minute speech which would certainly bring the loudest applause to ever rock that stage. I would be a mother hen to this flock, a Wendy to the lost boys (and girls) of this new Neverland.

And, as is often the case with my lofty ideas, it was a real pipe dream. In fact, if we are going to cite literature, *The Secret Life of Walter Mitty*, might be more appropriate.

For starters, most kids didn't read anymore, and if they did, it was rarely in print form. Further research into this subculture revealed it as a typical millennial group, proficient in cyberspace. They used Facebook and other means of social media to stay in touch and many traveled with smart phones to which GPS and weather station APs had been downloaded.

It was a brave new world out there, and one to which I would always be viewed as an immigrant. The more I pondered the holes in my newest plot, the more I realized the sad and bitter truth; I was in way over my head. Therefore, if I were to accomplish this newest goal, I would need a native to guide me.

I sat around and fussed and fumed over this stumbling block until mid-April. The summer was coming on, and I knew that time was a wastin'. I should have been on the road a month ago. So much to do, and so little time. Why, for all I knew, poor Old Dutch would miss a step and fall to his death. After all, he was no spring chicken anymore. Of course, neither was I, in more ways than one which brought me back to my original problem. Yeah, I needed an injection of some young blood; that was for sure.

Maybe I should post an ad to one of those Internet sites Leslie always talked about. Or maybe I should head on over to ManPower with her the next time she went to town in search of cheap labor. Who knows? One of those little Mexicans might do the trick. They had to be good at sneaking around all sorts of obstacles. Hell, hopping a freight was probably old hat to them. Plus, the cut-off line for those proficient with technology seemed to be anyone whose birthday postdated mine by a decade. So I didn't need to go too far into the cradle to find my guy. And yes, it would have to be a guy. Two chicks traveling the rails together offered an open invitation, despite the current hobo code which professed zero tolerance for violence to women.

It was a tall order, but one worth obsessing over. I had always believed in ask and you shall receive.

And so I conjured him, and so he came.

He wasn't a Mexican, though the road dust covering him sure did darken his skin tone a few shades. But other than this, he fit the profile to perfection. Young and athletic, about ten years my junior, and an apparent whiz with the technology which had infiltrated our planet like a bad case of AI. And best yet, he came with a sterling track record, as it soon became apparent he was no stranger to my friend and benefactor.

"Why look what the cat drug in!" Leslie exclaimed after opening the door one stormy night. And the cat smiled a Cheshire grin which revealed a few teeth that would soon require some serious dental work.

He didn't even need to speak. I knew I'd found my guy.

Chapter 13
Stitch and Doe
On the Road
April 2018 to August 2018

Noone/Doe Speaking

Wow, guess Leslie already has a full house. Gee, this visit may be shorter than I'd originally anticipated. Well, maybe not that short because one look at the Biafran specimen Leslie had taken in assured me that my competition sure wasn't eating much, which meant there should be plenty left over for me. And boy, oh boy, had I ever worked up a hunger crossing the country.

So that was that. But there was something else too. A weird little thought that itched in the back of my brain. Because a second look at the bag of bones Leslie was harboring brought about a deep sense of déjà vu. I couldn't help the feeling that I had seen her somewhere before. But where?

I racked my brain for clues, but came up empty-handed. Or empty headed as it were. So after awhile, I just gave up and went with the flow. It was a hell of a lot better than the triathlon style swimming *I* had been experiencing for the past few months. I had to admit I was still hurting, rocking over Aniel's abject rejection of my affections. And if that wasn't bad enough, there was the way her whole operation had picked up stakes and left me stranded in the middle of the high desert with nothing more than my smartphone and the clothes on my back. Yeah, that had been the icing on the cake, especially since there'd been something downright uncanny about the whole deal. Oh well, best not dwell on it too much.

Nonetheless, once I'd settled into the routine of assisting Leslie with her baby girls, I came to realize that the past six months had taken its toll, and I was not only starving for food and affection, but was bone tired as well. My reaction was to eat more and work less. Thank God my job description focused mainly on an industry that was known for encouraging down time.

The Biafran, whose name was Stitch, was not much of a toker, which left me as the primary candidate for Leslie's late night samplings of her newest crop. And since her product was also known for loosening lips, it didn't take long for me to realize that something was in the wind.

It was typical night about a week into my stay at the farm. I was starting to get into a good rhythm. Leslie, who had never been too much of a harsh task-master, had slowed down even more with the addition of her extra years and pounds. Unless she was setting off for town on an errand, her typical day didn't usually start until well past noon. Then it was interspersed with numerous smoke breaks and visits to the lounge in the big house, where she relentlessly watched U-Tube on her TV.

"You'd be surprised at just how much useful information there is out there," she claimed. And I just shook my head because I knew better. Yeah, there was good stuff if you knew the right channels, but Leslie was allowing the Tube to predict her programming. If she ventured to close to a prepper apocalyptic site, then lo and behold, that was all U-Tube recommended for the next few days. If she got into alternative health, she was swamped with info on the next product to make her feel eighteen again. In fact, right now she was into Moringa, a so-called miracle tree, and was seriously considering opening up a section in the pig barn basement just for the cultivation of these tropical trees.

"They can't make it through our winters," she explained. But one or two would be all I'd need if I wanted to bring then indoors for six months. You keep lopping off the leaves. That's the part that's so beneficial. Tastes like spinach or so they say."

Yeah, you don't say, I felt like replying. *And I can't stand spinach.* But I held my tongue and let her have at it. As far as I was concerned, this topic was better than the other one which she'd broached earlier that morning.

"It's about Stitch," she'd begun, and as the lady in question was out and about on her daily walk, I guess Leslie found it safe to discuss her.

"Stitch?" I responded. "What about her?" *Besides the fact that she's one of the oddest little additions to your farm I have yet to see. Why sometimes she*

268

doesn't even seem human. More like a fairy child, except the crow's feet around her eyes are living proof that she's been around the horn a few times.

However, such thoughts remained locked up in the confines of my mind. Best to play impartial as Leslie never had liked me when I became too judgmental.

"Well..." my benefactor drawled. "It's just that I am really worried about her. She's got this wild idea to..."

And at that point, the door slammed to announce that we were no longer alone, meaning it was the end of the conversation.

For now.

But I had a funny feeling it would be rearing its ugly head again soon, and I had a funnier feeling that Leslie's plans for me went way beyond stripping a few leaves off her pot plants.

The old intuition was right, as usual. Wow, why hadn't it clicked in when I'd first seen Aniel scale the heights with her silks streaming out behind her? What was it about certain parts of the anatomy that annihilated any common sense? Oh well, let's not attempt to answer that one; let's just focus on the moment since I had a feeling it was bad enough.

It was another morning when Stitch had taken off across the hills. They were growing greener every day, a sure sign that the *summertime was a coming*. The phrase played leapfrog in my brain until it triggered a memory. It had come from one of my maw's favorite songs. She'd claimed it reminded her of our Scotch-Irish heritage—though I had always prided myself more on the one tenth of Indian blood that ran through our veins. Right, that bit about Scotch-Irish was a bit too much. Reminded me of another memory I had tried to stuff down the old rabbit hole, the one centering around those weird letters I'd found in maw's closet from some guy who'd claimed to be in the Secret Space Program.

What had his name been? MacIntyre? McCrady? Oh hell, it had been Mac'something, and most assuredly Scotch-Irish, causing me to wonder about the true nature of maw's relationship with him. It was another one of those things I'd rather not dig too deep into; just like the song in question, which was now coming back in full force.

Could it be my old Scotch-Irish intuition was trying to warn me about something that was coming? Perhaps it was a subtle alert to get out of the room before disaster hit in full force. If so, there was a slight obstacle, one which forbade a speedy exit. For we'd been taking so many smoke breaks that morning I was damn near immobile. So all I could do was hum along and pray, hoping if I didn't look at her, maybe she'd forget I was in the room.

But no such luck. *Yeah, the summertime was a-coming* indeed. And the leaves were surely turning, and the wild mountain thyme loomed across the purple heather. So will you go laddie, go?

I tried to pretend that I didn't hear her the first time. However this was a bit hard to do since she'd been talking for a full five minutes, relaying a tale of woe that just about topped mine. It, too, involved an estranged family. But in this case, death had not been the only culprit —although it had still been a force to reckon with, claiming both a father and a brother. However there had been other factors at play as well.

"I had no idea she'd been writing a book about them," Leslie moaned. "Or I might have asked to proof it before she sent it their way. You know that death does weird shit to people, makes them act real funny some times. And if there has been any sort of friction before hand? Well, it only makes it worse. And Stitch never did get along very well with that mother of hers, and now the bitch isn't even speaking to her. Said she was going to write her out of the will. Whatever. But Stitch sure does need a bit of cash. Not that she did very well with that big windfall the brother left her and..."

Leslie was bird-walking, but I knew the trail of bread crumbs she was laying out would eventually lead to the bakery. She was just building her sob story to a crescendo so that, when she got around to sticking it to me, I wouldn't be able to say 'no'. She had an agenda. A favor was in the wind, and it was kicking up to a mighty storm. And the worst part of it all was there was nowhere to seek shelter. I was trapped, and with a corral all around me which could only proceed down the chute to the slaughter house.

"So anyway," she continued. "She takes all that money and travels all over the place seeking some sort of spiritual Holy Grail, then gets some notion that she is supposed to write this expose on her family. She says its military history, but I read it and let's call a spade a spade. It's an expose. Well, needless to say, it goes over like a lead balloon. Plus, I don't think it's selling very well, mainly because Stitch is clueless when it comes to marketing this sort of thing. Oh, she'd good enough with a needle and thread; and if it weren't for her eyesight, she could probably just get by on that. But then there's her heart condition, and the two disabilities added together make her pretty much unemployable. Even to someone like me since she's really not much into the green gold I've been mining here. But to make a long story short..."

And here she took a long drag on some of said green gold product, one which resulted in a paroxysm of coughing.

"To make a long story short, she's got this new cockamamie scheme in her head. Says she wants to ride the rails and write about hobos. Says she's sure it will be a best seller. Well, first of all, the girl is hardly strong enough physically to go on that sort of adventure alone, and second, this is hardly an original idea. I looked into it, and it's been done before. Both in prose and poetry. Think Jack London and Robert Frost and you get my drift. And then there are scads of more scholarly social science writing. Why, there have been studies and dissertations galore, not to mention songs and movies. I think just about every creative base has been covered. But now, with the internet, there is a new captive audience. Only problem is the girl can't use the Internet very well, and I know she's been eyeballing you every time you go on that phone of yours. Watching your nimble little fingers find their way around a tiny keyboard and…"

She stopped and looked at me. I didn't need her to finish. I got the picture. There was a more than pregnant pause. Hell, we could have delivered triples in the time it took for me to answer.

"Did she put you up to this?" I finally asked and Leslie shrugged.

"No, not really. Or not completely. But I've known her long enough that I can read her mind, and besides it's fairly obvious to me. Both of you being on the road like you are, and her in need of a traveling companion and one who can start a blog for her, maybe even set it up so that you can get a bit of revenue from it. Then, if it goes viral, who knows? Maybe she will find someone to back her and publish it in hard copy, like that kid Brodie did with his photographic essay of these gutter punks. But for her to go it alone? It's more than just dangerous. It's a suicide mission. And let's get something straight. I love this girl. She's as much a daughter to me as you are a soul brother and surrogate son. So it only seems logical to pair the two of you up. Strength in numbers and all that…"

Yeah, logical. In whose book? Your jackass's? I stifled a laugh. I still got a good chuckle every time I thought of Leslie's other little cottage industry, the one she used to throw the IRS off her trail. *Jerkin the jack* was what she called it, and it sure was one of the weirdest ways I'd ever seen to hide the money. But this was no time to digress into the better moments on Leslie's Funny Farm. More serious matters were afoot, and I'd best keep my focus. To be honest, I'd had plans of my own, plans which hinged on how Leslie had referred to me. How had she put it? A surrogate son. Yes, I was in need of a new mom. This was for sure. Plus a place to hide and lick my wounds until I got out from under the radar of my own IRS woes and out from under the spell of one Aniel Miklanovich.

But how was I supposed to do this if my proposed benefactor had other plans for me. If I said *no* it would surely be the end of a long-time running relationship. And if I said *yes?* Well, I groaned at the prospect. Just how long was this little social experiment of Stitch's supposed to last? Would there be a time limit on my expulsion from Eden? After I paid my dues, would I be welcome back to the fold and given free rein to linger as long as necessary before I found some other path to pursue? These were pressing questions, and they hurt a head already swollen by cannabis. I needed time to think on it, and in the end that was the tack I took, one of stalling. But we all know how that goes. The sword of Damocles is never far from our noggins, and sooner or later we will have to shit or get off the pot over which it dangles.

I thought about it long and hard for a few days. I knew my fence-riding could not go on forever. Leslie demanded an answer and *sooner than later* was preferable to the *twelfth of never*. I weighed it all back and forth. Yeah, it was true that I had the skill set for the job, and it sure would be a good way to expel the demon temptress that continued to haunt me. Yeah, there was nothing like the thrill of a death defying act to take your mind off of a broken heart. No wonder so many guys bought motorcycles after a break up. It wasn't all about styling and trying to attract a replacement. It was more about a way to say *fuck it* to the old grim reaper. Yeah, go ahead and take me, you SOB! See if I care! See if anyone cares!

But those were the pluses. The cons were just as strong and mainly centered on how this little assignment would involve spending more than a few hours of quality time with a chick who barely mumbled three words a minute. And she called herself a writer?? Gee, maybe she was just internalizing it all, saving it up for her next big best seller. Not that she'd really hit the big time yet as, according to Leslie, she was a bit weak on her promotional skills. Besides, in the past I had always traveled alone, and it would be more than a challenge to endure the compromises that came with kowtowing to a companion.

Oh it was a dilemma, alright, and I rode its horns for the better part of a week until I swore they were drilling holes into my ass cheeks. But then something came along (as it always seems to) which swayed my decision.

Evening had set in, and I had just returned from the goat barn where we'd been trimming the leaf off the newest crop of budding beauties. I was almost up to the house when I heard music. At first I thought someone was playing an old Joan Baez album. I knew about Joan from my maw who claimed she was one of the few recording artists from the sixties who deserved a Grammy. However, when I got closer I changed my mind and named Emmy Lou Harris as the artist, mainly because I recognized the song. It was called *Boulder to Birmingham* and even a kid like me, who leaned towards heavy metal and grunge rock, could appreciate its merits.

But, whoa, wait a minute. Appreciate its merits made me sound like some scholarly critic, one with all *ass* and no *soul*. For this was more than just music. This was *half way to heaven with paradise waiting and just five miles away from where ever I am*. This was an angel band, a heavenly chorus, Beethoven's 9th—and yeah; I did have some knowledge of classical. Holy shit! Could it be?

The last notes of the refrain were being drawn out, and as I listened to them, I realized my eyes were moist.

I would rock my soul in the bosom of Abraham
I would hold my life in his saving grace
I would walk all the way
From Boulder to Birmingham.
If I thought I could see,
I could see your face.

It was too much. All the poignancy of loss was caught up in those few lines. Be it romantic unrequited love, or just the loss we experience due to separation from our creator, it was all there. And it was at that very moment I realized not only the identity of the artist, but my role in the Passion play she had written. Oh, yes, yes, and double yes. I would be honored to travel at her side, as lord protector and knight in grungy armor, guiding her way from Boulder to Birmingham while she pursued her own version of the Holy Grail.

It was similar to the way I had been bewitched when I'd first seen Aniel rise towards heaven on the silks. But this was different. This was hardly carnal. It was more like I had found a previously undiscovered older sister—albeit one who was more soul than biological. Therefore, orphan that I was, I'd be more than happy to tag along with her despite her chosen means of travel. In fact, I'd be ecstatic. That said, I almost ran back to the barn where I delivered those three fatal words which sealed my fate.

"I'll do it," I half-screamed at Leslie, who by now had turned up the music on her radio to full volume. Apparently she didn't care if she added deafness to her current roster of ailments. Not that I wouldn't have recognized the song playing even if it had been broadcasting at a volume quieter than a mouse. Its refrain echoed in my brain, a carbon copy of the one I had just heard up at the big house.

I would rock my soul
In the bosom of Abraham...

Yeah, it had to be. So why was I surprised? It was a sign from God, and when Zarathustra speaks, you'd better snap shit.

Leslie looked up. She didn't require any further clarification. She knew exactly what I was referring to and merely commented that I'd best prepare for departure early next week because, after all, *the summertime was a-coming* and time was a wasting.

And so it was settled. Leslie would help outfit me for the trip. Plus she would pay for my phone service plus x amount of data per month. But that was all. The rest was on me, and I would have to rely upon my paltry earnings from the past few weeks to see me through. Later on when we were deep into the recesses of our journey I couldn't help but ponder the irony of this set-up. Alas, like so many in my generation, I had endless Internet, but lacked a pot to piss in.

At any rate, I didn't have too long to prepare. First came a family conference during which Stitch and I sat down and mulled over the details. She wanted to go back to Cincinnati first, where she had a PO Box. Don't know what kind of mail she was expecting, but I played along, and why not? My role in the adventure was more watch dog than guide dog. The girl wasn't blind yet, though she sure did seem to have a few problems with her vision. But hell, I should talk. My own eyes had been succumbing to way too many days (and nights) spent behind a computer screen. For the past few years I'd had to resort to those glasses you buy at the Dollar Stores and couldn't help noticing that I'd worked my way up to the strongest setting. Gee, what was next? Bifocals? I cringed, shivering in the first frost of the inevitable winter that overtakes us all.

But speaking of computers, there was work to be done beginning with a shitload of research, some of which had already been accomplished by Leslie. Thank God she'd had the good sense to bookmark everything. However, I soon found that she hadn't dug deep enough into this sub-culture. She'd been right to assume there was so much more, a fine network of cyber-bums who communicated via the Net. All that ideology about the Internet keeping us in a bubble just didn't hold water in this case. Instead, as far as the millennial bums were concerned, it was all about connection.

They were organized, that was for sure. There were sites for job-hunting like Craigslist, and ones like couchsurfing.org which directed you to a cheap flop. There were group websites like squattheplanet.com and TravelerHQ.org. Then, there were other sites more specifically geared towards hobos like dumpstermap.com, wifi freespot.com and on-track-on-line.com. The last one gave out digital scanner frequencies for railroads, making it super valuable if you wanted to study the trains and hop one that was completely stopped.

It was impressive how tech savvy the current generation of vagabonds had become. Seemed like most of them had at least one mobile device aboard, a smart-phone or laptop being the most common. This should make us wealthy in the eyes of our fellow travelers because we would have both. Lulu, as she now wanted to be called, had insisted on taking her laptop which was a bit too bulky for my tastes.

"But I have to have something to write with," she moaned, and in the end I gave in, since this really was the point of it all. However, not before I put a plug in for smart phones, which were just as easy to post with if a blog was what you were after.

"But then, it would be in your words, not mine," she countered, and I knew she'd got me there. So it was agreed. She'd do the writing, then I'd cut and paste her words to an email which would be sent to me before I posted it to the Blog I was setting up for her. It was a bass-ackward way of doing things, but I had to remind myself that I was merely tech support, and she was the boss.

Unfortunately, her little victory came with a cost because in order to bring the laptop, she had to sacrifice one other rather large item. Her guitar. I had to admit this stung. I had been looking forward to spending many a night around a hobo campfire listening to that angel voice, and now the very thing that had drawn me to her flame need be left by the wayside. However, it was all about practicality, and I knew there was no way in hell we could pull off this adventure with Big Bertha in tow. Too bad she didn't play a ukulele, not that any delicate stringed instrument would have survived the rigors of the road she had chosen for us. Oh well, maybe if I was lucky I could cajole her into an a-cappella concert or two.

"We're going to need a scanner radio," I informed her in a feeble attempt to take her mind off the loss of her guitar. "I've already priced them at about one hundred bucks through Radio Shack."

She looked blank, so I elaborated.

"You know, a little hand held gizmo that will let us listen in on conversations between dispatchers and engineers. That way we can find out all sorts of stuff about the individual trains. Speed, number of axels, even outside temperature. And yeah, we have to make sure it comes with an antenna that's at least seventeen inches long. But what the hell... it's worth the investment. After all, it will really give us an edge..."

Lulu/Stitch Speaking

Give us an edge? Yeah, once we kicked in the auxiliary antenna, it would set us back at least hundred dollars, so it better. What did he take me for? Someone with money?

I looked over at the aging Adonis with bad teeth who had cornered me for what he referred to as a *family conference. And which side of the family,* I had wanted to say? The bride or the groom's. Because wasn't this somewhat of a marriage, albeit a shotgun wedding? Oh, I knew I had suggested it to Leslie, who in turn had commandeered Noone.

And who in hell has a name like Noone? No, from here on in I would be calling him by his CB handle, except that it was all about the NET these days, especially a site he called REDDIT. Yeah, apparently he was Doe/R/vagabond—the Doe being short for Dope which reflected the vast amounts of Leslie's cash crop he ingested while helping her ready it for market.

Oh, dear, what had I gotten myself into? Oh well, you've got to take the rough with the smooth, and I had to admit he sure was smooth with all that technology. Plus he was easy on the eyes. Not that this mattered much to me since he was a good eleven years younger than I, and my cut-off had always ended at a decade. Besides, I was in pursuit of a much more mature specimen. Wasn't that a big part of what this trip was all about. So why get distracted? Best to keep it all on a professional level, mainly since there was this weird little voice inside me which jumped at his mention of *family.* In a way he reminded me of my younger brother Davey, my only remaining brother at that. And when such an association grabs you by the arm, you need to stand up and pay attention. Why look a gift horse in the mouth, especially this gift horse? Thank God he didn't smile too often, or I would have to revise my statement about him being easy on the eyes. Wonder why he never got those choppers fixed. Give him another few years, and he'd have enough missing teeth to grant him honorary membership into the greybeard division of the hobo tribe. But right now, that root-rot he was sporting just gave him bad breath.

But beggars can't be choosers and as far as being a tech savvy little specimen went, he was the answer to my teenage dreams. So let's just get on with this planning stuff, which means I'll have to try to hit Leslie up for a loan. Maybe she can front me the cost of some of the expensive toys he seems determined to take on the road with us. Maybe I can offer up my guitar as a pawn. Boy, does it ever hurt to leave my Stella behind, but I knew he was right on that point. The poor thing would probably just bite the dust the first time we tried to hop a train, and what an ignominious end for such a grand old girlfriend.

So, my resolution finally achieved, I mumbled something about how the hand-held gizmo was probably a good idea and went back to writing down a list of stuff we'd need before we embarked on my great adventure. And then, like many a good international traveler, I crossed off half the items. After all, wasn't this all about whittling it down to the lowest common denominator? So why bother with a sewing kit, or nail clippers? I doubt if Dutch possessed either one in his rucksack, and if I planned on making a good impression on him when we finally met, I would have to weigh in a pound or two lighter.

Later on, I would come to regret my decision to throw a few articles off the train, so to speak. Like the time I found a hole in my one and only sweater. Gee, I sure could have used that sewing kit then. Noone's comment? Only that the hole would last longer than the sweater. That was all he had to say about that.

"Something my maw used to console me," he'd explained.

I had come to learn quite a bit about Noone and his mother by then, and had found some comfort in the fact that he, too, was without a family. It somehow strengthened our bond. However, his means of dealing with loss were so much more cavalier than mine. The sky could be falling on this guy, and he'd pretend to rejoice in the fact that he'd not been hit by one of the chunks. *A little trick I learned from my maw*, he'd claim. *She always was one to look on the glass as half full.*

Yeah, well maybe there was something to that. After all, the apple doesn't usually fall too far from the tree. Plus, maybe his childhood had toughened him and forced him to be happy with the crumbs. Lord knows, it had sounded pretty hard scrabble prior to his *Maw* inheriting some little house in a place called Coolville. Now, whoever lives in a place by such a name?

But I'm getting ahead of myself. Time to backtrack and hit the road properly; and this involved a proper send off from a proper Wiccan benefactor.

"They call it Beltane," Leslie informed us. "And you have got to stay to celebrate with us. What are a few more days when you're beginning that journey of one thousand miles?"

And at this she gave me her customary *no ifs, ands and buts* look, and I knew the matter was settled.

The timing for this celebration fell on the first of May, and it had long been a big day for the Wiccan crowd that frequented the farm. One of the eight pulse points of the year and midway between the spring equinox and the summer solstice, it symbolized the coming of the growing season. Therefore it was celebrated by summoning the spirits of all things lush and green, and judging from the previous years of bounty on the farm, they had been pleased to be front and center on the guest list.

However, preparing for their arrival involved a bit of planning. A tall Maypole had been set up in the front yard and then festooned with a crown of colorful ribbons. These would be ceremoniously entwined by the members of Leslie's coven as they danced around the pole.

But first there was the invocation which involved a series of chants and readings. All the cardinal directions were represented by their corresponding spirits of earth, water, fire, and air, as were more powerful entities and elementals. Then, the guest list in place, everyone chose a part. Some had done the ritual so many times that they had their lines memorized. However, both Doe and I were a bit weak on all this stuff—he more than I—so we had to retain the crutch of a small slip of paper which we referred to when it was our time to speak.

Then we stepped up to the plate with our lines and our props. Each speech involved some sort of representation of the entity which we summoned. Peppermint scented liquid for water, incense for fire, soap bubbles in a jar for air, and some sort of fairy dust for earth. These were fired up, sprinkled, and scattered as magic words of incantation were pronounced. Everyone had a part; some even held two, but in the end the invocation was complete.

And then as a grand finale, the Maypole was wrapped by an eclectic group of modern day witches and warlocks. Some wore ornate costumes with tons of tie-die and intricate beadwork. Others wore caftans, turbans, tutus, and miniature fairy wings. One showed up in a bat cape which she was forced to shed due to its impracticality while wrapping the pole and one poor guy—who must not have received the memo—simply showed up in jeans and a tee shirt.

But regardless the dress, all seemed committed to blessing the coming season, and even though I have never been ritualistic when it came to spirituality, I had to admit I could feel the force of their collective intentions.

Then, the pole well wrapped and all prayers in place, Leslie's colorful coven convened to the porch. Here they would take on the serious business of ingesting all the goodies and provender that had been so laboriously constructed for their dining pleasure. As I checked out the seemingly endless selection of appetizers, main courses, and desserts, my stomach groaned. No way was I going to be able to fit even a smidgen of all that stuff into my pint-sized frame. So I opted for sampling of a few of the dishes which looked the best to me, making sure I saved some room for that chocolate truffle cake which was whistling Dixie from the dessert tray.

Not so with Doe, however. Good Lord! Where did that guy intend to put all that food? He was a good foot taller than I and fairly muscular, and I knew he was still a growing boy... but seriously??? Well, whatever the case, he would be occupied for some time, and the flagon of mead in his free hand indicted he might also be willing to communicate about something that wasn't computer related. So I decided to take advantage of the situation and spend a little time trying to get to know him better. After all, we'd be joined at the hip for the next few months, so we may as well get past the tech talk.

No, wait a minute! Not joined at the hip! I sure didn't like the imagery that evoked. Let's just go with hitched to the same plow; that had a much better ring to it.

So, that decided, I poured myself a generous glass of mead and took my meager meal over to where he was attacking his well-stocked plate.

"Anyone sitting here?" I asked. And to my relief, his mouth was too full for one of those famous dental carries smiles of his. So he merely grunted and motioned for me to sit down.

It took awhile until the contents of his plate began to thin, but eventually he shifted around to the serious drinking side of the bar and we had our very first non-work related conversation. It started with small stuff, a brief recap of life history—anything too personal being deleted, of course—and eventually shifted to philosophy and its bastard sister, politics.

As I well suspected, his leaned more towards the cyber side of the force. He was well versed in all these websites which spouted conspiracy theories, although he refused to call them that.

"Do you know where the whole concept of the conspiracy theory originated?" he asked in between mouthfuls of truffle cake.

He still hadn't slowed down on the food intake, and I wondered if, like a camel, he was stocking up for the forced fasting we would no doubt encounter while on the road. But I made no comment to that effect and merely shook my head in answer to his question.

"JFK," he declared. "The assassination. And, yes, the poor guy was offed, be it by the mob, or the Cubans, or the CIA, or maybe just by our soon to be President LBJ. Did you know that Kennedy was getting ready to take us back to the gold standard? Just like Kaddafi in Libya or Assad in Syria, he didn't want his country to be part of the petro dollar economy anymore. That's the real reason why they went after Syria, and Libya, and now Iran. Because they didn't want to play ball with the big oil cartels. And you know what? Those are also the same countries that refused to comply with the global chem-trailing program."

And at this he this he paused to give me a look one might expect if one was still in kindergarten. Whatever did he take me for? I might not have my head buried in the Internet during every breathing moment, the way he did. But this didn't mean I was ignorant about what was going on with the planet, and perhaps it was because I wasn't buried in a box day in and day out that I looked up occasionally.

Yeah, I was hip to chem.-trails. In fact, since I had been on the planet a few years more than he, I could still remember a time of robin-egg blue skies. But that seemed a thing of the past. Now it was all milky white with a touch of opaque clouds, induced by a chemical soup, the likes of which will probably cause our skin to fall off our bones. So, just to impress him, I started to name the ingredients of the toxic stew which rained down upon us daily.

"Strontium, barium, aluminum…"

Not that he let me finish before he interrupted with a suggested website.

"Dane Wittington of geoengineeringwatch.org," he insisted. "He's the ultimate authority on all this stuff. And yeah, I don't know who your sources are, but you're *dead* right. Oh, I know that's a bad choice of words, but Dane has conducted studies all over the world. Taken soil and water samples and the results are damned scary.

"And he's one of the few guys out there I trust. So many of them are just windbags, and so questionable that they are probably trolls and shills employed by the very same deep state they badmouth. It's all about controlling the narrative and getting people to run around chasing their own tails to the point that they don't even realize that somebody's been pinning the *tale o*n the donkey all along. Or should I say, the jackass!

"Take for instance the question of why this is all being done. Some say they are trying to keep something out. This is the global warming contingencies who claim the sun's rays are getting hotter because we've destroyed our atmosphere with fossil fuels. Though I have a hard time believing there wasn't just as much—if not more—crap in the atmosphere back in Jurassic times. Consider all the rotting vegetation and dinosaurs farting, and you get the picture. But that's beside the point. The global warming contingency glosses over all that and tries to convince us we need a barrier so those nasty rays have a hard time getting through. That way we can just keep pumping CO^2 into the air and partying till we puke.

"But then there are the folks who still believe in global warming, but don't really feel it's all man-made because, according to them, all the planets are heating up. However, just try to find any kind of valid documentation that supports this, and you'll wear your eyes out looking. Because the global warning guys are determined to blame the problem on us naughty children who surely need to be punished with a nice fat carbon tax.

"So that's one side of the story. However, there is another whole group who claim the clouds are being seeded so as to keep the heat in;

that we are really going into another ice age. They call it the Grand Solar Minimum and it all centers on sunspots and solar flares. According to this theory, the sun is in a cycle of powering down, so we are heading for a deep freeze. And after last winter, I would tend to agree.

"But Dane claims the freeze is being manipulated by those in power so that it is only taking place in certain parts of the country, populated places like the northeast and west coast, and that way people will be inclined to pooh-pooh global warming and continue to run pell-mell down that road to environmental destruction. And I'm not really sure if I buy into that one either. It's right up there with the guys who claim we're being terra-formed for an alien species to take over. Kind of like that movie *The Arrival*.

"Anyway, see how complicated it all gets, and yeah, both these theories, be it keeping heat out or keeping heat in, will point you to some scholarly document that supports it to the max. Which, in a nutshell is the Internet these days. Lies, damn lies, and statistics, as Mark Twain would say. It's enough to make a boy's head spin."

And, at that, he took a deep slug of his mead, which was surely another way to make a boy's head spin.

Wow, was all I could think. He sure does have a heavy head. No wonder he has to work out so much, just so that body of his can hold it up. I sighed, feeling I wasn't contributing much to the conversation. And then, I remembered a little philosophical point I often fell back on.

"Occam's Razor," I mumbled, and his ears perked up.

Realizing I had his attention, I went on.

"You know? That logical principal which came to us courtesy of some medieval philosopher? It states that, since too many assumptions spoil the broth, you should stick to the simplest solution because it's probably correct. Anyway, I feel like it applies here. So I'll just go with first scenario of global warming, the one which would have us mask the sun's rays so that we can continue on down the fossil fuel road to destruction. In fact, I'm adamant enough in my belief to put my money where my mouth is. Or in this case, withdraw my money. Because after I read about how much fuel airplanes burn up, I've decided not to fly anymore."

Actually my boycott of the airlines had more to do with lack of funds than excess of convictions, but I let it go at that. Besides, his next statement one-upped me to the point that no further response was necessary.

"Yeah," he concluded. "So just let all those chem-trail spewing airplanes take control of the skies. Why not? They meet with Agenda approval."

And that was that, the way most of our conversations went. I had to concede that he was more knowledgeable about current events than I was. My education was primarily classical, and since I was not a Net-aholic, I just wasn't up on half the stuff he talked about. If it hadn't found its way into hard copy, it probably hadn't found its way to my lap. Not that his excessive knowledge of global events bothered me. Quite the contrary, as I had always tried to stay open to new information. It was just that, if anything, I considered myself a lukewarm liberal. So a lot of the tangents he went off on were a bit too militant for my tastes, too left side of the brain for my right sided reality.

Whatever the case, my days and nights with him would never descend into terminal tedium. This was for sure. And as I left the table that day, I gave thanks to the forces which had brought me such an interesting and entertaining traveling companion.

Noone/Doe Speaking

All my raps on chemtrails aside, the day we left was one of the prettiest days we'd had for some time. I took it as an omen, despite the fact that I wasn't really into such crappola. However, Lulu was, so I humored her when she made archaic references to King Arthur and Guinevere and how they were always going *Maying*.

"*Maying*," I repeated as I loosened the straps on my pack. All the food I'd ingested during my stay at Leslie's had taken a toll on my physique, causing it to bulge a bit around the midriff. But what the hell? I'd be shedding those pounds soon enough, so may as well be comfy in the interim.

"That's right," she continued, looking pleased to have knowledge hitherto unknown to me. "The weather in England was always so damp and nasty during the winter months that when spring came, it was a real celebration. So they'd saddle up the horses and gallop around the countryside in search of the perfect spot for a picnic."

Well, sister, I felt like retaliating. *This ain't gonna be no picnic. But, then, I guess that shouldn't come as any news.* However, I just smiled my imperfect smile, the one which strengthened my resolve to take some of the money Leslie was paying me for my escort services and invest it in some serious dental work. Yeah, if I ever did find Aniel again, I sure didn't want to bowl her over with my rotten breath. Who knows? Maybe that had been the icing on the cake, or *la frutilla del postre* as they say in Espanol. Maybe that's why she and the rest of the gang booked out in the dark of the night, leaving me heartbroken and empty pocketed in the middle of the high desert.

I sighed, not wishing to dwell on that memory, and also knowing full well that her exodus had little to do with the sweetness of my breath. Besides, the entire train of thought had brought up another point I wasn't necessarily proud of, the fact that I was indeed a gun for hire on this little excursion. It had been part of the deal I'd cut with Leslie, the other part having to do with pretty much permanent employment once the gig was over. The whole notion of what I was doing might have sickened me two years ago, but this was before I'd discovered the TDA shit-skid in my knickers. Hell, I had to do something for cash, and I sure wasn't going to be too employable in the open market. This meant I had to stick to stuff that was under the radar—like pig/pot farms—and if *el jefe* of said enterprise decided to tack on *escort* to my job description, I sure as shit was going to get paid for it. Of course, one of the contingencies of our arrangement was that any financial remuneration would come once the job was finished. Guess Leslie didn't really trust me enough to allow for a cash advance.

That said, the bulk of the funds needed to finance our operation would have to come from Lulu, who claimed she had enough money to cover most of the expenses. Good thing, since I was pretty much broke, having left the farm with only a few hundred dollars and a pack stuffed with a smattering of supplies, which included some hand-me-downs, a couple of high tech gadgets, and my recently purchased gear from a local camping outfit. However, as was my MO, I refused to focus on what wasn't in the jar. Shit, a few hundred was a far sight better than what had been in my pocket upon my arrival.

Yeah, the jar is always half-full.

Or is it? Because our first stop was one which tested my resolve to remain positive at all costs.

It was really just a hop, skip, and a jump from our place of origin, but due to a run of bad weather—and yes, that perfect May morning was soon blasted out of the water by a wicked low which blew in from the Gulf—this short journey of several hundred miles took us over two days.

Since this involved an overnight, we had no choice but to camp out in an open field surrounded by a host of hay rolls. They looked like looming white mushrooms in the evening gloom and provided very little shelter, forcing me to break out my bivey tent if I wanted to beat the drizzle falling from the leaden skies.

As I unfurled my tiny home, I caught something like green envy in the dark eyes of my traveling companion. Her look convinced me that, in her haste to strip down her pack, she had thrown out the baby with the bath water.

"Guess you don't have your own," I noted.

"Well...." she drawled. "It seemed unnecessary."

Unnecessary?? I was stunned. Good lord, woman! What kind of traveling have you been doing?

And as if to answer my unstated question she went into a long explanation about how she'd always ridden buses before... and oh, yeah, the occasional plane, back in the days when she wasn't boycotting them because of all the fossil fuel they burned up.

"OK, OK," I stopped her. "Enough, already. I get the picture, but it's one that needs to change. Come on. Let's rig up something using one of these here hay rolls."

And I took out my blade and stripped the white plastic off the nearest mushroom. Then using a retractable camp saw, I carved a pint sized impression into the hay roll, a place for her to stick her head and upper body to keep it out of this infernal drizzle.

"There," I stated, my handiwork complete. "Now you have a home-made bivey. Keep the plastic for later. It might come in handy. Or else we can pick you up some lighter weight stuff at the next hardware store."

The entire operation had taken all of twenty minutes, but it would be worth it. No sense courting pneumonia this early in the game. Surely *the summertime that was a-coming* would eventually show up, and bring with it a puzzled farmer who would be pissed when he saw what I'd done. But we'd be long gone by then, so what of it?

She seemed grateful, and so was I since it meant I didn't have to offer up my own accommodations for the night. That sure would have been a mighty tight squeeze.

However, as I drifted off to sleep, I couldn't help but wonder if this was but a precursor of fuck-ups to come. Despite having introduced herself as a well-seasoned traveler, perhaps little Lulu had been away from the wind and rain for a bit too long. Maybe having the security of her brother's bucks had softened her. Hopefully not to the point of no return though, or else this adventure would be over before it ever began.

The next day only strengthened my ill feelings. The weather had cleared and improved the mood of all. People who had sped past us in the funk of yesterday's gloom now seemed inclined to offer assistance, and on account of their generosity, we were able to make it to our destination before it closed. The place was a small post office in a suburb of Cincinnati, the size of which the government was always threatening to close due to lack of clientele.

But Lulu sure was about to give them a bit of business. I almost had to physically restrain her after she inspected the contents of her PO

Box. I knew she'd been expecting a good sized tax return from the IRS. Instead she merely received a letter stating that an audit was forthcoming.

"What the fuck?" she shouted, and I had to hush her before we got kicked out of the place. Indeed it was a bitter pill to swallow, but later, when she told me more, I could hardly blame the Feds. They never did like it when you tried to pull one over on them, be it with fraudulent TDA accounts or simply out of ignorance of the law.

"No one told me I had to declare that insurance payoff as income," she later moaned.

Oh yes, dear Alice. So sorry. Alas and alack, but such are the rules of Wonderland.

However, as the contents began to spill out of the box, there were other disappointments. A letter from her credit card company claiming she was in arrears and they would be turning her account over to a collection agency. Letters from several doctors claiming the same. A curt doozy from her mother which contained an updated copy of the old girl's will, one which cut poor Lulu to the bone. No other missive here, just the legal document with a sticky note attached claiming that *since I can't seem to locate you, I have sent this to your last known address.* (And indeed the envelope did bear evidence of forwarding from a street address nearby.

That last letter sent my traveling companion into a renewed fury.

"Yeah, bitch, we'll see about that. Last one you'll ever know!!!" And at that, she'd marched into the PO office to cancel her account. While there, she set up a new box, one in a small town in Illinois.

"It'll be closer to the train yard," she whispered to me by way of explanation. But I just nodded, not wanting to appear too interested in her personal affairs—which was somewhat of a lie since the two cash bombs that had come in her mail were somewhat disconcerting.

However, just as Pandora's Box had retained a glimmer of hope, so had Lulu's, and clutching a single envelope, one whose return address bore the stamp of the Ohio State Treasury, she spoke the first good words I'd heard her utter all day.

"I need to find a bank," she commented. "Before they slap a hold on this, too."

And that was exactly what we did where we cashed in the check inside the envelope for the lofty sum of $267.56 in cash. Not much if you have rent to pay, but Lulu had chosen to toss all correspondence from her former landlord, meaning that we were in the money now.

Humpf! Well, the silver lining is that it's never good to travel with a lot of cash in your pockets. It just paves the way for petty thieves and muggers and—added to the two hundred bills I still possessed—her windfall put us close to what I considered as *a lot of cash*. Mine was stashed in my boot. So they'd have to kill me in order to gain access, and then, who cares? However, I was a bit appalled to find hers being roughly stuffed into a zippered compartment on her rucksack.

"Don't you think you should bury that stash a little deeper," I suggested, but all I got was a wicked look suggesting that I should mind my own business. Guess she wasn't too good at taking orders or even following advice.

Which lead to the next narrowly avoided fuck-up of the day.

For some reason Lulu wanted to hitch over to a small town nearby. Well... when I say nearby, this was pushing it since, as it turned out, the place was a good two hours drive if you were privileged enough to own a car. However, the distance wasn't what bothered me. It was the name of the town that got me going. It was one I was familiar with, having been there a time or two during the days when I'd been trying to pawn off my maw's junk, and as it was small postage stamp kind of town, it was bound to be one in which my presence would be noted. Then, as I continued to ply my companion for details, the entire scenario got worse.

"What the hell do you want to go up there for?" I'd asked, and the answer I received was far from one I wished to hear. I should have guessed. I'd often felt that Lulu and I had been ships passing in the night prior to our hook-up at Leslie's farm, and this only confirmed my suspicions.

"I have a friend there," she started in. "She helped me get my book to print, and I wanted to clue her in to my next project. Oh, I know it's going to start out as a blog and all that. But eventually, I will want a hard copy, and she did a really fine job with my first novel and..."

Her mouth was going a mile a minute, which was rare for her. Did she suspect a conflict in that uncanny way twin souls have when they are about to step on the other one's toes? Was that why she appeared nervous and too anxious to explain her little detour? Whatever the case, it was time to come clean.

"Your friend," I interrupted. "Her name just wouldn't happen to be Kady, would it?"

She stopped what she was doing and stared at me, once again amazing me with the intensity of those myopic eyes.

"Why, yes. Do you know her?"

I sighed. How was I to proceed without revealing more than I wished to about my current situation? Then she gave me the out I was looking for.

"Old girlfriend?" she asked and winked.

Yeah, that's right. An old flame extinguished in an ungracious way—like pissing on it. I grinned sheepishly.

"I'm going to opt out on this one," I explained and let her draw her own conclusions. It was best if my sins remained those of omission.

So that was how I came to spend another night in the damp and drizzle while little Lulu slept in Kady's feather bed. Or at least I assumed this to be so. I don't know because it had been a long time since I'd seen the interior of the house inhabited by my old partner. Such details were irrelevant as was my discomfort. I only cared that there be no mention of my presence to the tattooed friend of my youth.

"Not a word," I made Lulu swear, and to her credit she was good at keeping secrets. It wasn't my fear of what Kady might do if she knew my whereabouts. After all, she'd been playing around with the TDA accounts as well. So let's just say I wasn't the only guilty party. However, she'd been better at covering her tracks, and...oh yeah, at using me as a guinea pig to see just how far she could push the Feds. Whatever the case, she was hardly about to rat me out. To do so would threaten her head as well as mine.

No, my reluctance for a reunion with my old *flame* stemmed more from Kady's own suggestion. Hadn't she been the one to advise me to stay low and remain under the radar? That said, I was just following orders, albeit from a Captain who would be the last to lead the light brigade. Indeed, Kady had cared more about her own ass than anyone else's, and it was her abject selfishness which caused me to come to my next conclusion, one which held that partners in crime should still be partners. And partners shared Intel and did not keep secrets, at least not secrets vital to the operation.

For that reason, as I swatted mosquitoes and attempted to dry out my boots, I made a resolution to share a bit of my sordid past with Lulu. After all, via Leslie, I knew way too much about my present companion, so it was only fair she knew the truth: that her traveling companion and knight-for-hire was a wanted criminal. Who knows? Maybe it would scare her off this crazy quest and she'd call it quits, which would allow me to return to the green fields aplenty in Leslie's basement. Ah, yes, but dream on, for I was soon to find out that the girl was as stubborn as she was stupid.

I told her the following night. I began my confession in a round-about way through a long dissertation about an Alt-news personality by the name of Thomas Williams. (Though I had lately come to call him Thomas will-o'-the-wisp Williams.) Tommy was the progenitor of a several websites, all of which he proudly and long-windedly announced at the beginning of each of his talk shows. Among them were the People's Club and Think Different, both which held links to his many broadcasts.

Some of these were done on a weekly basis, during which time he would devote three hours to the fine art of bullshitting, dividing his show up into what he called Intel (often coupled with a long line of statistics), question and answer sessions, and op-ed pieces. Then he would culminate the show with at least a half hour of berating of his audience for being part of the problem and not the solution.

Oh yeah, he also would spend long hours outing others in the Alt Media. No one was spared, from name-brands like David Wilcock to the more obscure individuals like Simon Parkes. No matter whom they were or what they said, they were charlatans and fakers, and he bad-mouthed them unmercifully. His condemnation was so intense that, by the time he was done, one might think Tommy was the only guy in cyberspace whose shit didn't stink. And speaking of stinking, I smelled a CIA plant—someone conveniently placed into position to peddle Hopium, so the alternative sheeple would do nothing but sit on their butts and feel like all was going according to plan.

This was OK, if that's what got you through the night. So I listened to the guy anyway, and some shows were actually pretty powerful containing unusual takes on world history and its effect on current events. These were the shows that originally hooked me, ones like *Humanity Unplugged* and From *Russia with Love*. However, as time went by, the narrative changed; and then it really hit the skids of credibility when Thomas introduced some babe by the name of Kim, AKA Kimpossible. (You gotta love this play on words, but remember, I did maintain that Tommy was a Hopium peddler.)

At any rate, this woman supposedly—and this word needs to appear in all caps as in SUPPOSEDLY—held the banking codes to all the money in the world, a lofty sum which had been rounded up into one fund entitled the Manna World Holding Trust. And since Kim was a white hat, she'd be going to bat for humanity using said funds as collateral.

Yeah, right.

Poor Thomas and Kim. You'd think they spent every breathing moment securing the Trust from the greedy clutches of the banking cartels who were always seeking to take the money and run. Of course, since they were always under attack, it was impossible to transfer funds out of the trust in order to assist the downtrodden of the world. However, the day was coming (and so was Christmas) when this would be made possible. So Thomas was taking applications from his members for projects that would benefit humanity, and when the lucky day came, these select folks would be the first to receive el *dinero*.

"And Leslie and I actually sent in one of these applications," I confessed to Lulu. "Of course, Leslie made me join the People's Club first. But what of it? A moving target is hard to hit. Anyway, we had this idea for going big time with the farm's real source of revenue—if it should ever become legal in Kentucky. So we typed it all up in a nice tight business plan and submitted it. What the hell? Maybe the guy is on the up and up. But I really don't trust him. I tend to look at him as a hope peddler—that's the opposite of a fear monger—and then I swear I read someplace that he used to work for the NSA. At any rate, I can't help but wonder for the life of me. Here are two people who are laying claim to all the money in the world, and they are running around scot free. Yet you've got Heather Tucci Jarraf and her unlucky sidekick Randy Beane, and they lock these two up for life and throw away the key?"

My final words were inserted as a conversation bomb, and they had their desired effect. The response I got was the one I'd aimed for. Lulu's eyes opened wide, and her brows arched in a question. Not that she had to verbalize it; I knew what she was she was going to say, and it was my cue to come clean.

"Yeah, Heather Tucci Jarraf, or HTJ for short. Poor girl, she really tried to do the right thing with the One People's Public Trust and all those Courtesy Notices, the likes of which require a pretty lengthy explanation. But let's just say they really stuck it to the man in a place where he's most vulnerable, his pecuniary nerve. But then she got too bold and started in on directions for accessing our TDA accounts. Those are the ones that are set up at birth and then traded relentlessly on the Future's market; and yeah, they really do exist.

"Ask Randy Beane. He was able to purchase a brand new mobile home with them, the price tag of which was just shy of half a million. Not that his high rolling lasted too long. He didn't even get to drive the thing very far. In fact, the Feds were waiting for him at the dealership the day he went to pick it up. Just like they would have been for me."

I paused to let my final statement sink in, before I went on.

"But don't think for a minute I came up with the whole plan because I had a little help from my friends. One in particular lived back in that poor excuse for a town we just left, and I guess she didn't stick her own pretty little neck out too far. Cuz it still appears to be attached to her body."

There was a long silence before Lulu murmured the expected word.

"Kady?

It was more of a question, but one to which she already knew the answer. Then it was her turn to shock me.

"Gee, maybe I shouldn't have given her a down payment on the new book."

You've got to be kidding!!! was all I could think. But I was so stunned I didn't even put my thoughts into words. So I picked at a scab and bit my tongue. I could only pray that Lulu hadn't forked over too much to our formally tattooed friend. Wow! What memories that image brought back. Wonder what new persona Kady was up to these days? Oh well, I would never know, so why care? And THAT was becoming my latest mantra.

Turning on my side, I signaled that the conversation was over. Yeah, good night and good luck to all.

Lulu/Stitch Speaking

I know he thinks I'm stupid. First the deal with the bivey tent, and now the thing about Kady. But I'd known all along she wasn't just some ex-squeeze. Call it a sixth sense, but I've always had an uncanny knack for reading between the lines. Then came my little bout with Ayahuasca and it kicked into high gear.

However, when Doe had first refused to accompany me, I had allowed him to believe I accepted his feeble explanation. And why not? A person needs their secrets and should only reveal them when good and ready.

Still I was glad when he'd come clean, just as I had been thrilled when he'd built me that little bivey shelter. It all pointed in one direction. The source field had sent me the perfect traveling companion, and though I had always been one to travel alone—believing that he who travels alone, travels fastest—this was not the time or place for platitudes. I knew it was a rough road I had chosen, and was glad I did not have to walk it by myself.

Or should I say *talk* it, because as we proceeded to hitch our way to the Chicago train yards, our days and nights were anything but silent, being lubricated by the bottles of wine he insisted upon buying. Funny, since I'd never pegged him for an alky, more a stoner than anything. Oh well, maybe he was trying to get me drunk enough to carry on a conversation with him. Or maybe, having broken the ice with some truth serum, he was just determined to fill me in on Alt-media stuff. It was, after all, his language and what do you always do when confronted with a foreigner? Why, you try to teach them a few words in your native tongue. What else?

Since he knew I wasn't too big on the Altnet, he made it his mission to educate me as to the likes of some of the major players. Over the course of our journey west, he introduced me to Simon Parkes, a mild mannered Brit who reminded him of Mr. Rodgers. Then he went on to diss some guy he called Benjamin Full-of-it Fulford and puzzle over another by the simple moniker of Cobra.

"You know," he explained. "It's hard to sort them all out. Most are suspect and seem to have their own agenda. So the trick is to take what you need and leave the rest. There are only a few who seem to shoot straight. David Icke being one…"

David Icke? My eyes lit up at that name. Finally some common ground.

"I've read some of his stuff," I ventured. "And, yeah, I think he's got quite a bit of the total picture, and he was one of the first to tie it all together. You know, I always knew something wasn't quite right on this planet. And then, as more knowledge came my way, I began to connect the dots. My source of revelation was books. So many contributed to my education I don't know where to begin. Frank Herbert with *Dune*, Philip Jose Farmer with *Riverworld*, and of course, all of Carlos Castaneda's stuff. And Tolkien and C.S. Lewis and…"

It was a long conversation for me and destined for interruption.

"*Dune*," he commented. "Yeah, saw the movie. Also saw that *Riverworld* stuff on the sci-fi channel. And everyone's seen LOTR. Never read it though, nor those other guys you mentioned. Seems like you like a lot of woo-woo stuff. Me, I stick to politics."

"Does that include exopolitics?" It was one of the few millennial words I was familiar with, and as I'd always been a big fan of Ancient *Aliens*, it was now a term in my arsenal.

"Exopolitics?" He repeated the word, turning it over on his tongue as if it were some new tender morsel offered for his culinary pleasure. "What's that?"

"Oh, you know…extra-terrestrial politics. Like the Secret Space Program."

"Oh." He seemed a bit put off. "Yeah, I believe they've probably got one. The Nazis had it during World War II, and we stole a shit load of their technology which the elite on this planet are using for their own benefit and screw the little guy. But bases on the moon and Mars? Woo-Woo stuff. Like the flat earth theory and the hollow earth believers. Yeah, woo-woo stuff." And he punctuated with a healthy swig on the bottle we'd been sharing, then continued to caress it as if it were a long-lost lover.

"Well," I continued after a long pause. "I'm not so sure about the flat earth stuff, but I do think the interior of our planet may hold a few mysteries."

I wanted to tell him of some of my experiences, like the one I'd had years ago near Mt. Shasta. And then, there was always my fascination with caves. But it was too soon for any of that; and besides, he had a look on his face suggesting we might be on dangerous ground. Indeed, it was never good to tax a person's belief system when they held the bottle, and he seemed to be in a combative mood.

So I'd simply sighed, and as I did so, he released the bottle containing the last of the Gallo. It had been a good choice for our final night before reaching the train yard. After all, it was the chosen elixir of hundreds of bums and hobos before us, and they could hardly be wrong when it came to getting for the biggest bang for a buck. However, I suddenly realized I'd enough. So I waved him away.

"You finish it," I instructed. "I'm done."

It was a tough call for a former borderline alky, but I knew the truth. Tomorrow would be big one by all accounts, and I wanted to be in top shape. For tomorrow I would be putting my life on the line for the love of my life.

They say heroin addicts are always trying to recreate that first high, but it is as elusive as fairy dust. So, try as they might, they can never again achieve the lofty heights of their first excursion into Neverland. This is the reason why so many overdose. Because they continue to pump more and more poison into their veins in a vain attempt to feel as fine as they did at the very first pinprick. Yes, all of this is common knowledge, but not until one experiences it firsthand does it make any sense. Not unless you can find a similar addiction to throw you under the train. Well, I had and thank God, it didn't throw me under the train, but landed me instead, conveniently in one of its cars.

I had no idea it would be like this. I should have been scared shitless like my companion. I could tell he was having a real hard time with the whole deal. He'd spent hours researching the place on his phone using Google Earth as a guide, but no itty-bitty map Ap could do the place justice. To say it was huge was selling it way too short. Gargantuan? Mammoth? Massive? Colossal? Herculean? Titanic? Shoot, a Thesaurus couldn't hold enough synonyms to describe the sprawling wasteland of iron and steel that spread out before us.

"Maybe we should have started out slow," he'd murmured.

But it was too late to turn back now. In fact, two weeks ago it still would have been too late. Here it was with May half gone already which meant it was a little over three months until the annual Hobo convention out in Britt. Wow, this sure left a lot of miles to cover, not to mention words to write if I was to have anything to crow about come August. So we'd better get cracking.

"Forget that!" I countered. "Let's just do what we came for. Come on! Time's a wasting!"

My heart was pounding in a strange way, not in the sickly Afib style I had come to dread, but in a way suggesting high adventure. No doubt about it; my adrenal was pumping and sending powerful rushes through my body. However, I forced myself to wait. Doe had already informed me that sometimes you had to scope out a train yard for several days before finding your ride. Of course, that only applied if you were specific about which direction you were going, and this was hardly an issue. North, south, east, or west; it hardly mattered to me. For this was a trial run, and since it was also a trial by fire, I was in no mood to be selective. Any train would do, just as long as we were on it when it left the yard.

It took awhile to sort the place out. Hell, it took most of the afternoon during which time we remained hidden in a clump of scrubby trees at the edge of the yard. Then night fell and our train appeared as if by magic. It was a junk train, one of the ones which haul stuff that isn't considered too valuable—like fruit, coal, grain, or oil—and it was going by pretty slow, leaving the departure yard like an old man wheezing up a flight of stairs. But it was still moving at about 5 MPH and picking up speed every moment.

"That's our train," Doe whispered, nudging me. I could almost taste the fear in his voice; it was that palatable. "Come on! It's now or never."

And though I had a funny feeling he would have almost preferred the latter, I rose up and grabbed my pack. Had it become heavier in the last five hours? I doubted it, but boy, it felt like a ton of bricks. How fast could I run anyway? I can't remember ever clocking my time, never having been one of those jock girls who sport spandex and tank tops during the Boston Marathon. No, I was just plain Lulu, and though I'd done a lot of hiking in my day, I'd never had to sprint to catch anything other than a bus. And that sure hadn't involved the kind of risk I was contemplating now.

But then something strange happened. Something un-Lululike kicked in and when it did, it did so with a passion. I was up and over to the side of the train before you could say Jack Robinson—or Flying Dutchman as it were. Then I was hoisting myself onto the ladder that led to the car within, and two seconds later I was inside. I didn't even check to see if my companion was hot on my heels; I'd been in that much of a hurry, flying on an automatic pilot I didn't know I possessed.

In fact, I'd been so preoccupied with my mission I hadn't noticed that I'd caught the tail end of the train, and was now riding on the rear deck of what turned out to be a grain car. Oh my God! I was *riding the porch*! That's what Connecticut Shorty had called it, and she should know.

Though now an aging septuagenarian, she'd once ridden the rails with a passion that reflected her lineage. Progeny of a famous hobo named Connecticut Slim, both her brother and sister had followed the family tradition, as had she. And her first ride? Why, where else but on the rear-deck of a grain car. You couldn't get any better than that. It was destiny. The cold wind in my face, the clickity-clack of the train on the track... it all spoke of a freedom I had never yet tasted, and one I feared I might never get enough of.

I turned around. Doe had made it. I guess I should have thanked God for that, but instead I was communicating with a different sort of deity. A pale moon came out from behind a cloud and illuminated my face and ...

Noone/Doe Speaking

Jesus H. Christ!!! She looks like some sort of grungy Madonna. Almost beautiful in a scary sort of way. Fucking A!!! I could hardly believe my eyes. In fact, I could hardly trust any of my senses at that point because hadn't I just been blown out of the water by watching a half-pint halfling fly by me at a speed unknown to man before hoping a train which had to be going faster than she could run? Sweet Jesus! I still can't believe she made it, and to my shame, she did so a good ten seconds before me. Oh well, ladies first and all that. Guess I underestimated her. There must be a rod of steel running down that skinny spine. And a jet propelled unit that kicks her into overdrive upon the push of a button. One that reads: *Press here if you're an adrenaline junky.*

Gee, I never would have figured her for this. But, then again, by the look of her face, never did she. Holy fuck! What was I witnessing here? Whatever it was, I sure didn't like it. Nor had I liked the hop. Christ Almighty! I'd almost shit my pants.

Despite the fact that I'd drunk half a bottle of Gallo the night before to ease my nerves and had researched the whole thing meticulously, I was still shaking in my shoes once we arrived at the yard. Then the yard came into sight, a sprawling megalopolis which appeared to extend all the way to the horizon, and I felt the butterflies descend in mass into my stomach.

I'd tried to postpone what was becoming the inevitable. I'd followed all the advice I'd received from Reddit. First I located what surely must be the classification yard, the point from which the cars would come and go, often without warning. It was the danger zone, a busy area swarming with bulls and ripe with surveillance, and hardly the place to be. Instead I focused on the departure yard. This was where you'd find the main lines and where the trains ran through real slow, and it was here where we'd hop our train. But not until nightfall, or so the instructions went. So we needed to hole up awhile someplace where we'd escape notice.

I'd found some trees near the edge of the yard and headed for them, and that was where we'd spent a good five hours waiting, waiting, waiting. There hadn't been much to do but change our clothes to darker colors. That was easy enough since we both embraced black as a fashion statement.

So there you have it. The check list had been completed. Let's see. Avoid the bulls. Travel light. Make sure you have water. Wear black. Don't drink. (Well, at least not immediately before the hop.) And... let's see, what else? How about the part where you take a healthy dose of Prozac? Why hadn't anyone mentioned that?

As the hours wore on and the sun did its daily sinking, my panic attack had accelerated. I'd been so bent out of shape I'd found it impossible to sit still and had paced the small enclave of trees like I was some jungle cat getting ready to pounce on its prey. At least that's the image I'd hoped to convey to her. Didn't want to let on that I was scared shitless. No, that wouldn't do at all.

And then, the big moment had come, Beelzebub had arrived in a coat of rusty iron, sporting graffiti and belching toxic smoke. As slow as he'd been going, I knew he was no hot shot. Those are the trains that carry the expensive shit and fly by at seventy MPH. Instead he was of the lowly junk train variety and ripe for the hopping. If that is, the hoppers were ready and willing.

I'd watched him ease on down the track and when I felt we were a decent distance from the front of the train—where we would certainly be seen and reported by the conductor—I made my move.

"It's now or never," I'd told her, and though I would have gladly chosen to bag the whole deal, I rose to meet my doom. And that's when some sort of fucking miracle happened. For my torpid traveling companion—the same one who'd been struggling to keep up with me as we ran for the rides we'd flagged down—was up and on that train so fast it would take ten minutes for her underwear to catch up with her. If I hadn't been in such a hurry to follow her ass, she would have left me standing, gaping from a clump of tress in one of the busiest train yards in the country. But I knew that such was not an option, as did my fragile male ego. So all I could hope for was that this was a fluke, a one-time deal, and that in the future, she'd settle down to a more ladylike pace. Yeah, dream on!

As luck would have it, our first train took us back east to Louisville. I'd looked upon that as an omen. This journey was now officially over as we had somehow returned to our point of origin. Who cared that it had taken a little more than a week? It was good enough. We were home; or should I say, I was. I'd fulfilled my contract to Leslie, brought Lulu safely through the fires of her first baptism, and now I could rest on my laurels while she wrote about her experience.

Right. All of one page.

Sadly, I knew this was not what had been expected of me. Lulu was going to need a whole lot more than one page if she was going to survive the coming years until she was old enough to claim Social Security. Good God, it was fairly obvious that she was about as useful as tits on a bull. Leslie claimed that she hadn't done jackshit while hanging around the farm all winter, and I knew Leslie. She was business woman, and though she seemed to love us both as a sister/daughter and brother/son, she had no use for dead wood.

So Lulu was going to have to do something in order to feed herself for the next few decades. Oh, there was always SSI. Surely she'd qualify with that eye problem of hers, not to mention the heart condition Leslie had described. But SSI took lawyers, and lawyers took money, and Lulu had little. So what was a girl to do?

Well, maybe she could just ride the rails for a living. Hook up with another bum, a professional one this time, who shared her adrenaline fired hobo hobby. But for the immediate present, I knew I was all she had, and once I accepted the fact that going home to Leslie's was off the table, I steeled myself for fulfilling the rest of my contract. Maybe my nerves would settle down, maybe this catching *out* business would be like murder and get easier the next time around. Yeah, fat chance.

One of Lulu's heroes, an old babe named Connecticut Shorty who had ridden over five thousand miles, bragged that she'd never been afraid. Good for Shorty. Just as I'd prayed that Lulu's initial enthusiasm would wane, I also expected my first-time jitters to let up. Not so. In fact, quite the opposite, and as her reckless abandon gained momentum, so did my dread. Both increased at such an exponential rate that it didn't take long until they were off the charts.

It was hard to hide my fear from Lulu. Though I'd always prided myself with being an eternal optimist, I found myself descending into dark moods, especially right before a jump. Afterwards was a little better, if you can call sleeping in an open car filled with wood shavings any sort of an improvement. But at least the ride would give my stomach a chance to settle down, before the inevitable happened.

Meaning that trains, like all means of transportation, have an ultimate destination and once reached, are sure to be parked for a spell while they unload. This means that there will always be another hop, and another, and another, all of which will be associated with a plethora of risks and fuck-ups.

First and foremost were the railroad yard bulls. Then, came the crazy people. I'd read on-line that one old hobo had his legs broken by a punch of punks one night. No particular reason. Just some bullies out for a good time. But if that weren't bad enough, there were the trains themselves. Wicked two ton barrels of rusting iron, so heavy their wheels could peel the metal right off the tracks, the result being something akin to a rain of shrapnel. And speaking of those wheels, a hopper wanted to avoid them like the plague least they lose a limb right then and there.

Oh, it went on and on, my list of grievances against my latest job, and it sure did make me miss my mom's basement and all my wondrous gadgets, the like of which had long ago been sold down the pawn shop river. Alas and alack. So this was *living large with very little* as Lulu so joyously blogged one day. Fuck that! All I could hope for was that we'd stay clear of an early grave. That way, we could still *live* to tell about it.

That said, I did my best to keep us out of harm's way. First off, I tried to sneak into stopped cars whenever we could. This involved avoiding the railroad bulls, by always keeping a train or two between them and us while in the yard. In fact, as much as possible I avoided contact with anyone we met near the trains. I didn't even stop to chat up the workers, who on a good day might give us a tip about schedules and destinations. Instead, I worked the Net for Intel, seeking the trains that would provide us with the longest ride. It became a number's game, all about reverse probability, for this was one instance where one did not want to hold a whole bunch of raffle tickets. I figured the fewer jumps we made, the less chance we had of dying during one. It was a cockeyed philosophy, but statistically sound.

And then the lucky day came when we were down to our last few dollars. Hallelujah! My prayers had been answered. Never did I think I would ever get down on my knees and pray for poverty, but this was one time when it just might save the day.

"Lulu," I began one night while we lay in wait for our next ride. "I don't know about you, but I've got about five bucks left."

Then, sure that I'd put the fear of the Lord into the lady, I let it go at that.

But nooo... She was not about to be stopped. In fact, her behavior for the past month reminded me of my maw's favorite ballet. (And yes, maw had not totally neglected the classical side of my education.) It was known as *The Red Shoes* and featured some hapless ballerina who had become bewitched to the point that she could not stop dancing; and although her shoes remained in pristine condition, their wearer soon fell by the wayside. Talk about dancing until you dropped. Poor girl; her passion had done her in. Just like Lulu's was doing.

I examined her face. It was covered with grime and gaunter than ever. Plus, I swear that she'd dropped a good ten pounds in the last five weeks. No, make that a *bad* ten pounds because she didn't have much to spare. Tiny to begin with, she needed all the fighting weight she could muster. Hell, she needed a hot meal and a warm bed!

Then there was the matter of her vision. One of the lenses to her pop-bottle eyeglasses had come loose and had fallen out during a jump. So she was more visually impaired than ever. I'd tried to help her out with my reading glasses, but they, too, had suffered a mishap, meaning that I'd lost them. (Again.) So, until we got someplace where I could replenish my stock, we were down to one lens between us. The fact that we had to share and share alike had already led to a few arguments. Despite functioning more like a huge magnifying glass than anything else, that one lens was still essential if I were to peruse the various train schedules on-line. So I was always trying to borrow it. However, doing so deprived Lulu of any ability to see straight, so she was none too compliant with my request.

I'd tried to inject some humor into the situation by reminding her of an image from mythology, that of the Fates who were unlucky enough to share only one working eye between six sockets. But it hadn't worked. She needed an optometrist, and the cash to pay for one, which brought me back to my original concern, that of our pending poverty.

So I waited for her response to my declaration of empty pockets, hoping she'd concur with me that, it would be best to call it quits before we were literally down to our last nickel. But I guess she had other ideas, for her reply was simply that *we should go to New Mexico then because…*

"I have that PO Box set up there, and it's sure to contain a royalty check by now."

A royalty check? Yeah, in what reality? Probably the same one where my dog just had kittens.

I was stunned. So she was still priming that dry hole. Didn't the girl get it? No one read anymore, and if they did, they read stuff which had been approved by The New York Times, and more than likely they accessed the stuff via a Kindle or even better an Audible account. (That's the one where they read it to you, thus sparing you the eyestrain which the Blue Screen of computers had become infamous for.)

And did she have either? I doubted it, although Kady might have been kind enough to set her up an e-book version of her book. For a few extra bucks. Yeah, Kady never did anything for free!

But even so, the competition was fierce out there, so fierce that many self-published authors spent more time marketing their book than even writing it. And was Lulu doing that? No, instead she was off on a wild goose chase, the likes of which was supposed to ultimately win her a Pulitzer Prize. In bullshit maybe, but not much else! Yeah, I didn't really see such kudos happening anytime soon. After all, I was her blog-master, and the number of hits we'd had on her daily ramblings never had made it out of the single digits. No one was biting. There were already a bundle of websites and videos out there on her topic, and many were a lot more interesting than the quasi-spiritual dribble she'd been having me send into cyberspace. Stuff like:

We've all been fed a line of bull and made to feel like naughty children, manipulated by guilt. Be it the Judeo-Christian version of heaven and hell where he died for your sins or the eastern version of karma-to-burn and lessons-to-learn, it's all the same pack of lies. The bottom line is that, until we stop identifying with the drop of water, we will eternally remain separate from the ocean. Yes, we must never forget that we are children of God and children grow up to be like their parents.

Right. Great stuff, but what exactly did it have to do with the price of trains in Chicago? And then there was this little gem.

Did it ever occur to you that we might be on a reincarnation loop? That it is all a program brought about by our controllers? That they have an agenda and they plan to drop us back down here accordingly, all the while convincing those of us who are half-way cognizant that we might have more than one life and that we are being dumped back to where we are because of the activities we engaged in during our previous incarnations? It's all the old guilt grid. We can check out multiple times, but we are never allowed to leave.

Well, you know what? That never did occur to me. But it sure did occur to a bunch of other people, including David Icke and those guys from The Eagles; and do I smell a bit of plagiarism here? Did Lulu really think she was inventing the wheel? Hell, everyone from Tommy Williams to Simon Parkes sang this song, and it was bad enough coming from their lips. At least they could carry a tune in a bucket. Lulu? Her metaphysical eloquence was right up there with Alvin and the Chipmunks. Sorry sister, but what you said just didn't make a good deal of sense.

Good Lord, I can't believe I was putting my name to this sort of dribble. Of course, I had taken care to cover my own tracks so that nothing could come back to haunt me. Still, it was a matter of professional pride that I produce something more worthy of the cloud than this. Which brings me back to the overload of posts and blogs, and especially videos that line the library shelves of Cyberspace about her purposed topic at hand.

I wish I'd had more time before we'd embarked on this little adventure to do more research. But I'd been too busy with the nuts and bolts of preparation to bother watching hour-long videos sporting footage some dude had captured out of a boxcar bound to St. Paul from Seattle. And let me tell you, that about sums up half of the videos posted, just boring wordless dissertations featuring close-ups of the insides of rail cars and long shots of the world surrounding the tracks. Most of this shit was barely suitable for skimming, and its only saving grace came from a Go-Pro, the camera of choice for any bum lucky enough to afford one.

That's right, a Go-Pro. Wow, I'd give my eye teeth for one of those sweet little gizmos. But it hadn't even made it past the first of our budget cuts.

But, whatever the case, a cat could look at a king; and when I finally did get around to watching some of the stuff generated by our competition, I came upon a few three star productions. Some were hokey, and I could tell the people involved were just wanna-be riders, kids out for a cheap thrill or a way to supplement their college fund. These guys had all the best equipment—new Jansport Packs and small solar panels with which to charge their phones—and once again, I became green with envy, especially when confronted with all the techi-toys they carried.

However, the real McCoys would have scoffed and berated them for all the extra weight. Or else, if they were kindly, they might have cautioned them as to the dangers associated with such a sport. For instance, take the one video I watched about a guy who'd been sent to prison for train-hopping.

Prison??? And here I thought the worst you could get slapped with was a NO TRESPASSING misdemeanor. However, I was soon to be enlightened. Apparently, it's only a misdemeanor if you hop a stopped train. Other than that, it's a felony. Oh well, still no reason to send an eighteen year old punk to prison, and that had been the age of this blogger at the time of the incident.

It had happened in Alliance, Ohio, a town way too close for comfort in regard to my own past. I knew the place. It was near where the tracks split, one going north to Chicago and the other west to Cincinnati. Poor guy. All he'd been doing was trying to hitch a quick ride home from a skateboard competition, one where he had apparently won accolades. The idea of riding the rails had seemed fast enough, and the romance of it all caused him to talk his buddy into giving it a whirl. So they caught a train. Ecstatic at their early success, they did anything but keep a low profile, and it didn't take long for railroad security to catch up with them. With a show of force formerly only used for the likes of arch terrorists, nine cop cars greeted them at the Alliance yard, wielding tear gas, guns, and handcuffs. Then, before you could say Osama Bin Laden, the boys found themselves being whisked off to a maximum security prison. Not good. Thank God the judge—who incidentally appeared via

TV screen—saw the story for what it was and ordered their immediate release or the kids would have ended up in Gitmo.

So at least that story had a happy ending, one which allowed it to resurface later as a cautionary tale to other riders. But not so with some of the other stuff I found while foraging around in the shadow world of the modern day hobo. Some of it was dated and you only had to pray the culprits had been apprehended because it was pretty bad.

We'd known when we started out that this life attracted all sorts of misfits, and despite my attempts to avoid contact with other riders, we'd happened upon our share. Some were old timers like the gray-haired drunk we'd found cramped into a corner on an empty grain car. I had to admit that despite his odor, which was just shy of overpowering, he was some pretty fine entertainment. Not only were his stories right up there with Jack London's, but he had a funny way of punctuating them by popping out a glass eye.

"Had the red threads in it ordered up special," he'd bragged. "Since I'm rarely sober, I figured I'd better get the new eyeball to match up with the old one."

And then he'd wink, his eyelid heavy with enough alcohol to run a small lawnmower, and would continue on with his next tale from the railroad car crypt. Usually it would have something to do with an organization entitled FTRA. That would be Freight Train Riders of America, a group which according to Wikipedia had **supposedly** been founded by some Vietnam vets back in the 80's. (Sorry, but I just had to emphasize that adjective, since like most of his stories, the bullshit about the FTRA beggared believe.)

At any rate, these guys frequented the Chicago to Seattle line, and *squattheplanet* referred to them as a bunch of harmless old farts from the 90's. They'd been blown up to look like arch villains in an attempt by the media to discourage folks from riding the rails. However, they'd never committed any worse crimes than food stamp and benefit fraud, so what's the big deal? What anarchist amongst us has not played that game? All it took was getting hold of a few extra Social Security numbers. No problem there if you were a good enough hacker, not that this fit the description of our octogenarian Scheherazade. So I ruled out any possibility that he might be a member of said nefarious group, and continued to listen idly to his numerous attempts to impress us with his plethora of travel tales.

Yes, those had been the harmless encounters, and though there had been a few which bordered on suspect, there had been none yet that were out and out dangerous; none yet which hinted of darkness and unspeakable acts.

I wonder if the unlucky bums who had encountered Robert Silveria (AKA The Boxcar Killer) or Dirty Mike Adams had any inkling of the evil sitting next to them. Did they suspect that both men would end up serving multiple life sentences for killing up to four dozen people during their time of riding the rails? Indeed, both Silveria and Adams had gone down in the books as serial killers of an almost unstoppable kind. They had taken the authorities on quite the man hunt, one fueled by the old adage that a moving target is hard to hit. It was only luck and persistence which landed them both in jail, making the rails just a little bit safer for newbies like us. However, this didn't mean that dangerous people weren't still out there, and as far as I was concerned, the less I saw of my fellow travelers, the better. In fact, the less I saw of this whole lifestyle, the better.

Ergo, when Lulu suggested checking in on her PO Box near Taos, I jumped on the idea. Oh, I confess I had my own agenda. While wintering down near the area just months ago, I had renewed a few old contacts. One was a guy who'd been a fellow woofter back in the good old days and who now owned little bug-out shack up in the hills. Since the guy was still on the woofting circuit, he wasn't always around, but he made it clear I was welcome to drop in whenever I was in the neighborhood and stay for a few days if need be.

"It isn't much," he'd confided. "Just a shack with a privy out back and a wood stove. But it's a roof over your head should you need one…"

And boy, oh boy, could I use a place to rest my bones about now, especially one that wasn't rolling down the tracks at seventy-five MPH while providing me with no roof but the stars over my head.

Yeah, that sure sounded good, and if I was lucky and played my cards right, I might be able to talk my tiny princess into pausing for a moment in her head long dash over the train yard cliff. Perhaps after she checked out her PO Box, I could get her to agree to spending a little down time in the New Mexico hills. I would bill it as a chance to catch up on her editing. I knew she was trying to build a book out of the blog we'd been posting, and this would take some quiet time, time without piercing whistles and screeching brakes.

And when she was done? Well maybe, just maybe I would be able to sweet talk her into calling it a day. After all, the end of the summer was rapidly approaching and that little town in Iowa which was her ultimate destination would soon be hosting its annual Hobo Fair. What she hoped to accomplish there was beyond me. On this point her lips were sealed, but I couldn't help wonder if it might have something to do with a guy. Or maybe even a girl in her case. But then, perhaps I was just seeing things through the lens of my own myopic vision, because I had to admit that a return to New Mexico brought with it the possibility that I might, just might, manage to re-hook up with a certain carnival. It was one which had left me in the lurch, stealing away in the middle of the night with the love of my life aboard, a magnificent specimen of a woman who dangled from its death defying heights.

Aniel. Dare I whisper the name?

Yeah, I can dare. Lord knows I'd been getting a lot of practice lately.

Lulu/Stitch Speaking

Amazing. He seemed to relish my plan to hop the Santa Fe line down to New Mexico. I'd started to wonder about him. He sure didn't seem to be enjoying himself much. Oh, he was handy enough with his smart-phone, posting my daily ramblings to that blog he'd created for our travels. And he sure was good with the nuts and bolts stuff like choosing which train went in what direction. Plus he was somewhat of a boy scout, and I had come to rely on his back woods survival skills. He could start a campfire with one match and keep it smokeless enough so as to not draw too much attention. Then, his pack—which by all means was smaller than my own—was constantly amazing me as he drew one survival tool after another from its grungy depths.

When I'd asked him how he learned about all this stuff he'd gone into a long dissertation about how he'd spent a lot of time woofting around to various organic farms, many in third world countries.

"Yeah," he'd claimed. "You get real good at shittin' in a bucket. If that is, you are lucky enough to find one." Then he'd laughed.

I guess he'd been trying to impress me. Little did he know I'd done my own share of wompassing around the planet, albeit under slightly more sophisticated circumstances—thanks to Brother Joe's money. Oh well, why bother to fill him in on all the details? He seems content with the knowledge that I have culled my stories, keeping many of them to myself. This is fine with me since I've been saving them up for my next book, the one I will write when this is all over.

Of course, this all came as somewhat of a revelation to me. You see, my original intent when I had started this journey was to simply publish the blog I'd been posting. But as the days worn on, a better idea had come to me. Why not personalize it and start with Joe's death? For wasn't that where the whole odyssey had begun? There was so much I hadn't put in the last book, all that business about the power places of the earth and the Merkaba grid; and let's not forget the ayahuasca revelation. Yeah, I sure had experienced quite a lot while working on my first book, so why not commit my experiences to paper.

After all, my mother had gotten her day in the sun the last time around—or should I say, her *day in the shade*. So now it was my turn. And what better way to serve my rebuttal to her heartless cruelty? I would bare her britches for all the world to see, and then they would know just what I'd been up against.

It was perfect and the more I thought about it, the clearer it became. Not that I was forsaking my original plan to hook up with Dutch. But I figured it might be a good idea to have a plan B just in case he didn't pan out as a soul mate. Indeed, regardless of what Doe might think, my mama did not raise a fool.

I knew Doe thought I was ditzy. Since I sure didn't say much, allowing him to do most of the talking, there was no way he would ever understand the complex process of the gears which whirled about in my brain. They were pretty much non-stop these days, perhaps motivated to perpetual motion by the clickity-clack of the trains as they rolled on down the track. And the song they sang was one that needed to be put down onto paper.

Yes, paper. A forgotten medium of exchange and one that would, hopefully, still be around when the terrorists finally hacked the system and cyberspace fell from the sky. I knew it was coming. It was inevitable. Like Michael Crichton explained in *Jurassic Park*, it was all about Chaos Theory. The bigger a system gets, the harder it falls. And the system we relied on at the beginning of the 21st century sure had become gargantuan. So unless we managed to skip a few stages and went straight to communicating via telepathy, we were going to be royally screwed if some terrorist managed to set off an EMP blast above our hapless heads. Yeah, Doe might think he's pretty smart with all those gadgets, and he probably is—at least a lot smarter than me. But as a famous man once said, smart does not always equate with wise.

Besides the more he shared his world view with me, the more I came to realize that he was dogmatic pragmatist who, though knowledgeable about many things, seemed to lack a spiritual direction. This I gleaned from his nightly ramblings during which he attempted to enlighten me to the intricacies of the political scene.

He'd go on and on about various Internet personalities, many who he would bad-mouth, claiming they were all capitalizing on confusion to make a buck. There was some guy named Tommy Robinson who the whole alt-media was up in arms about, since he'd been unjustly thrown in prison. Then the word had come out over the wires that Tommy wasn't in prison after all and… So, what's a guy to believe?

Case in point was another guy who called himself Daniel Cannon, though it was never very clear where the *ali*ases left off and the asses began. This guy went by the sobriquet of *Logic before Authority*, and oh, how I loved the names of these guys—neatsey cutesey, stuff like Serial Brain and DahBo777. Guess that, like the rock groups back in the 60's, all the good monikers had been taken, forcing them to resort to the bottom of the barrel.

But that's beside the point. Back to Daniel, who Doe considered an OK kind of guy—at least until he started talking about flat earth theory. No wonder some other internet troll had slaughtered Daniel in a foul mouthed call-out. And speaking of which, let's not forget Thomas Williams who was always *outing* everyone else except his own people! Good Lord, didn't Doe get it? They all had their own agendas. They were all trying to get the most hits, and the most clicks on their Donate buttons.

And as far as *outing* went, Doe did his own share of casting folks out of the circle of trust—although there were a few for which he held some degree of hope. One of these probably wasn't even a person, but a collective intelligence, and possibly even a computer. However, there were rumors that it was really JFK Junior.

JFK Junior? I thought he'd crashed and burned decades ago, not long after he'd started that men's magazine *GQ*. And now Doe is insisting that he's back at it, operating from some incognito bunker where he posts regular prophetic blips to the Internet?

We were watching the bland countryside pass by, the flatlands that preceded our journey to the Land of Enchantment, and we were both bored. So Doe had decided to entertain me with what was usually reserved for his evening entertainment.

"Yeah, he goes by the handle of Q, and in the military that stands for top level security clearance, stuff so secret only sensitive compartmentalized access is allowed. That's why so much of it is in code."

Code? My ears perked up since I had always relished a good mystery, and that had been my signal for him to continue.

"I came across this stuff on an obscure Internet channel where all the posts were anonymous. It made a big stir when it first appeared since it seemed to be predictive. Or at least half of what it forecast came to pass—which is an OK ratio, but not enough to make a true believer out of me. But then it got deeper, and every one and their brother began to analyze the posts, picking at tiny details like time stamps, gematria, and numerology, and they lost me. But I have to admit there was something to it all, and what they were finding couldn't have been purely coincidental.

"So I paid casual attention to it, becoming a quasi-follower with just enough interest to keep my feet wet. But as my passion waned, so did everyone else's mushroom until folks at Trump rallies were even sporting Q placards. This led to my seeking more analysis, some of which attempted to put the whole phenomenon into some semblance of order. First off, they talked about how it all began with the military, which would explain the code. That alone was enough to get me to stand up and pay attention because I began to worry if the military was now running our government."

When did it ever stop? I wanted to say, but sat down until the mood passed, allowing him to ramble on.

"Anyway, the story goes that there was a faction in the military who saw what was going on in the world and didn't approve, didn't want to sign their name to it anymore. So they got Trump to run for office as a populist President, one who would make America great again. But behind the scenes, the royal Trumpnees would still answer to this patriot faction of the military, the ones attempting to wrestle America away from the clutches of an evil which has permeated the world for eons.

"I guess you'd say it boils down to patriots versus globalists, which is somewhat of an oversimplification. But that's the way I understand it. However, it's not supposed to be about politics. Left versus right; Dems versus Republicans. The priority was to unite the people and to initiate a deep cleaning when it came to the swamp that our political scene had descended into. Plus, it was supposed to be world-wide because this evil is embedded globally, and the US will just be the first domino to fall. Yeah, round up the pedophiles, and expose the crooks at the top level of government. Then serve them with indictments and send them all away for a long long time. And I've got to admit this all sounds good to me.

"But is it happening? Oh, I know about all the hoopla with the Catholic Church and yeah, it seems every day some new sex trafficking ring has been brought down. And then we lost both Daddy Bush (the evil Emperor from *Star Wars*) and John McCain. But both were old and could have died from natural causes. So I'm torn here. I'd like to believe we are heading down a better track, but I don't see where Trump has united this country. In fact, it seems just the opposite, that we are more polarized that ever. So the pessimist in me wonders if this wasn't the real reason why he was put into office, just to perpetuate the same old divide and conquer. Just keep the people bumfuzzled and they won't pay any attention to the man behind the curtain.

"I mean, where are all those mass arrests and sealed indictments that the Internet pundits have been blabbing on about forever and ever? Oh, they say there are consequences to be paid for moving too fast, that we need to expose the truth slowly or the sheeple will panic. Yeah, timing is everything. Trust the plan and all that. Still, I can't help but feel we're all just being played. Again. Because the only people that are reading these Q posts are the ones who already get it. Maybe Q is trying to get everyone else on board. Maybe he does want us to question and expand our thinking. But what about your average Joe on the street? All he cares about is making another rent payment and maybe having enough left over to tie one on over the weekend. Let's face it. We really aren't a nation of deep thinkers."

"Anyway, I remain skeptical that it may be all a psy-ops, a way to trick us into a false sense of security, one where we trust the plan so much we just sit on our butts and do nothing and let the big brass take control."

He took a breath before concluding.

"But boy, is sure would be something if all this stuff was true and Q really is JFK Junior, who faked his own death and who will be revealed as still alive (along with Princess Di and Groucho Marx and John Lennon). And yeah, John Boy will come back from the dead to run alongside of Trump in the 2020 election, and we'll all be saved by a new dynasty, one that will replace the Bush-Clinton cartel. Yeah, but why is that so great? Gee, I might as well toss my hat in the ring with the ET's, who are all going to come down to save us. Of course, that's a topic for another day."

And with that, he turned and gave his full attention to the flatlands of western Texas, a landscape whose monotony was punctuated only by oil rigs and tumbleweeds. Too bad, I might have liked to continue in the vein of the ET's. Now that was a topic I could sink my teeth into. But it would have only precipitated an argument. I could sense a doubting Thomas when I saw one, and no way in hell was I going to try to enlighten him with some of my cosmic experiences. It was, as he said, enough for one day.

Of course, tomorrow was another day, and as we pulled into the Santa Fe yard the following morning, I was struck with the realization that it was going to be a good one. No ambiguous Q posts here, no weird populist plots, no code, no bullshit… and oh yeah, no car, no pool, no pets, ain't got no cigarettes. And maybe that wasn't so good.

I examined my pockets. They still held a couple dollars worth of change, but that was all; meaning I was at risk of becoming destitute. So why did I feel so elated? Could it be the feeling in my bones which insisted my luck was about to change? If so, it was a strong motivator, and it got me moving enough to push us through the train yard in record breaking time. Then, in keeping with the cheery little song that was tickling my throat, our first ride took us directly to the center of the small town where I had set up a PO Box months before.

I marched in there like a conquering hero. I was so certain victory awaited. But then I took one look at the bulletin board which greeted me upon arrival, and my helium filled balloon developed a bad case of lead feet.

Jesus H. Christ and God Bless America! You've got to be kidding! She wouldn't! She didn't! But there it was in big glossy celluloid, the proof of the pudding that my mother was a bigger bitch than I'd ever given her credit for.

MISSING PERSON
Have you seen this woman? If so, please contact the number below.

And there I was for all to see in all my high school glory, horn-rimmed glasses, over-permed hair and all.

Woman? You have got to be kidding. Boy, she really was trying hard to find me, wasn't she? I was puzzled at first. But not for long since didn't I just mention that my mother hadn't raised a fool? I smelled the rat of an ulterior motive. This was no grieving mother trying to find a long lost daughter. Nope. This was more the work of a conniving schemer who knew the rules of life insurance policies: that a missing person has to be absent for x amount of years in order to be declared dead. Then and only then can their benefactor wrangle the big payout. I thought of my mother with her dear old fixed bitch face. Surely she knew the ropes, and what better way to fulfill the requirements of the life insurance policy she'd taken out on me as a child than to post my mug shot in every PO Box in the country. She'd probably been really burned when Joe had cashed his in and then taken out a new one, naming Davey and me as the new benefactors.

Guess this was her way of getting back at me for The Book. Right. The Book. That's what she called it, spitting out the words as you would a stream of spent tobacco juice. The Book, indeed. The sum total of my life's work so far, and yet the poor thing wasn't even allowed the dignity of a valid title. What a slap on the face!! And now this!!!

Well, we'll see about that. We'll see just how well her little scheme plays out, especially once it's documented that someone is picking up the royalty checks for said *book*. That should throw a fly into her little poison pie.

I ripped down the poster, not wanting to court the chance that some casual post office employee might do an age adjustment and recognize me. Not that there was much chance of that. Good Lord! She could have at least paid homage to my adult form instead of using old pimple face's high school yearbook poster. But that would have been defeating her purpose now, wouldn't it.

Trying to control my rage, I strode over to the wall which held the PO Boxes. Then, releasing the necklace of keys from around my neck, I selected the one that fit the lock. Doe was looking at me. After I'd shown him the photo, he'd been all about doing a quick exit. Guess he was worried someone would recognize me and call the cops. Strange, since he'd been the first to agree that the picture bore little resemblance to my current self. But I'd noticed a growing nervousness in him. He was jumpy about everything these days, and had even suggested that we needed a *vacation from our vacation.* Maybe so, perhaps it would bring back that playful spirit I had first pegged him for.

At any rate, it was an idea worth considering, for I was also getting weary of the road. Maybe it was time to hole up somewhere for a while and get started on my new book which up to that moment had been nothing more than a gleam in my eye. But that would take a bit of start-up cash and, shit, who knows? Maybe providence would smile on me here.

Nervously, I turned the key and reached in to secure the contents of the box. Much of it was the usual drivel and was immediately tossed into the waste can. But then, there it was like the grand finale allowed to Pandora—gleaming in all its golden splendor—a letter from the LULU publishing house. And by the looks of it, it had to hold a check.

I tore open the envelope and barely restrained myself from letting out a whoop and a holler. However, no need to draw any more attention to our presence. Lord knows, the stench arising from our unwashed bodies was enough. Not to mention our overall appearance, which was right up there with some poor soul straight out of *The Grapes of Wrath.*

But still I could barely control my elation at the sum within, a whopping seventy-five big ones. Well, hallelujah! My first big pay off, and I knew it would not be my last. My good mood of the morning flew right back in that window and landed square on my shoulders. It was time for a celebration.

"Dinner's on me," I assured my companion and lead the way out of the PO to the main street of the town. There was dusty diner nearby, right next to a pawn shop, one which featured a line of guitars in its window. I paused and considered entering. It had been a long time since I'd held a guitar next to my heart, and I missed it. But then my stomach growled, and I decided to wait. First things first and all that. But later? After we'd eaten our fill? Well, that was different story. After all, what's the point of having money if you can't enjoy it a little bit?

Noone/Doe Speaking

I can't believe she spent twenty-five bucks on that old guitar! My God! That was one third of her total take, and then dinner had gobbled up another ten spot. Jesus! At this rate, we'd be back to skid row in no time! And hell's bells, why did that cop car keep cruising by? Fuck a duck! All we needed was to be arrested for vagrancy.

It sure looked grim, about as grim as the landscape around us. When we'd pulled into the Santa Fe yard, I'd been struck with how gloomy it was. Sinister. Spooky. They were all worthy adjectives to describe my first impression of the place. Oh, I'd been in New Mexico before, recently even (and at that, I had been forced to groan at the memory). But either the place had changed, or I had.

On the way in, we'd been engulfed in a fog so thick I'd fantasized it would engulf the train and transport it to some other dimension. Yeah, New Mexico. Home to Area 51, Roswell, and Taos. A place where cell phones don't work and GPS is often on the fritz. A true Bermuda Triangle. And I was seriously considering staying put here for a couple of weeks?

Yes, I was. Especially since I'd been able to get her to agree to it. I had broached the topic over dinner, a good time to make plans, and surprisingly, she had taken to my suggestion. Guess she had her own reasons, but why inspect a silver lining for a storm cloud. Just be happy she didn't spend any more money on that fucking guitar cuz we would need whatever was left for a grubstake.

My plan was to take up my old buddy's offer of hospitality. But first we'd stock up on a few essential items, enough beans and rice to see us through until my application for food stamps came through. That's right. After years of false pride, I had finally succumbed to the dole. It was both the bane and the boon of the impoverished, depending on just how much integrity you possessed or just how far you'd sunk into poverty. Actually, I might have considered it long before because then we could have spent what little cash we had on other items, like data cards for my phone. But the problem with any sort of government assistance is that you need a permanent abode, and a boxcar on the City of New Orleans wouldn't do. However, my buddy's generosity would provide us with a physical address. That said, we'd be in the running for all the government assistance we could gobble up.

Of course, I couldn't use my own name and number on the application, as it wouldn't do to clue the government in on my whereabouts. Nor could I use Lulu's since it now appeared she was now wishing to travel incognito, at least until two years had gone by. That was the amount of time required to officially to declare her MIA. At that point she would have to come in from under the radar. Either that or allow her mother to cash in on one big insurance policy. And if I knew Lulu, she would sooner take a beating with rubber hose than do anything to assist that woman.

So I was in somewhat of a dilemma. Until that is, I remembered that old bum's rap about the FTRA and one of the reasons why they had been branded as dangerous anarchists. It all had to do with their uncanny ability to possess more than one social security number, a little obstacle which some serious hacking could quickly overcome. Oh, it might be hard to get all the ID assembled that we would need in order to stay on the dole for any length of time. But when I had suggested a vacation from our vacation, I wasn't talking about years. So with any luck we'd be able to use a couple of fake social Security numbers just long enough to get us some temporary relief from the hunger pains which had been assaulting our midriffs. Then, after we'd sorted some of this out, we'd just move on.

Yeah, just move on. This was the part of my plan I didn't really like too much. But at best, it would buy me some time. Britt, Iowa and the Hobo Festival which was Lulu's final destination were growing closer with each passing day. And if I could just keep the girl away from those dangerous train yards for even a few weeks? Well, that would bring me closer to my own goal which was the annulment of my contract with Leslie. I had, after all, agreed to take Lulu only so far, and anything else was above and beyond, a wild blue yonder where I did not intend to go. Surely Leslie would understand. I knew she'd been reading the blog, so she had to know the sorry details of our walkabout. I knew she hadn't expected me to do this indefinitely, and hopefully, once I deposited Lulu in Britt, the girl would be off on a different tangent, one that would free me to return to those green rolling hills of eastern Kentucky. And then, I suppose I'd be about as close to home as one can get this side of Jordan.

I sighed. I guess I'd never realized up until that point just how much I'd missed my maw. But that wasn't all I missed.

The money spent on the guitar had been worth every nickel. From the first strum to the last echoing chorus, it reinforced my commitment to my current cause. For hadn't this been the deal breaker all those weary weeks ago? Hadn't I tossed my hat into the ring for this very reason? So I could hear this celestial music played out again and again as the angel who uttered it warmed the chilly New Mexico nights better than any campfire ever could?

Boy, had I ever missed the sound of her voice. When she spoke without the benefit of song the result was almost irritating, a nasal twang which sounded like someone might be harboring a serious sinus infection. But there was something about the force of the music rising through that skinny frame which changed all this, and caused me once again to feel she had chosen the wrong muse to follow. I even said so at one point, asking her why she had never considered a career in the performing arts. But she'd just smiled her ambiguous Madonna smile and had gone right on strumming.

Many of her songs were unfamiliar to me, and I figured they must be originals. However, others reminded me of the stuff my maw liked to listen to, which only added to my listening pleasure. Sometimes I felt like I was back in that Coolville basement again, tapping my feet to the tunes which drifted down the stairs from mom's old turn of the century stereo. They were often traveling songs, sung to the rhythm of the rails, and I couldn't help but wonder if this was where her passion for the life of the hobo had come from.

> *Freight train, freight train, going so fast...*
> *If you miss the train I'm on...*
> *You can't jump a jet plane, like you can a freight train...*
> *And the sons of Pullman porters and the sons of engineers, ride their father's*
> *magic carpets made of steel...*
> *I hear that train a coming, it's coming round the bend...*

Her repertoire was as diverse as it was endless, and I couldn't help but wonder if she was getting me back for some of the long winded raps I had entertained her with while on the road. The whole idea made me smile; but then again, I couldn't blame her. I sure had treated her like an Internet ignoramus who needed some serious education as to the wicked ways of the cyber-world. However, a lot of my spotting off had really been more for the purpose of blowing off steam. I had to admit I had been pretty stressed out for the past couple months; and when I am stressed, all that tension comes right out the old pie-hole. I'd even delivered some pretty scathing comments concerning my own personal philosophy, and in retrospect a few of them have been a bit harsh for polite conversation. I cringed to remember one of my last dissertations on how the world has demonized the white Anglo-Saxon male. I must have been close to the end of my rope to go on as I had. Even now bits and pieces of the conversation came back to bite me on the ass.

"And well he might be demonized for what he's done. Not just to others but to his own people. In fact, that's why a lot of us immigrated to America. Then, once here, we just continued the process of abuse by inflicting genocide on the native population. Yeah, it's somewhat of a pattern on this planet, and the bottom line is that it's all perpetuated by one thing and one thing alone: man's infernal desire to reproduce—which leads to his inability to put a plug in it."

Boy, I must have been on an anti-sex rap that day, probably the fallout from one of my graphic dreams about a certain silk swinging maiden. Yeah, put a plug in it. Easy enough to say for a guy like me who had just been emasculated by the lovely lady of his dreams. But it had gotten worse as I went on to itemize how man's ego played into the reproductive crisis on planet earth.

"And then there's some guy in India who is determined that child number nine is a male so as to carry on the family name. And some whoremonger in Malaysia who is raping some twelve year old. And even a hapless yuppie from NYC whose sperm count is almost nonexistent. So he and the missus opt for artificial insemination. And let's not get into the gay couple that does the same thing, just so when junior pops out, he will carry on their own personal brand of DNA. Criminy, what is there about this planet that we feel this infernal compulsion to reproduce? Do we think we are gods trying to make a mini-me in our image?"

I'd been on a roll, that was for sure, and these were the times when it was a wonder she didn't throw me off the train. But maybe she sensed that I, too, had some raw wounds to tend, and this was my way of rubbing salve into them. True, it was easy enough to come off as a disciplined monk in full control of their sexual urges when one has recently had their weenie slapped down as hard as mine had been. Who was I kidding? All my pious posturing was merely the sour grapes of a guy who hadn't gotten any in almost a year. (And who may never get any ever again—because the only woman who will ever do has gone and flown the coop.)

Did Lulu suspect that she was traveling with the broken-hearted? Was that why so many of her favorite songs featured the theme of unrequited love? It was hard to tell because she'd been about as guarded with her past as I'd been. Still, I have to admit it was strange in a way to have traveled all these miles together and yet know so little about each other's lives. However, all that was soon to change.

It happened on one of our last night's there. We'd probably overstayed our welcome having been holed up in Bubba's rustic cabin for well over three weeks now. The food stamps had come in, and the job Johnny was reaching critical mass with the residue from many an extravagant meal. Both of us were eating like there was no tomorrow, and indeed there may never be. Since in two days time we would have to expel ourselves from this temporary Eden and return to life on the rails. The blog had fallen by the wayside, being superseded by Lulu's constant clacking away on something she'd referred to as the next *War and Peace*.

Her fervor had put me at risk of falling into terminal boredom. The Internet at the cabin was dicey and often nonexistent, which led to some fairly monotonous nights. I'd been reduced to reading—yes reading—some of the moldy paperbacks left by the owner. It was ancient stuff, mostly sci-fi with a bent towards Star Wars type material. I'd never been much into the outer space stuff, but here in the wilds of New Mexico with a ringside seat to Chicoma Mountain (regarded by the Pueblo People to be the center of the universe) it was easy to get waylaid by the stars. The sky was so clear at night you could almost see past Jupiter to the outer planets, and I began to wonder what might lie beyond.

There were many Internet contingencies which swore to a Secret Space Program, one that may even be the precursor of a break-away civilization. The concept made sense. We sure had fucked up this world, and I could clearly understand why those with enough cash would just throw up their hands in disgust and take off into the wild blue yonder. Whatever the case, it still sounded like a whole lot of bullshit to me.

Not that I was one of the few remaining humans who felt we were alone in the universe. That would have been taking xenophobia just a little bit too far. It was just that I liked my home planet, regardless of man's attempt to completely destroy it, and I was happy to keep my distance and only participate vicariously in the worlds above my head.

And so I devoured them, one right after another, their yellowed pages at risk of crumbling into dust as I turned them. The complete works of Arthur C. Clarke (of which I only made it through the first three). The *Dune Trilogy* (I'd liked the movie better). And, of course, *2001, Space Odyssey* (and beyond). The last was the one which really got to me. I'd seen the movie there as well, so I was able to follow some of the esoteric nuances of what was going on. Yet the whole deal still baffled me. What was it we were meant to come away with here? That we were seeded by a giant monolith and that was where our quantum leap came from? Hell, I preferred the Internet buzz about space aliens that came down here to mine gold eons ago, and seeing the potential on this Planet of the Apes, decided to exploit some of its population for the purpose of free labor. However, before that was possible a bit of DNA tweaking was in order, so they tinkered and manipulated until, voila, you had your current dominant life form, a life form which unfortunately became too smart for their own good. This led to some serious wine tasting of forbidden fruit which in turn lead to their expulsion from the *easy* life of a slave.

That's right. Get the fuck out of here. Go make your own clothes and bake your own bread if that's what you want!!!

Yeah, I can just hear God now sounding like some petulant patriarch, dismissing his know-it-all children as he condemned them to a life of toil and hardship.

And here you thought high school was tough. Just wait and see what it's like when you have to mow all the grass and pay all the bills!!!

It was a funny picture and one that had me chuckling to myself as Lulu typed away on her laptop. I would have liked to have shared some of my revelations with her, but she was even more unapproachable than before. Guess that's what happens when you stuff a writer in a garret for the better part of a month and instruct them to write or else. She was approaching this task with the same fervor she had devoted to our railroad adventure, and I began to wonder if the girl did not possess somewhat of an obsessive compulsive personality.

Maybe that's why I suggested our little outing, or perhaps I was just getting tired of my own little diversions. One can only stuff so much outer space between their ears before it begins to ooze out of their eyeballs. Or it could have simply come about due to a bad case of synchronicity. You know the drill. It's what happens when you put out a vibe into the universe, and the universe decides to throw you a curve ball right back.

OK, sucker. So you're bored? Feeling stagnant? Well, here's a little something to kick you back into high gear. Get your heart a pumping and your bowels a moving. Yeah, watch what you wish for and all that...

I'd been idly surfing the net. It had actually made a guest appearance, and I'd been so shocked I'd been willing to follow the first You-Tube video recommended to me. It centered on a Renaissance Fair, which immediately sparked my interest. Earlier, I had been searching for stuff about these odd little gatherings, thinking that surely such a place was where I might be able to link up with the UniverSoul Circus. There had been several occasions when we had piggy-backed off the Renaissance Fairs, tag-teaming with the town that sponsored them. And why not? Wasn't that sort of stuff right up the UniverSoul alley? After all, weren't we, too, all about extravagant costumes and propelling our participants into a mystical world where dragons and unicorns frolicked together on the green field of the town commons?

Yes, it made sense as a place to start my search, but so far it had proved fruitless. It was as if the UniverSoul had disappeared off the surface of the earth. Gee, maybe our world really was flat, as some of the other internet pundits claimed, and my little carnival had sailed too close to the edge. Here they had been sucked into the yawning mouth of the Midgard Serpent, never to be seen again. Alas, all things were possible when it came to the Internet. So why should it surprise me if my beloved comrades had apparently slipped into another dimension?

At any rate, my former searches had lead You-Tube to bless me with a little bonus known as predictive programming. It goes like this: you give the couch surfer what he wants—*yeah, the guy wants to look at stuff about Ren Fairs, so let's sock it to him*—and since I was of the mind that something was better than nothing, I followed the Tube's lead. After all, if you can't have the cream, you may as well have the milk.

So there I was, scrolling through a host of videos about Ren fairs—all the while hoping I might catch a glimpse in the background of a colorful banner advertising the UniverSoul Circus—when lo and behold, I came across a fair which appeared to be located not that far away. At first, I couldn't believe my eyes. A Renaissance Fair? Here in good old north central New Mexico? How very strange. Usually they were clustered closer to major population centers, not stuck out in the boonies like this one seemed to be. Well, I never! And within a short hitching distance at that. Boy, this could be fun.

Or so I thought until I clicked on the video and realized a small drawback, one which brought me back to my musings over milk and cream. For indeed, if dairy has been left in the bottle too long, bad things begin to happen. First comes the curdling and then comes the putrefaction and then, oh my God, the end result may not even be fit for the chickens.

Such had been the progression of this particular sad little Renaissance fair. Guess building it in the boonies had not been such a good idea after all. Thank God it hadn't been very big or the investors really would have lost their shirts because, like a lead balloon, the poor thing just hadn't been able to make it off the ground. Construction had begun, then halted when a serious recession—the one that hit so many us in the old wazoo—had come along and bankrupted the company in charge. So that was that. No Ren Fair. Just a host of half-built buildings that had been meant to host medieval knights and ladies, but which were now home to Gila monsters and scorpions.

In retrospect, it didn't look like much of a field trip, but what the hell? The fact that I even considered it might give you some indication of just how far I had stooped into lethargy. But I guess I wasn't the only one as Lulu's reaction to my proposal was soon to confirm.

"It'll be fun," I started to say as I showed her the tiny video playing in my phone. "Might even prove inspirational for your writing." (Though I had no idea just why this might be so.)

And that's when she shocked me by grabbing her pack, which she proceeded to stuff with apples and granola bars.

"Let's call it a picnic," she explained. "It will be our excuse. Besides, I'm at a good place to take break."

So that was that. It was morning, and the day was young. We had plenty of time. Or so we thought.

We damn near strolled down the rutted driveway leading to the feeder road that would put us on a highway. Here we could best ply our trade, the one which centered on our big thumbs. We were a bit better looking than when we'd first arrived. I'd even clipped off some of my dreads, and the ones remaining were stuffed under a baseball cap. Long ago I'd learned that the preppy hitcher gets the ride, and it also helped if the dude has bathed sometime in the past nine months. Lulu had followed my lead and wore clean clothes and had tied a bandana around her neck to hide that hideous rope tattoo. So I figured it wouldn't be long before some helpful soul came along and catapulted us off in the direction of our quest.

Quest? Yes, *quest* was an adequate descriptor since I was already looking upon this little excursion as an almost spiritual affair. I felt You-Tube had sent the information my way on purpose and surely, here in the wilds of New Mexico, not that far from where I had lost my love, I would find her sweet smile once again.

OK. Dream on.

The day started out auspicious, and then turned sour. We got a ride with the second car that passed by, and he was gracious enough to deposit us less than a half-mile from our destination.

"I used to go up there myself when I was a kid," he explained. "But then they started to crack down on trespassers. So be careful. I don't think they patrol it too much anymore though since the place has really fallen into disrepair. In fact, I'd be more concerned about rattlers and tarantulas that I would about getting busted by the man." And at that he chuckled the sardonic chuckle of one who figures he has put the fear of the Lord into another.

Which he had. Rattlers and tarantulas? Well, now, I hadn't really signed on for that.

Lulu looked at me. I knew what she was thinking. Hell of a place for a picnic. But I just ignored her. We'd come this far so we may as well go all the way. Besides, maybe it was time to pay her back for all the adrenaline she had cost me during our trek through the train yards of America. So I hoisted my day pack on my shoulder and positioned signaled her to follow or fuck off.

She chose to follow.

The place was all it had promised, a royal dump. The video had warned to *prithee, go not to this fair Faire*, and they sure weren't messing around. To say it was a ghost town would have been giving it more credit than it deserved. A ghost town suggested there had actually been warm bodies that roamed the streets here, parents whose children screamed with glee as they met with unicorns and fairies and college students who guzzled tankards of ale after cheering themselves hoarse during jousting matches.

But none of the above had ever taken place at this shit hole. In fact, all it had seen was a bit of illicit sex and underage drinking, and most of that had not been recent. The place had an air of true neglect. Even the No Trespassing signs had crumbled into ruin, suggesting that no one had bothered to enforce them for a decade. Rot and ruin was everywhere from the crumbling turrets and watch towers to the doors which lay half off their hinges. Nature had begun to encroach on the site and many of the half finished buildings were covered in some sort of vine I didn't recognize, but one which gave the whole place the feeling that they might encounter Sleeping Beauty at any turn. The overall effect was one of Spookesville, and in less than an hour we'd had our fill.

"This place is dangerous," Lulu began, and I nodded in agreement. What could I say? She was only reporting the obvious.

But dangerous has its degrees, and I was just about to find out that it doesn't always hinge on death defying acts, or snakes and spiders, or running from the IRS. No, danger can manifest itself in much more subtle forms like that flyer over there.

Now why did it look so familiar, and better yet, why in the world did it look so new?

That's because it was, you dodo! Both familiar and, by all appearances, freshly printed within the last few months. The wind and rain had taken its toll on every other piece of paper in the joint. Much of it had been shredded by field mice, and even the paint on the graffiti was faded to a point where it was barely legible. So how on earth had this one little poster survived, and why was it drawing me to it across a mine field of unapproachable debris, insisting that I take a closer look?

Why? Well, do I really need to tell you? Haven't you figured it out by now?

No? OK, then. I'll shout it out in big bold letters.

UniverSoul Circus

That's what it said. But that's not all. Yeah, as if that wasn't bad enough, upon closer inspection I was able to make out the date. It was one that had already passed, thus dashing any hopes I had that maybe, just maybe, she had slipped into this shit hole in the dark of night to leave me this breadcrumb. In fact, the date displayed was that of our very last gig together, before we'd retired up into the mountains to wait out the winter.

Lulu caught me staring.

"What is it, Doe?" she asked. "You look like you've seen a ghost."

I turned to face her.

"Let's get out of here," I whispered fearing that if I spoke too loud, the demons which inhabited this place would awake.

She didn't need a second invitation. I think she'd been ready to book the minute we'd crossed the threshold of the first crumbling structure. Picnic be damned; I could tell she'd much sooner dine in an outhouse than in this dung heap.

I followed her this time, retracing our steps through the overgrown paths. The only blessing was that we had not disturbed a rattler or two, it probably being way too hot for the old fellows to show themselves. But night was now coming, and this was no place to be spending the bewitching hour.

Now where had the day gone? I felt like I had been thrown into some inter-dimensional time warp, and my head began to throb. It throbbed all the way back to the cabin which meant it plagued me for some time since our return took at least twice as long as our departure. By the time we'd finally crested the hill which brought the cabin into sight, it was well into twilight. Huffing and puffing, I paused, the path leading up to the place being much more demanding than the route down. For a brief moment, I took it all in. The broken railings, the cardboard filled windows, the blackened chimney outlined against the evening sky, and of course, that infernal job Johnny. Yeah, it sure wasn't much to write home about. But even though the place had never been a candidate for *Better Homes and Gardens*, I was never so glad to see its gnarly frame.

"What a day," I murmured half to myself, and then turned to Lulu to see if seeking her forgiveness was in order. I almost felt guilty at that point for suggesting this whole debacle. But then again, she didn't have to agree. A picnic, indeed.

However, when I caught the look on my companion's face, I stopped dead in my tracks. Her gaze was distant, focused on a point directly above Chicora Mountain, and as I followed it, I was in for the second big surprise of the day.

This time it had nothing to do with small posters tacked to decrepit wallboard. No, this time it was much bigger since the sky was the backdrop to this particular painting.

The clouds—determined little fuckers that they were—had moved in as they often did at sunset and <u>had</u> decided to stay on well into dusk, providing a hint of the rain that would fall in the morning. But it wasn't the clouds which caused my own eyes to widen in disbelief; it was the gap they made as they clustered around a bright glaring object. It was almost as if someone (or something) had rent the fabric of the sky and provided the viewer with a ring-side view of one of the brightest stars I'd ever seen. The effect was profound, looking for all the world like the vision which must have greeted those three wise men so many long years ago, and I could not help but stare. Then, the moment passed and pragmatist that I was, I had to deliver a comment by way of explanation.

"Must be a planet," I noted, knowing this was a plausible explanation for such a glitch in the matrix.

But, nooooo...The star...or planet...or whatever it might be...wasn't about to let me off the hook that easy. Somehow I knew this wasn't over. In fact, it had just begun. So I turned my gaze back in mock reverence, determined to pay the same homage to the phenomenon as my companion. And that's when something really strange began to happen.

The thing began to rise up, slowly at first, and then picking up momentum until it reached the edge of the cloud bank above it. Then, with a flicker and flash, it simply disappeared.

Yeah, that's right, disappeared. No, it didn't dash behind a cloud since the cloud bank was still far above it, and there was plenty of room before it ascended that far. It was merely swallowed by the firmament. Poof, you're out, as if it was never there in the first place. And if I hadn't had Lulu beside me for confirmation, I surely would have assigned the whole incident to the nebulous category of being all *in my head*.

I looked at her. She looked at me, and together we breathed a sigh, though it was hard to tell if it was one of relief or sadness. What had we just witnessed? To most folks it would be a no-brainer, a simple close encounter of the third kind. But, hey, this guy didn't really truck with that kind of stuff. Such explanations were for the woo-woo crowd on the Internet, and though I didn't deny the possibility of Extraterrestrial life, I often questioned the credibility of the accounts posted to cyberspace. Because what do they say? Lies, damn lies, and the Internet? Hmmm. Well, I think that last word is really supposed to be *statistics*.

Oh, what the hell. Who cares anyway? Cuz hadn't I just experienced a similar event with my own eyes? And what about Lulu?

Yes, what about Lulu? Because it would appear that the Event was not one hundred percent over. In fact, so far all we had witnessed was a visual disturbance. The auditory was yet to come.

Did I mention that there were caves in these here hills? Yeah, well probably not since I sure hadn't found much reason to explore them. You would have thought different. That sometime during the past few weeks—as I paced the floorboards on the cabin's porch, being careful to avoid the rotten ones—I would have succumbed to a casual curiosity and taken a hike in said direction. But the truth of the matter was simple. I just didn't like caves. Oh, I'd explored a few here and there and could appreciate their divine coolness on a hot summer's day and speculate about them being the perfect bug-out shelter in the event of a nuclear attack. But visiting them alone, sans guide or rope barriers to keep me from falling into their murky black depths? Nope. No way. Spelunking was for the birds. Or in this case, for the salamanders and bats. Or whatever else might naturally inhabit the deep dark places of the earth. So these alleged caves, which were within a short hike of the cabin, had simply been placed into the off-limits category. But now it would appear that after weeks of neglect, they were clamoring for a return to center stage.

The glow started about half-way up the mountain, and grew deeper with intensity the longer we stared. Lulu seemed transfixed—as well she should be, considering what happened next. The initial sound began as a whisper, and it could have easily been confused with the wind in the pines.

OOOOoooooo, it began, and at first it was hard to make out any definite syllables. But then it picked up speed and distinction.

Looooo ooooo

Loooo Looooo

Until at last, it became quite apparent just who the critters in the cave were trying to contact.

Her face seemed to glow in the after light. It was almost too dark to make out her features. So I couldn't tell if she was terrorized or mesmerized maybe a little bit of both.

And then, as quickly as it had begun, it stopped. It was almost as if someone had turned off a fountain of sound, leaving us in the stillness to scratch our heads in disbelief.

I don't know about her, but I was ready to seek the nearest light source, one that I would set into motion with my own hand. Hightailing it for the cabin door, I reached the steps in three seconds flat. The matches were just where I'd left them that morning, and within moments, I had a kerosene light underway, its warm glow throwing familiar shadows around the room.

Lulu stumbled in not far behind me. She immediately took a seat at one of the rickety kitchen chairs.

I could tell she was spooked, but I didn't know how to approach the situation. Finally, after a long pause, I sat down next to her.

"Do you want to talk about it?" I asked, and she answered with a knit to her brows.

"Do you?"

And that did it. The locked box was unsealed and out of it poured decades of days, some well spent and others better forgotten. We talked way into the night. And when it was over, I felt we'd both completed a fairly accurate excavation into each other's souls. I loved her then, not in any carnal sense, but as a sister, fellow traveler and comrade, and like Old Faithful, it was a love that came from deep within. Its origins were as boundless as the infinite, and its presence provided me with more comfort than I had experienced for quite some time.

Lulu/Stitch Speaking

"I've got this theory that all this tech, all this addiction to gizmos, is nothing more than a way to condition us to live without Gaia, our mother and to dwell instead somewhere in deepest space, in some self-contained little bubble, our faces buried in a box and the only hint of greenery being found in the virtual reality of a hollow deck. But what of it? Who needs green grass and trees? We never gave it much attention when it was all around us, so why bother now? Just bury yourself in a box. The way you do all the time with that little phone of yours."

He looked up.

"Oh, yeah, look who's talking. How about that laptop of yours? The one you've been hauling around for months. It's still a box, albeit a bit smaller one. Besides, looks like if I'm going to bury myself in a box, you'll be burying yourself in a cave."

"Is that so, Starman? At least I don't do the Facebook thing and sacrifice my privacy on the altar of the NSA. Yeah, you moronic millennials just step right up to the plate and offer up your entire life history on a silver platter. Guess you'll stop at nothing just as long as you can get a captive audience for your daily bowel movements!"

"Oh, yeah? Spoken like a true troglodyte! Guess your only means of immortality will come from cave art!"

And so we'd bantered back and forth, our tennis balls of mock insult landing only momentarily in each other's courts, only to be slung back before touching the ground.

It was all harmless play, a way to diffuse the intensity of the events which had transpired that day. They'd been cathartic enough even when you didn't factor in the subsequent purging of our inner guts which followed. The hour was late, but we still weren't ready to call it quits. There was too much energy coursing through our collective veins. I had told him things I had never shared with any other, and I had the feeling he had done the same. I knew all about the demise of his mother and his ensuing descent into bankruptcy. He'd explained the best he could about a nasty little scam called the TDA accounts, and though they'd seemed valid enough, I could tell they were a hot potato, not to be touched unless one sought a serious burn. Then he'd gone on to agonize over his time following a small circus. Here his days had ranged from pursuing mundane tasks like shit-shoveling to fruitless ones which centered on unrequited love.

I'd recognized the name of the circus from the flyer we'd found at the Ren Faire and now understood his hasty retreat. Her name had been Aniel, a very lofty sounding name for a lofty dwelling lady, and I'd felt sorry for him. My guy, the Dutchman, was much more down to earth, which made him approachable. If that is, I was still so inclined.

But I'd realized during the course of our dialogue that Dutch no longer held the same mysterious allure to me. He was more like an old lighthouse shining in the distance, sent to steer me off rocky shoals and provide me with a safe passage home.

Not that he'd fallen from an exalted status. He still retained a hint of the mystical. In fact, I could have sworn I'd heard his voice just hours ago, emanating from that cave half way up the mountain. It was the same voice as one belonging to a man I'd met in a dream years ago while camping near Vedauwoo Rocks in Wyoming. Then it had resurfaced later as I struggled up Mt Shasta. Here I'd been accosted by an asexual entity who had claimed to be my soul family. At that point I'd been told I still had work to do. However, I'd also been informed that I would only be contacted one more time. Then it would be too late for me to join something called the Argarthian Network.

At the time I'd had no idea what they had been talking about, but now I was a bit more knowledgeable, having taken the time to Google the term, a task which I deplored and which I often did poorly. But I still liked what I'd read. It fit right into my profile. Yes, I was a trogdolyte, a cave dweller who preferred the cool pristine places of the earth's interior over the rapidly polluted ones on its surface. Here, I would find my true soul mate, though not in a single individual but a whole host, a family the likes of which I'd always craved while topside. Together we would dwell in the depths, emerging periodically to direct and influence mankind as we fought the spiritual war which had been waging on this planet for centuries.

Yeah, it had been something worth aspiring towards all these years, though I felt I may have gotten a bit sidetracked, especially with my writing. However, as I looked back on my first book, I realized it had been primarily exorcismic, an attempt to cleanse myself of the debris left by my earthly family. Of course, all my efforts had only led to my alienation from its remaining members. They had not—could not—accept the book in the spirit in which it had been written, but had instead, wanted me to candy-coat the entire experience.

True, it had emerged as somewhat of an anti-war epistle, and yes, that is a real no-no for anyone associated with a military family. But in essence, that had been its purpose, and I know now that I had been just as destined to pen its pages as I was to complete my current project, one which was far more esoteric and personal. However, I also knew I was at an impasse with my current creation, as it lacked direction. Sadly, its main character (i.e. me) had failed to accomplish any degree of growth, and yet this was the hallmark of any worthy work of fiction.

Was this the reason they had given me one more chance? They had told me back on the mountain that they would only contact me one more time. Well, if that little light show in the high desert hadn't been a contact, I don't know what else it might be.

I shivered as I remembered the sensations it had evoked. I had chosen to keep them a secret and had not described them in detail to my present companion. I'd known that despite our new-found intimacy, he was still the flip side of my coin, the Felix to my Oscar of *Odd Couple* status. Though there was much we shared, we were coming at our world view from two opposing perspectives. His was so much the doubting Thomas, whereas mine revolved around blind faith. Well, maybe not that blind because I sure had witnessed my share of the inexplicable.

So what was the point? Why had I been shown a brief glimpse into that inner sanctuary with its scintillating orbs of diamond radiance and bifurcating brilliance where shards of light were split into infinite prisms containing every color of the rainbow? (And a few which probably hadn't been recorded yet.) And why had the voices I'd heard there—an angel choir of overwhelming sweetness—repeated their message? Why had they made it plain (once again) that I was still not ready to gain admittance to the forbidden kingdom?

Well, the answer was simple. Because I clearly did have some more work to do. So the forces that were reckoning with me had decided to give me one more opportunity to finish what I had come here to complete. A final task had been assigned to me, and I now knew its essence, knew it so well that the writer's block which had been plaguing me for the past few days disappeared like dew in the morning sun. In short, I knew how my current (and final) book would end. All that remained was to put that knowledge into good use.

Endings are never that great. The writer has been chugging along, page after page, first getting to know his characters, then developing them and running them through a school of hard enough knocks to effect some kind of change. However, once their characters have developed to a suitable point, it becomes time to cut the cord. And that's when the going gets really tough. Forget the writer's block. That was small change. Likewise the hours spent working on one's myopia and carpal tunnel. Hey, the end is now in sight; and boy, isn't that wonderful.

Well, no…not necessarily. Because with all endings come goodbyes, and we all know how difficult that one simple word can be, so difficult that many have come up with novel (no pun intended) ways of mitigating its effect. Farewell, adieu, see you later, bon voyage and *vaya con dios* all come to mind. But in the end, one can only call a spade a spade, and this time I'm not referring to the black figure shaped like an inverted heart which is commonly found in all good decks of cards. No, this time I am referring to its other meaning, as a flat bladed digging tool with a long handle. And guess what it is digging? Well, let's just put it this way. You've got to plant those major characters somewhere. Whether they all died and went to heaven (or hell) or lived happily ever after, it is now time for those two magical words to appear at the end of your manuscript, that is to say THE END. And they are particularly poignant when an author realizes that their main character is none other than himself.

Nevertheless, it is sad but true. We all have to face this impasse sooner or later, and as one of my songs said:

> I have blown in on the wind,
> Someday I'll blown back out again
> A winter candle in springtime rain,
> I'll cut my losses and count my gains

Alas, I sensed a closing coming up, a denouement as the French so delicately put it, and though I didn't know if it would follow closely on the heels of the climax of my little story or appear several chapters down the road, I still knew it was inevitable. My only consolation lay in the final chorus of the song I had just quoted, words written to comfort me and place it all in its proper perspective.

> I've heard it whispered on the wind,
> To end is to begin
> An endless cycle of days and nights
> Another chance to make it right.

OK, so enough said about that. No more lamenting. It was time to march into battle, and we all know that many who enter the fracas do not live to tell about it. But those celestial powers couldn't have made it any clearer. It was time to tie up my loose ends, roll up my sleeves and get to work. Then, if I finished my task in time there might actually be a pot of gold at the end of the rainbow waiting for me. In some circles, this is called a be-all/end-all, but in literary ones it is merely known as a *sequel.*

That said, I could hardly wait.

Noone/Doe Speaking

Jeeze, Louise. She's been hard at it for days now. I can't believe her fingers haven't fallen off by now. Her only breaks have come when we fire up the generator long enough to recharge her laptop, and boy, oh boy have we gone through a ton of gas. My own arms are about worn out hauling it all the way up from the nearest gas station which is a good five miles away. Of course the first four and a half are hitchable, and who wouldn't pick up a guy who has a gas can under one arm?

Yeah, that's one of the silver linings to all this. It's small change though compared to the biggest boon, one which came as a true blessing in disguise. Because apparently the force that compelled her to write almost nonstop day for days, has also canceled her other plans. That means no more *freight train, freight train goin so fast*; no more Wabash Cannonball. In fact, the only glimpses I get these days of those rusty rails are when she stops to sing a few verses in their memory. Dead and buried, they are. And good riddance, as far as I'm concerned because our date with destiny in Britt, Iowa draws closer and closer with each passing day. It's my due date, the one when I'll be released from servitude, and I sure would like to be alive to enjoy the rest of my days. I still had plans to set out for Leslie's Fields a Plenty, and they would come a lot easier once we gave the train yards the retirement party they deserved. No more riding the rails, no more running from bulls, and no more sleeping with one eye open always on the look-out for crazies like Robert Silveria. But, best of all no more blogging, as apparently Lulu had moved on to bigger and better ideas. Of course, this caused me to wonder if Britt, Iowa was going to materialize at all since it looked as though our whole little project had gone belly-up.

I watched her as she typed away, her nimble fingers barely gracing the keyboard before the words appeared on the screen. I didn't venture to ask her what this was all about. I only hoped that whatever she was working on would take until the middle of August to complete.

In the meantime, I sure was left with a whole lot of time on my hands. I'd just about run through my buddy's library, for what it worth; and since the Internet faded in and out up in these hills, it was hard to get involved with recent developments in cyberspace. I'd been particularly interested in the Alt community and its coverage of one Heather Tucci

Jaraf and her sidekick, Randal Beane. But except for a brief and somewhat dishonorable mention by Thomas Williams, they seemed to have faded into the black hole of the American penal system, which is not a far cry from the Russian Gulag as far as gleaning any Intel is concerned. Oh, Thomas went on and on about his Kimpossible and their Manna World Trust, the one which *allegedly* held the codes to all the money in the world.

Yeah, a*llegedly*; how I love that word. But all semantics aside, when it came down to Randy's actual purchase of a very expensive motor home with some of those funds—which to me, is proof of the pudding they actually do exist… Well, Thomas's only response was to berate Heather for going after the wrong trust. *Stupid woman. She should have listened to him*, he chided; and then continued dragging his feet when it came to the release of any real money from the Manna World Trust.

Sorry, but something isn't adding up here. I kept wondering why Thomas and his cronies were still out running around scot free while Heather and Randy appeared to be locked away for life. Guess it all boils down to who's serving the hardest time; that's the true litmus test as to how close someone got to the real money. Indeed, always follow the money, or lack thereof.

Hmpff. It was a point worth considering, an idle occupation for a bored mind. But didn't I have better things to concern myself with, like whether or not they'd give us food stamps for another month? Britt, Iowa and its free hobo stew was still a couple weeks away and shoot, the larder was beginning to get a little too bare for my taste. Yeah, I should be snaggling over how I could continue to pull off some social security fraud instead of concerning myself with old will-o'-the-wisp Williams.

However, there was still something about the whole deal that bothered me. You know how it is. One thought provokes another. Oh, it may be buried deep within the brain it originated from. Nonetheless, it is still present, a kernel of sand irritating the great big oyster it inhabits. And it doesn't always turn into a pearl. Sometimes it goes the other way and festers and festers until it creates a real problem, a pus filled sack that can only be relieved via the surgeon's needle.

Such was the niggling thought that my detour into Thomas William's and his *alleged* funds had brought forth, and it continued to bother me, insisting I stand up and pay attention least I miss something important. Oh dear, the things the brain will get up to when bored. I continued to watch Lulu clack away and wished I had some sort of gainful occupation to pursue as well, something better than chasing wayward thoughts through the convolutions of my gray matter. But it was a slow day and good for nothing better than mental gymnastics. So I pondered and pondered until my head it was sore, all the while feeling like an octogenarian who is struggling in vain to connect a face with a name.

OK, it has something to do with why Thomas is free and Heather is not. And don't tell me that Thomas can run faster or is more adept in covering his tracks because...

Oh please, the guy has regularly scheduled radio shows and a bunch of irregular ones. So he is getting himself out there and should be an easy target for the goons he talks about. No, there was another reason why Tommy was not rotting in a federal prison, and it all came down to the simple fact that the feds did not consider him a threat. However, Heather was another story. Heather was right up there on their on their Ten Most Wanted list. And I took this to be proof of the pudding again.

So what did that have to do with the price of tea in China? Oh, there was a connection. This was for sure. But it had nothing to do with tea. Instead, it concerned itself with letters, letters found in a simple shoe box in a dusty closet in room whose door had been closed to me for some time.

It all came rushing back, my foraging excursion into the depths of maw's closet in my vain search for anything I could but a price on. Odd how the end results had been **priceless**.

I forgot the guy's name now, but he'd claimed to be associated with some secret space program. Now this was not generally something you bragged about on your resume. However, the dude had made the mistake of spouting off, either on account of his conscience or a desire for Internet woo-woo fame. Whatever the case, he lived to regret it because he found himself locked away for life and all for a murder he did not commit. Oh, I guess they could have offed him, which would have only turned him into a martyr; and that, my friends, just wouldn't do. So they discredited him and branded him as one of those conspiracy nuts and... Oh well, you know the rest. There he sits, and there he'll sit for all eternity.

Of course, at that time the mystery had centered on why he was writing to my mother. Didn't she have better things to do? Like playing at Scratch-Off and feeding the birds? What had been the connection anyway? When I'd researched the guy, I'd discovered he was married, so it wasn't anything like that. So what was going on in the old girl's mind?

Oh well, her motives were own her business, and as they so succinctly say, that's all been dead and buried. Yeah, dead and buried. Though I confess the whole incident had sent me down some rather strange rabbit holes in the Internet. First there were the interviews with this guy, conducted over a period of years by a lady who was one hundred percent convinced of his credibility, and I had to admit he was consistent enough in his story to command my attention. This had inspired me to branch out in my search to include other whistle-blowers, and that was where I'd started to get suspicious.

Some of them whistled a good enough tune, but that was the point. They were singing canaries, and in the real world, isn't that grounds for divorce? Doesn't it amount to a bullet in the back of the head or, at best, a life time sentence? I began to smell not one, but multiple rats.

Not that this was always the case. There were a few out that got to walk away, guys like that English dude, Gary Mckinnon, who'd hacked the Pentagon and found all sorts of files relating to spaceships and aliens. Kalabunga! What a payload that had been with flight manifests both terrestrial and non-terrestrial that described cargo loads to the tee. True, his stuff had been pretty damn persuasive considering the source. Yet he had been allowed to go on with his life, but not until they'd turned it into hell for several years. There had been so many attempts to extradite him from England that I'm sure he became a nervous wreck. Apparently the Pentagon wanted to prosecute him for what he'd done, even though he had never downloaded any of the files, and that was enough to push him into the credibility camp in my book.

Prosecution meant that they took you seriously. Unlike a bunch of other guys who'd been allowed to spout off at will considering their time aboard the good ship *Enterprise*. Guys who frequented conferences like Contact in the Desert, and new-agey event which happened every year at some spa in California. (Where else?) Guys who were introduced into the Internet community by top-brand names like David Wilcock of *Ancient Aliens* fame. Guys who seemed to be jumping on the ET bandwagon with the same intent as hobos hopping freights during the depression: to seek a means of livelihood.

And who could blame them? A man's gotta make a living somehow and when so many of the so-called good jobs have been shipped to Malaysia? Well... let's just say that P.T. Barnum had offered some pretty good advice when he'd claimed there is a sucker born every minute. So if you are charismatic enough and if your line of bullshit stays consistent, you may be in for a pretty good run. Plus, given that you are an obvious hot air balloon, the government goons leave you alone.

So, once again, we get right back to the proof of the pudding, perhaps an oversimplification on my part, but it went like this. Those who were full of shit were allowed to continue their defecations in order to confuse the issue. After all, this is a topic that the folks in power want to marginalize and demonize. Heaven forbid! If there were ET's out there, the next obvious question would center on how they got here so fast. Oh, oh...not good. We don't want anyone speculating on that hot potato! If so, we'd have to fess up to the possibility of alternate forms of transportation.

You mean to say they didn't burn a ton of rocket fuel to make the jump? You mean there might actually be other sources of energy bigger and better than fossil fuels? Well, do tell.

No, don't tell. So lock up the real McCoys and make them into crack pots, and let the little guys spout away. In truth, they are playing right into the non-disclosure narrative. Get a bunch of them out there and make them sound crazy enough, and sooner or later anyone who has the utter balls to suggest the possibility of a deep space program will find themselves drowning in a sea of bullshit.

It was your classic tactic of mudding the waters to the point that no one was guaranteed any successful fishing, and it is why I'd given up on my own pursuit of the matter. But here it was, coming back to haunt me on a hot day in northern New Mexico as I idly watched a busy little bee type away. Maybe that was the ticket. Idle hands are the devil's work. Maybe I needed to find something better than mere speculations to occupy my time.

I sighed and picked up another book, a really rag-tag one this time. *The Green Hills of Earth* by Robert Heinlein. Yeah, that's should do the trick. Keep this stuff up and I'll be shitting green instead of brown, just like those little green men. Oh well, when in Rome, do as the Romans; and though this probably didn't include reading crap about off-planet events, it looked like I didn't have much by way of choice.

Later that day, I was down at the local diner. My boredom had assaulted me to the point where I'd been willing to walk the two miles into town just for the sake of a few bars of wireless.

I'd left her in the same spot she'd been occupying for over a fortnight, and as I paused to say goodbye, she responded with a cursory nod. The interaction or lack of it gave me plenty of reason to ponder on all that had happened following our return from the Renaissance Fair. Had we really opened up like that and spilled the collective beans of our tortuous pasts? Or had that all been a dream, one lost at the dawning of her current frenzy. Whatever the case, we sure weren't communicating much these days and though my feelings for her had not changed—she was still a soul sister and comrade in arms—I had to admit I was getting a bit starved for company. Enter one dubious Internet connection at a diner that specialized in greasy spoons and greasier food.

I stirred my lukewarm coffee and watched as globules of fat spilled into the surrounding water. Jesus! It was a wonder the health department hadn't shut this place down, but as it was the only show in town—and the only town for miles around—it was drink up and shut up. So, I plugged my nose, closed my eyes and took a drink (as the old song liked to instruct). Then I opened my phone, clicked onto the local network and began to surf.

It had been a few days. Oh, my gosh! It had been almost a week, something unheard of for members of my generation, and I found myself salivating as the little circle which heralded the arrival of the Internet began to spin. Think of all that must have happened in that eternity of time. What had I missed? Surely Facebook had gone down on account of my inactivity! I'd best get crackin out there or lose my place on the web!

Such were my thoughts as I began to access some of my favorite sites, but if it were national news I craved, I just should have looked up to where a television was now blaring in the corner. The waitress, a wizened old specimen who looked old enough to have come over on the Mayflower, was turning up the volume. Not that one needed words, the pictures displayed were worth a thousand.

There's a quote by Tesla to the effect that we will all live to   see man-made horrors beyond our comprehension, and as I watched slide after slide pass through the studios of CNN and later NBC, it kept returning to my thoughts. The only glitch was that I wasn't supposed to view this carnage as *man-made*.

They called it the Camp Fire, a nice little play on words which brought to mind hot dogs, marshmallows, and all that is good about a Jamboree. Except this time the dogs weren't just roasted, they were terribly toasted, and guess what? They weren't canis familiaris, but homo sapiens.

The photo shoot was past shocking and featured charred remains of the innocent victims. They were still in their cars, escape vehicles they had counted on. But the highway they'd used to flee the scene had recently seen its status reduced from four-lane to two, causing it to bottleneck into a death trap.

My God! How had this happened? The inability to conduct a hasty retreat was one thing, but why had everyone waited until the last minute? Hadn't these folks been given any advance warning? Truth be told, the firestorm itself had blown through in the early morning hours when most people were still in their pajamas. However, as the story soon revealed, the threat of fire had loomed for days. So what was the deal? Why hadn't the place been evacuated before it was too late?

Yeah, there sure were a ton of unanswered questions, each one more inexplicable than the last. But that was nothing compared to a highly observable fact, one which had little to do with bungling bureaucracies or asleep-at-the-wheel emergency broadcast systems. And this fact centered on the condition of the cars themselves.

I watched in disbelief as the news portrayed these sad excuses for getaway vehicles, many of which were burned beyond recognition. Yes, you heard me. Beyond recognition. Their tires melted, and their steel frames in pools upon the ground.

Steel? Wasn't that supposed to burn at twenty-eight hundred degrees Fahrenheit? Just how hot was this forest fire anyway? And speaking of which, if it was a forest fire, why were the trees still untouched? Why was this convoy of escapees winding down through a forest of green, a forest populated by petrified rabbits which looked suspiciously like the frozen statues found in Herculaneum? How very weird! And it didn't stop there.

The photographic essay went on to display pictures of entire neighborhoods where homes had been flattened. Everything was gone. Houses and all their contents had been reduced to nothing but ash. The devastation was total and included window-glass—which burns at 2600° F—and toilets and tubs—which are generally ceramic and burn at 2000° to 3000°F. Indeed, the plot thickened, or sickened as it were.

As the news anchor continued to babble on about forest fires, I continued to marvel over the presence of the tall green pines which stood sentinel in these devastated neighborhoods. How could this be? Wasn't anyone else seeing what I was seeing? That all this was against the laws of physics? Were they so busy lachrymosing over the plight of the victims, that they didn't see the forest for... Well... the trees?

I knew it was time to quit. Change channels to some real reporting, the kind I wasn't going to get on CNN (though later I had to hand it to the networks for having the utter chutzpa to display some of the pictures they had). What did they take us for? A bunch of dumbasses who had been fast asleep in science class? OK, don't answer that. It doesn't really dignify a response. Just like CNN and NBC and CBS don't dignify my continued attention. I turned to my phone and sought out the real news.

Oh, don't get me wrong. CNN is good for some honest reporting. They did do a special on something called Electro-magnetic Frequency Weapons. And the History Channel had seen fit to inform us about the presence of DEWs in a nice little documentary they had recently aired. Oh, and just in case you were wondering, DEW is short for Directed Energy Weapons. Yeah, talk about predictive programming!

So predictive that it actually goes back to 1985, the year of my birth, when a so-called comedy was playing in the theaters by the name of *Real Genius*. Even though I was but a babe in diapers at the time, I still got to watch this masterpiece again and again since it was one of my maw's favorite movies.

In the film, a group of young geniuses are attending a school tailor-made to exploit their talents. They are assigned to a project which has stumped everyone else, one which has to do with cutting edge technology. Their task is to develop a working power source for a powerful laser, one which won't ignite its delivery system, and they work diligently towards this end. But somewhere along the way, they start to put two and two together as they question just what this delivery system might be used for; and from there on in, the fun begins. At least, it would be fun for them, but not necessarily for whoever ended up at the working end of that laser beam.

Anyway, starting to get the picture yet? That's right. The whole project is under the umbrella of the military who—surprise! surprise!—are seeking to weaponize it by attaching the whole kit and caboodle to a space-shuttle and incinerating targets from outer space. The beauty of it all is that their victims will have no clue what the hell ever happened. It was perfect subterfuge, and the minute I saw the pictures of this so-called fire I knew deep down in my soul that the weapon portrayed by this decades old movie had come to pass. Three story homes flattened and reduced to dust. Football fields bifurcated into precise patterns by a line of fire which defied the current wind direction. And, oh yeah, let's not forget the house that was neatly cut in half. That's right. One side was just as the owners had left it; the other was completely gone. And all this accomplished by a simple forest fire?????

Wow, maybe maw was in deeper than I had ever suspected! For one thing, chem-trails sure had been one of her pet peeves, and one of the sites I was currently accessing had already started to connect the dots back to them. Mind you, this fire had not just happened, and since the news of it was close to a week old, there had been plenty of time for postulating and theorizing by pundits on both sides of the aisle. As I drank my greasy coffee, the guy I was listening to insisted it was a perfect storm which had created this apocalypse, one which he referred to as a Weapon of False-flag Environmental Terrorism. This weapon was made up of a variety of components including chem-trails, Smart meters, Microwave towers, and of course the evil DEWs. Alas, put 'em together and whaddaya got? Bibitty, bottity, boo. And the joke's on you. But seriously, they fit together like a glove.

For starters came the chem-trails that had been used for decades in California, a state which has long served as a testing ground for many an evil project. Recently it has come to light that these aerosol sprays contain a chemical cocktail of shit which is really bad for you (and for the planet). Included are barium, strontium, and aluminum oxide, which are unhealthy enough ingredients when taken separately, let alone together. However, it is the last one which plays into the fire scenario due to its remarkable ability to impregnate the soil and the atmosphere, thus causing it to become increasingly flammable over a period of time.

Then, enter the Smart meters which have been known to catch on fire. And gee, if their digital signatures could possibly be triggered from a remote location—kind of like the same way we blow up terrorists with cell phones—that would explain the exploded houses (more like *imploded*) that are surrounded by perfectly intact trees, yet devoid of one single possession inside. Mainly because there is no inside and outside anymore, just a vaporized hole where a three story house once sat.

And, while we're at it, let's not forget the Microwave towers which are everywhere now, another key component in helping to make the area more combustible. Oh, and the fake firefighters who were actually setting blazes instead of fighting them. (Although this last claim was a bit of a stretch for me.)

At any rate, it was perfect firestorm waiting to happen, not to mention a perfect place to initiate it cuz we all know that California's north woods are primarily conifers and ones that have been attacked by enough devastating pests to make for a lot of dead standing timber. Add to this the fact that California had been in a serious drought for years and years, one which may or may not relate to weather warfare. In essence, it all added up. All it took was a spark. So enter one DEW which could be surreptitiously deployed from drones, helicopters, or planes (or maybe even from much higher up as in my maw's favorite movie). Yeah, enter the dragon. In truth, this would explain the cars bursting into flames as they headed down a highway where no other fires were visible.

No such animal, you say? Well, then, ponder the following ripped from the pages of Reuter's, an international news organization with two hundred locations around the world, courtesy Mike Stone August 21, 2017.

The United States Air Force awarded a team of Boeing, Northrop Grumman and Lockheed Martin a $1.1 billion contract to develop and demonstrate a revolutionary laser weapon system to defend against the threat posed by theater ballistic missiles such as the Iraqi Scuds used during Desert Storm. Under the terms of the Program Definition and Risk Reduction (PDRR) contract awarded in November 1996, the three companies, working together as Team ABL, will build and test an Airborne Laser (ABL) weapon system mounted aboard a Boeing 747-400F aircraft. This system will be capable of destroying missiles carrying chemical, biological and nuclear warheads almost immediately after launch and before they would pose a threat to civilian populations and military assets.

Indeed, put that in your pipe and smoke it.

The Camp Fire that blew through Paradise claimed eighty-eight lives, though one hundred and fifty-eight people still remain missing. That's the official statement. However, other assessments placed the number at closer to six hundred, many of whom were elderly folks who could not exit their homes in time. By the time it was finally put out, it burned across 153,000 acres and demolished 14,000 dwellings, making it one of the most devastating fires in California history.

Those are the stats, but for those of us who choose to explore a bit deeper, they only scratch the surface. I guess if we are to entertain some of the thoughts I had just recently been exposed to, then the next obvious question would become one of *why?* Here the speculations ran wild, only united by their conviction that it couldn't have been the Russians. If so, the media would have been all over them like flies to stink. For what better way to add insult to injury when it came to all that **Trump**eting about Russian collusion? So, if it weren't the commies, then who?

The Chinese? Yeah, maybe. It's said they own California anyway and maybe they wanted to clear a bit of land for their own purposed development. Of course, this line of thought leads us to further speculation. Some said that Paradise was in the way of a High Speed rail route, and the town had been selected for a brutal version of eminent domain. However, others believed that it was all part of a plan to clear out rural California so the UN's Agenda 2030 could be implemented. (Agenda 2030? Oh, just go look that one up! I'm not going to get into it here!) However, should this be the case, then it smacks of an inside job, a global agenda run by a select elite who have their own ideas as to where we peons should be spending the bulk of our remaining days. Think rabbit hutches stacked sky high in the city of *their* choice and you get the picture.

Of course, all this lead down a rabbit hole of horrendous proportions, one so nightmarish that it is small wonder the masses simply turn their backs and accept the national party line. Despite such a compelling compilation of evidence, the general reaction was one of your typical NIMBY. After all, it wasn't in my backyard now, was it? (Though it may soon be coming to a channel near you.) Oh well, what of it? Let's just see what's on the Sports Channel, pop a few more Denitals, and hum along to another of my maw's favorite songs.

Too much of nothin' can turn a man into a liar
It can cause some men to sleep on nails, another men to eat fire.
Everybody's doin' somethin', I heard it in a dream
But when it's too much of nothin', it just makes a fella mean.
Say hello to Valerie, say hello to Marion,
Send them all my salary, on the waters of oblivion.

That said, let's just go with my favorite explanation as to why all those folks—be it a mere eighty-five or a whopping six hundred—had to die. Because according to one internet pundit (and I won't discredit him by naming names) they were all aliens and getting ready to hit the world with total disclosure. OK. That's where I leave off. Time to get back to the ranch and share a bit of my new-found knowledge with my significant traveling companion, one who failed to surprise me when I encountered her a good hour later, standing on her head and looking liked she'd been there too long.

"And just what the fuck are you doing now?" I bellowed.

But she only calmly descended and just as calmly announced that she was celebrating the completion of her second offering to the dubious world of self-publishing, a novella this time, but still a work worthy of a Pulitzer.

Oh, oh. I knew what this meant. We no longer had an excuse to hang out here in our own little paradise. Oh well, I knew this day would come sooner or later, and to tell the truth, it was getting a bit old. However, I sensed another ending coming on and for some strange reason this one seemed to come with a capital **E**.

Now don't get me wrong. I know that endings are inevitable and often necessarily. Life can't just go along the same track forever and ever. Something always has to give, and change always has to come. It's just that endings are sometimes a tad traumatic, especially when one is propelled away from one's comfort zone and hurled back into the unknown.

For this reason, I paused for a moment and considered my next words carefully. I didn't want to appear the coward, but then again, I sure had suffered enough of the railroad tramp lifestyle to last me a lifetime.

However, miracle of all miracles, she beat me to the punch and did so in a way to confirm my belief that we had truly experienced a Vulcan mind melt.

Lulu/Stitch Speaking

"We'll be hitching this time," I informed him, and then realizing he needed a little bit more by way of explanation, I went on.

"I don't want to risk losing my laptop to one of those railroad bulls or, worse yet, some young bum who will just pawn it for a line of coke. And now there's the guitar to worry about..."

Ah, yes, the guitar. My trump card. I could tell by the way he was church mouse quiet wherever I got to strumming that he approached my music with the same reverence devoted to the holy of holies. I had to admit I was flattered. Ever since it's rudimentary origins in the Ayahuasca mallocca, no one had honored my music in such a way. That's why I was surprised when his next words suggested what could only amount to an out and out sacrifice of my dear friend Stella, the nickname I had given to my recently purchased pawn shop guitar.

"That's OK," he began (though I knew it wasn't). "It's just a quick hop from Santa Fe to Des Moines and from there a short hitch to Britt. Why risk being late for an important date? After all, you know how it gets with hitchhiking sometimes. Besides, I can carry the guitar. *No one*'s about to fuck with me. I can do that quite well, thank you."

Then, hiding a grin at his play on words, he issued a mock growl and shook his Maori mane. I guess he was still trying to convince me that the rails did not scare him to death. It's amazing what the male ego will do in order to maintain its fragile hold on a person.

Here I thought I'd been offering him a chance to save face, and what does he do? Why, what else but present me with a counter proposal too juicy to refuse. I tried to argue, but it was futile. Just the thought of hearing those rails singing beneath my feet again set my heart to pumping and pumping hard. I couldn't help myself. I really missed the life, and it would be hard to pass it over in favor of a tamer one. But I really had no choice. It would be necessary to pursue some heavy duty marketing if this newest book was ever to jump off the shelves. This meant I would have to settle down somewhere—maybe even Britt, Iowa— and find a shit job, one that would tolerate my disabilities. Then I could contact Kady and send her the files needed to put the book up on LULU, and then? Well, then the fun began. The writer's conferences, the book signings, the library readings.

And as for Dutch? Well, he'd served his purpose. However, I still wanted to meet the guy. I had a funny feeling our story wasn't over yet, and who knows? Maybe he was worth a few chapters in a book yet to come.

Yeah, I had it all figured out. There was only one thing I hadn't factored into the formula, and it was so obvious that if it were a snake it would have bit me. Come on, Lulu! If such a marketing approach hadn't worked with your first book, just why in the world did you expect it be any different the second time around? Yeah, what do they say about the definition of insanity? Something about doing the same thing over and over again and expecting different results?

Oh, but it had worked, remember. There had been a nice little royalty check to greet me when we'd pulled into New Mexico. All of a whopping seventy-five bucks. And surely that was just the beginning. Surely once the heavens opened up, the manna would pour from down above. Either that or the rain, though I refused to consider a single negative thought. Not on that day of all days.

So I swallowed my true feelings and conceded to Doe. Oh, there had been a brief argument, staged to allow him to feel as though he'd achieved a real victory here. But the truth was more the other way around. It was a clear case of appearances being deceptive. For in the end, I had gotten exactly what I wanted.

However, had I known my stray thought about rain would ever manifest itself in such a wicked way, I would have stood my ground and insisted he accept my offer to forsake the rails and use our thumbs for travel instead. Indeed, in that case we might have shown up late. Yeah, late, as in better *late than never.*

Ah, but alas, we all have our own stumbling blocks, and mine was the adrenaline rush of the rails. Yeah, spoken like a true junky, and now there was no turning back. Events were set, the die was cast, and the barrel set in motion for its ill-fated tour of the Niagara River. It was full speed ahead and damn the torpedoes, famous last words though they may be.

The train ride itself was not what set us off balance. Actually, catching a ride was a piece of cake, despite all our collective anxiety. Mine had primarily centered on my precious guitar, but Doe had proved true to his word and had guarded it as if it were his little papoose. His fit of the nerves, however? Well, I probably don't need to go into the plethora of reasons why riding the rails stirred up the butterflies in his stomach the way they did. Any fool could see that catching out was a dangerous sport and not for sissies.

Not that Doe fell completely into such a contemptible category. The life history he had revealed to me during our baring of the souls had convinced me that he was a risk taker on many levels. Hell, he had actually been a surfer, and surfing was a sport I viewed right up there with sky diving—which is understandable given my inability to master the basics of dog-paddling. Then there had been all those years spent in banana republics, places known for exotic diseases and even more exotic creepy-crawlies, not to mention political unrest and drug related murders.

By comparison, my travels had been somewhat tame, especially once they'd been tempered by my brother's money. However, even before that windfall, I had sought out the tourist train when it came to excursions south of the border. That said, despite our mutual fondness for feeling the wind in our hair and the sun on our backs, our journeys aboard Spaceship Earth had been quite different.

Of course, he was a guy, and it was much easier for men when it came to roaming around unprotected. Plus they are expected to be daredevils, whereas we women are presumed the weaker sex, one in need of a champion. Well, I guess I'd blown that expectation out of the water, especially in consideration of our current pastime. But that hadn't helped Doe any, and I'm sure he felt a bit upstaged by me when it came to the life on the rails.

However, I'd let all this slide, refusing to make an issue of his shortcomings. Who cared if he was a pansy-ass when it came to making a hop? After all, his presence had been indispensable in so many other ways, most of which centered on his millennial-styled magic with technology. I had to hand it to him. He'd been top of the line when it came to reading the on-line charts and had rarely screwed up a schedule or a transfer. That was why I had been shocked when for his last hurrah he'd managed to set us on the wrong train, one bound for Texas, instead of north to Iowa. Texas??? Whatever had he been thinking? Had our little vacation caused him to become that rusty? Or was he just losing his edge, so traumatized over the notion of hitting the rails again that he flubbed up in a big way?

Good Lord! Now we would have to ride the rails all the way to Houston, where with any luck we could find a northbound heading in the right direction. And that, my friends, didn't look like a plan which would hold water. Or should I say it might hold a whole lot of water because word had been coming in over the wires that Houston was in for a pretty rough ride.

Yes indeed. Ever since he started going into town to listen to all that crazy stuff about the fires in California, Doe had been obsessing about the weather, following forecasts like a hawk. I guess he feared that whatever had happened in the Golden State might jump to the Land of Enchantment. And it was a distinct possibility since by its very nature the Southwest was also primed for dangerous forest fires.

But up to the day of our departure, the horizon had remained clear. If there was any smoke around, it had been from the small fire we'd lit in the pot belly stove in an attempt to ward off the chill of the New Mexico nights. However, old habits die hard and during our hitch back to Santa Fe, Doe had insisted on checking in with his weather AP, and that's when I realized fire was not the only force we might have to reckon with.

"There's a big hurricane brewing out in the Gulf," he informed me. "They named it Harvey, and can you believe it? It's the eight named storm of the season, and we're barely into August. They say it's going to be a big one though, a possible Cat 4 with sustained winds of 130MPH. So we definitely want to avoid that mess."

Yes, we definitely did. So how in God's name had we managed to get on this train that was heading in the exact same direction we were trying to avoid?

Well, I can't answer that. No rhyme, no reason, I suppose. Sometimes it just is what it is, and I have to confess that if the choosing of trains to hop had been up to me during these past four months, we would have probably found ourselves bound for Katmandu.

I looked over at Doe. He had gone from sheepish to miserable. A light rain had already begun to fall, and here we were in an open boxcar. We'd tried to set up some kind of shelter out of that piece of plastic he'd bought me months ago, but it had just been whipped around by the ever-present wind. So there we sat, huddle in our ponchos, counting the minutes until the train pulled into the station. Of course, by that time, we'd be exiting the frying pan and cast into the fire. Or should I say, exiting the fish bowl only to find ourselves immersed in the ocean?

Noone/Doe Speaking

Lulu was singing, her voice a thin reed against the wailing of the wind as it whipped around our lonely boxcar. I don't know how she'd managed to make any sound at all considering the obstacles imposed by our surroundings, especially since she hadn't even attempted to unclothe the guitar from its protective trash bag. No, the song was carried on the strength of her voice alone, and I felt a bit guilty knowing she was taxing her vocal chords on my account. She should have spared them as the words she sang were not ones which brought me any degree of comfort.

Corn stands crackling in the sheaves
The wash flaps in the wind
Across hot pavement scurry leaves
As the hurricane hurries on in

Across the Gulf of Mexico
Up through the Florida Keys
Whipping up to a mighty gale
What was just a gentle breeze.

Changes in the weather,
Omens in the sky
1000 unanswered questions
Will I find out when I die?

Here I sit just a little child
Waiting out the storm
Feeling those cosmic forces
Watching them take form

Waiting for a plan to unfold
In a formless plan
And wondering just what God expects of man

1000 unanswered questions?

Yeah, the song brought it all back home. For starters: just how in hell had I managed to fuck up as bad as I did when selecting our train of the moment. And then there was that bit about *finding out when I died,* a major life event which may arrive a bit sooner than expected.

Oh dear. Despite all it had been a good good song, and I had to admire her for spinning straw into gold when indeed she had no straw to spin. I guess you'd say we were at an all time low. The scanty news I was able to pick up on my phone did little to calm me.

Harvey was a complex and dangerous storm and was going to pack a real punch, not just to Houston but to the industrial sprawl of petrochemical plants that lined its outskirts. God help the environment if all that crap got inundated to where it formed the great flood of 2018. I sure wouldn't want to be swimming in **that** pool, but come to think of it, I wouldn't want to be swimming in any pool about now, given my drenched condition. The only good thing about the drenching rain was that it kept the soot from clinging to me the way it always loved to, so that by the time we arrived in the yard I would look a little less the gnarly vagabond. However, none of this would alter my appearance enough to disguise my homelessness; and if what I was hearing on the Tube was any indication, now was not the best time to be homeless in Houston.

The news wasn't good. The shelters were already bursting at the seams, filling up with people who would have evacuated except for the Governor's refusal to give the order. But despite all the predictions of widespread flooding, he had stood firm in his decision not to send his citizens into the hinterlands. Guess a similar plan had been used during Hurricane Rita, and it had led to disastrous traffic jams. As I recall, at least one hundred people had died while trying to escape the wrath of a storm which hadn't been half as bad as predicted. But what could I say? That was a different storm, and this was not my call to make anyway. Maybe the governor was right; maybe it was best to ride it out. After all, Houston was the fourth largest city in Texas, and it would sure be a nightmare to move all of its inhabitants to higher ground. The only problem was that their presence in the shelters would mean less room for railroad bums like us, and it looked like we'd be staying for awhile. No way in hell were those trains going to keep running. In fact, it was nothing short of a miracle that ours hadn't stopped in its tracks. Just our luck, to be catching the last train to a war zone!

The wind, which up to this point had been gusty, responded with a hurricane force blast strong enough to rattle the slats of the boxcar. We weren't far from the yard now, and anyone with any sense had already left town, despite the governor's wishes. Either that or they were hunkered down in their homes with their candles and a three day food supply, one which would be a whole lot better than the swill they'd be shoveling out at the shelters. If that is, they would even take us in.

Yeah, that was a true concern, especially since the first one we tried refused us access. The policeman at the door cited having no known address as a reason, and I sure wasn't about to give them Leslie's. But holy fucking Jesus!!! Men in blue? Policing a shelter? However, considering what happened during Katrina, maybe it wasn't a bad idea after all.

So we thanked the guy for his service—it never hurts to be polite when you look like you've been train hopping—and went on down the street. The rain was already beginning to blow sideways, and at this point I wished we'd just found a better boxcar. But we were almost out of food and water, having not anticipated this hop to last as long as it had. Boy, oh boy, had I fucked up, on more than one front! I could have kept shaking my head over my stupidity, but the way the wind was now blowing, I might have experienced some serious whiplash.

Then I saw it, a van with permanent tags on it and the FEMA insignia emblazoned onto its side. The cop at the last shelter had told us to be on the lookout for it since this was our only hope of finding shelter from the storm. Still, I cringed when I saw its bright blue logo, the one featuring the American eagle holding the fasces, a bundle of sticks that was the ancient Roman symbol for authority. Although I knew they'd take us to an approved FEMA location, one specifically designed for the homeless, I sure wasn't too willing to step up to the plate. But then, what choice did I have? I scratched my head, a subtle gesture that was morphing into a bad habit, and right on schedule, the wind responded with a timely moan. That was all it took, and I made my move.

"We're going to have to swallow it, and take the ride," I shouted at her. "What do they say about any port in a storm?"

I was trying to make light of the situation, but it was hard. There had been so much on the alt-web about FEMA camps and none of it good. Not only were there pictures that looked straight out of Dachau, but they were often accompanied by photos of mass graves and the make-shift coffins to fill them. No, FEMA didn't have the best reputation. Even in its early days critics had blasted it as being a sorry bunch of bureaucratic assholes who could screw up a two car parade. And that was before Bush and Obama got hold of the organization and morphed it into the scary piece of homeland insecurity it was now.

But, once again, what were our options here? For folks like us, it looked like it was the only show in town. Besides, I consoled myself, it was only temporary. Hurricanes never lasted long and usually blasted through in less than twelve hours, or twenty-four at tops. So we'd be out of jail in no time flat, enjoying the crystal blue sky which often follows head on the heels of such a great grandmother of a storm.

I looked at her, she looked at me. The van was starting to pull away from the curb.

"Better run for it," I nudged, and we did, oblivious to the fact that we really should have been running in the opposite direction.

Ah, yes, how I wished that foresight superseded hindsight instead of the other way around.

I sat on the dirty floor of the dilapidated building which served as a holding tank for the destitute. We'd been in the joint for a full four days, during which the relentless rain had continued to pound the Texas coast. We'd been carted off on the eve of the destruction to the coastal city of Port Arthur, which struck me as a pretty weird place to ride out a storm. But, as usual, FEMA had its reasons. Maybe the Houston shelters had all been full, or maybe there was something about my name that did it. Because when I showed the guy in charge my ID, he had gone to the front of the van where he'd conferred with some great computer in the sky. Then he'd returned and informed everyone that they would be taking a little ride, but not to worry, they would just love their new accommodations.

Yeah, nothing to worry about here. A crumbling army barracks that resembled chicken coops more than anything else. Quarters so cramped that only ten people could be housed in one room, and guess what? The men were segregated from the women unless, of course, they could produce the proper documentation that verified a marriage sanctioned by church and state. Lulu was devastated, and so was I although I tried not to show it.

"It's only for a day or so," I assured her, and that had been four days ago. Four days of waking up to the sight of an armed guard patrolling the premises. Four days of shit on a shingle to eat, and an overflowing bathroom for the end product. Four days during which we were not allowed to see the folks in the neighboring barracks, four days during which we'd been denied permission to even leave.

I guess I should have considered myself lucky. I had managed to retain my phone, when most of the others had been confiscated. How I'd escaped the attention of the guards was beyond me. Maybe it had just been an oversight, or maybe they figured a kid as grubby as me would never possess such a toy. Whatever the case, I was careful not to be caught using it since it was my only link to the outside world, my only way to make any sense of all those alarms and sirens going off in the distance—and worse yet, the sound of gunfire.

Gunfire? Yeah, well it had been four days, and though the initial punch of the storm had passed, it had stalled and remained trapped between two weather systems. So it just sat there spinning and spinning, dumping gazillions of gallons of rainwater on an area that was prone to flooding under the best of conditions. After it had gotten done with Houston, it had meandered over the entirety of East Texas where it had lingered like a three-day old house guest who just doesn't know when to leave. So, that said, the sound of gunfire should not have surprised me one bit.

They say that, given any natural disaster, the population has about seventy-two hours before even the most morally minded of us reverted back to our carnal natures. And given that it had now been close to one hundred hours since the storm had hit, and given that Port Arthur had some pretty rough neighborhoods, it was easy to put two and two together and figure out that some folks might be getting deep sixed.

The news that I was receiving via my contraband phone confirmed my suspicions. There had been looting, and some of the people found floating in the floodwaters had even been shot in the head. It was so bad that some asshole on a jet-ski had even been spotted flying around with a pistol in each hand, firing into the homes of defenseless victims. Gangs were out in full force, stealing rescue boats from the Cajun Navy and then dressing up like officials so that they could better gain access to the folks who were trapped in their homes. It became the Wild West, and many of the bona fide boats had at least one government sharp-shooter on board, armed to the teeth, so what was meant to be a rescue operation often morphed into a hunting expedition.

But other than that, the government folks weren't helping much. Although there were a ton of them down in the area already—most belonging to those three letter agencies we have come to hate—they were mainly running around like chickens with their heads cut off, shutting down roads and adding insult to injury. Supplies meant for disaster relief had been stolen, guns were confiscated from law abiding citizens, and many were lucky to receive anything from FEMA other than a loaf of bread and a case of water. So that in the end, it was the Texans helping other Texans that saved the day. Thank God for a few patriots or else this country would be in a heap of trouble.

Actually it was from these patriots that I learned all of the above as they were blogging and vlogging relentlessly in an attempt to fill in the gaping holes in coverage left by the mainstream media. Yes, the rainfall did exceed fifty inches, and yes, an area the size of DC was flooded, and yes, there will be billions of dollars in damages. But when it came to the so-called body count, I fear that a mere seventy-five was low-balling it considerably. For if my patriot friends were to be believed, it would probably be closer to the thousands.

And the possible reason for this miscount was what really got to me. It began as a rumor, and rumors by their very nature are to be taken with a grain of sand. But given the circumstances perhaps this one should not be taken lightly. However, until I got more conclusive proof, I was going to have to hope and pray that it would remain nothing but Internet buzz. Lord knows, there sure was enough of it out there right now.

Take, for instance, the belief that the intensity of the storm resulted from weather manipulation. One guy had even posted a video which clearly displayed radar footage proving that there was a point in the storm where it looked as if a massive horseshoe cloud came in from the southwest. It formed quickly and appeared to have an object in its center, and moments after its appearance, it seemed as if a bomb had gone off. Yeah, a weather bomb, cuz immediately after that happened, Harvey exploded into a mega-storm.

OK, I can buy that, especially since weather modification has been around for decades. I refer to a project funded by DARPA that took place during the Vietnam War whereby excessive rain was generated in order to keep the North Vietnamese in check. And that, my friends, is a documented truth. As is the fact that geo-engineering has been confirmed by the likes of prominent scientists like Dr. Kaku, who went on CBS to state boldly that yes, man-made hurricanes have resulted from a government weather modification program. The skies are first sprayed with nano-particles, and then the storms are activated via lasers, using a technology which reminded me a bit of what had just happened out in California. Except it was water this time, and not fire. So it didn't surprise me that the monster we were stuck inside of might not be one hundred percent natural. Such shenanigans were not beyond our controllers, and proof of their existence had ceased to shock me.

But then, there was the other piece of news coming in from cyberspace: that FEMA had brought in floating barges in which to house the overflowing refugees from the flooded coast. Now THAT had shocked me, and caused even my flesh to crawl.

The mayor of Port Arthur called them riverboats, but they sure didn't seem like no fancy Mississippi Queen to me. In fact, despite their claim to providing three meals a day and satellite TV, they more closely resembled a prison, another holding tank where such amenities are available. I looked at the pictures of these floating hellholes and prayed for the poor slobs who would end up there; and well I should, since I was destined to become one of them. However, this brings me back to that unsubstantiated rumor I was picking up from the web, one that I cringed to even consider. It went like this:

Houston was flooded. A given. But that nasty little storm just wouldn't go away, so something had to give, or neighborhoods which up to this time had been spared the worst would become irretrievable. So what could be done? Well, the three-letter agency heads got together and conducted a plan. Why not flush the toilet on Port Arthur, use I-10 as a makeshift dam and release excess water from the regular dam, one which just so happened to protect some of the city's more marginal neighborhoods? It would be a controlled release of course, which meant that the residents would be given time to evacuate.

Well, some of the residents. Others would just have to swallow some tough titty, especially since many of the highways leading out of these neighborhoods had been locked down. But the bottom line was that this would get rid of another pressing problem, all those bodies with holes in the head. How convenient to just wash them out to sea where the fish would politely dispose of them. That way, no elected official would have it on their watch that they'd mismanaged another disaster. End result? Hundreds would be left to drown just so a political career or two could be saved.

Of course, God help you if you were in the line of fire of such a nefarious plan, and being the homeless, and therefore being about as disposable as diapers, all the inhabitants of Chicken Coop Central were up for a quick trip down river.

I didn't want to believe this rumor. I balked at its authenticity and fought it every inch of the way. Funny how I had accepted the worst about the fires in California, but when it came down to my own precious hide, I resorted to an infernal disavowal which insisted that *they would never do such a thing.*

So I struggled, stuck between my denial and my intuition, the latter of which caused my heart-rate to elevate and my stomach to churn. I just didn't want to believe what I was hearing on this one vlog; I had to fact check the guy's You-tube channel to see what else he was into. Was he a government plant, sent to muddy the waters with outrageous accusations and out and out lies, all so that true conspiracies would never be given any credibility?

God, how I wished I could have gotten in touch with Lulu, but she was housed in a barracks twenty feet away and up a small rise from my own riverside view. Oh, well, if it were true, at least the girl might have a fighting chance, since the flood waters might not reach that far. I was trying as hard as I could to retain some of my maw's old optimism. Yeah, she always was an opti-mystic, maintaining a cheery view of the future no matter what. So what had happened to me? Oh maw, I wish more of your good humor had rubbed off on me. Heaven help me, if you could only see me now. Or not, for no one in their right mind wanted their parent to witness their demise.

And as if on cue, the waters began to slip in from under the locked door.

The guard was as efficient as he was taciturn. No muss, no fuss for this guy. They were herding us up a narrow stairway to the roof, and the best I could get from him was that the whole place would be under six feet of water within an hour. I figured that since we were closest to the water, we were the first to get our ticket to ride on the train to safety. All well and good. But when I overheard mention of some three story barges that had been parked in the Port Arthur harbor, my merry mood evaporated. It couldn't be, yet I knew in my gut the exact nature of our new housing. It would be a true step down, a frying pan to the fire experience.

However, once again I found myself in the pitiful position of having no choice. Gee, what happened to free will? Guess it went out the window with my former sunny disposition, one which sure had been put to a test during the past few months. First that stint on the rails, and now this. I felt my sphincter tighten and somehow knew that all of the above had been a slow high school dance compared to what was coming.

By that time I was on the roof, dodging the whirling blades of an army helicopter. It was probably some derivative of the Huey, although I didn't really know my choppers. But I did know they only held eleven to fifteen passengers a piece, and as there was only one of them and about one hundred people housed in this complex, I began but wonder just how they planned on evacuating the place in one hour. Jesus! It would take at least fifteen minutes to get us over to our destination, another five to unload, and then fifteen more back again and that made for a big NOT GOOD. The numbers just didn't add up. There was no way in hell they were going to get everyone out in time.

I looked out the window. We were flying close, almost too close to the barracks where Lulu was housed. I looked out the open back of the carrier and saw her frightened face peering from a dirty window, and even though I knew she couldn't see me, I felt like I had to do something to reassure her. So I mouthed the words *see you soon* into the rain drenched air.

Right, *see you soon*. Little did I know what a ridiculous statement that would turn out to be.

.

Lulu/Stitch Speaking

I watched as the helicopter pulled off towards the east. I knew Doe was on it because I'd seen him herded towards that particular barracks on the day of our great separation. It had been an awful day, the kind reserved for great loss. We had grown so close over the course of our travels that he had achieved a special status in my book, one which was about as close as I'd ever come to soul mate or twin. It wasn't a sexual bond, mind you. More of a mind melt and one strong enough that I could hear his words in the back of my head. Something about *sooooon*, and the sound brought to mind that weird little experience we had shared on the night of our great bonding, when my name had been projected in long drawn out syllables across the New Mexico hills.

OOOOoooooo

Looooo ooooo

Soooon

But just as I had sensed the content of his message, I had also known that it was way too optimistic. In fact, I had the distinct feeling that sooooon was going to morph into a long, long time, if not forever. It was the opposite of a warm fuzzy feeling, and one that is probably more appropriate when confronted with the death of a twin. I felt empty inside, as if a significant part of me was now winging its way into a murky sunrise, one which may never see the light of day.

As I continued to follow the path of the chopper which carried Doe towards an unknown future, I cursed myself for two things. Number one: why hadn't I tried to learn more about technology during our time together? If so, maybe I could have emailed the guy, for it looked as if the barracks had some sort of Wi-Fi available—at least if the chatter I was picking up from a couple of the women was of any worth. Although most phones had been confiscated, a couple of us still had alternate means of contacting people on the outside. Weird since these are the homeless we're talking about here, a sub-culture that are not usually privy to maintaining a fleet of high-deck toys. But remember, this is 2018 and even dogs have their own webpage—unless they happen to be techno-phobes such as myself.

At any rate, these two women—really girls by the looks of them—seemed fairly proficient in bringing up mundane shit like Facebook and the weather channel on their snappy little Samsungs. I watched them like a hungry dog in search of a bone, hoping they might offer me some assistance. All I needed to know was how to get online. Then via email, I could send a message over to Doe who was but a mere quarter of a mile away. In that way maybe I, too, could access news about this crazy storm which just seemed to spin and spin over our heads, dropping enough rain to scare the likes of Noah.

However, the *girlz* seemed more concerned with gleaning tidbits of irrelevant information about so-and-so's cat and their cousin Bob's new Dodge Charger than about anything which might shed some light on our current situation. It was almost sickening to watch them. They seemed oblivious to where they were or anything that was going on outside their little boxes. It was truly the invasion of the body snatchers, and after a while I pegged them as runaways, truculent teens who had probably been grounded sans techno-toys. Seeing the storm as an opportunity to get out from under daddy's authoritative thumb, they had hit the streets in search of the first Wi-Fi cafe and had somehow got caught up in the homeless round-up. So, finding themselves among hardened criminals and hookers, they were clinging to the only lift raft they had—their newly purchased state-of-the- art Samsung tablets—and excluding all others, had gone on to form a techno-club of two.

When it soon became apparent that there would be no help from this quarter, I withdrew into myself, a habit I'd had a lot of practice with, and that led to my second stupid move. Long story short, I just wasn't making any friends at a time when forming alliances equated with survival. You would have thought that such an experience would bring people together and that I would break from my usual stand-offish mode and reach out to others. However, with the exception of the two teens, all the rest of the women in my quarters were tough looking street veterans with missing teeth and vacant stares, leaving me few candidates for forming any bosom buddy relationships.

So I retreated to a shelf of books some well-meaning matron had donated to the shelter—many of which were way beneath my dignity—and proceeded to wait out the storm. It was tough, boring and confining, and my only relief came from my dreams. If you want to call it relief.

Each night was pepper-sprayed with weird disjointed images, from which, upon awakening, a real doozy would emerge. On the first night I woke to realize I had just been in one of the many clothes closets of my youth. Because we moved around a lot, it was hard to remember which one, but it had emerged from the pack somehow as a favorite. There had been ample space for tons of clothes, and since I had hit this place during my teenage years, I was in hog heaven. Rack upon rack was filled to the brim with department store purchases that I had raided my babysitting wages to procure. It had been my one and only attempt for straight and normal in my life, and I was playing it to the hilt.

But in my dream, something was wrong. There was stuff in the back of the closet that needed to go. It had been there way too long and would have to be liquidated if I was to have room for all my new garments. Alas and alack, it was a time for reckoning, and I woke up confused, not knowing what to leave in and what to leave out.

So that was dream #1, not much of a no-brainer to any shrink worth their salt. Number two was a bit more complex and bordered on prophecy. In this case, I was on the last train to Clarksburg. (Don't know where the name of the town came from unless it was that silly song by an even sillier group, *The Monkeys*.) Anyway, this little snip of a girl, barely five foot in her stocking feet, had convinced me that we had time for a quick excursion before my family came to visit. Now, why on earth I should care about being present for such an ignominious event was beyond me, but I was. However, when we got to the town in question and after we'd done it up proper, it turned out that, not only was our return ticket at least fifty bucks more than the one we paid to get there, but the next train would not be leaving until the following day. Ultimate outcome: I would miss my rendezvous with my two remaining relatives.

It was a strange dream, though I guess most dreams are. But what struck me about this one was that I really did feel bad about diss'ing my family. Maybe I shouldn't have run off like I had on such a wild goose chase. Perhaps I should have paid more attention to practical matters like finances and timetables. Would they ever forgive me? Or better yet: would I ever forgive them for not forgiving me?

Oh well, not too much I could do about it now except in the words of Dr. Dwayne Dyer: perhaps *I could change the way I looked at things, and the things I looked at would change.*

But wait a minute. We're not done yet. There was a grand finale coming, and it occurred the night before I caught my last glimpse of Doe as he disappeared over a far horizon. And, later on, I realized that—yes— we had managed to communicate after-all. For what it was worth.

A flood was coming. Well no shit, Sherlock! Except this was a flood within a flood. The waters were rising, and we were trying to escape to the roof. But just when it looked as if we might make it out, something horrible happened. The waters, which were tsunami-like in their strength, ripped the house we were in right off its foundation, and we were set adrift amongst the flotsam and jetsam. Everyone looked at each other, faces white with terror. But what could we do? We would just have to ride it out, allow ourselves to be carried downstream until we came to rest somewhere. Yeah, anywhere would do. So we sat in the cold and dark and waited, and then the worst happened. The floorboards beneath us began to buckle, and the beams above our heads to creak.

"She's coming apart!" someone screamed, and seconds later, the water rushed in to second the motion.

I woke up shaking, though oddly enough I also woke up with a song on my lips.

> *The river, she runs deep,*
> *and the waters they'll be rising,*
> *and there's no turning back once you cross over.*
> *But when I swim it in my sleep,*
> *it really ain't surprising,*
> *that it flows on down through banks,*
> *of thistle and clover.*

In the dim light of dawn I found my guitar and hugged her to me. Guess we all have life rafts.

Later that day, the dream slipped it bonds and drifted into a dark reality. Doe had departed over an hour ago, but as of this moment, the helicopter had not returned to carry anyone else to safety. We watched, we waited, but there was no sound of the chop, chop, thump, thump of its surly wings. Only the ever-present rain.

And then, a new sound began to infiltrate the room. It was a subtle sound at first, the kind a sneak-thief would make as they attempted to gain access to a locked door. Then it began to pick up speed and when it did so, it emerged in a new light, one that was almost pleasant. The gurgling of a brook as one sat beside it on a summer's day, it was the kind of sound that brought back memories of childhood and picnics by the old millpond and…

Wow. It was becoming so real I could almost feel the water as it lapped my fingers which were draped over one side of my cot. I'd been reading, probably one of those disgusting novels left to placate us, a Danielle Steel or Nora Roberts, where the heroine always emerges victorious from the perils of Pauline. I'd been immersed in the shit, and why not? It was my only means of escape. But it didn't take long for me to figure out that I'd better come up with a much better plan. Because the waters definitely were rising, and they were rising fast!

Holy shit! I jumped off the couch to find that there was already a good half-inch of water on the floor. Since I was closest to the door and on the low side of the room, I was the first to sound the alarm. Suddenly, all these sorry-assed women, including the two nubile teens, took on a new light. They were no longer throw-away items to be rejected and ignored. Instead they were my flock, my responsibility, and I was no longer little boy blue asleep in the hay. It was time to blow that horn and blow it loud.

It's funny how in the face of disaster even the most xenophobic will pitch in and work with others. The more mobile amongst us found sheets to stuff under the door, and the *girlz* immediately got on Facebook to put out a plea for help. Not that this should have been their problem, that task being the duty of the guards who had been watching over us since day one of this whole disaster. But speaking of which, where were those guards? We looked out the windows. Hell, we beat on the windows and on the door—at least until I put a stop to that nonsense, fearing that too much impact might cause the old piece of shit to come off its hinges.

Yes, we tried to get proactive. Tried and failed. For we were up against a power greater than ourselves, a power even greater than drugs and alcohol. We were up against Mother Nature, Gaia in all her fierce beauty and gutsy glory, and we were on the losing side of the game.

The water came in so fast it quickly saturated the bedding we'd piled up to stop it. In less than an hour it was touching the bottoms of the cots, a sanctuary to which several of the more infirm had already retreated. It came in down and dirty, and it came in spades, rushing gushing, and swirling until the bottom of the barracks resembled a filthy swimming pool that even a pig would have found repulsive. And then it stopped, just as suddenly as it had begun, and our collective sigh of relief could have been heard in the next county.

But wait, the show wasn't over yet because, as we looked out the window, we could tell that we were no longer on an island. Instead, we were part of the stream, and not only was that stream flowing pell-mell down river to a hot date with the sea, but with a tremendous creak and a groan, we found ourselves along for the ride.

In short, the barracks, which was probably of pre-Civil War construction, was one which would never have passed any current hurricane code. Instead of a strong foundation, one attached by rebar to footers sunk deep in the ground, it had simply been placed haphazardly atop some crumbling cinderblocks. So it didn't take an engineering degree to figure out what would happen when said structure was hit by a wall of rabid water. Think *The Borrowers Afloat* and you get the picture.

Oh, not familiar with that allusion? Well, I'll fill in the blanks. The borrowers were little people who generally who lived in old houses and survived by…well, *borrowing* from the big folks. Usually this went on for decades without a hitch, but sometimes they were found out which would result in a hasty relocation. One family in particular came to live in the great outdoors and was stupid enough to set up house-keeping in a discarded tea-kettle by the side of a stream.

Need I say any more? The first flash flood found them careening madly down a raging torrent, and though our present predicament was not quite that dramatic, we were definitely afloat.

As I peered out the window to watch the detritus of civilization pass us by—old bottles, milk jugs, chicken coops, dog houses, and an assortment of other stuff ripe for the landfill—my heart sunk. Then it hit rock bottom when my eyes fell upon what could only be a dead body. It was so bad I automatically crossed myself, resorting back to a habit cultivated at my mother's knee.

But no amount of prayer was about to get us out of our predicament. In fact, the only thing to do was ride it out. I mentally calculated the odds. Though adrift, at least we still had the barracks to buffer us from that raging torrent. So all we had to do was follow it down stream, where surely at some point it would come to rest—hopefully right next to a good motel where we could get a shower and a decent night's sleep before   strolling over to their breakfast buffet.

Yeah, dream on. But still, there was a measure of security in Plan A, a plan which essentially had us doing nothing. I gazed back out the window. It seemed as if the current had slowed down as well it should since we were approaching a wider body of water. Shit, at this rate we would be out to sea in no time. I tried to remember just where we were in the world. I knew we'd been taken close to the coast, but how close? The hodge-podge of items borne by the water began to thin out, and as they swirled around us, it brought to mind an image from *The Wizard of OZ*, the one where Dorothy finds herself inside the tornado. I half expected to see Elvira Gulch as she turned from spiteful spinster to wicked witch. Would we end up smashing the bitch? Was that our ultimate goal?

But no, though we certainly weren't in Kansas anymore, neither were we bound for OZ. Ozymandias, maybe. But definitely not OZ. The words of Shelley's famous poem rushed in from somewhere deep in my grey matter, a remnant of some long forgotten class in English literature.

> My name is Ozymandias, king of kings:
> Look on my works, ye Mighty, and despair!'
> Nothing beside remains. Round the decay
> Of that colossal wreck, boundless and bare
> The lone and level sands stretch far away.

They were right on target and signaled a change from bad to worse. It began with a slight moan as if the barracks were complaining to have found itself evicted from its previous resting place, only to be jettisoned towards God knows where. Then, the mild complaining morphed into an outright bitch fit. The barracks was pissed, and it was about to let us know it. Rusty nails that had been happy to remain in rotting wood were now seeking the quickest exit. Floorboards which had borne the weight of many a stinky feet were sick and tired of being stepped all over, and windows which had previously provided only a quick peek were about to go from preview to main feature. It was rebellion in it finest, and one which was reserved for jilted lovers who were determined that *if I can't have her, no one will.* So let's just put a gun to her head and be done with it.

Bang! Crash! Boom! And there went the back wall, which caused a gaping hole to open through which we lost at least three of our party. Party? Why that makes it seemed like a real fun get-together; and this was more like an execution. So let's just call a spade a spade. The house was lining us up in front of the firing squad as if to ask for volunteers. *Who's next,* she seemed to say. (And yes, she had to be a woman, to be acting the way she was.)

Oddly enough, there were two volunteers, the truculent teens who mumbled something about their chances being better before there was a true *there she blows* situation. So in tandem, they grabbed their tablets and ran to the nearest window, which they proceeded to exit, rats deserting a sinking ship. I watched them go, two Bobbsey twins bobbing on the surface of the water like life-sized corks, and considered following them. However, I hesitated, rationalizing that it would be better to wait until the whole deal went down. That way, there would be less house to hit me once it joined its remnants in the waters of oblivion.

It was faulty thinking really and one that resulted more from my inability to swim than anything else, but I stuck with it. At least until the barracks which–deprived of one wall for stability–decided to list seriously to one side, thus allowing a clear pathway for more and more water to enter. It didn't take a rocket scientist to know what would happen next. Every child has played this game in a bathtub or two. It's called *Sink the Bismarck*, and it's sung to the same tune they played while the Titanic was going down. We had to get out that window and fast before it was impossible to reach.

I tried to communicate this to the four remaining women, but to no avail. Only one of them wasn't too sick, too old, or two strung out to give a shit. I guess they just figured they'd go down with the ship. The one who joined me was a hefty gal who needed a lift in order to gain the window sill. I pushed and shoved until her corpulent frame hit the water with a big splash. I had a feeling she'd sunk, and was glad I couldn't see out the window as such sight would not to bolster my confidence. I could have chickened out at that point, but adrenaline would hear nothing of it. Funny how the old girl will take over when confronted with demise.

Pulling me up to the windowsill was tougher than any train I'd yet to catch, but I made it. I sat poised for a moment considering the murky waters below. I'd been right, the two ton heifer was nowhere to be seen, and the Bobbseys had bobbed right out of my life. I was alone.

Oh well, I always knew I'd die without fanfare. What the hell? Given the choice, I would rather fight the wind and the rain than die in the prison behind me. I took one last look at its dinghy interior. The water within was rising fast, inundating four days of bad dreams and dashed hopes. Here goes nothing.

I closed my eyes, plugged my nose and fade to black.

The log had been both my undoing and my saving grace. It was a big hunk of oak, a tree native to Texas. In fact, Texas boasts housing at least sixty different kinds of oak trees. Not that I much gave a shit about such trivia at this point in my life.

It was enough to say that I was still alive.

I opened one eye. The other was swollen shut, having been hit pretty hard by the tree limb as it crashed into me on its way downstream. To this day I don't know how I managed to find myself clinging to the back of this baby, but when I awoke I was draped over it like a drunken cowgirl on my way back from an all-night bender at the local saloon.

Then I saw her. At first she was just a placid eye and a toothless grin, and the rest was all grey. However, as my good eye began to come online, I realized my confusion had nothing to do with my inability to focus but reflected more on the coloration of its owner. Sleek, slippery and now chattering that characteristic chirping sound, I finally saw her for what she was on the totem pole of life. A dolphin. Yes, a dolphin. Savior of many a hapless sailor lost at sea, or so the stories went.

I looked at her; she looked at me; and the chattering ceased. We no longer needed any verbal means of communication. It was all taking place on some other level. From the bottom of my heart I thanked her for rescuing me and nudging my limp form onto the log. She responded with what could only be an *oh shucks, that's what we dolphins do best*, and then she began to nose the log I was on.

A bit unnerved, I wondered if I had read her wrong. Was she just playing? Was I but one more floating toy sent her way by the unexpected flood? But then I understood. She was trying to get me closer to shore.

Away from the maelstrom of a current which would most certainly take me out to sea.

Because I didn't want to appear completely helpless, I dug my arms into the water and offered my assistance. Together we pushed and pulled and finally broke free of the eddy. Now all we had to do was paddle, paddle, paddle until we reached that shimmering shore.

It was shimmering, wasn't it? Or was that just an optical illusion brought about by the goose-egg on my head? And how about those clouds, the first ones I had seen for days that weren't the color of my friendly dolphin. White and dappled, they looked exactly like a herd of prancing ponies clip-clopping across the sky, going from west to east; and suddenly, the words to yet another song popped into my head.

I see my light come shining,
From the west down to the east,
Any day now
Any way now,
I shall be released.

And that's when I got it. God was alive, and magic was afoot, and best to just let it play out the way it had been prophesized from day one. After all, I was only fulfilling my destiny. How hard was that?

Oh, but there was one more task to perform, one more question to answer, and as soon as I saw his kind eyes smiling down on me, I knew a response would soon be expected.

The sandbar stuck out into the gulf like the fickle finger of fate it must have been for many an unfortunate vessel. It probably needed a lighthouse, but given its shifting nature and shaky foundations, it never could have housed one for long. However, that didn't mean it had remained unmarked.

He stood there like some Colossus of Rhodes, though it was apparent upon approach that he was merely a man. A tall man, no doubt, but nowhere near lighthouse stature. But the biggest thing about him had nothing to do with height. It was his smile, which was a bit toothless, except for an occasional bicuspid or incisor.

Or was it those eyes, so infinite in their Krishna blue that a person could fall into them and end up on the far side of forever—eyes that were both foreign and familiar at the same time? Now where had I seen them before?

Perplexed, I would have scratched my head if my hands hadn't been so busy scrabbling for land. The sandy beach was peppered with mud, making it hard to walk on, and my footprints sunk as I struggled to rise. Then he was before me, extending his hand, and I knew.

He was the spitting image of his picture, the one I'd come across all those long months ago when it shown from the glossy pages of *The Smithsonian*. And at first, my rational mind tried to make sense of his presence on this distant isle. Had he also taken a wrong turn somewhere and ended up in the wrong place at the wrong time? Had he, too, been rounded up with the rest of the homeless, only to find himself collateral damage of a fucked up federal emergency system? Gee, what a coincidence if that were so, and what a way to finally meet! Golly, I wouldn't have to go to Britt, Iowa after all. For Britt, Iowa had come to me.

But even as I contemplated such nonsense, I knew I was full of shit. Goddamn, is it ever hard to accept the inexplicable, that the universe is a mysterious place and a lot of what happens makes no apparent sense at all.

I smiled a smile weakened by trauma and a split lip.

"Dutch, I presume," I managed to mumble with the same aplomb Dr. Stanley must have used when confronted with Dr. Livingstone, and he nodded in assent.

There was a moment of perfect silence as if neither of us wanted to break the spell. Then our Mexican stand-off ended, and I asked the obvious question.

"So where do we go from here?"

"You already know," he replied. "You were given the details a long time ago."

I was? This time I really did scratch my head.

He went on.

"Mt. Shasta? The Agarthian network?"

He was humming a few bars, hoping to jog my memory. It didn't take long.

"Oh yeah. So you are?"

"One of them." He filled in the blank. "And the last time you met us, you were given a choice... which you took. And you were also given more time, but the sand is at the bottom of the hourglass now, or in baseball terms, the bases are loaded and someone's got to walk. However, before we go on, a question or two."

Oh, oh, here it comes, I thought and began to mentally prepare myself as if gearing up for a really important exam.

And truth be told, it was probably the most important exam of my thoroughly over-educated life! Also one which had been impossible to study for. All the coursework had been completed out of class, while on the road, while riding the rails, while drinking ayahuasca, while writing a book and experiencing rejection and...

OK, it was that last one that was the clincher.

I thought for a moment and his eyes reflected patience. However, I knew I didn't have forever.

Then, it came, not as a bolt from the blue, but more like a gentle wave of calm realization.

I looked back into the depths of those new-born blue eyes and spoke the words that would seal my fate.

"I'm supposed to forgive her for not forgiving me, aren't I? That's what it will take to get to the next level, isn't it?"

"Is that a question, or a statement?" he asked.

I paused.

"Statement, definitely a statement."

And his tooth-deprived grin lit up the sky.

But we weren't done. There was another long pause before he held up two items. Now how in the world had they survived the tortuous trip down river?

Oh, right. I got it. This as one of those *lady or the tiger* moments, except that I get to see what was behind door number three.

In his hands were two items formerly belonging to yours truly. The right held a slightly used pawn shop guitar and the other a shiny new thumb drive.

"The choice is yours, but you can only take one," he said, although no explanation had really been required. "Sorry to say, but the next leg of the journey requires you to travel light."

I sighed. I'd suspected it would come down to this. OK, let's see. The thumb drive was quite literally the less bulky of the two items but....

Boy, was this hard, and I wished it could have been different, but I knew better.

Again he waited, and again the pause drew out to incorporate an eternity of moments. Then a note sounded somewhere in my brain, and I knew. He did too, and held out his left hand.

"Good choice," was all he said as a tunnel opened up beneath the sand. In its center was a door which opened slowly. I looked into his eyes, though I needed no further encouragement, and together we descended into that cool delicious darkness.

Noone/Doe Speaking

My new digs weren't much better than the last. As I had suspected, the chopper had winged us out into the Gulf where one of those disreputable prison barges sat awaiting our arrival. We were dumped off unceremoniously upon its deck and then it left again, presumably to return later with more refugees. At least this was what we were led to believe, but I never did see old thumper again.

I couldn't help but think of poor Lulu, back in that floating coffin, and yeah, the barracks had probably come loose from its moorings by now. I'd been hip to the incompetency of its construction the first time I'd set foot inside the door, and it sure wouldn't have been my choice of a place to wait out a storm.

But the choice had not been mine. In fact, that word had not even been allowed to enter my vocabulary for nigh on a week now, unless you counted whether I wanted to eat *shit on the shingle* or a *slab of lab*. It was a funny thought, and I began to smile the toothy grin of the truly loopy.

Then, I immediately wiped it away. Good Lord, what was I thinking? I might as well dance on her grave because there was no doubt in my mind that was where she'd ended up. A watery one, mind you. No six feet under; no perfumed casket. In fact, I half expected her to float by during one of my exercise times on deck. That's right, exercise time. Like they give you in prison.

The only difference was that my cell was not locked. It didn't have to be. For where was there to go? We were completely surrounded by water with no land in sight. So even if I had decided to swim for it, I would have been clueless as to which direction to take. Nope, I was in it for the long run, and at the rate my companions were disappearing, the long run might not be too long at all.

I considered this last thought, turning it over and over in my mind in an attempt to release some of its toxicity. There *had* been more of us yesterday, hadn't there? I wasn't sure because, unlike the former barracks, we were housed in individual cells—yes, cells—where we were expected to stay unless it was one of our established meal or exercise times. And since such times seemed to cycle on an irregular basis, you never knew who might be joining you for either dinner or a stroll around deck. I had really only seen my old bunk mates a handful of times. So it was hard to tell just how many of us remained on board.

But if we weren't there, where exactly had we gone? There had been no visible traffic—either to or from the platform—for the entirety of my time there. And then there was that one truly disturbing image, courtesy of our so-called exercise time.

We'd been walking the lower deck, and I had glanced at the turbid water only to witness a body floating by. Although I had been gazing in the direction of the sun and the glare on the water had hidden any major features, I could have sworn I recognized the water logged Hell's Angel jacket it wore. Could it have been Rodney, the burned out biker guy who'd been bunking next to me back in the chicken coop? A bona-fide free spirit, perhaps he had decided to take his chances with the waters and had jumped overboard during his time top-side. Jumped? Or had he been pushed?

Whatever the case, the image didn't do much to improve my mood, and I retreated further and further into my own shell. My phone was useless, for unlike my previous quarters, Wi-Fi was nonexistent. So I was really cut off from any news, alterative or mainstream. The only Intel I got was from the guards who assured us that soon we would be sent back to dry land.

Soon? I'm not sure I liked the sound of that. Soon could be anywhere from two minutes to two months. Two years even. Shit, soon could be anything it damn well pleased.

Soon. God, how I hated that word as it reminded me of my final pep talk to Lulu, mouthed from a speeding chopper in my final attempt to find a silver lining in this endless landscape of dull-assed grey.

I began to keep track of the days the same way inmates have done for years, by scratching hatch marks onto the walls of my quarters. I had to be careful to avoid the spots where the paint was peeling, but after a while my little art project began to take shape. Not that this was a good thing, since a headcount of the results soon revealed that I was way up over a week. More like two and counting. Yeah, *soon* was at it again, displaying its old nebulous self. And at that point, I would have welcomed the deep six. Anything had to be better than this infernal waiting game. Just what did they intended to do with all of us? Sure, we weren't the cream of the crop or the pillars of the community. Still, we deserved a fair shake. At least some of us, the ones who hadn't attempted to rip off the government for millions of bucks.

Of course, this brought up another concern of mine. It had to do with my credentials. For the longer they had to examine them, the worse off I was. I began to have nightmares in which my cover was blown, at which point this prison or one just like it would become my permanent home and not one I would be getting out of any time *soon*.

And then my wildest fears were realized.

They came for me in the middle of the night. Of course, they did. It couldn't have been a respectable hour like after breakfast or even while I was striding the sterile decks of the Good Ship Lollipop. Noooooo, it had to be the bewitching hour, and as I was to find out later, it all had to do with symbolism. They loved that kind of stuff.

I tried to mumble some sort of protest.

"Come on, guys! Couldn't you at least have waited until I finished my wet dream?" (I'd been actively engaged with a bodacious aerialist at the time and sure didn't want to break the thread.

But noooooo, again. It was *time*.

Time? Time for what? Oh, never mind. I figured I was going to find out, like it or not.

They marched me from my holding cell to the public showers where I was ordered to strip and bathe. Then, they sprayed me with a substance which could only hold some sort of de-lousing agent. Finally, I was escorted to a small room deep within the bowels of the ship. There was a single table where one seat sat facing a row of five others. In them sat five pompous looking military types, complete with a uniform I had never seen in the armed forces. The final seat was vacant, and guess who got to occupy it?

They grilled me for some time. There was no reason to argue. Or lie. I knew my gig was up, so why bother? Sometimes total transparency will get you a little leniency.

If there had been a clock on the wall, its hands would have rotated more times than I would have cared to count. But the whole place was Zen-like in its austerity and sterile as a hospital room. Later I would learn that it had to be so, in order to not contaminate the occupants.

After awhile I began to grow weary, sleepy even. And for good reason as it was almost dawn, and I'd been awake all night. How I knew the time was beyond me, but something in my bones alerted me to the hour. Just like it told me that said hour was growing late. The interview—for this was certainly what it had been—was drawing to a close. And here came the clincher, the job offer as it were.

"Noone McCumbers."

One of the guys was addressing me, and I got the feeling he was head honcho. So why had he called me by the wrong name? McCumbers? McCumbers. It was another thought to turn over in a vain attempt to rid the room of its deadly implications.

For I knew that name. In a rush of realization it came flooding back to me. Those letters in the back of maw's closet and the real reason why she'd kept them all those years. I always known, just hadn't wanted to accept it.

"Noone McCumbers," he repeated, and I turned to face him.

"Yes," I responded and for the first time in my life, I knew I was answering to the right name.

"We'd like to offer you a deal," he began. "Seems like you've committed various crimes against the state, crimes which could see you locked up for many years to come. However, there is another option. You can work off your time with us and, better yet, we will even pay you a small stipend. Plus I think you will find the work fascinating, a real challenge for your obvious technical skills."

His eyes met mine, and I nodded. Yeah, I'd heard of such things. Just about every hacker worth their salt comes to a similar impasse. I couldn't help feeling flattered. I was actually getting indoctrinated into the Hacker Hall of Fame, the one reserved for such greats as Gary McKinnon and Julian Assange. Boy, oh boy, if maw could see me now!

However my elation ended when the gory little details were explained to me. My assignment would be with an agency only known as The Dark Fleet, who were based off-planet, specifically on Mars.

Whooooaaa!!! Hold the horses! Did he just use *based off-planet* and *Mars* in the same sentence.?

I must have looked shocked because his next words were meant to scare me back to center.

"Of course, there's always Leavenworth, but it sure doesn't come with the glamour of the Red Planet. However, the choice is yours. It always has been."

And that's when it all sunk in. The letters, my last name, my geeky nature, my love for adventure, my reckless ways. It had all been gearing up for this moment, this one big moment of decision, and it didn't take a crystal ball to figure out which way that wind was a gonna blow.

"I'll take the deal. I'll do it!" I exploded, uttering my assent with the same zest I had used when taking on the task of Lulu. They were my three favorite words when it came to sealing my fate, and I regretted them to this day.

Chapter 1
Private N. McCumbers of the Dark fleet
(AKA Noone)

"McCumbers. Are you finished with that blueprint yet? Command needed it two hours ago, and they don't like to be kept waiting. So hurry it up unless you want to incur another penalty."

Her sharp little words chirped in my ear, and the only thing worse would have been to find her standing right beside me. Lord knows, with her buggy eyes and carrion breath, she sure wasn't my idea of warm and cuddly. But they'd solved such higher management problems in the eight by ten cubicle in which I now labored. The trick had been remote viewing which led to remote control via an implant that was embedded just below my left ear. Get your work done in a timely fashion, and you were rewarded with a sensation that mimicked a sensual backrub. Piddle around and you would incur a penalty. Rack up enough of these and you would find yourself reeling from one hell of an electric shock.

And if that weren't bad enough, get more than fifty of these babies during one pay period and you might find yourself ejected from an airlock. Yeah, they were that brutal, and we, the help, were that disposable.

Oh, they still tried to convince us that we were there under our own free will and, yeah, I guess when faced with jail-time on an exotic planet or incarceration at Gitmo, you might say that you had come under your own volition. It was supposed to be part of their MO to offer you a choice and divulge full disclosure of its terms. However, the contract, when there was one, was so cloaked in rhetoric and legalese that the best lawyers on Earth would have been baffled by its bullshit.

Take that crap about pay for instance. Though I entered into my contract as a Private, my pay grade was nowhere near that of my counterpart back on Earth. In fact, it barely bought me a few cigarettes at the cantina, a place which I was getting ready to head to as soon as my handler got off my case.

"I gotcha, I gotcha," I mumbled to the voice in my ear, and as I spoke the words, the schematics I had been working on came into view on my screen. Something to do with cyborgs—always something to do with cyborgs—which were big business in the department I'd been assigned to.

"There, happy now?" I asked the lovely insectoid that was blissfully only present as a disembodied voice.

There was a brief silence during which the creature inspected my work; then I felt that weird sensation that heralded her notion of an atta-boy.

"Whoa, not now," I countered. "I'd rather a smoke break."

Yes, alas, smoking was a dirty habit I'd picked up in the past few months. Since we weren't allowed my favorite blends like Northern Lights, Girl Scout Cookies and Blue Dream, I had to settle for plane old Camel's or Marlborough's. But, hey, it ain't whatcha want, but whatcha get that makes you fat, right?

I guess I may have offended her. But not everyone enjoys being on the receiving end of an insectoid's loving claws. I'd rather save my atta-boys up for a real massage by a member of my own species.

However, if she was miffed, she soon swallowed it.

"You have ten minutes," she crackled, and I rose to make the best of them.

Strolling down a hall of hobbit sized windows which looked out on a barren red landscape, I contemplated how it could always be worse. My maw had raised me well, to be a hope-springs eternal optimist, and I was trying to apply my lifelong buoyancy to my current situation.

I knew there had been a hell of a lot worse assignments. I could have been impressed into service as a soldier and sent out to fight the green reptilians on the surface of the planet. They were always harassing the colonists, and gee, we damn well knew that the colonists came first. After all, hadn't they paid a hefty sum to be transported off-planet to this break-way civilization where they would be spared the nuclear war which all us space monkeys knew to be inevitable?

Hell, some of my co-workers were even convinced that our home planet was already toast, an uninhabitable cinder. But I sensed that story was just a bunch of bullshit, put out to further control us and eliminate any thoughts we might have about returning home. Not that this was difficult as usually all it took was one thought of the old home place to bring on a crippling migraine. I should know; I'd had my share.

Yeah, it could always be worse. At least I had been recruited, then given a choice; whereas I'd heard rumors of others who'd simply been abducted, and usually as children. They'd started off on earth in various government mind control programs where they'd been broken by heinous practices like drowning pools and electric chairs. It was torture they often didn't survive, especially that little game called Daisy whereby their handlers pulled the petals off the flower in question. Then, if the last one indicated that he loved them not, the poor kid was treated to a bullet between the eyes. Oh, but no problem. This just led to a regeneration chamber where they were brought back to life and then subjected to the same grisly shit over and over again. Gee whiz, no wonder these kids were fucked up!

Oh, the theory was that it was all done for a purpose, to desensitize them to pain, both mental and physical, which is a trait I guess you are going for when you are gathering an army of psychic weirdos. Remote viewers, pre-cogs, time-travelers, inter-dimensional travelers...their skills were multi-faceted and required a thoroughly nerve-deadened psyche. Indeed, such could have been my fate, had they decided to grab me at an early age; and to this day, I never could figure out why I had been allowed to live a normal life on Earth as long as I had. Maybe they had wanted me to hone my techno-skills first. Perhaps they sensed that my psychic ones were clouded by my disbelief. Whatever the case, I guess I should be grateful that I've got a few good memories.

At any rate, I thought they were still mine. I looked down at my body. It was same old lean and lanky frame I'd been blessed with all my life, and its muscles bulged with many a work out in the compound's gym. After all, just because I was in a place where there were few human females to impress, that didn't mean I should let myself go to pot. Yeah, to pot. Boy, I sure would have liked a pipe-full of that right now. I smiled and caught the reflection of my new pearly-whites in the glare of a window.

"Well, at least they fixed my teeth; I'll give them that much," I muttered to myself.

And hopefully that was all. Hopefully, that wasn't just the first stage of turning me into one of the cyborgs I'd been designing the software for. But then, that wasn't how it was done. By one step at a time. No, instead, they would first remove your soul and place it in a some sort of electrical field holding tank. Then they'd bring another body in, usually a cyborg super-soldier, and transfer your soul to its new accommodations.

Weird, huh? Well, it gets worse, because often these cyborgs weren't even kept in the fleet, but were sold to ETs, so God knows where in the galaxy you might end up.

It was a chilling thought and made me glad for my own measly little life, and for the dubious rewards it brought me. Like a ten minute smoke break in a cantina which resembled the waiting room in a doctor's office. Yeah, it had that much personality.

The door was locked as was always the case , and I had to use my key card to gain access. Nothing like maximum security. It went with the over-all ambience of the place. Hardly snug and cozy.

I hurried over to the cigarette dispenser. It was built to resemble those back on earth, their one little attempt to make the place feel homey. But it was actually a replicator where you programmed what you wanted, stuffed your cash chip in, and watched it magically appear. You were only allowed one cigarette at a time, and the things sure did eat away at my pay. But, hell, since I never could develop a taste for the battery-acid they tried to pawn off as alcohol, they were my one indulgence.

Of course there were the girls. But, dear Lord, let's nor even go there!!! Because they weren't even real girls, but some sort of robot designed to mimic the moves of the real thing. God help me, but I couldn't even tolerate the smell of them. All plastic and silicon glue. Although I had heard that the higher up you went in the ranks, the more realistic they became. Oh well, by the time I made it that far—if, that is, I was still breathing this recycled air—I'd be so old all the Viagra on the planet wouldn't have inspired me to do the dirty deed.

I sighed and began to take deep drags on my smoke. It tasted faintly of licorice because I had decided for some reason to break with training and try something new, some fancy little French knock-off that was supposed to resemble a Gauloise. Gee, all I needed now was a shot of espresso, and I could fantasize that I was in some cozy café on the Left Bank, a place which had long been on my bucket list while back on earth.

Working the fantasy for all it was worth, I strolled over to what we commonly referred to as The Wall of Shame and tried to pretend I was in the Louvre checking out famous works of art. But in truth I knew it for what it was: a rogue's gallery of defectors and freedom fighters which served as the Dark fleet's Most Wanted list. No doubt, it had been set there as a reminder that all resistance was futile. For boy, oh boy, did they love to put a big red X over a face when it was no longer considered a threat.

That means dead, of course. Exterminated. Snuffed out, deactivated. Call it what you may, but what's gone is gone is gone.

Yes, in my time here I'd watched many a brave man, woman, or friendly ET bite the dust. However, the effect it had on me was opposite the one intended, for instead of prompting despair, it reminded me that —in the words of a famous hobbit—*where there's life, there's hope.* Such thoughts had always been my own personal light in this time of darkness, and today was no exception.

Or was it? Because today the wall seemed to glow with a brilliancy previously reserved for dreams alone. It was as if a star had landed and taken up residency on its dismal bulwark.

My curiosity aroused, I picked up the pace. Time was a wasting, and I needed my morning fix of Hopium. Gee, maybe this would even deliver a double dose because, as I drew closer, it soon became apparent that one particular mug shot was about to burn its way right into my brain.

Must be a Pleiadian, I thought, for they always did stand out amongst here amongst the mere Earthlings, tiny Arcturians, and hairless Andromedans. The morning star of the cosmos, they were the ones who rarely surfaced on the wall, and when they did, I always rued the appearance of the inevitable red star across their fair features.

Not that this always happened. Sometimes the mug shot was simply taken down—especially if it had been up for awhile—because our controllers sure didn't want us to think that maybe, just maybe, the war wasn't going in their favor. No, that wouldn't do at all. It might just give us a measure of hope. Heaven forbid!

But what is this? Why is my hair beginning to stand up on my arms like it does when lightning is about to strike? And what is it about our newest arrival that is drawing me in despite the awful feeling that I'm about to be fried?

I walked as though on automatic pilot. I didn't care at that point what the end-result would be. I just had to get up close and personal with that face. For it was a familiar face, a face which had languished long in my memory. A face I had both lusted after and worshiped as a goddess. A face untouchable, yet so deeply a part of me that to forsake it would tear my life apart.

Three feet, two feet, one foot, and then I was touching its lines, tracing its curves and hollows. The eyes strode out of the picture and circled my wagons. I was surrounded, captive once again, and could only speak the one word that would buy me freedom.

"Aniel," I whispered, and as I did so, I knew all this had been but a preamble. The real story had only just begun.

Daniel Rose

Acknowledgments

Page 168 Bono Joshua Tree

Page 334 Mike Stone August 21, 2017 *Reuters Magazine*

Page 356 Bob Dylan *I Shall be Released* 1967

Page 363 Lord Shelley *Ozymandias*